THE UP AND UP

ALSO BY LEE IRBY

7,000 Clams

To Maureen and Joe,
Great friends, great neighbors, great
people! Thanks for all your support —

R Seeley   July 2006

THE
UP AND
UP

a novel

LEE IRBY

DOUBLEDAY

New York London Toronto Sydney Auckland

PUBLISHED BY DOUBLEDAY

Copyright © 2006 by Lee Irby

Book design by Cassandra J. Pappas

Library of Congress Cataloging-in-Publication Data
Irby, Lee.
The up and up : a novel / by Lee Irby.
p.   cm.
1. Florida—Fiction. I. Title.

PS3609.R47U6 2006
813'.6—dc22
2005054806

ISBN-13: 978-0-385-51500-9
ISBN-10: 0-385-51500-6

PRINTED IN THE UNITED STATES OF AMERICA

1   3   5   7   9   10   8   6   4   2

First Edition

For Iris and Jay

Acknowledgments

Thanks again to Jason Kaufman for his continued support and friendship. Nat Sobel and Judith Weber provided insightful feedback and astute suggestions. Jenny Choi saved me from many embarrassments. Karla Eoff did a stellar job copyediting the manuscript. Arva Moore Parks bent over backward to help me re-create old Miami. Paul George's work on the history of criminal justice in south Florida proved indispensable. Marvin Dunn helped me understand Miami's history of fractious race relations. Patsy West's study of Musa Isle is a groundbreaking piece of scholarship that richly deserves its praise. George Faust at the Miami-Dade Public Library assisted me above and beyond the call of duty. Shannon Burke and Suzan Harrison had the thankless task of slogging through early versions of the book. Olivier Debure guided me through the French translations without laughing in my face. Antonio Melchor graciously found the time to clean up my Spanish. Beth Forys gave me the straight dope when I needed it and the space to make it happen.

THE UP AND UP

It has been further disclosed that this lack of morale in the [Miami] police force has contributed in no small degree to the amazing growth of unlawful practices in the territory served by them. . . . We have been subjected to much information involving and connecting some branches of the police department with Miami's underworld. We have become thoroughly convinced that the open violations of law on the part of gamblers, bootleggers, and houses of ill fame are permitted because of an unquestionable alliance with many law enforcement officers.

—Final Report, Dade County Grand Jury, May 7, 1928

MALE AND FEMALE

J oseph P. Kennedy leans his sturdy body over the tracks and peers through round spectacles at the approaching train. It moves slowly across the flat terrain, spewing sooty smoke into the cloudless Florida sky.

A whistle sounds.

The platform of the West Palm Beach train station springs to life. Porters snap to attention, a small band strikes up a catchy tune, and the others who've been waiting for the *Florida Limited* begin to press forward. It is January 12, 1928, and another tourist season has commenced. Lavish parties, dancing till dawn, gossip over omelets, shopping on Worth Avenue—for the next two months, Palm Beach will bustle and hum, transforming a sleepy seaside village into the world's wealthiest sandbox.

"Right on time, sir," chirps Eddie Moore, Joe Kennedy's personal secretary, trusted friend, and keeper of secrets. Both men are attired in white linen suits and white straw hats. Both have sunburned faces from the round of golf they played yesterday. The resemblances stop there. Eddie Moore is older and stooped, with thinning white hair and the stern expression of a well-trained guard dog, whereas even now, on vacation, Joe Kennedy exudes the august impatience of a man in a hurry on his way to the top. He is pacing around like his feet are on fire, displaying the boundless energy that took Joe Kennedy from the rough and tumble of East Boston to the pinnacle of American finance—and, more recently, to the enchanted land of Hollywood. At thirty-nine, he is the father of seven children, although his wife, Rose, is expecting again and due to give birth in a few weeks. She hasn't been very pleasant to be around, which is why he came to Palm Beach in the first place.

He wipes his face with a handkerchief and then glances at Eddie Moore. The stout aide hitches his trousers confidently, as if he knows the answer to a riddle.

"I've taken care of everything," he says calmly, giving his boss a pat on the back. "You got nothing to worry about."

"And the orchids?"

"Her room is like a flower shop."

Joe Kennedy nods. The black steamer glides by, its brakes squealing. Next come the passenger cars, and he examines each hopefully. On one of them he spies a pretty woman waving. "That's her!" he barks, trailing after the car. Instead of waiting for her to disembark, he bounds onto the train once it stops, rushing headlong up the stairs, pushing past a confused porter.

He moves swiftly down the corridor with the illogic of a determined child, chest out, jaw set tightly. It's hard going, because the other passengers are trying to exit. But he's been thinking about her since they first met last November. He took her to dinner at the Savoy. He wanted her then, and now, months later, his desire has multiplied like a crazy adding machine.

Then a petite woman emerges from a compartment and waves at him. "Hi, Joe!" comes her strong, clear voice. Her teeth are a dazzling white. Her brown hair shines like patent leather.

"Where's Henri?" Joe replies.

"He went to meet you."

The sight of her sends him charging down the narrow corridor, where they meet in a collision that sends both back into her berth. He pushes her gently into a closet, knocking off his glasses when his forehead bumps against the luggage rack. He presses his lips against hers. She tastes like candy.

"I missed you," he says, wiping off her lipstick with the same handkerchief that he used to dry his sweaty, nervous face. "I just wanted you to know that."

"I missed you, too. Now come meet my husband."

"Oh, absolutely."

Seconds later Joe Kennedy is back on the platform, issuing orders at the porters while chatting amiably with Henri de la Falaise, Marquis de la Coudraye, otherwise known to the world as Gloria Swanson's third husband.

■ ■ ■

A movie star like Gloria Swanson, who has played opposite Valentino, Barrymore, and Reid, who has had three husbands and numerous lovers, who is considered to be the most glamorous woman in the world, doesn't normally allow a single kiss to upset her balance. After all, she's twenty-eight (give or take a few years) and knows very well the particular oddness of the male species. But there is something about this Joe Kennedy that sends her blood to boil.

A kiss? They are supposed to have a business relationship. And business it must remain.

"Milt Cohen resigned," she finally says, in a voice not much louder than a whisper. She's riding in a car with Joe on the way to the hotel. Henri has gone with Eddie Moore in another car. "He sent me a telegram."

The car starts to bounce across a rickety bridge. Skiffs sway gently on the placid water of Lake Worth separating the Palm Beaches. West Palm Beach houses the laborers, the maids, the cooks, and the gardeners, while Palm Beach exists as the ultimate playground for the rich. Joe promised her the time of her life.

"At least you didn't have to fire him. Firing people isn't pleasant but you'll have to get used to it. You have a bunch of worthless hangers-on sucking you dry."

"Like who?"

"I'd get rid of all the deadwood. Your dressmaker, your production manager, your accountant. Milt Cohen is just the start."

She knows he's right. But Milt had been her lawyer for the past five years, and she trusted him. Yet like the others Joe mentioned, she couldn't keep him on permanent retainer. Rather than accept this change, Milt resigned instead. His telegram made her cringe. REGRET YOUR ATTITUDE EXCEEDINGLY. It hasn't been easy, carrying out the changes Joe suggested. But what else could she do? She was nearly broke, and Henri isn't in a position to help. A title sounds nice, but being a marquise doesn't pay the bills. And the bills! They kept piling up, so high it felt like she'd never dig out.

"There it is," he says, nodding toward a huge building. "The Royal Poinciana."

The enormous wooden hotel, painted a vivid lemon yellow, extends some six stories above the palm and pine trees that surround it. It seems to stretch across the land like a giant who has decided to take a nap. Hotel? By the looks of it, an entire army could stay here. No wonder Joe likes it so much: it is bold and brash and rich, just like he is.

They pull into the long driveway that leads them through a grove of coconut palms. It takes several minutes to reach the front entrance, so vast are the hotel grounds, every inch perfectly manicured. Finally Gloria can see what awaits: a crowd of bellhops and other uniformed personnel has gathered on the stairs of a grandiose front colonnade that resembles something out of ancient Athens, except bigger. Much bigger.

"Everybody in Palm Beach is lining up to meet you," he tells her, his voice lilting like an excited Irish lad. "It'll be the same way tonight down in Miami. Remember that party the chamber of commerce is throwing in your honor?"

"Do I have to go?"

"They're paying you a thousand bucks to smile and wave."

A thousand bucks to smile, when so many toil away just to put bread on the table. She'll never forget how magical it was to open her first pay envelope as a professional actress: $3.25 for an hour's work for Essanay Studios. It was a wedding scene. Gloria brought a bouquet of flowers to the picture's star, Gerda Holmes. Then the director yelled "That's it!" and it was over. Days later the studio hired her as a stock player for twenty bucks a week.

Joe pulls to a stop, and even before Gloria can step out of the car, the hotel manager presents her with a corsage of orchids. She accepts them graciously. But she doesn't particularly care for orchids. They are too delicate and hard to care for. She likes durable plants, the ones that can survive with little water or sunlight.

But she says nothing, because Joe is beaming. The orchids were obviously his idea, and he is quite satisfied with himself. Women should always let men try to make them happy. Sometimes they actually succeed.

SURE THING

In a parking lot of crushed shells, some Seminole Indians have set up a makeshift booth to sell trinkets, mostly bird feathers and raccoon pelts. They stand in impassive silence, wrapped in colorful patchwork blankets, watching the white people pass by.

"Are they the real McCoy?" asks Frank Hearn, trying not to gawk. He's only been in Miami for a few months and some aspects of the city still thrill him. The white sand of the beach. The mansions on Brickell Avenue. The tall hotels along Biscayne Boulevard. It's a city where anything can happen. Like these Seminoles. They wrestle alligators, man against beast as only Florida can offer. That would be a hoot to see. Frank, though, could see only half of it. He wears an eye patch to cover his missing left eye.

"Probably," sniffs Parker Anderson Jr.

"They look real." So much for the small talk. The two men didn't drive out to this dusty corner of northwest Miami on a lark. There's business to take care of. But Frank can't help it. His nerves are jangling and he feels dippy tonight. His feet crunch against the shells as he walks. His throat is parched and he needs a drink. Up ahead is an enormous building four stories high and half a block wide, sitting on a barren swath of undeveloped land. A blue neon sign blazes in the night: PALMETTO JAI ALAI FRONTON. Frank has never seen a jai alai match before. Doesn't know the first thing about the sport, other than you can bet on it.

And that's the problem.

"Jeepers creepers, are you sure about this?" asks Frank, his handsome face twisted in confusion as he glances down at Parker Anderson. Frank stands well over six feet with an athletic build. Parker is almost a foot shorter and is as round as a beach ball. He looks soft but isn't. Parker knows how to play every angle in this city. It just seems like he plays them all at once.

"Sure I'm sure. I told you, it's been in the works for a month. And tonight's the night."

"I hope you're right."

Parker's squeaky voice drops an octave. "This is a sure thing, Frank. I'd never give you a bum steer. These poor spic jai alai players don't make two dimes to rub together. They hate the owner of this place. He treats them like slaves. They want in on this, trust me." Then he chuckles. "You could say I'm doing this out of the goodness of my heart."

"I didn't know you had a heart."

"Maybe not, but I have a brain. And this is on the up-and-up, old boy."

Parker pops a Marmola Diet Tablet into his mouth and starts chewing. He eats those things like candy because he wants to drop fifteen pounds of girth. His pants always seem like they're about to bust open, and his shirttails never stay tucked in. Frank, on the other hand, stays thin from all the scrambling he has to do every day to make a dime in the real estate business. There's barely time to eat, he's been so busy pounding the pavement.

The two men pay their admission of twenty-five cents and proceed in. The lines at the betting windows are short. Overhead, on a large tote board, an urchin is poised on a ladder, wiping away the old odds and scrawling the new ones with white chalk. Most sets of eyes are fixed on the board. Others study programs in anguished silence.

"Let's see." Parker scans the tote board. "The third match just started. The one we want is the fifth. Do you remember what I told you?"

"The play is Garate straight."

Parker nods emphatically. "You got it, old boy."

"Garate straight in the fifth," repeats Frank slowly, as if he doesn't believe the sound of his own voice.

"Mack!" Parker waves over to another young man, one of his college buddies most likely. There are legions of them, and most are cut from the same cloth as Parker: friendly, pampered, jovial. This Mack turns out to be no different than the others, a quick smile and slicked-back hair. Frank cuts out after the introductions are made. His throat is parched and he could use a drink of something.

A nice-looking doll hands him a bottle of what looks like beer. Frank drops a dollar bill on the counter. She smiles at him and he tells her to keep the change.

"It's my lucky day," he grins, always glad to leave a nice tip. There might be plenty more nice tips in his future—if Parker Anderson isn't cheesing him, that is. Word is that the fix is on in the fifth, and those in the know will stand to rake it in. Frank can see on the tote board that Garate is currently listed at six to one. Not bad odds, and a $300 bet will turn into a nice clump of kale. But those three hundred bones in Frank's pocket, that's all he's got.

Out of the corner of his good eye he can see Parker guffawing and backslapping with his old chum. He's got a smile nothing can wipe away. Happy-go-lucky, that's Parker Anderson Jr. But is this jai alai match really in the bag? Frank has seen Parker lose his shirt at the Hialeah racetrack, putting his faith on dope that turned out to be bunk. Every man has a weakness, and gambling is Parker's.

Frank drains his beer. The tote board still lists Garate as six to one. Parker is jawing away, merry as ever. Frank sucks on his cheeks, studying Parker carefully. He recalls the things Irene Howard, his fiancée, said about Parker. *He's swell and sweet, a good egg from what I can see.* Irene is a keen judge of character, mostly. They both liked Parker from the moment they first met him. It was in Italy last spring, on the beach in Rimini. They saw this young American tourist wearing purple espadrilles and a Basque beret, painting watercolors of the Grand Hotel. They got to talking to him, realized he was a good sport, and then the three of them spent a month getting drunk.

Turned out Parker was from Miami. He was a recent college grad having some fun on the Continent, but soon enough he'd be heading back home to get set up in the real estate biz. And that got Frank thinking. After all, real estate was the reason he came to Florida. He was going to make a killing in the Sunshine State. The first city he tried was St. Pete but things didn't go as planned, to say the least. He got mixed up in something stupid and lost his eye and all his money. But he found Irene and two years later there he was, floating through Europe on Irene's dime. Sure, it was swell, but he didn't have a career or even the whiff of one. And he was turning thirty. He was getting antsy, ready to stake his claim in this world.

Why not head back to Miami and go into business with this smooth talker, the son of a former mayor? With Parker's contacts and Frank's rakish charm, they could make a fortune. Then, when he married Irene, Frank would be his own man.

The fourth match has begun. It's time to put up or shut up. Frank makes his way to a betting window. Then the urchin wipes away the six-to-one odds by Garate's name and changes it to seven to one. Parker said the fix was solid. The owner treats the players like slaves. They hate his guts and want to stick it to him. As good as gold, that's what Parker said.

A thin, dour man with green eyeshades waits wordlessly for Frank's wager.

"What'll it be?"

Frank takes a deep breath, like he's getting ready to jump off a cliff. "Garate straight in the fifth."

"How much?"

"Three hundred bucks."

A mutuels machine prints out a ticket, just like at the racetrack in

Hialeah. A modern improvement over bookies, that's for sure. Nice and orderly, win or lose. As far as Frank can see, wagering is the only thing in Florida that works like it's supposed to.

Parker Anderson comes waddling over, face flushed and sweat dripping off his brow. "You do it?"

Frank shrugs his large, square shoulders. "Yeah."

"It's on," whispers Parker. "It's definitely on. That fella Mack I introduced you to, he's putting money down for the players. They're in on it all the way."

"So it's a sure thing."

"It's wrapped tighter than a Cuban cigar."

Ah, hell, Frank decides. What's the worst thing that can happen? He'll lose a couple of C-notes, which will hurt real bad. But he'll learn something about Parker Anderson Jr.—whether the guy can be trusted. Because Frank's not so sure anymore. Funny things have been happening around the office. This city is full of liars and thieves, and Parker seems to know them all by name.

■ ■ ■

The crowd cheers lustily for reasons Frank doesn't altogether understand. "What just happened?" he asks helplessly, with the unpleasant suspicion that things aren't going according to plan. He now understands the basics of the game. The court is a rectangle about a hundred feet long and thirty feet wide consisting of three walls and a wire-mesh screen to keep the ball from killing someone in the crowd. Six players are competing to win six points. They face off two at a time, throwing a ball against the front wall and catching it with a long glove before it bounces twice. The winner of the point keeps playing. A kid is keeping score on a chalkboard.

"Uranga won another point. He needs one more and he'll have six and be the winner." Parker sounds like a kid who just found out there is no Santa Claus.

"Uranga the winner?"

"Just wait."

Looks like Parker'll be taken to the cleaners after all. Frank grits his teeth and feels his muscles grow taut. Why did he fall for it in the first place?

"Just wait," says Parker again, without much conviction. He's a balloon that's slowly losing its air. Frank sighs and settles back to watch the young men in long white pants throw a ball against a wall and catch it. Under different circumstances he might have actually enjoyed himself. The sport of jai alai is keen. The ball moves so fast you can't see it most of the time, but these fellows sure can. They're prancing and hopping all over the court like they're doped up on something. You have to give them credit: they sure look like they're giving it their all. A few of them have gone tumbling head over heels trying to catch the ball. One even went crashing into the screen. If the fix is on, these guys deserve to be on Broadway for their acting ability.

Now it's Garate's turn to take on Uranga, who needs just one point to win.

"Come on, Garate!" Parker shouts, getting caught up in the atmosphere. Uranga reels in a serve and launches a drive high off the front wall. It skies over Garate's head and bounces off the back wall, but Garate is ready for it. He scoops up the ball on one bounce and whips a vicious drive into the corner where the side and front walls meet. The ball goes rocketing at a severe angle toward the screen. Uranga makes a stab at it but doesn't get close.

"Atta boy, Garate!" Parker shouts, jumping out of his seat. Pretty excited for a man who knows the outcome. But Frank feels like yelling, too.

Garate serves to the next man and wins that point, too.

"One more!" shouts Parker.

▪ ▪ ▪

A few hundred miles away, the SS *Wilhelmina* churns toward its destination: Havana, Cuba. On board is Irene Howard, who's so excited and nervous that she can't sleep. She rests her head on a fluffy pillow, her ink-black hair spilling over the white satin case. It's grown a bit longer since Frank saw her last. Few women in Europe bob their hair anymore. Most favor a bolero swirl or permanent wave. She'll decide later what style to wear for her wedding, still six months off.

Irene blinks her eyes a few times, moist lips pursed in apparent consternation. What if Frank only likes bobbed hair? What if she's gained too much weight? She's just two pounds heavier, nothing on a frame of five feet, nine inches. All her clothes still fit the same. She looked at herself in the mirror after her bath. Everything appeared in good shape, no flab or rolls anywhere. She still is the same trim and athletic girl Frank said good-bye to four months ago.

Oh, she'll never fall asleep tonight! But she needs her rest because soon she'll arrive in Havana and at dawn she'll hop on the early ship to Miami, the *Shawnee*. She'll have to hustle to make it in time, but getting to Miami earlier will allow her to spend precious hours alone with Frank before her parents arrive. If the *Shawnee* has telegraph service, she'll wire Frank about her earlier arrival. He's not expecting her until tomorrow afternoon.

She sighs into her pillow. The satin sheets feel smooth against her skin. But such first-class comforts are no substitute for Frank. They've been apart for several months, but soon they'll never leave each other's side, because come June 10, 1928, in Greenwich, Connecticut, they'll become husband and wife. Just six more months, and so much to do! The invitations have to go out, and that means coming up with a guest list, which means haggling with Mummy about every little detail. The woman can be impossible. And Daddy's going to meet Frank for the first time tomorrow evening. Hopefully they'll hit it off, although that's no sure thing. In his last letter, Frank promised he'd repay the money he borrowed from Daddy to help him get started in the real estate business. That gesture will go far in the eyes of Seddon Howard. So there's hope.

■ ■ ■

This is it. If Garate wins this point, he'll win the match. Frank clenches his hands into fists. Garate serves, but it goes too long, bouncing over the back line. Frank glares down at Parker, who looks like he just snorted a schnozzleful of battery acid.

"Wait," warbles Parker. "He gets another serve."

True enough, and this time Garate makes it count. Then he catches the other man's shot, and fires the ball toward the front wall. They trade a few more shots, and then Garate uncorks another one of these wicked corner shots to win the point, his sixth.

Parker Anderson exalts by lifting his arms into the sky and screeching like an owl. "Let's go collect our winnings, old boy," Parker sings, face ruddy from the flush of success. "Huh? What did I say? A sure thing."

Frank keeps looking around, waiting for the cat to jump out of the bag. This was a little too easy, and suddenly Frank's got that queasy feeling in his stomach, the one he gets whenever his nerves start jangling. But all he sees are folks headed to the lobby, and most of them seem glum.

Not Parker, who practically runs back to cash in his winner and nearly knocks over a stooped crone with a cane. He's a little bundle of energy again, a live wire bursting with glee and good cheer. Frank sees again the reasons he decided to go into business with Parker Anderson. He brims with confidence and knows everyone who counts. But Frank can see the other side, too. The cocksure swagger, the misplaced invincibility. Parker Anderson is burning a candle at both ends, and soon enough he'll get torched.

There aren't many winners in line so it doesn't take long to reach the window. As Frank hands over his ticket, he notices an angry-looking man with a cigar clenched in his teeth, rubbering every winner like a vulture, eyes narrow and hands on hips. Seems as if he would reach for a rod any minute. Frank doesn't trust the looks of that goon, the sort of lantern-jawed slugger who'd deep-six his own mother over a fin. Must be the owner of the joint, not wanting to pay out on a long shot.

"Pick a winner there, did ya, Anderson?" the man rasps as Parker waits for his money at the window next to Frank.

"Every dog has its day, Delaney. You've taken me for plenty."

The man just puffs away on the cigar, glaring as the cashier counts out the greenbacks. Frank collects his winnings and stuffs the bills into the inside pocket of his jacket. Then he turns to leave. No use staying here a minute longer than necessary.

Parker catches up with him outside.

"Hey, wait up, Frankie! How about if we bop over to the La Vida Club to see Ollie Hodges and His Dancing Sweethearts? I'll spring for the couvert charge."

Frank glances at the Seminoles, still selling those trinkets in the parking lot. "I don't know. I was thinking about heading over to the Deauville. You know, they're having that party for Gloria Swanson."

Parker pats Frank on the back. "Let's celebrate, old boy. One drink, for old time's sake. For Rimini! For us finally hitting the jackpot!"

Frank exhales, feeling a pit in his gut the size of a boulder. He doesn't really want to go, but he won big tonight, thanks to Parker. "Sure, one drink."

HELLO, SUCKER

L a Vida Club is a juice joint Frank Hearn knows well, because it's housed in one of the few buildings standing in Hialeah except for the racetrack. The developers, Glenn Curtiss and James Bright, thought that ham-and-eggers galore would buy lots just to be close to the ponies, but few wanted to own land near the Everglades canals that flooded over at the drop of a hat. So the sandy lots mostly sit empty, and word is that Curtiss and Bright have lost their shirts. Frank sure can sympathize, because he's about lost his, too. He tried selling Hialeah but got nowhere. The only development that moves consistently these days is Coral Gables, but the action out there is hard to come by.

Of course, you can make plenty of money selling swampland but that's something Frank won't do. Times have been tough in Miami, ever since the hurricane hit in 1926. Sharks have been circling and now everybody thinks you're playing a con. No one is buying. Hell, no one even bothers to come to Miami anymore. The old-timers can't remember a worse tourist season than last year, but maybe this year will be different.

"Here's to Garate!" shouts Parker Anderson, lifting a dry martini as ashes from his Fatima cigarette fall onto his cobalt-blue tie. Onstage

Ollie Hodges's Dancing Sweethearts are kicking up a storm, long legs lifting through the smoky haze, gimcrack bangles tinkling and garters flashing. "See the third one from the left? The redhead?"

Frank scans the revue and spots the dish Parker is gushing about. Even with one eye, Frank can tell she's an eyeful. "What about her?"

"I'll be seeing her later. Maureen. Sweet Maureen."

Frank nods in appreciation because the doll is a cutie, no question about that. Parker doesn't look like the sort who'd be a sheik with the ladies, but he's always mixed up with one skirt or another. It's hard keeping track of them all.

"I hope you two make some beautiful music together," says Frank, reaching for a sawbuck to cover his share of the drinks. He stayed for three instead of one. A few more and Frank will get drunk. The last thing he needs is a hangover tomorrow.

"What's the big idea? Are you leaving?"

"Afraid so. Irene's coming tomorrow."

"That's right! You must be hyper, huh, old scout!"

Frank can't hide the grin that spreads across his face. He must look like a dumbbell but it's been too long since he's seen Irene Howard.

"Hey! Who's the sucker now! Look at us! Good morning, nurse!" Parker lifts his glass and toasts their good fortune.

"Yeah, thanks for the swell tip."

"I'd never steer you wrong, Frank! What'd I tell you in Italy? Huh? We're gonna cash our chips, the two of us! Things are looking up for us, huh, old boy! You're a good man, Frank. A hell of a good man. Give my best to Irene. Maybe one night I can take you two lovebirds out for dinner."

Frank is surprised by the emotional tone of voice coming from Parker. It's like he's getting all choked up, which is unlike the cheerful little fireplug who wisecracks with the best ribbers around. Frank doesn't know what to say. So he smiles and stands up, figuring Parker is just getting fractured on giggle water.

Ollie Hodges is swinging his arms wildly as his Dancing Sweethearts turn in unison and shimmy their rumps at the audience, lifting up their dresses for a quick flash of satin undies. Frank lopes toward the entrance, stepping aside so harried hostesses can get past with their heavy trays of cocktails. He doesn't notice the men in dark suits standing by the hatcheck counter. He's got other things on his mind, like getting home.

■ ■ ■

"That's one of them right there."

Gene Delaney blows smoke toward the ceiling of La Vida Club. He's going to get to the bottom of this. Who did these lousy mutts think they were? Working a fix in his house, the fronton he built with his own hands, when everyone in Miami told him he was a deadhead. He'll track them down one by one, starting with that one-eyed mutt who just left.

"Let's take care of them two pills," growls Delaney, snuffing out his cigar. He turns to face two young men, Lonigan and Figgins. Boo Boo Hoff sent them down from Philadelphia last summer. Lonigan had a murder charge hanging over his head and Figgins is the son of an old friend who got plugged during an ambush a couple of years back. Boo Boo said the boys had potential, especially Lonigan. So Delaney is teaching them the ropes, although he'd prefer not to. But no one says no to Boo Boo. He owns Philly now, and most of the Jersey shore. Delaney grew up with Boo Boo in Society Hill. He helped him open his first gambling joint. The code back then was: take care of your own. So Delaney agreed to take the two punks in.

"You packing some heat like I told you?" asks Delaney quietly but firmly.

"Always, boss," answers Lonigan. He's got a sharp nose and sharp cheeks, and a ready answer for everything. Figgins is another story. The kid sits there nodding his head, with watery eyes that make him look like he's about to cry. His cheeks are puffy, as if they're stuffed with cotton, and his bushy eyebrows belong on an owl. Didn't much resemble his old man. Lou Figgins could cut a man down with one look. The last time Delaney cried was at that funeral. The little boy was about ten. Didn't look like he understood what was happening. Still doesn't, ten years later.

"Okay, boys. Let's see what you're made of. You two go get that mutt and take him back to the office. I want to find out what he knows. Go on now."

Figgins silently scurries away, trying to catch up with the one in the eye patch. But Lonigan hangs back.

"What about Anderson?" he asks. Delaney pats him on the shoulder.

"We'll take care of him later. Get moving."

Delaney lights another cigar, staring over at Parker Anderson. That little chub is having a gay old time spending the money he stole. "Live it up," he snarls under his breath. That little chub was born with a silver spoon in his mouth and thinks he can do as he pleases because his daddy used to be mayor. He'll find out different soon enough.

Delaney hops off his stool and exits through the kitchen. He walks stiffly, chin jutting out like a fist at the bottom of his wizened face. Lately he's been wearing a body brace because of his bad back. But the contraption rubs against his nuts. Getting old is hell.

But that's life. You get old and then you die. Some go quick and some wither away bit by bit. You get a little fatter, a little slower. Then the young Turks think they can pull the wool over your eyes. Parker Anderson and the rest thought they could bamboozle him and get away with it. He'll have to teach them a lesson. The players, too. Some of those spics have hard heads. Maybe a few of them will have to be cracked.

▪ ▪ ▪

Frank jumps into the back of a cab and tells the driver his address. The Crozier. Fifty bucks per month. The landlady said it used to run fifty bucks per week. But that was before the hurricane. It's a different ballgame now.

He rolls down the window as the cab pulls out. It's January and it's balmy. Frank thinks about how much he used to hate the cold, those miserable winters in Asbury Park, when the wind would blow in off the frigid Atlantic. That last dump he lived in didn't have a radiator, so he had to steal firewood to keep from freezing to death—and that was one of the nicer places he lived. He's been on his own since he was fourteen. While the other kids studied geometry, Frank got his education down on the boardwalk. He was big and strong and could fight. He got in good with the local bootlegger and loan shark, who used him for muscle. Frank also rubbed a few cops the wrong way, and they hauled him in for sport. Eventually Frank realized it was either stay on the shore and do a long bit in jail, or try something else. So it was off to Florida, the Sunshine State.

From Palm Avenue the cab heads south to Okeechobee Road, an unpaved lane that runs parallel to a canal that leads back into the Everglades. Along the canal's north bank houseboats are moored, and most of them look like they were made out of matchsticks, ramshackle huts half sinking into the murky water. But lots of homes were destroyed by the 1926 hurricane, forcing people to live anywhere with a roof. That was one hell of a blow, so Frank has heard. Boats were washed up onto Biscayne Boulevard, and out on the beach two feet of sand covered Collins Avenue. Nothing has been the same since. Now FOR SALE signs dot the land like tombstones commemorating a bloody battle. Nobody is buying, everyone is selling, and the great Florida land boom has gone bust.

Maybe things will turn around soon. The North American Life Insurance Company is holding its convention next week. There might be some good prospects in that group.

For some reason the driver starts humming that Irving Berlin song "All Alone." Then he actually starts crooning: "I'm all alone every evening/All alone, feeling blue." Frank winces like someone just stabbed his ears with a fork, but damn if that song doesn't get stuck in his head like a broken record.

Then headlights appear, suddenly shining in from the back. Frank turns to look. Some rube is right on their tail. An engine roars and the

car speeds past. But not too far. The next thing Frank sees are two red
taillights. The car has stopped in the middle of the road. The cabbie
slows down.

"Don't stop!" yells Frank, too late. The cabbie stops. Frank sees an
ape get out of the car and walk back. He's got a piece in one hand and
a look on his face like he'll use it.

"I don't want no trouble," the cabbie cries, stepping out of the car
and raising his hands.

"It ain't you I want," the ape says. "It's him."

Frank can feel those thousand bones in the pocket of his jacket. A
sure thing, on the up-and-up—but this stinks like a setup. Who's behind it? Parker? Is that why he wanted to buy him a drink at La Vida
Club so bad? A fool could've seen that one from a mile away. Frank almost begged out of it. But he wanted to be nice. Instead he was a
sucker.

"Hey, you, in the back. Let's go for a ride."

Frank steps out of the cab and keeps his hands up. He gives the
ape a friendly smile. "I don't know you, pal," he offers, even as his heart
thumps away.

"Get in the car." Then to the cabbie: "Get lost. You call the cops,
you're a dead man. I got your cab number."

The cabbie hops into his car and drives away, kicking up sand and
dust that tears Frank's good eye. "We can settle this right here," Frank
says, wiping the eye with his shoulder. "Who do you work for? Delaney? That's his name, right?"

The ape points the roscoe right at his spleen. "I said get in. No
more monkey business."

"I think I know what you want. There's no need for rough stuff. Just
take the kale. It's in my jacket."

The ape opens the back door on the passenger side and waits for
Frank to get in. Frank keeps his arms up.

"Take the money."

"Get in or I'll fill you with lead!"

The ape is standing there like a chauffeur. There's another goon behind the wheel. Two against one. Those aren't good odds. If Frank gets in the car, he's a dead man. If he doesn't get in the car, he's also a dead man. They could kill him here and just the crickets would know. There is one building nearby, a decrepit houseboat sunk so deep in the canal that only its roof juts up. On the other side of the road, way off in the distance, sits the city's waterworks, surrounded by a high fence. The lights of downtown Miami glow faintly on the black horizon to the east, so far away it might as well be on the moon.

"Don't get your skivvies in a knot," says Frank, walking toward the car. The ape with the roscoe is standing behind the door, leaning against it a little, the hand with the gun resting on the top of the door frame.

"Get the money from him first!" the driver barks. The ape with the rod turns toward the sound of the angry voice.

"What?"

That's all Frank needs. He acts like he's going to duck into the backseat, but then gives the door a quick and powerful blow with his shoulder and elbow. The force of it sends the ape staggering back and Frank takes one long stride and vaults headlong into the murky, brown water of the canal. He hits the surface where a big clump of water hyacinth is growing, and that and the roof of the houseboat shield him. He dives down with the current, wildly pumping his arms and kicking his legs. His heart is pounding and his lungs ache, feeling like they could explode. But he can't come up for air or he'll get plugged. Another twenty seconds go by. He can't hold his breath much longer, and he can't stop himself lifting up. When his head breaks the surface, he's gasping for breath.

A shot rings out. It hits the water upstream from where Frank is. The apes don't see him! Frank submerges again, this time heading back in the opposite direction, against the current. When he needs a breath, he very carefully lifts up and takes a quick gulp, trying not to make any noise. Frank sees the glow of the Chrysler's headlights, shining above him like a corona of angels. He reaches the bank and scrambles up it, his water-soaked pants almost ready to slide off him. He crawls along the ground like an alligator, using his elbows.

The apes are a good fifty yards away, looking for Frank downstream.

Frank races for the Chrysler and hops in. The keys are still in the ignition. He guns the engine and goes tearing off, new tires squealing as he turns left abruptly at Le Jeune Road. A bullet explodes the back window. But the shot misses Frank—by a few inches.

■ ■ ■

Frank steps on the accelerator, not sure of his next move. Going to the cops is out of the question. They'll start sniffing around the jai alai fronton, and Parker Anderson and whoever else is in on the fix will get hauled in. Frank grips the steering wheel tightly as he turns right onto Okeechobee Road. His instincts tell him to drive back downtown and ditch the ride a couple of blocks from his apartment.

He cruises past the jai alai fronton, its neon sign now dark. The parking lot has emptied, and the Seminoles selling trinkets have headed back to the swamps, back to a simple life. Eating, sleeping, making babies. Doesn't sound half bad, considering the stew he's in now. What in the world was he thinking? How could he have let Parker talk him into this nutty plan?

He eases off Okeechobee Road and goes east on Thirty-Sixth Street, but after a few blocks he realizes his mistake. He'll end up far north of the bridge at Flagler Street, so he needs to head south back toward River Drive.

Then he sees a sickening sight: the red lights of a police cruiser flickering in the rearview mirror. The siren sounds like the howls of a wounded animal.

"Damn it!" He hits the steering wheel with the heel of his palm. These Miami cops are the worst. Should he try to get away? He checks the rearview mirror once again. Two cops. One looks like a bruiser and the other looks like a kid.

Don't be stupid, a voice tells him. So he eases the car over in front of a boarded-up garage and waits for the cop. Heavy shoes grind against the sand-swept street.

This doesn't look good. With a shot-out window, the cops will think Frank's driving a stolen car. Unless he can think of something fast, he'll have to start crooning about why it was someone wanted him dead.

Then comes a voice: "What's your hurry, son?"

A Southern drawl. Frank looks up at the scowling face. Bushy mustache, eyes set close together, and a few missing teeth.

"No hurry."

"What happened to the back window?"

"I like the fresh air."

A disbelieving grunt. "You got a license?"

The license holder on the steering column is empty. Something tells Frank that this cop isn't in the mood for a long explanation. In Asbury Park, a hundred bucks would be plenty to smooth out any confusion. Money is the universal language of let bygones be bygones.

"Sure thing, officer." Frank digs into a pocket. "Let me get you something that'll explain everything." He fishes out five double sawbucks. He hands them over to the cop, who examines the wet bills like he's never seen Andrew Jackson's face before.

"Get out of the car."

Frank flashes a sheepish grin. "Will twenty more do the job?"

"I said get out."

Frank does as he's told, but his mind is racing. The younger cop comes over and pats him down.

"I don't got a piece and I'm not looking for trouble," says Frank, dreading what he knows is coming. Sure enough, the kiddie cop finds the rest of the cash.

"Lookit this!" he gushes.

"I'll book that into evidence," the bruiser intones, taking the money and stuffing it into a pocket.

"Wait up," protests Frank, spinning around. Before he can utter another word, a nightstick smacks him on the side of the head. Frank doesn't go down, but staggers back, blood pouring from a gash by his eye patch. Another blow catches the back of his head, and Frank drops to a knee, head spinning. The bruiser cop pushes him down onto the sandy pavement and presses a knee against his back.

"This is how you take someone into custody," the bruiser tells the kid.

FAITH HEALER

A very large crowd has gathered around a very large swimming pool at a very large hotel on Miami Beach. The Deauville swirls with glamour tonight, men in black tie and women dressed to the nines, as if expecting royalty. The person everyone wants to see hasn't yet appeared. All eyes are on the lookout, including those belonging to a young woman wearing a magenta feather boa. "I don't care about meeting Coolidge on Saturday at your uncle's little party," she tells her date.

Bryce Shoat laughs like a polite and earnest seagull. "Come on! It'll be a hoot! Silent Cal! What could be better than that?"

She rolls her kohl-rimmed eyes in exasperation. "Gloria Swanson, that's who."

"Coolidge has more sex appeal."

"You're such a simp."

But Bryce doesn't take offense. Janice Pendergast is rich. Filthy, stinking rich. And she likes to drink. At least they have something in common.

He lifts a sweating highball to his sun-chapped lips and gulps the rest of the watered-down gin and tonic he paid a lousy two bucks for, but everyone knows the drinks at the Deauville Hotel are weaker than a sissy's handshake. The only place on Miami Beach you can get a decent cocktail is the Nautilus, but Bryce isn't allowed to drink there anymore. Nor can he frequent the Roney Plaza or the King Cole. Same goes for the Pago Pago Room and El Chico. Just about the only place he can buy a drink is the Roman Pools, where you bring your own booze and they charge two bucks for splits of ginger ale.

"Mother wants me to volunteer for the Free Milk Fund. She thinks all children should drink milk." Janice bats at a mosquito and then sighs. "I hate milk. I never liked drinking milk."

"Well, I'm a firm believer in drinking."

Her face lights up and she giggles at him. She loves the fact that he's the black sheep of the Firestone family, nephew of Harvey himself, baron of the tire industry. And Bryce loves the fact that she is filthy, stinking rich. "It's good to believe in something," she gushes.

"But I don't believe in anything."

"Not even free milk for poor kids?"

"I'm gonna do it! God, Bryce, what do you make me for? I like helping poor kids."

He leans over and kisses her. She's a pretty girl of twenty-two, with creamy white skin and pouting lips. Her nose is long and delicate, and her figure is trim and well proportioned. But her ears are larger than average, an unhappy fact which Janice is convinced makes her ugly. Her hair covers them up so that you barely notice them. Bryce doesn't, that's for sure. They've been dating for two months and what he notices most about Janice is the size of her trust fund.

"Breath Heart?" Janice offers him a tin of mints.

"We're having fun now, huh? If I could get drunk, I could actually enjoy this lame party."

The reason that so many have gathered at the million-gallon pool of the Deauville Hotel is to tell the world that Miami's 1928 season will be stupendous, considering that 1927 was a complete dud. Movie star Gloria Swanson has been brought into town so that photographers can snap some shots of her beaming beneath a hokey banner that reads MIAMI BEACH IS ALIVE AND WELL. The banner is festooned above the band playing below the cupola where Bryce and Janice stand, both of them leaning against the rail in quiet contemplation.

"Who's stopping you?" Janice replies, still sucking on a Breath Heart and scanning the crowd below, consisting of Miami's smart set. Most are swaying to "Don't Bring Lulu," a stupid, sappy song that they both happen to despise. Janice starts singing along, in a satiric tone: *"You can bring Nan with the old dead pan, but don't bring Lulu . . ."*

An older couple shoots them a disapproving glance. Bryce smiles and waves.

"I want to get boiled for this, too," Janice announces gaily. "Make yourself useful. Get me another."

She hands him her empty highball. Bryce stares at it.

"Do you have any money?" he asks quietly.

She gives him her purse. "I think there's some in there. Hurry back! I want to start dancing!"

He unclasps the purse and paws through the myriad containers of mints and lipstick, finally locating a twenty at the bottom. He's about to leave when Janice's eyes grow wide as saucers. She points a trembling, red-nailed finger down toward the swimming pool. "Look! There she is! Gloria Swanson!"

Sure enough, the crowd starts to part and through the throng steps a nice-looking skirt getting trailed by a couple of photographers. Doesn't look like Gloria Swanson, but no one looks the same in a moving picture as they do in real life. The better question is why those morons at the chamber of commerce paid money to bring her down—like Gloria Swanson could revive the real estate biz. That's a pipe dream, and a pathetic one at that. People will do anything these days to sell land—even if it's in the middle of the Everglades. That was Parker Anderson's gig. The little tub of lard actually convinced Bryce they could clean up by swindling dupes from the Midwest who wouldn't know any better. But what happens? The little tub of lard gets caught red-handed. He says he's got the feds convinced it was all Frank Hearn's doing and they're in the clear. But Bryce knows better than to trust a born liar.

Bryce threads his way to the bar, pushing through the adoring crowd clamoring to get a glimpse of the silent-screen star. She's probably a kook, truth be known. Most actresses are. They're easy, though, real slutty.

He's about to head down the stairs to the pool when he hears someone call his name.

"Bryce?"

He knows that voice well. A squeal that makes his eardrums throb. He never breaks stride, not hesitating even for a split second. He can hear her footsteps behind him, clanking against the steel steps.

"Bryce?"

He still doesn't turn around but shoves his way past the photographers in front of the stage. Gloria Swanson is standing beneath the banner now, waving and smiling, black cloche hat pulled tight against her head, chin jutting confidently, but something in her eyes expresses weariness. They are flat, almost lifeless. A heavy coat of mascara only adds to their hollowness. She moves stiffly, looking right, then left, always waving. The crowd buzzes like a swarm of bees, and Paul Whiteman has his orchestra strike up "It Ain't Gonna Rain No Mo'." The flashbulbs pop, and Jessica Dragonette begins to sing, her strong, clear voice a bracing tonic of hope for all those who've suffered since the hurricane blew away the Florida dream.

■ ■ ■

The girl trailing Bryce stops to listen. Nina Randolph has heard Jessica Dragonette a hundred times on the radio, just like she's seen all of Gloria Swanson's pictures. It's so exciting to be here, even if she had to come alone. Bryce is on a date with that rich girl. He says he doesn't love her. He says he's going to dump her. Then they can be together. But when? That's what is killing Nina, the not knowing. She couldn't sit home with Mother again. Not tonight. Not with everything that's happening, not with all the emotions boiling inside her like a teapot.

She just needs to talk to him for a second. One little second, to convince herself she is doing the right thing. So Nina follows him, breathless, nearly sobbing, eyes moist with tears. One second and then she'll go.

Bryce ducks into the lobby of the Deauville and steps behind a potted palm. She approaches him carefully, lower lip quivering, like a little girl lost in a department store. All that's missing is her teddy bear.

"I'm sorry I came but I needed to see you," she says softly.

"I told you a thousand times, baby. We can't be seen together."

"I love you, Bryce."

He puts a finger to his lips and hushes her. Then in a low tone tells her: "We can't be seen together, Nina. You're smarter than that. I'll come by the office tomorrow to pick up the files. You can get them, can't you?"

"I'll have them. Come by in the morning."

"That sounds copacetic."

"Do you love me?"

He suppresses a sigh and manages not to slug her in the jaw. What a screwy skirt this one is! Jesus H. Christ, won't he be glad once this is all over, and he won't have to make nicey-nice with this ditz again. If Janice were to see them together like this, it would ruin everything. He's got to get rid of Nina. But he can't give her the cold shoulder. He needs the files she can steal from Parker.

"Sure," he tells her, trying to sound sincere. "There's so much I've got to tell you. Janice is driving me nuts."

"Leave her! Leave her right now and come with me!"

"I can't, baby. Not yet." He winks at her knowingly. "Not until I soak her for some spending money. We'll need that in Bimini. I can't stay. I'll see you tomorrow."

With that he leaves Nina standing there. She turns and watches him go. How handsome he looks in his white dinner jacket. Like a prince. A Firestone prince. How often she's driven by the estate on

Miami Beach, marveling at the high wall surrounding it. She would try to imagine the unseen splendors the wall concealed, the elegance and riches. Who could have ever guessed that she, Nina Randolph, might one day actually live there? A Firestone princess.

Ha!

Who is she kidding? He doesn't love her. He's a liar. Just like Parker Anderson is a liar. A couple of rich snots who think they can beat on her like a snare drum. Bryce will go running back to Janice Pendergast because she's loaded and vapid and went to finishing school. She can lift her pinkie finger and the world snaps to attention. Girls like Nina Randolph need to do things differently if they want to get ahead.

Bryce had better soak Janice Pendergast for plenty, because tomorrow he's going to need every penny. Every damn penny.

■ ■ ■

Joe Kennedy pats the marquis on his narrow back and intones in a playful, manly voice: "Has anyone ever told you that you look like Adophe Menjou?"

Henri winces and manages a wan smile. Who wouldn't want to be compared to a nattily attired actor? Both are slender men with trim brown hair, neat mustaches, and kind, soulful eyes. Onscreen Adophe Menjou portrayed elegant aristocrats. Henri de la Falaise is portraying one in real life. He can delight a party in five languages, play Mozart on four instruments, and look dashing in a piqué vest, but tonight Henri wears a strained expression. He examines his new friend, this rich and blustery Joe Kennedy, sandy haired and eyes of bright blue, and imagines him making love to his wife, Gloria Swanson. Being married to Gloria Swanson hasn't been easy, and the marquis has watched many men flirt with her—and she with them.

After all, Adophe Menjou was always the sidekick of the leading man.

"You could be twins," Joe Kennedy adds.

"I'll take that as a compliment."

"You should! That Adophe knows how to dress. The man has real grace."

"Indeed he does."

"I'm glad we finally got a chance to meet. Gloria is just nuts about you. She'll go on and on about your noble character. You should hear her."

Up onstage Gloria is waving at the crowd. She looks very tired. She has been under much stress of late, mostly due to their precarious financial situation. That's where Joe Kennedy comes in. He's helping Gloria out. He's being the husband Henri can't be. The Falaise family fortune melted away long ago, leaving only the residue of aristocracy. Charm, grace, erudition: these the marquis possesses in abundance, in amounts sufficient to sweep Gloria off her feet four years ago while she was in Paris filming *Madame Sans-Gêne*. She even left a husband for him, and in the bargain became a marquise. A title he could give her; money he could not.

"She looks beautiful in that dress," says Joe Kennedy, trying to sound like he's admiring a new car. "Did you pick it out for her?"

"Of course not." A trembling hand brings an ivory cigarette holder toward his thin lips. "I wouldn't dare. You know how she loves clothes."

A masculine guffaw. "Do I ever. She spent twenty grand on dresses last year and tried to write it off as a business expense." Joe Kennedy laughs lustily, gazing at the world's most desired woman. This man knows everything about Gloria's financial life, details even Henri has never heard.

"She likes the finest of everything," replies Henri.

"She sure does. You're one lucky man."

Gloria is now waving down at them, the flashbulbs popping. Henri lifts a limp arm in salute and winks at her. He feels the hard barrel of a gun poking him in the ribs. It's in his dinner jacket, along with his cigarette case. A Smith and Wesson .22-caliber ivory-handled revolver, very small and sporty. To kill a man, one must be in close range. A well-placed bullet would do the job. The temple or the heart, either would suffice.

It's been many years since Henri has killed a man. But one supposes it's like riding a bike: once the art is mastered, it is never truly forgotten.

■ ■ ■

"Who was that girl?"

Bryce has walked Janice Pendergast to the front door of her Brickell Avenue palace. Pink oleander bushes hide the porch from snoopy pedestrians who want to gawk at how the other half lives on Millionaire's Row. What the Pendergasts need is a big fence, like the one that surrounds Uncle Harvey's estate.

"What girl?"

"The one you were talking to."

"When?"

Now he knows why she wanted to leave the party and why she wouldn't drive out to Silver Bluff with him so they could make out. She saw him talking to Nina. This is no good.

"When you went to get me a drink, I saw you talking to a girl. She was blond and very pretty."

"I don't know what you're talking about."

A light snaps on inside. That's Mrs. Pendergast's shot over the bow. Time for Bryce to evacuate. But he can't leave now. Not until Janice is convinced she was seeing things.

"You don't?"

"Someone asked me for directions to the bathroom—is that who you're talking about? Was she blond?"

"But you were talking to her for a long time."

"She didn't understand English or something. She was pretty dumb, I guess."

"I guess."

"Janice, don't be mad at me for something I didn't do."

"I'm not mad. But I'm not blind, either."

"No one said you were."

He reaches out and brushes her cheek. Then she pulls him toward her lips and they kiss. She tastes like those mints she's always sucking on. But he's breathing easier now.

"You're so beautiful," he whispers in her ear. "Maybe tomorrow we can go for a drive."

She kisses him again, running her hands through his hair. Then the door opens and her mother comes out onto the porch.

"Hi, Mrs. Pendergast." Bryce waves. The matron regards him sternly. It's like the old hag can see right through him with those eagle eyes of hers. He searches for something to say. "Nice night, huh?"

"Janice, it's getting late," she says, ignoring Bryce.

But Bryce won't give up. "Won't you both come to the polo match tomorrow? We're playing Palm Beach."

"I will be volunteering for the Free Milk Fund," answers Mrs. Pendergast. "We're having a bake sale."

"What time? Maybe I can help."

"It starts at eleven."

"In the morning?"

"Yes, in the morning."

"That sounds dandy. Janice was telling me of her volunteer plans just tonight."

"Have you been drinking, Bryce?"

"No, ma'am! Well, good night! See you tomorrow at eleven for the bake sale! I'll have cook make some cookies!"

Bryce waves one last time and then starts off down the walkway, feeling like he just dodged a bullet. Tonight was a close call. Nina almost ruined everything. Nina! He's supposed to meet her tomorrow but that'll be for the last time.

He kicks at the walkway in disgust. It will be wonderful when all of this finally goes away. After Nina steals those Sweetwater files from Parker, Bryce will be in the clear. He'll get rid of Nina and then propose to Janice Pendergast. Together they'll while away the rest of their days getting drunk and spending her money.

■ ■ ■

Delaney snuffs out his cigar and grimaces at the full ashtray. The cleaning woman is starting to slip. Can't anyone do anything right anymore?

"Boss, I'm sorry."

Figgins can't stop apologizing. He's like an idiot parrot that only knows a few phrases. That cube head of his keeps shaking like it might fall off. His watery eyes flow like sprinklers. But there's one question Delaney wants an answer to. It's a simple question.

"Why didn't you just stuff him in the car?"

Figgins nearly jumps out of his chair. "We tried!"

"You didn't try hard enough! It's a good thing I was a friend of your old man's. I'll forgive you this time. Next time I might not be so understanding." Lou Figgins is turning over in his grave. His boy is a pussyfoot.

Figgins falls into a morose silence.

"Just next time, do what I tell you. It's easier that way."

"I can't do nothing right."

"Don't say that, kid."

A Tiffany lamp on Delaney's desk casts an eerie glow off the paneled walls. On them hang photographs of Delaney holding fish. Tarpon, amberjack, pompano. Right behind his desk is the biggest prize of all: a huge blue marlin. He fought that thing for hours but nothing gets away from him. Nothing, that is, except the man in the eye patch.

"We need the mutt's name, is what," Delaney sighs. "We don't know nothing about him except he wears an eye patch, but he knows we're after him. If he goes to the cops, we're cooked!"

"I'll get his name," Figgins says unconvincingly, eyes downcast. A mope. That's what this kid is.

"How? Tell me that."

Figgins draws a deep breath and his face contorts in agony. "I could go back to the club and ask around, see if anybody knows him."

Delaney claps his hands. Figgins unleashes a hundred-watt smile. "Good thinking, kid. I already got Lonigan on it. You're always a day late and a dollar short."

"Sorry, Uncle Gene."

Uncle Gene. He hasn't called him that in a long time. But Figgins knows he futzed up, letting the mutt with the eye patch get away.

"Get out of here, kid. We got work to do."

In the silence Delaney closes his eyes. A terrible night this has been. The players are locked down tight in the dorm, doors barred shut. Not even a tank could bust them out. Still, a mouse got in. A mouse named Parker Anderson. He'll pay for it, too. And so will Garate. Stupid kid. It wasn't two years ago Garate was sweeping streets in Havana, and now look at him. Clean place to live, hot food to eat, money in his pocket. And who provided all that? Who plucked the kid from the streets and helped him out? Gene Delaney, that's who. If you needed it, he'd give you the shirt off his back. Just last week he gave Father Bocci fifty smackers so he could send some canned food to Argentina. Never even hesitated. How many kids has he helped over the years? Kids like Figgins and Garate, the ones going nowhere. *Uncle Gene.*

Delaney's eyes stay closed.

■　■　■

"Take your clothes off."

Parker Anderson leans back against the wicker headboard and kicks off his patent-leather shoes. They fall to the hardwood floor just as Maureen O'Bannon lets out a girlish howl of delight. She's still wearing her Dancing Sweetheart costume, a short dress studded with rhinestones and spaghetti straps that seem too thin to work effectively. Her dress looks like it's ready to fall off anyway, so might as well let nature take its course.

"You're naughty," she scolds him playfully.

"I know, but I'm a dying man so grant me a final request."

"What are you dying of?"

"I have a condition."

"Horsefeathers. I don't believe you."

"Do you want me to show you?"

She giggles again, covering her mouth with her hand. This skirt is one hunk of snatch! Fresh from the cornfields of Iowa, hoping to see her name in lights like all the others who've driven down the Dixie Highway in rusty flivvers. Maureen has done better than most, finding work with Ollie Hodges. The others who aren't as pretty or lucky end up turning tricks on Flagler Street. But Maureen's got something special. She's young, but she knows what she wants. She's learning fast about life in the Magic City. Self-respect, dignity, moxie, call it what you want, but Maureen O'Bannon has got it. She won't be flipping her dress for long at La Vida Club, that's for sure.

"Yeah, show me, Mr. Parker Anderson. Show me your problem."

"Okay, I will."

He stands up and begins to unbuckle his pants. She's giggling riotously now, so that her bobbed red hair is shaking like a palm tree in a squall. But she stops suddenly when she sees the barrel of a gun appear in the open window behind him. Before she can even scream a bullet tears through Parker Anderson's head. He crumples to the ground in front of her, and she starts crying hysterically.

"Don't kill me! Please don't kill me!"

A bullet slams into her face. A silencer muzzles the report. Not that anyone could hear the shots. Parker's bungalow sits off the Tamiami Trail, in a subdivision called Sweetwater. It is the only home out here, five miles west of downtown Miami. Most of the surrounding land is submerged in the vast swamps of the Everglades. There is no electricity out here, no running water or sewer lines. Just this one bungalow that Parker uses as a model home and as a place for romantic trysts. Candlelight dances off the newly plastered walls, and a gentle breeze lifts the curtains like the soft breaths of a sleeping child.

TOLD YOU SO

The SS *Algonquin* has heeled to port a few degrees, plying the waters off the coast of Charleston, South Carolina. The lights of the city glow faintly against the black horizon. A waning half-moon has just risen in the sky, and a gentle wind blows from the northeast. Conditions are perfect for a midnight stroll along the promenade. An attractive older couple has taken advantage of the calm, and stand wordlessly against the rail to regard the ocean. The woman has a mink coat wrapped around her thin shoulders, as the night is crisp, although appreciably warmer than it was when they left New York yesterday. The man is wearing a black dinner jacket and has his hands thrust into its pockets. On a table behind them, an empty bottle of Haut Brion 1918 stands between two empty champagne glasses.

"I suppose Harvey Firestone will want me to play polo with him," Seddon Howard tells his wife, Lauren. His tone indicates that he brooks little enthusiasm for the idea. She blinks at him glassy-eyed, tipsy from the champagne. It has been exactly six years since a drop of alcohol last crossed her lips.

"So don't."

He chuckles and grunts at her suggestion. "You don't say no to men like Harvey Firestone."

"So play."

"Perhaps I will. But don't forget about Coolidge's visit. I need to have a word with him about the situation in Nicaragua."

She slips an arm through his and closes her eyes. "You look so dashing when you ride."

"Is that so?"

She deeply inhales the salty night air. The *Algonquin* rocks gently on the calm sea. They had dinner at the captain's table, a gaggle of stewards endeavoring to meet their every whim. Their stateroom boasts Derby porcelain and a Wetherfield clock. There is a steam cabinet and soft chamois towels. Silk brocade damasks hang on the walls.

"It's lovely," she coos happily.

"For now."

She blinks her eyes open and gazes up at him. "Whatever do you mean?"

"Nothing, dear." But she knows him better than that. Something is bothering him but he won't say what. So Lauren Howard brushes his cheek, chilled from the crisp night air, and then grabs his nose.

"Tell me right now or overboard you go!"

"Ouch! Okay, okay, woman! You Southern belles don't like secrets."

"No, we don't."

"It's Irene and this Frank Hearn! There, I said it. I don't approve of this marriage. I have never approved."

"But you did! When Irene told us in London, you gave your blessing."

"Had I refused, do you think our daughter would be coming home to us? No, she would've eloped the first chance she got and then we'd be stuck with him. Wasn't her trip to Europe supposed to have cured her of Frank Hearn? How is it that they managed to remain so close? She's been gone for two years!"

Lauren arches an eyebrow at her husband. "Do you honestly want an answer?"

Seddon exhales bravely and puffs out his chest. "Had they illicitly consorted on U.S. soil, I would have had him arrested on a Mann Act violation! I should've sent a Pinkerton over there to watch Irene!"

"Really? Is that why you loaned Frank a thousand dollars?"

"Irene asked me to assist him and I granted her wish, although I knew it to be a mistake. You wait and see. He won't pay me back. He's only in this for the money. Why can't Irene see that?"

They fall silent, mystified by their daughter. That Seddon should be objecting now strikes Lauren as a bit foolish. After all, Irene has been carrying on with Frank in one form or another for nearly four years. By all appearances, a June wedding is still being planned. In Greenwich, no less. The groom will be attired in an eye patch. A glass eye would look a little more . . . civilized. But Frank apparently doesn't want one.

"Firestone has four sons!" blurts Seddon Howard, turning to face his intrigued wife. "Isn't one of them about Irene's age?"

"Seddon, we shouldn't meddle."

"Meddle, beddle. I'm not going to allow my daughter to wed some ruffian from the boardwalk of Asbury Park! Not when there are eligible men available who don't need her inheritance."

Lauren Howard doesn't say what she thinks. *You're the one who spoiled her all these years. You're the one who set up the trust fund she could start spending when she reached twenty-one.*

"Are you ready for bed, dear?" she asks instead. The champagne has caused Lauren to think of changing into a more comfortable outfit—like the silk robe she bought at Saks the last time she went shopping in the city.

"No, you turn in if you're tired. I think I'd like to sit in on a few hands of poker in the saloon."

Lauren leans up and whispers into her husband's ear: "Seddon, it's time for bed."

He breaks into a mirthful grin. "Is that an order?"

FIGHT OR FLIGHT

Nina Randolph is dressed and ready to go. She's eaten no breakfast because an hour ago she got a phone call that threw her for a loop. It was Frank Hearn. He said he was in jail and he wanted her to come down and bail him out. She said she would. After all, she doesn't want to arouse his suspicions. There's no reason she wouldn't help him out. She works for him. It's a favor a loyal secretary would do.

One last thing to do. She quickly addresses an envelope. Her hand-writing is neat and sure.

Nina Randolph
Box 48
Miami, Florida

She licks a two-cent commemorative Surrender of Burgoyne at Sarasota postage stamp and affixes it to the upper right-hand corner of the envelope. To be on the safe side, she decides to add another stamp. After all, the envelope is pretty heavy, at least an ounce. It's better to be safe than sorry.

"That's that," she whispers, shoving the envelope into her purse.

She takes a step and pauses, eyes roving across her tiny bedroom. Bed made. Nothing out of order. Suitcase packed and in the trunk of her car. The key to P.O. Box 48 is in her change purse. She checks again to make sure.

"Okay," she tells herself.

She walks from her bedroom to the living room. Mother is sitting on a worn sofa, smoking a cigarette that fills the house with an acrid odor. She's still in her ratty bathrobe and probably won't dress until much later. Then she'll powder her face like a doughnut, smear on scarlet lipstick, squeeze into a dress a few sizes too small, and spend the night at a blind pig with vile, disgusting men. Men who treat her poorly, like a doormat they wipe their feet on.

"You look nice," she hears Mother say. Nina doesn't turn around.

"Thanks."

"Is the dress from Burdines?"

"It was on sale."

"On sale, huh? Such a smart girl I raised. Owns her own car and has new dresses hanging in the closet, while her poor mother has holes in her stockings."

Nina holds her tongue. This is the last day she'll have to endure this. The kitty starts to purr. Poor Noodles! Nina can't leave the precious dear behind. She'll have to come back for her, after this is all over and before she leaves Miami forever.

"Are you still seeing the married man?"

"I'm not seeing a married man."

"Then why does he drop you off at the curb like a streetwalker?"

"Leave me alone."

Mother's voice rises up like the howl of a condemned prisoner at the gallows. "Don't let a man ruin you! Look at me! Don't make my mistakes, Nina! Look out for yourself, because no one else will."

"I am looking out for myself."

"Good. But don't forget about your poor mother."

This is it, the moment she's been dreaming of, when her life will change forever. She thought it would be easier to leave. But she's having trouble. She hates her mother, yet she has an urge to throw her arms around this unhappy, unwashed person and shower her with kisses. Nina's tried so hard to be a good girl. She made her mother breakfast on the mornings when she couldn't get out of bed. She was polite to the men who came and went, and dried Mother's tears when her heart was broken.

Suddenly she spins and goes over to hug her mother.

"What's this?" Mother asks, surprised at the display of affection.

"Nothing. I'm late."

"So go."

Nina tries to pull the door open but it is stuck again. It's like the house doesn't want her to leave. But nothing is stopping her. She'll do whatever she has to. No one will get in her way. One last time she pulls on the knob with all her might. The door pops open and she steps through the threshold. Already the air smells nicer.

■ ■ ■

"Hearn! Frank Hearn!"

A bleary eye blinks open, and a tall man pushes himself up from the hard concrete floor of the detention cell. His blue serge suit reeks of foul water and motor oil. The gash on his face isn't bleeding anymore, thanks to six stitches sunk in by a nurse in the infirmary. His head feels like it could split open and his stomach is queasy. An oppressive stench hangs heavily in the stagnant air of the Miami city jail. The one toilet doesn't flush and the air ventilators don't work, either. At 6:30 AM they dropped off brick-hard rolls and cold coffee, and the twenty men gobbled down these tasteless morsels, tearing at the grub like animals. A few fought over scraps. They could've killed each other and no one would've known or cared. Until now, there hasn't been a guard checking on them since the food got dropped off.

"Hearn?"

A pudgy jailer is jangling a set of keys in his small hands as he stands and waits for Frank to say something. But anger chokes back the words in Frank's parched throat. He's just spent the last nine hours dreaming of beating the snot out of every roach in a uniform.

"You Hearn?"

"Yeah. What of it?"

"You're going home."

"About time."

"How's that? You like it in there, Hearn?" The guard keeps futzing with the keys, like he just might not unlock the cage after all. Frank feels every muscle in his body clench. It takes a lot of restraint to keep his hands from reaching through the bars to wring that roach's flabby neck. "We got us a nice birdcage here in Miami, ain't we? You probably been in lots of jails, so you oughta know."

Frank smiles thinly and somehow manages to keep his trap shut. All he wants is out of here. Irene is coming today, and he's got a lot to do to get ready for her. She won't like seeing him like this. He's got to pull himself together. A shower, a hot meal, a nap. He can do it. He's got to do it. Her parents are coming, too. They're all staying at the Flamingo Hotel. They have dinner reservations at nine.

The cage creaks open. A drunken bricklayer staggers over. "When's me gone home?"

The guard shoves him back. "Is your name Hearn? Sit down!"

■ ■ ■

Frank stands at the booking desk and watches a stubby-fingered sergeant fumble with some paperwork. He goes from one pile to the next, in no particular order and in no particular hurry. Frank can't wait to get his mitts on his paperwork. On it should be some dope about the flattie who arrested him last night. After all, Frank doesn't even have a name to go on. The face, though, he'll never forget.

"I don't got nothing for you," the sergeant finally says to Frank, before stuffing a wedge of crumb cake into his mouth.

"What do you mean?"

The sergeant snorts like a constipated pig. Crumbs go spewing out and land on the desk. "I don't got no papers, wally! Is that a problem? You want to go back in the cage?"

Frank smiles like he was just given a key to the city. "Let me take a look at the arrest report, how about it? I'm entitled to that, right?"

"There ain't one."

"What?"

"No charges are pending, Hearn. The matter is now closed. If you don't like it, go see Officer Tibbitts at the complaint desk."

It takes a second for this news to sink in. At first Frank is relieved he won't be needing a lawyer, because last night it looked like he was getting charged with a host of raspberries, including grand theft auto and attempted bribery. Those are some serious charges. But now he's as free as a bird. How convenient. "Oh, I see. Somebody's pulling a fast one to keep my thousand bones."

"I don't know what you're blabbing about, Hearn. You should thank your lucky stars."

"It won't work. You can tell that to the son of a bitch flattie who roughed me up last night."

"Flattie? If I was you, pretty boy, I'd watch what I say. Now get out of here, you punk."

Before he heads off for the stairs, Frank makes sure to get this wiseass's name off the placard on his desk.

"Okay, there, Sergeant Flagstead. You have a nice day."

Flagstead. Easy enough to remember. Who knows, it might come in handy.

■ ■ ■

The cramped lobby of the City Hall Annex seethes with raw emotion. People are just getting out of jail or just going in. Shouts of joy commingle with angry curses as Miami's finest brandishes its version of justice. Frank stands for a few seconds, scanning the faces. Then he catches sight of his secretary, Nina Randolph. She is long-legged and shapely, a platinum blonde and a real knockout. Just the kind of tomato you want working at your front desk. Customers stop by solely to make time with her.

Frank gives her a feeble wave, full of chagrin. He didn't want to call Nina to come bail him out, but he trusts her more at the moment than he does Parker.

Nina comes rushing over to him. She puts an arm around his waist and presses up against him. She smells like a bowl of fresh-cut flowers, all clean and perky.

"You're hurt!" she cries.

"I'm fine," Frank says. "Have you seen Parker this morning?"

"No. Why? What's happened, Frank?"

"Ah, I'll explain it later. You haven't heard from Parker, have you?"

"Not a peep. Let's get you home and clean you up. You must be exhausted."

"I'm fine," he tells her again but she doesn't let go of him. Nina Randolph is a good kid. Parker is always complaining about her because he thinks she's some kind of chiseler. But she's never been anything except on the level as far as Frank could see. More than likely Parker made a play for her and got the brush-off. He was even making noise about letting her go but you don't fire a looker like Nina. She'll make a good bird dog this season, with her sex appeal. She ought to make hay next week, when those insurance salesmen hit town for their annual convention.

They step outside. Across Flagler Street towers the new Dade County courthouse, all twenty-some stories of it. Frank gazes at the monstrous building of gleaming white marble and tries to imagine how it must feel to be stuck in jail way up there. That's where the new city prison is going to be, right at the top. Fat chance of anyone busting out of there.

"I'm parked in the alley behind the Frissell Building," she tells him. "I hope I don't have a ticket."

"I'll take care of it if you do." Frank grimaces as he starts to walk. The cop got a good knee into his ribs before he stole his money.

"You sure you're okay?"

"I am now. Thanks, kid. I knew I could count on you."

"So if you weren't arrested, why were you in jail?"

"That's a good question. Maybe I should write away to Damon Runyon and ask him."

"Is he a lawyer?"

"No. He's a newspaper hack."

Nina frowns. "They beat you up, too?"

"Some cotton-brained bull got the jumps and let me have it."

"That's dirty pool."

"Tell me about it."

A couple of minutes later, Frank is easing his long body into the front seat of her flivver. No ticket on the windshield. This fact brightens the mood a little.

"Got lucky!" sings Nina.

It's been a while since a skirt drove him anywhere. Feels kind of strange. But Nina can handle herself. She left school when she was fourteen and has gotten by on moxie. She reminds Frank of himself, which is a little screwy if you think about it. Boy, he could use some sleep.

They stop at a light in front of the Bank of Bay Biscayne. A streetcar goes clanging up Miami Avenue.

"Frank?" Nina is looking at him, batting those big brown eyes with girlish concern.

"What's up, sheba?"

"You smell like a dead fish."

"That's good, because I feel like a dead fish."

They cross the river at the drawbridge at Flagler Street. Luckily they don't have to wait. A pleasure boat goes speeding beneath the bridge, kicking up a good wake. Looks like someone is having fun. After all, fun is the reason Florida exists. Those lucky bastards on the boat, all smiling from ear to ear. Maybe this Sunday that'll be him and Irene, cruising toward the Government Cut and then out to the open sea.

"You live at the Crozier, right?"

"It's on Twelfth Avenue."

She hangs a left on Twelfth and cruises past a bunch of small bungalows. A few blocks later she parks in front of the barbershop on the corner of Eighth Street because there's no place closer. Although the Crozier has only a few tenants living in it, the Lawrence Court Apartments next door is pretty full.

"Stay here a second," says Frank, getting out and eyeing his building and its environs. There's a chance Delaney and his goons have tracked him down, so Frank wants to be sure no one is waiting for him. Nothing looks out of the ordinary. No sleek automobiles or suspicious characters. Just rusting flivvers and the usual crowd of porch-sitters.

"What is it?" she asks.

"Nothing."

"Let me help you. You're waddling like a duck."

He and Nina walk slowly to the Crozier and then up two flights of stairs to his apartment, Nina with an arm looped around his waist while he leans on her like a crutch. She's a sweet kid, innocent enough so that you want to protect her from the creeps of the world, but she's no shrinking violet.

Then he reaches for the key to his apartment. Not in any of his pockets. Must've fallen out last night. He'll have to find the landlady, Erma Hayes, and ask her to let him in. So it's back downstairs, and one dirty look later Frank has a spare set of keys. He didn't bother asking Mrs. Hayes about breakfast, she wasn't going to do him another favor.

"Are you hungry?" Nina asks him once they're inside number 2. It feels good to be home but one look around at the dirty clothes and sandy sheets reminds Frank of all the chores still waiting for him today before Irene comes.

"The landlady isn't going to cook for me now, I guarantee it."

"I could make you some breakfast while you get cleaned up. I don't mind, I really don't. You've been so sweet to me, Frank. It's the least I could do."

"You've done plenty already, bailing me out of jail."

"Don't be silly. It's just breakfast."

"I guess you should get in touch with Parker and tell him what happened." Frank's voice drips with more sarcasm than he intended. No use airing the dirty laundry in front of Nina.

"You think he's in?"

Frank chuckles. It's not even nine o'clock. No way Parker made it to the office yet. And what's the difference anyway? He'll deny he had anything to do with setting Frank up. Parker can talk out of both sides of his mouth without really trying.

"Good point."

"I'll go downstairs to see if I can scare up something for you to eat."

"Sure, that sounds swell."

Nina leaves and Frank wobbles back to his bedroom. His head just won't stop pounding. Getting out of these smelly clothes will be a pleasure, and a hot shower ought to perk him up a little. He has a few hours to pull himself together. Of course, there's the problem of Delaney and his goons. Parker might have a few good ideas what to do next, but it's probably not worth asking him. Frank's got to get out of this mess alone. If he had the cash, he'd drive out to the jai alai fronton and return it. It was a stupid thing he did last night. If Irene ever finds out—Frank closes his good eye and starts undressing.

▪ ▪ ▪

Irene Howard doesn't notice the royal palm trees waving along Biscayne Boulevard, nor the sailboats cutting across the blue waters of the bay. The *News* Tower doesn't remind her of its inspiration, the Giralda tower in Seville, although she and Frank marveled at it last spring when they were in Spain. The sights of Miami make no impression because she's thinking only of laying eyes on her beloved Frank. For nearly two weeks she's been journeying toward him, and soon her journey will come to an end and into his arms she'll melt. They'll have several precious hours together before her parents arrive. She's getting goose bumps just imagining it.

After a short drive from the pier, the taxi pulls up in front of the

Crozier, a pink stucco building with a long candy-striped awning that stretches from the front door to the curb. It's not a fleabag, exactly, but not much above one.

"Do you mind waiting?" Irene asks the cabbie, heart racing, hand gripping the metal door handle. "The person I'm looking for might be at work."

"As long as the meter's running, you own me, miss."

"I'll check quickly. Thank you so much."

She steps out of the taxi, smoothing the flowered taffeta dress that falls to her knees. On her feet are Deauville sandals and on her head is a georgette hat, which were all the rage in London last season. Hopefully he'll like her outfit. She won't be wearing it for very long, if everything goes as planned.

She chuckles to herself. She's as nervous as a schoolgirl on the night of the big dance. But Frank Hearn has a way of quickening her pulse. Soon they'll be husband and wife. They're all grown up and before long they'll be parents.

But a little excitement never hurts, so surprising him like this will be perfect. It'll say to him: *We're older and getting married, but deep down, anything is possible between us.* And that's important in a marriage. The last thing Irene wants to become is as comfortable to him as a pair of worn slippers.

Irene ascends the stairs, smiling even as her stomach starts fluttering madly. Each step causes a delicious torment. What is waiting for her? What will he say? What if he's irked at her little surprise? But what if he takes her in his arms and carries her off to bed? "Please be home," she whispers as she stands in front of his door, number 2.

She knocks. No one answers. She leans her head against the door and hears the muted sound of a shower running. This ought to be a thrill, to catch him unaware in the shower. Hand trembling, she reaches down and turns the knob. The door creaks open, like an unearthed vault. A wicked grin appears as she minces into his apartment. This is better than she ever imagined.

Through the living room she breezes. Steam is wafting from the bathroom. He didn't bother shutting the door all the way. Men are so casual about their habits.

She stops at the threshold and sticks her head in. She can see the outline of his physique through the oblique shower curtain. It's definitely Frank, every sculpted inch of him.

"I have a telegram for Mr. Hearn," Irene calls out in a husky voice.

"Nina, is that you?"

Irene recoils as though punched squarely on the jaw. *Nina? Who the hell is Nina?* At that exact moment a young woman comes in carrying a plate of food. "Here you go! I bet you're starving!" the blonde calls out.

Irene's eyes burn with fury. The blonde, Nina, stops dead in her tracks.

"Who are you?" she asks.

But Irene doesn't answer because she can't talk. Her mouth feels stuffed with cotton. She hears the sound of loud bells clanging in her head. Her feet start moving but they don't seem to be attached to her legs. Faster and faster she goes, flying down the stairs with her Deauville sandals flapping like the wings of a large bird. She jumps into the waiting taxi without taking a look back.

"Go!" she yells. The driver throws the cab into gear.

AN OLD SAW

orace Dyer shudders at the unspeakable sight: two bodies soaked in blood, the victims shot at close range. Dyer's handsome, cherubic face has turned ghostly white, and he gulps for air like a drowning swimmer. His straight teeth and straight brown hair seem out of place amid the carnage. Horace Dyer is so well-knit and clean-cut that he belongs on the cover of *The Saturday Evening Post*. He's the kind of young man every mother dreams her daughter will bring home. But now he's standing in a bungalow in the middle of a swamp, inches away from a pool of blood.

"I appreciate your help, Mr. Dyer. I think it's going to take all hands to solve this one." Chief of Police Leslie Quigg radiates the professional detachment of a highly trained law enforcement officer. The badge on his blue uniform shines like a diamond. His white shirt is pressed and starched, garnished by a black bow tie. Two gold stripes and gold stars punctuate his shirtsleeves, at the ends of which two huge hands direct men to various positions. His black hair is combed straight back, framing a face with a prominent nose and a double chin. Hulking and muscular, the ex-boxer in Quigg isn't hard to discern. "With the president coming to town, the last thing the city needs is a killer on the loose. Not after everything we've been through lately."

Then the chief exhales thoughtfully. "Mayor Anderson gave me this job. I don't look forward to telling him that his boy is dead."

"I need some fresh air, Chief."

Dyer walks away from the dead bodies of Parker Anderson and an unidentified woman. He's never seen a murder victim before, even in textbooks. After all, Dyer isn't a cop, just an investigator out of Tampa on loan from the federal prosecutor's office. He's used to examining bank records and title transfers. When he got the call from the MPD this morning, he didn't know what to expect. He wasn't prepared for the carnage.

"You okay, Mr. Dyer?" asks Quigg, catching up with him by the front door.

Dyer knows he has to pull himself together. He can't come across as an out-of-town rube who's in over his head. Even though that's exactly how he feels.

"Who found the bodies?" asks Dyer. Photographers from the coroner's office begin snapping shots of the crime scene.

"A housepainter. Said Parker Anderson hired him and he was supposed to start today."

Dyer looks around. The interior needs some work. You can't sell the Florida dream without the pastel colors that go with it. Not to mention running water or electricity, neither of which this bungalow has. It sits in a subdivision called Sweetwater, a few miles west of downtown Miami on the Tamiami Trail. No one in his right mind would live in the middle of a swamp. But Parker Anderson could sell sand to an Arab.

"I'm just curious, Chief," Dyer asks cautiously. "How did you know to call me?"

"I found your business card in his wallet."

"Really?"

"I figured you and him had something worked out."

Dyer suppresses a bitter laugh. Only someone as reckless as Parker Anderson would keep that business card in his wallet. The kid really considered himself untouchable, being the son of an ex-mayor. In retrospect, Parker wasn't the best candidate to turn state's evidence. He was glib and told good stories, but maybe that's what got him killed: he couldn't keep his mouth shut.

"I had him on a 215 violation," explains Dyer. Quigg raises his eyebrows in apparent confusion. "Section 215 of the federal penal code. Congress passed it to stop the fraud in Florida real estate. An anonymous tip led me to Anderson. He was selling underwater lots out here in Sweetwater. You notice this is the only house that got built."

"Did you charge him?"

"Not yet." Dyer steps out of the way so a team with a gurney can pass by. "We were having conversations. Mostly about someone named Frank Hearn."

Quigg's bushy eyebrows lift in apparent interest. "What do you know about this Hearn character?"

"He was Anderson's business partner. But he's also a punk with a record and ties to organized crime. Bootleggers, thugs, triggermen, those kinds of nice fellows. He's from Asbury Park, New Jersey, and he hasn't been in Miami for long."

"Do you have a motive for why Hearn would've done this?"

Horace Dyer cocks his head nonchalantly. He's got to give Quigg something to go on, even if it means tipping his hand. From what Dyer has heard, the MPD is rife with corruption that starts at the top. But Dyer has a duty to assist in a homicide investigation. Who knows, with some extra help, Dyer might get to the bottom of the real estate cesspool. As his supervisor in Tampa told him, *You'll end up a hero or you'll end up dead. Maybe both.* Dyer took the assignment anyway.

"Anderson was spooning us good, solid dope on Hearn. He and Anderson were playing the C in real estate around here. Until Anderson got caught, that is."

"It doesn't look like he lived out here without water or electricity."

"I'd venture to say he used this bungalow as a love nest."

"You recognize the girl?"

"No. But there wasn't much of her face to recognize."

"So what you're telling me is that Hearn might have found out about Anderson and you, and he either iced Anderson himself or paid somebody to do it."

"Could be, Chief. It's worth looking at."

Quigg rubs his chin thoughtfully. "I think we'll pick up Frank Hearn and shake his tree. Maybe something good will fall out. Do you have an address for him?"

■ ■ ■

Frank hitches up a towel around his waist and hobbles down the two flights of stairs as quickly as he can, fighting the dizziness that threatens to topple him like a bowling pin. Nina is trailing him, tearfully asking him to explain what's happening. But Frank can't bring himself to talk. He just wants to see Irene, if he can catch her.

He steps into the bright sunshine. Out on Twelfth Avenue there's no sign of her. He starts walking east anyway, but it's like chasing your shadow. He stops after fifty yards and turns around. Nina is right behind him.

"Who was she, Frank?"

"She's going to be my wife. At least, she was."

"I didn't know your fiancée was coming!"

They begin drawing curious stares from people walking in and out of Lawrence Court. A man clad only in a white towel, consoling an upset young woman. Frank feels like crying, too. But there isn't time. He's got to find Irene and explain it all. She's supposed to be staying at the Flamingo Hotel in Miami Beach so he should check there first. Unless she's hopping on a boat or a train and heading as far away from Miami as she can get.

But then, right as Frank is about to return to his apartment to get dressed, a black-and-white pulls up in front of the Crozier and stops. Two flatties in uniform and a plainclothes detective emerge, squinting menacingly. They walk past, and a sudden flash of intuition stops him. He watches as the cops go into his apartment building.

He waits until they're inside, and then he grabs Nina by the hand.

"Come on, you got to get me out of here!" he pleads, pulling her toward her Model T parked a couple of blocks away.

■ ■ ■

Irene wipes the last tear from her eyes as the taxi drives across the County Causeway toward Miami Beach. A string of spoil islands lies on her right, dotting Biscayne Bay like white boils. Dredges continue to suck the bay bottom, deepening the channel so that larger ships can enter the port. On her left is Pine Island, where enormous yachts are docked in front of palatial homes of white stucco. Australian pines wave in the gentle breeze. The sun is bright, burning away the morning cool.

Maybe one day Frank and she could've lived in such a paradise, raising their children to be stalwarts of the sea. But no more. Not now.

Oh, stop it, she chides herself. She knows she is being overly dramatic. There was a pretty woman in Frank's apartment, and Irene jumped to conclusions because deep down she feared his infidelity, although he's given her no reason to mistrust him. Maybe there is an explanation. Maybe she should return to find out, now that she's starting to calm down a little.

"Driver?" she asks gently. "Do you mind if we turn around and go back to the Crozier?"

"You own me, ma'am."

"Thank you. I know I'm being a bother."

He executes a sudden left turn onto Star Island and steers the cab back onto the causeway now heading in the opposite direction. Irene's spirits start to lift a little. She should learn not to get jealous, because men don't like being second-guessed. A marriage can't endure if the husband and wife don't trust each other. The last thing she intends to become is one of those disputatious shrews who are unrelenting in their expressions of outrage.

It doesn't take long and she is right back where she was, pulling up to the Crozier. It feels like the rehearsal of a ragged performance, except now Irene gets the chance to play her part to perfection. Even if that little fawn is still there, Irene won't bat an eye. No, this time she'll waltz in and ask to speak with Frank in person, thank you very much, because such are the perquisites of a fiancée.

When she steps out, she notices the police car. That is the only different prop on the set. It's curious but not foreboding. She breezes past it and into the building.

Once again she ascends the two flights of stairs to number 2. She presses an ear to the door, and can hear movement. Someone is walking around, and by the heaviness of the vibrations, Irene deduces that it is not a woman.

She knocks and waits for the door to open. She expects to encounter the same little fawn but instead is greeted by the large features of a uniformed police officer, whose hair resembles a chinchilla perched atop his square head. His stomach protrudes as if he were in the last month of pregnancy.

"Can I help you, ma'am?" he drawls. A Southerner.

"I'm looking for someone."

"Who's that?"

Two more faces leer at her like she's on display at a zoo. Irene grows very afraid and starts to backpedal away from the door. She doesn't go far, though. The cops in unison invite her in to answer a few questions if she doesn't mind. One even grabs her by the elbow.

"Let go of me!" she snaps at him, jerking her arm free.

"Ma'am?"

It's the cabdriver calling out from the lobby. His voice echoes off the walls.

"I'm up here!"

"Should I wait?"

"You go on, boy," one of the cops says.

"The fare is over seven dollars."

"Let me pay him." Irene's voice conveys authority as she walks down the stairs like a zombie. Bewilderment clouds her head. What has Frank done? Is he in trouble? Are these cops trustworthy? What's the smart move she should make?

A sigh.

Why didn't they just elope in Europe? She wanted a wedding, that's why. She wanted to wear a long, flowing gown and have her father give her away. She wanted to eat caviar with her friends and go on a proper honeymoon. She wanted all the things that little girls dream of, and that's why she didn't elope. Stupid, stupid, stupid.

■ ■ ■

Frank can't go barging into the Flamingo Hotel wearing only a towel, so he'll need to borrow some duds from Parker Anderson. And while he's at it, he can get some answers, too. But Frank has the gnawing suspicion that he's not going to see Parker Anderson again. He's probably somewhere having a good laugh with his college chums. They dangled easy money in front of Frank and he jumped at it like a trained seal.

"You didn't know your fiancée was coming in early?" asks Nina, voice as flat as the bridge they're driving across.

"Nope." Frank sighs, head shaking in little abject twists. "She must've wanted to surprise me."

"I think I would've wired ahead."

"Irene likes surprises." He rubs his temples, thinking about the time in Athens she got him a goat for his birthday.

"Apparently so."

"You have no idea." One last chuckle, then he quickly snaps out of his reverie. "Jeepers creepers, I feel like a plate of fried pompano. Do you know where Parker lives?"

"No," she warbles anxiously. "I've never been to his house. Doesn't he live with his parents?" Her tone catches him off guard. Maybe she's just spooked. What normal person wouldn't be?

"Yeah, out on the beach. Take the causeway."

But she takes a wrong turn and they head toward Miami Shores. Nina has become a bundle of raw nerves, like she's seen a ghost.

"Sorry! Those cops back there, they made me nervous."

"Take a deep breath. Parker can explain everything."

"It's none of my business. I know the score. I don't butt in where I don't belong."

"You're not butting in. You're saving my hide, is what."

She steps hard on the gas and they go roaring back to the causeway. It's a white-knuckle ride the whole way to Alton Road. When he sees the glassed-in tennis courts of Miami Beach founder Carl Fisher, he knows they're getting close. Parker likes to sneak in there and play a few sets. He loves bragging about how he gets away with it all the time. But he'll get caught one day. Carl Fisher didn't build those fancy courts for everyone to play on.

"Slow down," he has to tell her when they turn onto Lincoln Road. The Miami Beach cops pull over speeders like there's no tomorrow.

"Sorry."

Mayor Anderson's Spanish-style villa sits off in the distance down Meridian Avenue. Surrounding the house is a sandy stretch of empty lots, allowing Frank to see the throng of police cruisers parked beneath the royal palms Parker was so fond of. Great for resale value, he claimed. Wowsers from Cleveland go gaga for palm trees.

"Keep going," he tells her, mind racing like a five-hundred horsepower engine. "I don't like the looks of this."

"What should I do?" Nina's voice is starting to crack again. Poor kid. Everywhere they turn, more cops. But why here at Parker's house?

"Just keep driving."

"What's happening, Frank? Tell me! Don't hold back."

"I'm not feeding you a line. I'm in the dark like you are. Take me to the Flamingo Hotel. Turn right here. We'll backtrack on Fifth Street."

"I'm scared, Frank. What were all the cops doing at Parker's house? Why did the cops come to your apartment? And why did they arrest you last night?"

"I can't explain it all to you right now," he sighs. A horn blares behind them. A truck wants to get past. "You got to help me. This will all make sense real soon. At least I hope it does."

■ ■ ■

"I will not answer any questions unless I have an attorney present." Irene knows better than to let these cops tear her to pieces. They're looking for Frank, that much is obvious, and they want her to help them. So there she sits, on a sofa cluttered with her fiancé's dirty laundry, facing a detective named Reeve who needs to trim the thicket of hair in his nostrils. Irene can't stand to look at him much longer.

"You don't need an attorney, Miss Howard," he replies in a relaxed manner. "We just need a little assistance if you can provide it."

"Well, I can't. As I told you, I arrived in town this morning. That is my luggage, as you can plainly see."

The detective doesn't look over. The other cops are searching through Frank's apartment, looking for who knows what. These are the rudest police officers she's ever seen; they all speak like hillbilly dirt farmers, with the manners of such lowborn trash.

"How do you know Frank Hearn?"

Irene returns an icy stare, saying nothing.

"Would you be more comfortable if we spoke downtown at police headquarters?"

Now her blood starts to boil. "Don't threaten me! If you so much as lay another finger on me, I'll have your badge. The last time I checked, it's not against the law to knock on someone's door."

"Ma'am, perhaps you don't understand. We're investigating a homicide."

Irene starts to feel faint. The room begins spinning like one of those crazy rides at Coney Island, and she clenches her jaw, breathing slowly through her nose. But still, she tries not to betray a hint of emotion. Not until she knows more.

"I see. Who was the victim?"

"I can't tell you any names. We haven't notified next of kin."

Irene nods, feeling very much like her mother, a woman who never loses her composure. "Frank didn't kill anyone," she says coolly.

"How would you know that?"

"Because I know him. He's not a killer."

"He sure does have a criminal record, though, for such a swell guy."

"That was a long time ago."

The detective grins at her like she's just told an off-color joke. "You sure seem to know a lot about Frank Hearn. Maybe you should come on downtown with us and answer some more questions. Huh? How about that?"

"I've told you all I know. I just arrived from Europe. Would you care to see my passport?"

"No, that's okay."

"I'm sorry someone has died, but I can be no help."

"Just the same, you aren't planning on leaving Miami anytime soon, are you?"

Irene stands up. "I'm staying at the Flamingo Hotel. You can contact me there if you wish."

"So if Frank calls you, you'll let us know, right?"

She smiles like a beauty queen. "Of course, Detective. Harboring a fugitive is against the law."

"It sure is, Miss Howard. We'll talk again later."

Irene picks up her bags and starts off for the stairs. Her Deauville sandals clack against the dusty floorboards, the sound growing fainter until she is finally outside.

■ ■ ■

"The Crozier?"

Lonigan jots the name of the apartment building down, a thin smile cracking his stern face. Took long enough to find Frank Hearn. Like looking for a needle in a haystack. Couldn't get an answer out of anyone at the office where Hearn and Anderson ran a shady real estate business. Neither man was listed in the city directory. Miami isn't a big town compared to Philly, but no one seemed to know nobody else. A city of strangers, almost.

So Lonigan really had to think. He started calling around different real estate companies saying he was looking for an agent with an eye patch by the name of Frank Hearn. Most people said they didn't know nobody by that name or description. Except this last guy, who was real suspicious. So Lonigan tried to sound like he was about to cry. *Our mother just passed away! Can't you help me find my brother?*

"I appreciate it, friend," Lonigan adds for the final touch.

"I think that's where I remember him saying he was staying. We were pretty soaked, though."

"God bless you." Lonigan bites his lip so he won't bust out laughing. He hangs up the phone and then rushes over to tell Delaney the good news.

HERO'S WELCOME

enri de la Falaise is sitting at a table in the hotel's Coconut
Grove, waiting for Joe Kennedy. They are supposed to go fishing today. Joe insisted last night that they engage in this most
masculine of pursuits, since the Florida waters teem with exciting sport fish like tarpon and swordfish. *Landing a big one, there's
nothing like it!* Who was Henri to disagree? Why not take the opportunity to study the man whose life you will be snuffing out. Yes, snuffing out. The words tumble through Henri's mind like glittering
diamonds. *Hoy el muere. Aujourd'hui il meurt. Oggi lui muore.* It won't
be hard because killing is easy. How many German boys did he kill on
the Somme? The certificate that came with his Croix de Guerre
claimed that "Colonel Henri de la Falaise, Marquis de la Coudraye,
killed ten German soldiers who were" blah blah blah "bravery in the
face of fire" blah blah blah, but the point is it was very easy. Pull the
trigger, watch them crumble like the burned crust of old bread.

So Henri must continue to play the part of unsuspecting cuckold.
They will let their defenses down, emboldened by his indifference.

He lifts a sweating highball to his thin lips and takes a long drink,
careful not to stain his mustache with the tomato juice. Nothing like
a nice cocktail to begin the day. Especially today. Things will be differ-

ent after today. There will be an arrest, a trial, but what jury would ever convict him, a wronged husband? Just look at the facts. A man with seven children and a pregnant wife comes to Florida to have an affair with a married woman right under her husband's nose. The Greeks have a word for it: *hubris*. The gods strike down those mortals who fly too high. Doesn't Joe Kennedy know this? Has he not read Homer? Typical American businessman, all dollars and cents, no knowledge of the soul. He is disturbing the basic elements of the universe, and he'll pay dearly for it—to the fourth generation, if those deep-drinking Greeks can be believed.

The private secretary, Eddie Moore, approaches, wearing a white straw hat and an enigmatic expression. Henri stands to greet him, although Kennedy's absence is disturbing.

"Hank, good morning, sir!" he chimes, blue eyes sparkling as he takes a seat. He resembles an Irish publican, square-faced and earnest. "You're looking very natty, like you're ready to catch some fish!"

"I have never been much of an angler. Is that the word? Angler?"

Moore snorts out a porcine laugh. "Beats me, Hank! Sounds about right, though. Say, what's that you're slurping down? Bloody Mary?"

"I believe so."

"Looks good. I'll have mine on the boat! We better shove off if we don't want to be late."

Henri blinks twice, unsure of what exactly is happening. "What about Joe?"

"Oh, he won't be joining us. He sends his regrets, though! He's got to take care of some very important business. You know how it is." Eddie Moore winks and Henri returns a twisted smile.

"Of course. A man like Joe Kennedy, I'm sure, has many pressing matters."

"Well, let's go catch some fish! Huh?" Eddie Moore slaps him on the back and the force of these friendly prompts sends Henri staggering forward, like he's being impelled by a great, menacing wind. There are plenty of men in his social circle who care not with whom their wives spend time. Most have their own mistresses, and governesses for the children. It is considered bad form to call attention to such indiscretions, so Henri must go shuffling along to the waiting car, because to call Eddie Moore what he is—a liar—would overturn the table of half-eaten moral crudités served at the riotous party of the soul. It doesn't take a genius to figure out what Joe Kennedy is planning to do. Didn't Gloria take a shower this morning and rub her feet with sweet-smelling lotion? Wasn't she wearing a flaming red kimono? *I'm going shopping for the kids*, she'd told him.

Her daughter, Gloria, and adopted son, Joseph, whom they call Brother. Henri loves them both dearly. They enjoy dressing up in costumes with him and roaring in laughter at his antics. There is no sweeter sound in the world.

Thinking of the kids only makes it worse. How could Gloria and Joe Kennedy do this to him? And without even thinking of a clever ruse? How stupid do they think he is? It only doubles the humiliation.

Today he dies.

"Lead the way," says Henri.

"I hear you're a war hero!" Eddie Moore thunders, his hand still nudging Henri's back as they lope across the emerald lawns of the Royal Poinciana.

CAN I HELP YOU?

rene joylessly trudges through the well-appointed lobby of the Flamingo Hotel located on the bay side of Miami Beach. It is a huge, hulking barn of pink stucco, with a decor that strikes her as relentlessly Florida: pastels, marine life, palm fronds. Everything is bigger than it needs to be, glossy to the point of smarmy, overbearing in its irrepressible invitations to "have fun" and "relax," and above all dedicated to the haughty display of wealth. Why wear one necklace when six will do just fine? These sunburned barbarians talk loudly, guffaw like baboons, and career about like they have been jolted with electricity. They're rushing across the lobby to and fro, porters nipping at their heels, and the poor concierge! A pack of them has surrounded the addled man, like they intend to tear into his flesh.

Never has she hated this state more than she does now. Why did Frank have to come back here? What is the attraction? Easy money in real estate? He didn't need to earn a dime! She told him a hundred times that she had plenty of money for both of them. If life has taught her anything, it's that time is precious and happiness should be cherished. He almost died saving her from a terrible situation—they've been given a second chance, and they shouldn't waste a moment of it. But he was insistent: before they get married, he wants to "stand on my own two feet." So he left Europe with Parker Anderson, and now the police are looking for him because someone is dead.

She steps into the elevator like a zombie. "What floor, ma'am?" the operator asks her.

She doesn't know. She stares at him blankly, before realizing she's holding the room key. Without speaking, she holds it up so he can read the number. A moment later, off they go. A porter stands at her side, towing her luggage that bears the stickers from her extensive travels. But she looks away rather than remember those glorious days when she and Frank had the world at their fingertips. She examines the silver walls, and in them she can discern a distorted image of herself.

She tries to imagine Frank pointing a gun at someone and pulling the trigger. He wouldn't do that. He left that world behind forever.

A leopard never changes its spots.

She hears her mother's stern voice, the one she uses when she wants to give Irene unsolicited advice or an unsought-for opinion. Of course, she prefaced this warning with: *I like Frank, dear. He's a brave man, a real fighter. But—* Then she delivered the verdict that's ringing in Irene's ears.

"Fifth floor, ma'am."

Irene steps out of the elevator, her legs less steady now, wobbling a little as she walks down the corridor, as if there is some enormous burden on her back that she struggles to carry. The weight is the confusion that has eaten her hollow. What has Frank done? Who was that woman in his apartment anyway? Why are the police looking for him? Her confusion turns back into anger. If she could just get her hands on that big brute, she'd pound him into pulp. She doesn't care how powerful his muscles are, she'll throttle him good.

By the time the porter drops her luggage off, Irene is shaking with rage. She can barely open her purse to get out a tip. But once she does, she is soon alone in the vast sweep of another luxurious suite, the furnishings of which seem oddly Biedermeier. A sofa, a table, some chairs, all probably expensive and all rather dull. Frank would take a look around and say: *Fancy digs.*

"Oh!" she shouts at no one, her fists balled up at her sides. She even stamps her foot, a gesture that strikes her as ridiculous. All of a sudden she's become Mary Pickford, testy that her Douglas Fairbanks is a loveable dunce who drove a car off a cliff. Oops!

Oops is right. She's going to find Frank Hearn if it's the last thing she does. And the first place she's going to look is the office he shares with Parker Anderson. She's going to find out why the cops are looking for Frank. She'll also learn—or die trying—the identity of that woman who was in Frank's apartment.

Wait till Mummy hears all about it. The japery that woman will unload on her—it'll be the worst sort of I told you so.

■ ■ ■

"You can drop me here," Frank tells Nina, who has pulled up in front of the Flamingo Hotel. He's still wearing just a towel but he'll worry about that later. Finding Irene is the most important thing in the world right now.

"Are you sure?" Her voice is still unsteady. Poor kid, she's been through the wringer this morning. She sounds frayed.

"You've done more than enough. Thanks a million, kid. You saved my bacon."

"Oh, Frank. I don't know what to do."

"Just go to work. Act like nothing's wrong. I'll call you later and we'll see if we can't figure out the score."

Frank slams the car door and starts off for the lobby, drawing curious stares from those who can't help looking at a very tall, very muscular man with a black eye patch, six stitches sewn into his face, and a thin white towel hitched around his waist. Frank's caveman attire stands in stark contrast to the regally appointed porters who look snappy in their vermilion uniforms with gold epaulets. The guests are dressed elegantly yet casually, women in loose-fitting charmeuse and men in sporty knickers.

Frank can feel the eyes boring into him, so he's starting to wonder about the frontal approach. Walking into the lobby and up to the front desk will get him nothing but trouble. But he's got to figure out a way to get Irene's room number.

He stands beneath an Australian pine and regards the hotel. It's plenty big, with doors and sidewalks enough for an enterprising man to find a secret passage. Getting in without being noticed shouldn't be a problem. What he's going to do after that—well, he hasn't gotten that far yet. First things first.

He smiles at an old woman who glares at him with smoldering, beady eyes. "Just went swimming," he chirps as he proceeds down a sidewalk canopied by a row of palm trees. He walks quickly past a row of Afromobiles, bicycles with wicker baskets hitched to them so Negro boys can pedal these fat cats around. Then it's past the tennis courts, where Frank earns a few curious glances from the prim and proper. Soon enough he's free and clear from the clutter of the entrance. Time now to get his wits back.

He's reached the southernmost corner of the hotel, where a breezeway connects the main building to an annex. In front of him glitters Biscayne Bay, where young men in white uniforms stand on gondolas to pole the guests on short pleasure rides over the still, blue waters. Maybe once he finds Irene, they can hop aboard one of those and go for a quiet little cruise, just the two of them. But how's he going to find her?

He follows a sidewalk and snakes through a grove of stubby palm trees that look like they just got planted. Now he's facing the hotel's rear but it looks equally imposing, like a fortress rising up into the cloudless sky. But he keeps on walking, mind racing, looking for any angle he can play. He approaches the back portico, where he can see a throng lounging around in the cool shade, reclining on cushions and getting served cold drinks. What a happy-looking bunch of swells.

He better come up with something.

Then he spots a phone sitting unused atop a small glass-topped table. A house phone! He'll just call her room! Why didn't he think of that earlier? Hell's bells, he's had a lot to gnaw on this morning, so he's not as sharp as he should be.

He strides manfully over to the phone and picks it up with an air of authority. He keeps the towel firmly grasped with his free hand because it really feels like it could slip off. That would gum up the works.

"Irene Howard's room, please," he tells the switchboard operator.

After a pause he hears ringing. His pulse quickens in anticipation of hearing her voice, realizing it will sound strange because they haven't spoken in so long. But disappointment quickly sets in because the ringing continues, with Irene never answering.

She's not there.

His head pounding and his stomach twisted in knots, Frank decides to sit down and collect himself before starting off in who knows what direction. If only Irene would come back, that would be a start. He slumps into a chair, imagining Irene hopping on a train for New York and away from him. He leans back and closes his eye, wishing for some good luck. Winning that money last night was about the worst thing that's happened to him in a long time. Go figure.

With his good eye closed, Frank doesn't notice the horrified look of the plump, red-faced woman sitting at a table opposite him. He doesn't see her stand up and call a waiter over, and point out what has so upset her. The waiter sees it, too, and hurries to fetch hotel security. Not a minute later, as Frank is starting to come up with a plan, he feels two hands grab him around the arms and pull him from the chair.

"Come on, pervert," one of the hotel detectives snarls at Frank, who is now hopelessly confused.

"What'd I do? Can't a man sit down?"

"You're sick, fella. Flashing women in public."

"I didn't flash nobody!"

"Come on, tell it to the judge."

■ ■ ■

So many birds. A million of them almost. Long birds, shorts birds, every kind of bird. In Philly all you see is pigeons begging for food.

"Stop the car," says Delaney.

Figgins pulls off the sandy path, driving over some saw palmetto.

They're a couple of miles outside Miami. First they went down something called the Tamiami Trail. It's the road that runs from Tampa to Miami. You can stop at a hut and get your picture taken with a real-live Seminole Indian. That would make a postcard. The boys back in Philly would howl about that.

Garate is in the backseat. His hands are tied behind his back and his mouth is gagged with an old smelly sock. Boy, that thing reeks!

Delaney spins around and looks at Garate. "You're a stupid kid, you know that? *Stupido! Muy stupido!*"

Delaney says some other junk in Spanish but it sounds like gibberish. Figgins watches a bird with a long sharp beak peck at the ground. Peck peck peck.

Figgins lets out a loud yawn. Last night was a long one. A real long one. One thing after another. But at least they figured out who the man in the eye patch was. Frank Hearn. Uncle Gene was glad to hear that. Now all they got to do is find him. That's what Lonigan is doing today.

"Get him."

Figgins opens the door and steps out. The ground is soft beneath his feet. The sun shines brightly through a few clouds. It must be easy to hunt birds in Florida. Like shooting fish in a barrel.

Figgins reaches in and grabs Garate by the arms. He's not very big. None of the spic players are big. His eyes are big, though. Big and wide and teary. He's trying to talk but he can't because of the sock. Delaney comes over.

"You do it," he says to Figgins.

"I don't have my rod."

"You should always have it! Always!"

"I left it at home." It's heavy to carry it around. Sometimes it pinches him in the stomach. Like he's getting tickled. He always hated getting tickled. Unless Daddy did it. "But sure, Uncle Gene. I will from now on."

"You got lots to learn, kid. Lots to learn. Let him go."

Figgins lets go of Garate's arms. For a second Garate stands there frozen. Like he's not sure where he is. Sometimes when blind people get their sight back, there's a minute when they're confused. It's like that.

Then Garate starts to run. His feet churn against the sandy ground. It sounds like a baby's rattle. Delaney waits a few seconds, then starts shooting. Garate crumples about twenty yards away. Birds go flying in every direction. It's hard to believe so many birds could live in one place. Some good hunting back in here.

"He got me in the back," says Delaney softly, "and I got him in the back." Then he starts yelling at the dead body but all the noise goes into Figgins's ear and it starts to ring. "You're a stupid kid, you know that! A stupid kid!"

THE KINDNESS OF STRANGERS

ehind Harvey Firestone's large oak desk, a ten-by-twelve-foot picture window perfectly frames the cadet-blue water of the Atlantic Ocean. On days when he is in a more cheerful mood, the tire baron will stroll out to the balcony that opens off his study and sit in a high-backed wicker chair, glass of sherry in hand, and watch the breakers roll in. He will pick up binoculars and observe the shorebirds scampering along the sand of his Miami Beach estate, Harbel Villa, a prodigious expanse of oceanfront property that runs from the surf back to Collins Avenue. Serpentine paths wind through sunken gardens and tennis courts, swimming pools and sundecks, two guest lodges and the servants' quarters. Until recently Firestone kept a dwarf hippopotamus on the grounds, but last year he had the beast delivered as a gift to President Coolidge. Now the old sluggard is coming to town on Saturday. Hopefully the hoopla of a presidential visit will give Miami a badly needed lift. And perhaps just meeting the president will steer a certain young man on a different path in life. Once again his nephew Bryce is causing Harvey Firestone to worry.

A soft knock on the door causes Firestone's smooth, tanned face to grow stern. His carefully parted brown hair has grown gray at the temples. This year he turns sixty, but on some days it feels more like a hundred. "Come in," he commands.

A head appears. "You sent for me?"

"An hour ago! Sit down. I need a word with you."

Bryce Shoat steps into the room as if he's trying not to make a sound, but his rubber-soled tennis shoes squeak against the hardwood floor. White shirt and white shorts complete his tennis ensemble. His eyes, though, are bloodshot, and judging from his stubble the lad hasn't shaved for days. One thing Harvey Firestone prizes is being well-groomed. A man ought to wear his heart on his sleeve, and show the world exactly what he's made of.

Bryce sits down facing his uncle. "Do you know who called me this morning?" asks Harvey Firestone in a voice that booms like a foghorn.

"No, sir."

"Maurice Zimmerman."

Bryce shifts uncomfortably in his Chippendale chair.

"He said you convinced him to invest in a subdivision, but the title you sent him was defective."

"I can explain!"

Harvey Firestone holds up his hand and closes his eyes. Bryce talks too much and listens precious little. He has an answer for everything and nothing is ever his fault. It's not that Bryce, still a young man at twenty-four, hasn't shown glimmers of promise. One of the best polo players on the East Coast, a crack tennis player, scratch golfer, and excellent swimmer, he is a tassel-haired, loose-jointed, handsome kid who badly needs direction. And that's precisely what Harvey Firestone intends to provide. Responsibility begets character and therefore is the basis of character building. He'll mold Bryce into a decent citizen even if it kills them both.

"No, Bryce, don't explain anything. I want you to call Maurice Zimmerman, right now, and explain to him what happened." He slaps his hand on the desk. The thud hangs in the air for a few seconds, but then Bryce Shoat swallows hard and learns forward in his chair.

"Uncle Harvey, I didn't do anything wrong."

"No, Bryce. I don't want an explanation. Call Zimmerman. But I give you fair warning: you're running out of chances with me. I took you in after your poor mother ran into difficulties with the understanding that you'd live up to the Firestone standard. But so far you haven't done much of anything. If you keep up this lollygagging, I'll send you to Liberia to learn the business of rubber! That ought to make a man out of you!"

"But I haven't done anything wrong, Uncle Harvey."

"Don't talk! Listen, Bryce. Listen to what I'm saying. You're down to your last out. One more indiscretion, one more embarrassing lapse in judgment, and I will personally throw you aboard the next steamer for Monrovia. Do you read me loud and clear?"

"Yes, sir."

Harvey Firestone regards his nephew with anger—and sympathy. It's hard for a boy to grow up fatherless, as Bryce did. But Bryce has been indulging himself for too long, and it is time for him to face the music. And now this nonsense with an old family friend, Maurice Zimmerman.

"I promise that I'll never flub up again for as long as I live. And today I guarantee we'll lick those pussyfoots in Palm Beach!"

Polo is Harvey Firestone's passion, and nothing gives him greater joy than sticking it to those morally decrepit louses from Palm Beach— but without Bryce riding as a number-three man, the task would prove difficult if not impossible. So the uncle smiles at his wayward nephew, who is a magician aboard a pony with a mallet in his hand, and the anger that was nearly choking him begins to recede.

"Just call Maurice Zimmerman and clear this matter up."

"It's a misunderstanding, is all. I'll take care of it. I'm sorry he's sore."

■ ■ ■

The philodendron on her desk has died because Nina Randolph never watered it. She didn't like the plant much anyway. The man who gave it to her, Vernon Silbert, was a blocky, ham-fisted chiseler who always had dandruff flakes on his shoulders and bits of food stuck in his yellow teeth. Every time he stopped by the office, Vernon Silbert made a point of chatting with her. Because he was a client, Nina had to pretend like what he had to say was interesting.

But she won't have to do that ever again.

The police have come by. They wanted to know where Frank was. One flattie looked like he was ready to sit and wait, which would have been disastrous with Bryce on his way, so Nina had said: *Frank just called from his apartment.* That sent them scurrying away.

She's standing at the window, peering between the blinds at the parking lot below. It is empty, except for her Model T and a Buick belonging to the man who works downstairs. Sometimes it gets lonely in the building since there are so few tenants. When Parker and Frank are gone, Nina must busy herself the best she can, with a radio as her only companion. But after today, she won't be stuck in here.

Is this really happening? Can she actually pull this off? When she was a little girl, she used to lie in bed, stomach twisting in pain from hunger, dreaming of the day she'd be rich. The kids at school laughed at her for wearing the same clothes every day: blue gingham dress with lace around the scoop neck, white patent-leather shoes two sizes too small. She tried to keep them polished, just like she tried to keep the dress clean.

Nina hated the laughter so much that she stopped going to school, and at fourteen, after her father died, she started selling flowers at the foot of Elser Pier. She spent all day gathering them from various gardens—hibiscus, geraniums, pentas, frangipani, whatever she could find growing. She'd stand on the sidewalk at the end of Flagler Street, hoping to take home a dollar. Some days it was more, and some days it was less. Afterward she'd trudge back to an empty two-bedroom cottage in Coconut Grove with a leaky roof and windows that were stuck in place. The screens had rips and holes in them, so palmetto bugs and mosquitoes came and went as they pleased. She'd try to sleep, but it was scary for a kid to be alone at night. Not that things got better when

Mother came staggering home drunk. When she brought someone with her, Nina would have to listen to the vile sounds, lying there on her musty bed in a room not much larger than a closet. She'd tell herself: *I'll be rich one day. I'll never live like this again.*

There it is, Bryce's Nash roadster, bedecked with dazzling swirls of chrome and shiny wood side panels. It's hard to miss that car. Parker Anderson drove one just like it. What a pair, those two. A couple of snotty-nosed brats who thought they could make her play fetch. But every dog has its day. Today is Nina's.

She watches as Bryce parks in the empty lot behind the building. He gets out, scowling up toward the window where Nina is standing. She hops away like a scared bunny. Fear grips her by the throat, and the enormity of what's happened feels like an anchor pulling her under the sea. She, Nina Randolph, is about to change her life forever. The girl nobody noticed until she blossomed last year, springing to life like a hothouse flower, one day skinny as a rail and plain as brown paper, and the next a tall, ravishing beauty—the girl nobody noticed is about to become rich.

She hears footsteps outside the office door. Through the opaque glass she sees his outline. Broad shoulders, Roman nose.

The door creaks open. His head pops in. "Nina?"

She runs to him and throws her arms around his neck, as though she were smitten. "I missed you!" she gushes.

He looks surprised. "Where is everybody?"

"They're not here."

"Must've been some night at the jai alai fronton. I'm almost sorry I missed it, except I hate being around that little tub of lard."

His riding boots clack against the floor as he scurries over to peer into Parker's office. He takes a step inside. What he's looking for, he won't find. She walks up behind him.

"Did you get the files?" he asks, turning around. "I got to scram. There's a big polo match with Palm Beach."

"Will Janice be there?"

He's standing over her now. He leans down and kisses her. His lips feel leathery and chapped, like an old football. There was a time when his kisses sent her heart into wild ecstasy. But not now.

"Who cares about her? Compared to you, she's a cow. So where are the files? Did you get them?"

Here's the moment she's been waiting for. This will let him know she isn't playing games anymore. "I need to tell you something. It's about Parker."

"What did that moron do now?"

"He was murdered last night."

"Murdered?"

"The police think Frank Hearn did it. They came by here looking for him."

"Did they search the place?"

"No."

Bryce's eyes dart around the office. He looks like a mouse trapped in a small cage. "You have the files, right? The ones from Sweetwater?"

"They're somewhere very safe."

He looks at her like she just spit in his face. His lips start quivering and his nostrils flare, and there's only one word that describes his attitude: contempt. Although she suspected he'd act like this, it still shocks her. Because she did love him once. She would've done anything for him.

"Where, Nina? This isn't funny anymore! Parker is dead! This is serious business!" He tries to compose himself and turn on the charm. She used to fall for that act every time, the cocksure smile and rakish wink. "I need those files, honey. My nerves are a little frayed. Sorry I yelled like that."

She walks over to her desk, keeping her head held high, so that her posture is perfect. Mother's back curves like the handle of a teapot, so Nina has spent years working on hers, walking around the house with a book poised on her head.

She reaches inside a drawer. He thinks she's getting the files. She can hear his relaxed breathing. She grabs the note, which is the part she thought would be the best. The look on his face when he reads it.

"What's that?" he says, trying to sound pleasant but he's still confused.

"Read it." She hands him the note, with its very simple message: "$10,000." She examines his face carefully, looking for that flash of recognition when he realizes he's not in charge anymore. A slight curl of the mouth. A lift of the eyebrows. A blush of red in the cheeks.

"What's this supposed to mean?"

"That's how much I want for the files, Bryce. In cash."

He bites his lower lip. She's never seen him do that before.

"You're blackmailing me, too? What's that about? Who put you up to this?"

"In cash by the end of the day. Meet me at the band shell at Royal Palm Park. Five o'clock sharp."

"Well, looks like you've stepped in it now, Nina. Did you think this crazy plan would actually work?"

"Fine. I'll call the police and tell them everything I know. And maybe I'll make up some junk, too."

He grabs her arm and won't let go. He's strong and very powerful, with muscles as taut as steel cables. The first time they made love, she was awed by his physique, so lean and tapered, like a Greek god. They were on the beach in Fort Lauderdale, and Nina was in love. But not now. She sees Bryce Shoat for what he is: a spoiled rich kid who can only think about himself.

"Let go of me!"

"I want the files."

"You can have them, for ten grand. Small, unmarked bills."

He lets go of her. "I thought we had something here, something special. At least that's what you told me."

"Now you know what it feels like to be used."

That comment catches him off guard. He seems stunned for a few seconds. "Yeah, well, you're wrong about me, Nina. I wasn't using you, in case you didn't notice."

"I noticed."

"I don't have ten thousand dollars."

"I thought you were going to soak Janice for it, so we could run off together."

He looks like a sad, wet puppy dog. But he's lying. He can get the money. He'll have to go begging for it. He'll have to get on his hands and knees.

"You killed him, didn't you?"

She shakes her head and sighs dramatically. "Who knows, maybe you did. You sure had reason to. After all, Parker wouldn't destroy those Sweetwater files. He wanted to hold them over your head in case you decided to start crooning to the cops. You even tried to get me to steal them for you. Poor, little me."

"All right! Just shut up! I'll get your money, you miserable slut."

"It's not nice to call people names, Bryce."

"Yeah? You'll get what you deserve."

He's all bark and no bite, a little poodle with a fancy leash. She gives him one last smile. "Don't do anything stupid. You wouldn't want Uncle Harvey getting mad at you. You better get out of here before the cops come back and start asking you questions."

■ ■ ■

In front of the entrance to Burdines Department Store, a group of well-appointed dames sits stiffly behind folding tables covered with white linen. On the tables are stacked an assortment of cakes, pies, and cookies. A sign inked in bold blue tells the numerous passersby that money is being raised for the Free Milk Fund. Each year the group throws a gala ball at the McAllister Hotel, in which prizes are raffled and some of Miami's most prestigious men and women vie for gewgaw trinkets as if they were treasures from King Tut's tomb. While the event is a highlight of the social calendar, it is hardly public. The bake sale at Burdines raises far less money but has the advantage of allowing everyday working people to make a modest contribution. As the sign reads: EVERY NICKEL HELPS.

Janice Pendergast crafted the sign just this morning. As she stands beneath the heavy awning, she keeps one eye out for Bryce, who said he would come but probably won't, and the other on the gorgeous crepe smocks hanging on the mannequins in the picture window of Burdines. Maybe once this is over, she can go shopping for a special something to wear to the polo match. She remembers Bryce saying the opponent today was Palm Beach. Who wouldn't want to look ravishing?

"Let's see, it all looks so good."

Janice knows that voice—it's Bryce! He came after all! There he is, standing over a plate of sugar cookies, wearing his polo uniform. He came! Janice waves.

"What did you make?" he asks her.

"The sign."

"I can't eat that." Then he smiles at her mother. "Hi, Mrs. Pendergast. How are you today?"

"Just fine, Bryce. And you?"

"Can't complain."

"How is your uncle?"

"He stays pretty busy."

"Give him my best, will you?"

Janice smirks at this exchange. Around her society friends, Mother treats Bryce like royalty. He's got the right family connections and memberships at the right clubs. But privately Mother thinks Bryce is a playboy. She claims to have heard rumors about Bryce. He gambles. He's a womanizer. He drinks alcohol. All so scandalous. Janice feels like saying: *And he gets the best booze in Colored Town!*

"Aren't you coming to the polo match?" he asks. Mother practically swoons.

"I think I'll be too fatigued. But thanks for the invitation. Aren't you going to buy anything for the cause?"

"Yeah, let's see. How about a cookie? Here's a quarter." He drops it in a tin can decorated with pink felt.

"Thank you, Bryce. That's awfully kind of you."

"Sure, Mrs. Pendergast. It's a swell cause, free milk."

He walks over to Janice, his cookie in hand, shooting her a know-ing look that says: *Please rescue me.* Nothing would suit her better than taking a quick spin in his Nash roadster. She's not mad at him anymore for talking to that blonde last night. Janice caught him lying through his teeth but it's not like there are scads of young men in Miami who like to dance and listen to race records. Bryce is fun, he's handsome, and he likes to loaf around. It's not like she's going to marry him—or anyone, for that matter.

"Can you take a quick walk?" he asks, sounding a little funny.

"Sure. I've done my duty to help the poor."

They head north up Miami Avenue toward Flagler Street, past the Biscayne Hotel with its doormen attired in deep purple uniforms. A streetcar rattles past, turning right on Flagler and stopping.

"I need to ask you . . . a favor," he stammers.

"What?"

But he doesn't answer her. He keeps on walking, his face growing more agonized with each stride.

"What is it, Bryce?"

He stops in front of the Kress 5-10-25 Cent Store. Inside there is a red-tag sale. But hardly anyone is shopping.

"I need to borrow some money." He turns away from her and runs his hands through his hair.

She pulls on the back of his uniform. Number 3. That's the hard-est position to ride in polo. "How much money?"

"I can't believe I'm asking you for money. This isn't right."

"How much?"

She's standing in front of him now, blocking his forward motion. He finally looks down at her. He really could use a shave. "I wouldn't ask you unless it was serious. You know that, don't you?"

"How much, you simp?"

He shakes his head warily. "Ten grand."

"Ten thousand dollars?"

"I can't go to Uncle Harvey—he said he'd send me to Africa! I don't want to go to Africa! They kill white people there! One of my cousins almost had his head chopped off!"

A black man goes shuffling past and into Kress. Bryce lowers his voice and pulls Janice toward the Woolworth next door. "I don't have anywhere else to turn, Janice. I'm in trouble."

"What sort of trouble?"

"Big trouble."

"I figured that out." His head is perfectly framed by the two Os in the painted Woolworth's sign on the large picture window. He looks like a strange animal with huge ears. Sort of like a mouse but not quite.

"Listen, I did something stupid. Last night after I dropped you off, I went by the casino at the Seminole Hotel. I don't know, I guess I was pretty gassed. I lost a lot of money and I have to pay it back by today or—" His voice breaks off and he wipes his eyes. His body falls back against the picture window, near the display for beach umbrellas. "They'll kill me."

"But you're a Firestone. They wouldn't kill a Firestone, would they?"

"My last name is Shoat and they don't care, Janice. They just want their money. I never should've stopped by that rotten casino. I'm some kind of soak, huh?"

"No."

"Can you help me out? I'll pay you back."

"Sure, Bryce. If you're really in trouble, I'll help you."

"Oh, Janice, you're aces!" He reaches out and pulls her toward him. He throws his powerful arms around her. Her face comes to rest against his heart, which she can feel beating wildly, like he just sprinted a couple of blocks. He's sweating, too.

"I wish I had time to thank you properly," he whispers, "but I've got to get over to the stables."

"Should I bring the money to the polo match after I get it?"

"That would be very, very decent of you."

"I don't mind."

"And tonight I promise I'll pick up a bottle of bourbon. How does that sound?"

"It sounds good."

He kisses her on top of the head. She'd like to kick him in the shins but something stops her.

■ ■ ■

Irene Howard tells the driver to wait and steps out of the hotel courtesy car. She surveys the nondescript Watson Building that houses the offices of Anderson and Hearn. It's a humdrum box of three stories painted a neutral shade of gray with a very large and very prominent FOR RENT sign hanging in a window on the first floor. The empty lots around the building are all studded with FOR SALE signs. One might surmise that the Miami real estate business is in dire straits. Frank's letters were vague on this point, if not misleading. He always maintained an optimistic tone. *Doing fine, very busy*, and the like. Apparently he's got a lot to explain, to the cops and to her.

She doesn't expect Frank to be here, of course. But Parker Anderson might have answers, if he's arrived at work yet. Nothing makes sense, and she fears that things will probably get worse before they get better. She feels like someone has turned off all the lights and she must now grope through the darkness, looking for a switch.

The lobby of the Watson Building is tiled in checkerboard fashion and smells of stale smoke. The barbershop sits in darkness, and a sign on the confectioner's door reads: WILL RETURN SOON. There is a land title company on the first floor but it doesn't look like it is conducting much business these days. She scans the directory for the room number of Anderson and Hearn, who seem to be the last remaining tenants on the second floor.

She marches up the stairs to the second floor, growing ever more apprehensive. She is on an absurd errand, chasing down leads to find her fiancé who is in turn wanted by the cops. The last time she felt overwhelmed by events was also the last time she was in Florida. What is wrong with this part of the world? A better question might be: What is wrong with her?

"No," she mumbles to herself when she reaches the second floor. "Everything will work out."

She begins looking for number 205, a short trek that takes her around a corner and down a hall. She sees the marbled glass door with the name Anderson and Hearn painted in block lettering. She opens it and the first person she sees is a pretty young blond woman sitting at a desk. It is the same woman she saw in Frank's apartment. His secretary, Nina Randolph, according to the nameplate. How convenient for him. Didn't need to roam far and wide to find a willing lover.

Their eyes meet. Nina Randolph shows no trace of recognition. A smile creases her smooth face.

"Can I help you?"

"I'm . . . looking for Frank Hearn," Irene stutters, mind racing. "Or Parker Anderson."

"Both of them are out for the moment."

"When will they return?"

"I'm not sure. Would you care to leave a message?"

You're good, thinks Irene, impressed by Nina's ice-watery ability to lie. She would make one fine actress.

"Yes." Irene is about to give out the name of the hotel where she is staying. But suddenly she decides that such information might be best left undisclosed. Nina Randolph doesn't need to know too much. Suddenly Irene doesn't know what to say to this woman. His secretary! How perfectly abysmal! Inside Irene's heart the chamber of love grows soot black. The lights have been shut off.

"I hate to presume, but are you Frank's fiancée?"

Irene nearly staggers from this question. The audacity of this wench! "Yes, I am."

"He's told me so much about you!"

"Has he?"

"Yes! I'm glad you made it here safe and sound."

"Do you know where Frank is at the moment? I can't seem to find him."

"He might be on a sales call. I thought he mentioned you were coming in this afternoon."

"My plans changed. I'll check back later, thank you."

Irene has had enough of this little charade and strains mightily to harness her anger. She turns to leave and nearly bowls into a man who is just entering the office.

"Excuse me," he offers politely, stepping aside. He's not quite as tall as Irene, but his clothes and manners suggest a person of some importance. His gray flannel suit appears to be tailored and his cuff links are gold. His soft blue eyes and neatly combed brown hair make him boyishly handsome. His build is athletic and he exudes an air of authority as he approaches Nina Randolph.

Irene leaves the office but doesn't go very far down the hall, because behind her she can hear the man introduce himself as Horace Dyer. He is some kind of special investigator. Then, as if on cue, two police officers come shuffling around a corner, talking in low, conspiratorial tones.

A few seconds later Nina Randolph starts crying. She comes out of the office and heads down the hallway and into the ladies' room. Horace Dyer trails behind. He looks concerned and compassionate as his eyes fall on Irene. "You guys go on in and get started. I'll be right there."

"Has something happened?" Irene asks timidly after the cops go into the office.

"Something has happened," Dyer answers softly. "Did you know Parker Anderson?"

"Is he dead?"

"Why would you ask that?"

Irene covers her mouth. Is that why the cops are after Frank? This is monstrous! Hot tears flush down her cheeks and she turns away from Dyer. Her body begins to move. She feels a strong hand on her shoulder.

"Ma'am, I need to ask you a couple of questions, if you don't mind."

But talking about it is the last thing Irene wants to do. Nothing makes sense. Parker is dead and the police think Frank did it. Frank was screwing his secretary and the tramp is just a few feet away. Last week Irene was in London shopping at Harrods. She was looking for a wedding dress.

"I can't talk right now," Irene replies between sobs.

"I understand. Just take a minute and collect yourself."

"I don't know anything anyway."

"You knew Parker Anderson?"

"Yes, but I don't know why anyone would want to kill him. Oh, please, I can't talk right now!"

"Can I just have your name?"

"It's Irene Howard."

"Irene, I'm Horace Dyer. I'm an investigator with the federal attorney's office. Here's my card."

Irene turns and takes the card from Dyer. His voice is smooth and reassuring, at all times in control. His demeanor has helped stop the flow of tears, and the shock is beginning to give way to another emotion—anger. Irene's eyes burn as she glares at the ladies' room door.

"Listen, Mr. Dyer, I don't know what's going on but if I were you, I'd ask a lot of questions of that secretary, Nina Randolph. She's up to no good as far as I can tell."

As soon as these words leave Irene's mouth, she realizes that she shouldn't have said anything, because now she's opened the wrong can of worms.

"Why would you say that?"

"I can't explain why right now."

"Miss Howard, this is a homicide investigation. If you know something that can help the police solve the case, you have to tell us."

"I'm not saying anything more without an attorney, Mr. Dyer."

"I can have you booked you as a material witness. Is that what you want, Miss Howard? To spend time in jail?"

"Of course not."

"Then we need to talk."

Irene is still glaring at the ladies' room door, waiting for Nina Randolph to show her face. She's in the middle of this, Irene can feel it in her bones. But where is Nina Randolph? "I'm not a cop, Mr. Dyer, but how long does it take for a woman to powder her nose?"

■ ■ ■

Nina Randolph turns on a faucet full blast. What rotten luck! She was just getting ready to leave. She was literally seconds from standing up and walking out forever and starting her new life, when the last person in the world Nina expected to see popped in. Frank's fiancée. She's going to tell the cops that she saw her in Frank's apartment this morning. The cops will think Nina and Frank were having an affair, and that might cause them to look at Nina as a suspect in Parker's murder. They might detain her, possibly even book her.

For the first time in a long time, Nina Randolph is scared.

She's worked too hard for this. At five o'clock today she stands to make $10,000. All she has to do is show up at Royal Palm Park and Bryce will have the money. But how is she supposed to get out of here?

There is a window. It's over the toilet and is already half open. Should she make a run for it? She has her purse. Her car is in the parking lot. She could drive to the hotel. The Sandman on Dixie Highway. But that's risky. If they catch her trying to crawl out the window, her goose is cooked.

If only that fiancée hadn't shown up! If only Frank hadn't been arrested! But she can't bitch and moan about rotten luck. You make your own luck in this world. Nina dashes over to the toilet and lifts herself up. It takes all her strength but she manages to pull herself up and then through the pollen-smeared opening. Now her dress is dirty. But ten grand will buy a gal plenty of dresses.

■ ■ ■

"Miss Randolph?"

Horace Dyer stands at the ladies' room door, tapping on it lightly with his knuckles. The faucet has been running long enough for Nina Randolph to take a bath. He knocks louder and raises his voice, but still there's no response from within. He motions for Irene to come over.

"Could you go in there and see if she's okay?"

"Sure."

Horace Dyer steps back and lets her brush past him. Even in the distressed state she's in, Dyer can tell Irene Howard is not just attractive but well-bred and high-class. Everything about her seems upper crust. Her skin shines like it's been buffed. Her nose is straight and elegant, and her neck is long and thin. Her black hair is all dolled up, and her shoes probably cost more than what he earns in a month. She exudes an air of refinement and aloofness that tells most men from the start they haven't a prayer—not unless their blood is blue and their wallets are fat.

"There's no one in here," Irene calls out.

"What?"

Irene comes back out to the hall. "She's not in there."

Dyer darts into the ladies' room. After a quick inspection he realizes that Nina Randolph might have slipped through the open window. But maybe he's imagining things.

"Let me try the office." Horace Dyer scurries over to the door. He pokes his head in and finds the two MPD patrolmen lounging in chairs. Some help they'll be combing through records. Dyer didn't want any help from the MPD but Quigg insisted, since Dyer isn't a real cop.

No Nina Randolph.

He steps back, perplexed. Why would the secretary scram like a bat out of hell? One person who might know is Irene Howard, whom just a few minutes ago voiced suspicions about the comely secretary.

"I'll be right back," he tells Irene. "Don't go anywhere." Then he gathers up the two cops and they all trot downstairs. A quick search proves fruitless. He trudges back upstairs, head still spinning from the possibilities. Now he needs Irene Howard's cooperation more than ever. At least she didn't run off. She's still in the hallway.

"It seems as though Nina Randolph has absconded," he announces dryly. Irene doesn't look altogether surprised. Her pretty face barely registers a change. An eyebrow lifts a millimeter, but that's all. "Perhaps you'd like to tell me why."

"I don't know why."

"Miss Howard, it's time to drop the pretenses. What do you know about Nina Randolph? Why would she avoid talking to us? What do you know?"

Irene doesn't answer. She throws her head back like he just told an off-color joke.

"Okay." He grins. "How about an easy one. Why are you here?"

"I've been asking myself that."

"Cute. But I'm running out of patience, not to mention time. You'd better start jawing or I'll have Tweedledum and Tweedledee haul you in. The jail downtown isn't exactly a resort."

She frowns at him. It only makes her more beautiful, showing the flame that burns brightly within her.

"You're awfully pushy," she tells him. But it sounds more like a compliment than a brush-off.

"I get that way when I want the truth."

"The truth?" She spits out the word like the pit of a rotten cherry. "The truth is, Mr. Dyer, that Nina Randolph is in love and love makes women do stupid things."

"I don't like riddles. Who are you protecting?" He pauses to answer his own question. It doesn't make sense but it's the only possible conclusion. "Frank Hearn? Is that who you came looking for?"

Tears begin to well in her eyes. So that's it. Irene Howard knows something about Nina Randolph and Frank Hearn, but she won't say what and how, and sticking her in jail wouldn't pry it from her, either.

She's too strong for that. He needs to coax her along gently and soothe her defenses down. There are worse assignments.

"You're in love with Frank, too. But he was having an affair with Nina. And you found out."

She glares at him. "I'm not answering any more questions."

"Hey—I know how it feels. I had a fiancée who took a liking to my best friend."

"Can I go?"

"How can I get in touch with you? And don't lie, because if I think you're lying, I'll just have one of these fine Miami police officers follow you around all day."

"The Flamingo Hotel."

"You're not from here?"

"Isn't it obvious?"

"Call me if you decide you want to do the right thing. I work late hours. You know, digging for the truth."

With that she turns around and leaves. As she goes, Dyer can't help wondering how she ended up in love with the likes of Frank Hearn. Now there's a question for the ages.

ON ICE

At least he's got on some clean clothes. The black-and-white stripes of a jail uniform fall across Frank Hearn's slumped body, merging with the shadows cast from the bars on the windows of Coney Island, also known as the interrogation room, where he's been sitting shackled to a chair for the past two hours. They still haven't given him anything to eat, besides a tin cup of tepid water that sits at his elbow. A single lightbulb hangs from the ceiling, and every so often it starts to blink like it's about to go out—kind of like any hope Frank has of getting out of this mess.

He sighs, and it sounds like a moan. He was just in this stinking place last night, but now the charges are serious. Homicide. The victim: Parker Anderson. It's rotten enough finding out your business partner has been killed, but to be accused of it to boot, on the same day your fiancée thinks you've been cheating on her—it's almost more than he can take.

But that's what they want. They want him to crack open like a walnut. That's why they keep leaving him in here, only to burst in and give him the third degree. The rough stuff should start any minute now. These flatties can beat him senseless but Frank Hearn will never admit to killing Parker Anderson. Never, no way.

His fist slams against the steel table. He's got to find Irene. She's the only one who can help him out of this jam. But the longer they keep him cooped up in here, the harder it'll be explaining everything to her. Not that Frank understands the situation himself. How could Frank have done the killing when he was locked up in this very same jail? The chief of police, Quigg, couldn't believe that one.

You're saying you were arrested last night?

That's right. After somebody almost killed me.

They're checking on it. And once they figure out he's not lying, they'll have to turn him loose. After all, what's a better alibi than being in jail? This should get cleared up, and then he'll have to start hunting down Irene again.

Finally the door swings open. Frank jerks up in his chair like he's been jolted by fifty volts of juice. Coming back in are Chief Quigg and a new wally Hearn hasn't seen before. He's carrying a raft of papers and a mug of steaming java. He looks like a choirboy who secretly enjoys killing rats.

"So?" asks Frank defiantly. "Do you believe me now?"

The two men sit opposite him. It's Quigg who starts.

"Hearn, I got some bad news. There is no record of you getting arrested last night."

"What?"

"We checked and there isn't a scrap of paperwork on you. So we're at square one."

Frank grimaces and then remembers how strange it was this morning when he was released. The desk sergeant didn't have an arrest report when Frank asked for it. They must've destroyed the paperwork after they stole his money, that much is obvious. What was the sergeant's name again? Flagstead! Remembering his name won't do much good. He'll just lie if they ask him. That leaves Nina Randolph. She can vouch for him, too. "Well, my secretary bailed me out. Her name is Nina Randolph. Ask her, she'll back up every word of my story."

There is some mumbling and then the choirboy introduces himself as Horace Dyer. He says he's a federal investigator from Tampa and he just wants to ask Frank some questions about the real estate industry. He tries to act real smooth and friendly, like he wants Frank to be his pal.

"We'd love to ask your secretary to back up your story, Frank," Dyer hums. "But there's a problem. We can't find her. Maybe you know where she's hiding."

"Hiding? I don't know what you're talking about."

"When we stopped by your office to talk to her, she crawled through a window in the bathroom and disappeared. Why would she do that?"

"I don't know. But she's not the only one who can back my story up. After Nina picked me up from jail this morning, she drove me home. My landlady saw her. Ask my landlady! Erma Hayes!"

"Anybody else see Nina with you?"

Frank doesn't like the tone Dyer used to ask that question. It makes it sound like he's talked to Irene and Irene told him that she thought he was having an affair with Nina. Dyer is setting a trap but Frank won't fall for it. "Who else do you need? I'm telling you the truth and my landlady will tell you I'm telling you the truth."

"Nina Randolph would do anything for you, wouldn't she?"

"She was my secretary. We paid her to do things."

That answer causes some snickering. Dyer clears his throat before he resumes. "Listen, Frank. You need to be honest with us. Lying won't help. We know you and Nina were involved, is one way of putting it."

"I never touched that girl! Never once!"

"Sure, Frank, that's likely. A looker like Nina. A young girl whose head can get some crazy ideas."

"I never touched her."

"Who is Irene Howard?"

That catches him like an uppercut to the kisser, Dyer moving in for the kill so suddenly. But Frank plays the chill and shrugs his shoulders. "She's my fiancée."

"Why would she think Nina had something to do with Parker's murder?"

"I don't know."

"Why would she think Nina was in love with you? Huh, Frank? Can you explain that?"

Frank doesn't answer, because he feels like someone just took a knife and cut out his heart. The Aztecs used to do that. The priests would slice up men and eat their guts. How could Irene tell the cops that? She didn't. They're lying and he won't fall for it.

Quigg starts in again. "Frank, things don't look good for you right now. When all the evidence is presented at trial, the jury will find you guilty of murder. There is no doubt of that. We will prove motive and opportunity. I think you killed Parker Anderson after you found out he was cooperating with Mr. Dyer's investigation of the real estate industry. And Nina Randolph helped you do it."

Frank's eyes narrow as he stares at Dyer. "I killed Parker because of what investigation?"

Dyer shakes his head like a disappointed schoolteacher. "Don't play games, Frank. I'm the only person who can save your life."

"He's right about that!" Quigg thunders. "If it was up to me, you'd hang."

"I didn't kill Parker and I don't know onions about any investigation," Frank says evenly, regaining his composure.

"It's in your best interest to level with me, Frank. Don't feed me any hooey. I want you to cooperate and give me the goods about the cons getting played in Miami real estate. Parker told us plenty about you."

Frank feels all the air rushing from his chest. "Parker told you what about me? I'm not running a C. I did everything on the up-and-up. Check my bank account. It's empty. Some con I am."

Dyer smiles and drums his knuckles on the table. "Frank, come on. I'm not stupid. Give me something I can work with. I know you weren't the big fish, just a minnow. I want the big fish."

"Yeah? I'm the wrong bait, fella. I came to Miami to make an honest buck."

"Yeah? Parker said you were knee-deep in Sweetwater." Dyer sounds like he's actually enjoying himself. "He said you had contacts with bus companies up north who brought the suckers down here. We were getting ready to haul you in—before you killed him, that is."

"I never did anything with Sweetwater."

"Who did?"

"You mean besides Parker? I don't know and I didn't want to know. I stayed clear of those scams. He tried to get me involved but I said no way."

"You're a real saint, Hearn. A real saint."

"I'm telling you the truth."

"Okay, Saint Frank, since you're a truth-teller, tell us what you know about Parker Anderson and Sweetwater."

"Not much. It's a subdivision out on the Tamiami Trail, in the middle of a swamp. Parker was selling lots there, and most of them were under water. If he told you I was involved, he was lying. And you fell for it."

"You better come up with something better than that, Hearn."

"I didn't kill nobody, and I can prove it. Find the cop who took me in. The bastard stole a thousand bones from me! Ask Delaney out at Palmetto Jai Alai! I won the money from him last night. So did Parker! Then he sent his goons after me. They drove a late-model Chrysler and now it's got a shot-out window! For all I know Delaney sent a goon after Parker." Spittle comes flying from Frank's mouth, and he falls into a sad silence.

"It's illegal to wager on jai alai in this city," says Quigg angrily.

"Somebody better tell Delaney."

"You shut up!" Now Quigg is really steamed. He stands up and hulks over Frank. For a second Frank is sure he's gonna get belted. "Now you're insulting my department! As far as I'm concerned, you can rot in hell for killing the son of one of the best mayors this city has ever had. But hell's too good a place for the likes of you."

Then Quigg herds Dyer out.

■ ■ ■

Quigg and Dyer are standing in the corridor outside the interrogation room. Quigg has calmed down a little after calling an end to the questioning. Why he did so makes no sense. Dyer was just getting on a roll and Hearn was starting to talk. But when the subject of jai alai and gambling came up, Quigg pulled the plug.

"Thanks, Mr. Dyer, that was useful."

Dyer feels his spine stiffening. "What's next?"

The chief sighs and checks his wristwatch. "I got to meet with Colonel E. W. Starling, personal attaché of the president, along with the mayor, the city manager, and the traffic director. I don't have time to waste on Hearn or anyone else. We got to get this city ready for Coolidge."

A reasonable excuse. So maybe Quigg would entertain a reasonable offer. Dyer isn't ready to take a backseat to the MPD quite yet. If he hopes to get anywhere with his investigation, all roads lead through Frank Hearn. "Shouldn't we try to find the secretary, Nina Randolph? She might be involved in all this. Maybe I can help dig into her background. I know as much about this case as anyone."

Quigg adjusts his bow tie. After all, he's got an important meeting to attend. "I wasn't aware the feds investigated homicides."

"I won't be. I need Nina Randolph for my Section 215 investigation."

Quigg gives him a solemn nod. "That's your business, Mr. Dyer. Rest assured I will alert my chief of detectives about Miss Randolph."

"What about Hearn?"

"Mr. Hearn will be confined in the jail at the new courthouse across the street, where our most dangerous men are kept. He'll be on the twentieth floor in an escape-proof facility, the most advanced of its kind in the nation."

Dyer feels like a fly buzzing around an elephant. Quigg keeps trying to swat him but Dyer isn't giving up that easy. "Are you going to check out his story?"

"What story?"

"The one about the jai alai game."

Quigg emits a satisfied laugh that sounds like someone banging on the bottom of a barrel. With a huge hand he smooths out his slicked-back black hair. "Mr. Dyer, I appreciate all you've done on the case but I suggest you stick to investigating real estate fraud and other violations of federal law. My suspicion is that Mr. Hearn will eventually confess to his crimes."

"That would be nice."

"Now if you'll excuse me, I've got to get this city ready for the president's visit."

As Quigg saunters away, Dyer looks in at Frank Hearn sitting at the table, his face buried in his hands. Something isn't right about this case. Quigg's solution seems to be in relying on a confession, one that will no doubt be coerced from what Dyer has heard about how this department operates. But that approach doesn't begin to explain anything. Why did Nina Randolph take off? Why isn't Quigg more concerned about finding her? Why isn't he more interested in Hearn's claims? Then there is Irene Howard. How could a man like Hearn win the heart of a woman like that and be a cold-blooded killer? Sure, plenty of women fall for the wrong man, but this case seems different. This city is different. Roads often lead to nowhere, and nothing is what it seems. The fact is, Frank Hearn might be telling the truth and there's only one way to find out. Check out his story and see if it adds up. Dyer doesn't need anyone's permission to do that.

NO MORE ORCHIDS

The shopping bags rest at Gloria Swanson's tired feet. She found some adorable outfits for Gloria and little Brother, her two children, her two delights, back home in Los Angeles with their nanny. She's already sent one postcard telling them how much she misses them, but perhaps she should send another. After all, she vowed to provide a better family life for her children. She hates it when they run crying to the nanny and not her. She wants to be home more often. But this year has taken its toll. Since she set out on her own, forming her own production company to make films the way she wants, Gloria has teetered on the brink of bankruptcy. It has required her to work longer hours, travel extensively, and literally fight for survival. She's put everything she has into making *Sadie Thompson*, and now the Hays Commission, that constipated board of censorious stiffs, is threatening not to endorse it. What prudery! It's a beautiful story from Somerset Maugham about a prostitute and a missionary who fall in love in the South Seas.

Joe says Bible groups in the Midwest will picket theaters that show it, despite the changes she made in the story to placate fussy Will Hays. She even went to lunch with the man and charmed him into letting her go forward. Admittedly, she had to tell a couple of white lies to convince him, but the bottom line is the film was made, when no one in Hollywood thought it ever would be. Now Joe thinks she should sell the rights to United Artists. He claims the picture won't make a dime outside New York and L.A., so it's better to take what you can get up front, rather than gambling on reaction from the heartland. Those were hard words for Gloria to hear.

And during this entire conversation last night, what did Henri say? Did he stand up and defend her? Did he offer to punch Will Hays's lights out? Did he try to console her, knowing that she faced an enormous decision? No. He just sat there, smoking an Old Gold cigarette, his flat expression unchanging as Gloria gnashed her teeth and pulled her hair. And then she agreed to sell the rights to UA, because Joe Kennedy understood the movie business in a way Gloria wants to but can't. It's the view of the mogul, devoid of emotion.

Movies are a commodity, like soap.

It's rather simple, really. Either you earn a return on your investment, or you don't make any more pictures. Art is wonderful, sure, but only money pays the bills. The dreadful sundry of the world, anathema to pure showmanship.

She sighs, looking at the shopping bags filled with clothes for children she hasn't seen in weeks. Maybe a long bath will lift her spirits. She pulls herself up from the chair, changes from her pink silk dress ruched with white trim into a red kimono. Then she hears a knock on the door.

It's him.

She knows Joe is coming. He never said he was, as they have no plans to see each other. But she can feel him, although his room is on the other end of the hotel. She can still taste his lips on hers when they kissed on the train yesterday, and it is that audacity she finds most attractive. Joe Kennedy takes charge of a scenario like a great director who is sure of every shot. He answers only to himself. His confidence brims over like champagne spilling after a loud, brash toast.

She glides easily to the door, nervous and yet willing to accede to the forces that brought them together. Seldom has she understood why certain men have become her lovers. She's read books on the subject of sex and understands in a vague way that she is seeking paternal approval. After all, Father was a horrendous drunk. But she still loves Father and seeks his advice on a variety of topics. So what drives her into the dark caverns of desire? Is it simply that she adores being adored?

She throws open the door and finds a hotel maid standing there, three dresses in hand.

"These are ready, miss. All nice and pressed."

"Thank you. Please hang them in the closet."

Silly thing, Gloria chides herself, stepping aside to let the maid pass. Then the phone rings. Leaving the door open, she goes to answer it. It is the hotel manager.

"Mrs. Swanson, Mr. Kennedy asked me to call you and inquire what color dress you'll be wearing to the Stotesbury's party tonight. You see, Eva Stotesbury has bought up every orchid in Palm Beach and the few we have left for your corsage might not match your dress."

"I don't like orchids, I'm sorry to say. Mr. Kennedy doesn't know that. A simple carnation will do fine. But, please, no more orchids."

"A carnation, yes, ma'am."

When she hangs up, she sees Joe standing in the open doorway, wearing white flannels, an argyle sweater, and two-toned shoes. He allows the maid to pass through, then steps in, shutting the door behind him.

"So now you know," she says playfully. "I don't like orchids."

But he doesn't say anything. He stands frozen in front of the closed door, staring at her. She can tell by his eyes what's on his mind. She feels her face grow warm as she drops her hands by her sides. He takes a long stride toward her, reaching out with one hand to hold the back of her head. With the other hand he begins to caress her body, forcing her kimono to cleave open and then fall to the ground.

With two strong arms he lifts her up and carries her to bed.

■ ■ ■

Nothing is biting. Then again, it's exceedingly difficult to catch fish without dropping one's hook in the water.

"Aren't you gonna at least try?" asks Eddie Moore, voice straining to maintain that forced amity Henri has long since tired of. "Have you ever reeled in a swordfish? Those bastards'll fight you for an hour! Right, Cap?"

The boat's captain grunts in the canine way of unlettered American men, which is still leagues better than the false joviality of Eddie Moore. The captain is interesting. He is short, stout, and bug-eyed. He also likes to drink rum punch. Henri is just finishing his third glass, perched on the gunnels and squinting from the bright sun dancing on the waters of the deep Atlantic. Seas are running at two feet, and the boat gently rocks along the rolling swells.

"The silver king! What a beast! Come on now, give it a go."

Henri stands and makes his way to the ice bucket, where the captain keeps the rum punch chilled. He pours another drink and goes back to the same position.

"Huh, Count?"

"Tu es un connard d'américain."

"Does that mean you'll do it?"

"Please, you've done your job. Let me be."

"What job?"

Henri closes his eyes. The sun is warm against his face. The sea is so inviting. What if he were to just lean back and fall in? Would he sink to the bottom?

"I'm not working a job! I'm trying to catch some fish!"

"Can we go back?"

"Go back?" Eddie Moore sounds like he just swallowed a cricket. "What for?"

"I'm fatigued."

Eddie Moore checks his watch. He looks so earnest, so sincere. "How about an hour, Count? That'll give us enough time to see what's biting."

"No, I'd like to go now."

"We just got here."

"Pardon me, I'm ready to go."

Eddie Moore looks helplessly at the captain, who has been watching the two men with an amused smile. "We can't leave! We haven't caught anything. Right, Cap?"

Henri's next words surprise himself. "They're finished by now, don't you think?"

It's very bad form to allude to such matters so openly. But nothing like rum punch to render one impolite.

"Who's that?" croaks Eddie Moore.

"My wife and your boss."

Eddie Moore's face turns crimson. He reaches back and unfurls a long cast, the sinker plopping into the water with the same sound of one uncorking a bottle of champagne. The captain smirks as his eyes scan the undulating horizon.

"His boss is screwing my wife," Henri tells the captain calmly.

"That's not true!" Eddie Moore interjects with such vehemence that any doubt has been obliterated. "You shouldn't say that or even think it. Mr. Kennedy thinks you're aces."

"*C'est un enculé.*"

"What's that, Hank?"

"*Je vais flinguer ces deux fils de putes.*"

The captain erupts in a fit of volcanic laughter, having learned to speak French during the five years he lived on Martinique. It's been that long since he's heard anyone call a man an "asshole" or a "son of a whore." *Flinguer:* that means something like "destroy." This has become an interesting trip. The captain wipes tears from his eyes and, winking at Henri, says: "*Seule une lavette ne le ferait pas.*"

It's true: only a weakling would allow another man to make love to his wife. Henri can't disagree with that.

THE NEW GUY

A guard leads Frank Hearn on a walk past a desolate row of solid steel doors, each with one sliver of an opening at eye level to allow the guards to inspect the goings-on in each cell of the new county jail. They are on the twentieth floor of the Dade County courthouse, an almost-completed ziggurat towering above downtown Miami. Citizens have proudly watched the edifice rise up for the past two years, as if with fervent dreams of grandeur they willed it so. Nothing could shake the city's faith in its new courthouse. It would be gleaming, progressive, and efficient—in short, qualities the civic-minded leaders of Miami desired the city to have. The equation is simple: new courthouse equals new city. But the past isn't easily swept away. It echoes down every hallway like the shouts of a lonely child at midnight.

Chains cut into Frank's wrists and ankles, so he must shuffle along like an old man. "You'll like it here," the roach assures him, swinging his billy club like a majorette. "It's real comfy."

"I won't be in here long," Frank says under his breath.

"Yeah? Got some plans tonight, do ya?"

Frank holds his tongue, because one place where talking will get you killed is in college. So silence will be golden from now on. He'll keep to himself and stay out of the way. He served a few months up in New Jersey, and that's exactly how he played it. He didn't mess with no one, and no one messed with him. But he knew when he was getting out. Now, he doesn't know anything—except that Quigg and Dyer want him to be a crooner and sing like a canary. Or they say they'll send him to the chair. What Frank needs is a good mouthpiece, but no one has mentioned the chance of him placing a telephone call. No, they want to let him soak in this cesspool and see if he won't crumble. That's why they threw Irene in his face. To burden him down like an old mule. To see how much he could carry before he collapsed.

They were lying about her. She can't think he's guilty of murder. She knows him better than that.

Doesn't she?

"Here's your new home, Hearn." The guard pounds on the door with his club. "I'm coming in!" Then he swings the door open.

A stench hits Frank like a two-by-four across his face. It smells like old socks dipped in cow manure.

"What the hell's going on, Jonesy?" a voice growls from deep within the cell.

"Got a new man for you bums. Come on, Hearn." The guard pulls him along like he's leading a dray horse. He unlocks the shackles and for a second Frank feels no pain.

"We don't want no new man! Ain't room enough in here already! Take him to the county stockade!"

"Just following orders. Trust me, this ain't my idea."

With that last statement, the guard shoves Frank inside and tosses a sheet and a tin cup at his feet. Then the steel door shuts in Frank's face. There is no lonelier sound in the world.

A young man with a harelip and a squeaky voice jumps down from the top bunk and points a bony finger in Frank's face. "You a stool pigeon, huh? Coming to spy on us?"

"Not exactly."

Frank looks past this four-flusher and finds himself in a rectangular cell about eight feet long and six feet wide. Against the back wall hangs a small sink and next to it sits a john. Pretty spiffy digs.

"Spying with one eye, what the hell is that?"

Frank doesn't bother replying. He picks up the mutt with the big bazoo and throws him like a sack of potatoes against the steel door. The mutt hits it with a thud, letting out a groan that sounds like a duck quacking.

"Don't talk about my eye," Frank says with his fists clenched. "I don't want no trouble. I'll leave you alone if you leave me alone. And I'm no damn spy. Where's my bunk?"

"You're standing on it," says a man lying on the bottom bunk, hands wedged behind his head. Acne scars have ravaged his cheeks, leaving swaths of rough, leathery skin. A little tuft of hair rests above his forehead, but the rest of his scalp is bald, except for around his ears.

Frank looks down at his feet. The floor is his bunk? It's bare cement and stained with blood and God knows what else. But wordlessly Frank spreads out his blanket and sits down, his back leaning against a concrete wall. The one he just threw into the door steps over him and crawls back up to his bunk.

"What you in for, Hearn?"

"Murder."

"Who'd you kill?"

"I didn't kill nobody."

The man with the leathery face starts cackling, but Frank doesn't say anything.

"I'm Buddy. Up top there is Theodore Roosevelt Wilson. He likes to be called T.R."

"You can call me Mr. T.R."

Buddy laughs and it sounds like a mule braying. Then he sits up and leans forward, moving within a foot of Frank's face. The glare of the overhead bulb makes Buddy's face even uglier. It looks like somebody set fire to it.

"You know why they put you in here?" he asks, his voice a bare whisper, eyes as wide as saucers. "I'll tell you why. They think we'll scare the snot out of you. Because we're bad men, Hearn. We're killers. Ain't that right, T.R.?"

"Hell, yeah."

Frank keeps a straight face. "Thanks for the dope."

Another cackle. "Keep on laughing now, Hearn. You won't be after they finish with you." Buddy leans back and closes his eyes. "They'll put me on trial next week and then they'll send me to the electric chair. It happens that fast, Frank. You ain't from around here, I can tell that. You don't know how justice works in Florida."

T.R. starts howling like a delirious wolf. "Nah, you don't know! But you will."

Frank sets his jaw firmly. "How does it work?"

Buddy sits back up. "Like this. They'll kill you in a week, like me, with a fancy trial and a rigged jury. Or if they want to, they'll just take you out to the Everglades and kill you with a bullet to the head. The gators'll munch you down and there won't be no dead body to find. You probably think I'm lying. No way that could happen here. But trust me, it happens all the time. Even to white men."

"It sure does," T.R. echoes.

"Do yourself a favor, Hearn. Sign whatever confession they want. You'll get a life bit at Raiford instead of the chair. It ain't easy to bust out of Raiford. People've done it. But if you're lucky, they'll send you to a work camp. That's how I busted out."

"Me too," chimes T.R. What a Mutt-and-Jeff show this is.

"No way in hell am I confessing," Frank grumbles, leaning back against the cool concrete wall. "I'm not letting these crooked cops carve me up like a Thanksgiving turkey. I haven't talked to a mouth-piece. I haven't appeared before a judge. I know my rights."

"Rights!" T.R. snorts. "You ain't got no rights in Miami!"

But Buddy holds his tongue. Frank can feel the man's eyes burning into him, like he's inspecting a car at a dealership. Kicking the tires, looking under the hood. Then Frank notices something else strange.

The mattress Buddy is lying on looks like it's stuffed to the gills and ready to pop.

▪ ▪ ▪

Nina Randolph lives in Coconut Grove with her mother. She is twenty years old and a graduate of the Miami Business College. Her father died when she was young. She has never been arrested. These facts are not much to go on, but Horace Dyer can feel it in his bones: the missing secretary is the keystone to the case. It doesn't make sense that Frank Hearn tore off all his clothes and then had Nina Randolph drop him at the Flamingo Hotel so he could expose himself in public, if in fact those two had just conspired to kill someone. And why would Nina run away if she didn't have something to hide?

It takes about fifteen minutes to drive south five miles to Coconut Grove, a strange little community that until recently was a separate city from Miami. Dyer hasn't spent much time there but he was always meaning to take in the sights. Grab a bite to eat at the Hamlet and watch a show at the new playhouse. Just park the car and walk around beneath the banyan trees. But his days as a tourist will have to wait.

A few minutes later, Dyer parks in front of a small, low-slung house with a tin roof and what looks like a palm tree growing up through it. Rotten grapefruits litter the sand-swept yard. A few have been sucked dry by rats. What a shame to let such a delicacy go to waste, but it's obvious this house hasn't been taken care of. The roof buckles and the screens need replacing.

He knocks on the front door. He hears someone stirring within. He has his badge out to answer any questions.

The door creaks open. "What?" a woman rasps, stinking of booze. She is a homely, flabby woman with skin the color of rotten meat and a wild nest of black-and-silver hair.

"Are you Mrs. Randolph?"

"I've already talked to the police. I don't know where my daughter is. Leave me be."

"Ma'am, I won't be a minute. My name is Dyer and I'm with the federal government."

She inspects his badge and frowns sourly at it. Dyer doesn't flinch.

"Talking to me is the last thing you want to do right now, but I intend to get to the bottom of this."

"I thought they arrested a man already."

"I'm here regarding another matter. May I please come in?"

She eyeballs him carefully, breathing heavily through her nostrils. Cautiously the door swings open and she steps aside to let Dyer in. A cat comes purring up to him, rubbing against his leg. The woman goes over and sits down on a sofa, in front of a bottle of rotgut.

"Drink?"

"No thanks."

"Are you gonna arrest me?" She pours herself a stiff belt and downs it.

"No, ma'am, I'm not. I just want to ask you a few questions about your daughter. I understand if you don't want to talk to me. But if she's in danger, I want to help her."

"She ran away from the police. What does that tell you?"

"It tells me she's in trouble."

"And her boss was murdered, too."

"Did you know him?"

"No."

"Do you know Frank Hearn?"

"No. Nina never tells me much. She keeps things to herself. In her mind she's better than me."

Dyer slows down, scribbling away in his notebook. This woman will start blabbing soon enough, thanks to the booze and the fact that she's lonely. He doesn't need to press her.

"Does Nina have a boyfriend?" he asks quietly.

"Lately she's been seeing someone who drives a fancy car. You know, a roadster."

Parker Anderson drove a Nash roadster. Frank Hearn owned a used

Olds sedan, which is no roadster. Was there something going on be-tween Parker and Nina? "Do you know his name?"

"No. He never saw fit to come in and introduce himself. Nina was embarrassed by me, her own mother."

Dyer keeps on scribbling and nodding. Was Nina in on the Sweet-water scam, too?

"Did Nina ever talk about her job?"

"Not much. She said she liked it. She was saving money to move out and get her own place." The woman downs another drink.

"Did she ever mention anything called Sweetwater?"

"She didn't talk much about her work. She went to the movies. She loved Gloria Swanson. She loved buying clothes so she could pretend to be Gloria Swanson."

Dyer smiles as cheerfully as possible and puts his notebook away. "Do you mind if I look in her room? I don't want to intrude, but there might be a very important clue to figuring out what happened to her."

"The cops already tore everything up. It took me an hour to fix it back!"

"I won't make a mess, Mrs. Randolph. My mother raised me to be neat."

"You seem like a nice young man. Not like these Miami cops. They're ruffians!"

She stands up unsteadily and shows Dyer Nina's small room, barely large enough for a bed and a dresser. Unlike the rest of the house, the girl's bedroom is neat and clean. Pink drapes on the only window and a pink blanket neatly folded on the bed. Dyer looks in the drawers of the dresser. Many are empty.

"Didn't you say she loved clothes?"

"Her things are gone!" The woman sounds genuinely surprised.

They both check her closet. Only a few dresses hang in it.

"Was she planning a trip?" Dyer asks.

"No. Not that she told me."

Dyer stares a few moments at the small closet. Wherever Nina

Randolph was going, she had planned on leaving today. And talking to the cops wasn't on her agenda.

■ ■ ■

The last chukker of the polo match between the Flamingo Club of Miami Beach and the Four Horsemen of Palm Beach has just ended, with the Flamingo squad on top by seven to six. It was a rollicking affair, marred by many fouls and much swearing, which the ladies in the grandstands of the Nautilus Fields could plainly hear. While Harvey Firestone relished the action, he must speak to his sons and his nephew about their language. Spirited competition is good for the soul, but not at the expense of good manners.

Still, what a glorious afternoon! The sun has begun its descent in the cloudless western sky, leaving a slight cool that smells like rosewater and feels like chamois against the skin. The groomsmen are leading the horses back to the stables Harvey Firestone designed himself to evoke the bucolic charm of his beloved Ohio farmlands. As is the custom, the losing side must spring for refreshments at the nearby Nautilus Hotel, hovering in the distance. Nothing makes Harvey Firestone happier than basking in the post-match celebration on someone else's dime. Conversely, nothing sinks his soul like having to pay for another man's triumph. But both of the teams he sponsors, the Flamingo and the Chagrin Valley Polo Club, seldom lose, sparing Harvey Firestone the indignity of treating.

He spies Bryce speaking to a group of attractive women, most of whom Harvey Firestone recognizes as the daughters of his Miami Beach acquaintances. Inwardly he beams. Marriage would be just the remedy for what ails Bryce. Nothing shapes a man's character like matrimony and fatherhood. There's Janice Pendergast, whose face radiates a felicitous sincerity. A fine match that would be.

"We showed them, huh, Uncle Harvey?" Bryce calls out, in a voice brimming with masculine confidence. The lad scored four goals and assisted on the others, single-handedly winning the match.

"Indeed, my dear nephew. Let's go rub it in, shall we?"

"Oh, not me. I've got some work to do."

Harvey Firestone scratches his chin. "I don't recall ever hearing you use that sentence before, Nephew."

The girls titter playfully. This is welcome tonic, proof that Bryce can be molded into a real Firestone. Making men is no different than making tires: in both cases, you turn unformed goo into something useful.

"I guess all your lectures are starting to have some effect, Uncle."

Harvey Firestone nods. "Don't forget that Aunt Roberta is arriving today. We'll be having a party in her honor. Invite your friends, if you'd like."

"Sure thing, Uncle. Go give those chuckleheads from Palm Beach what for!"

Harvey Firestone waves and saunters past on his way to the Nautilus Hotel, built by his close friend Carl Fisher, the man who more than anyone else invented Miami Beach. Fisher thought a fancy hotel would turn his swampy mangrove island into a jewel, but Harvey Firestone sold him on a better idea: to build some polo fields, too. As soon as the plans were announced, lots started moving like hotcakes, attracting the right sort of people. Now Miami Beach is known throughout the world as a luxury resort. He'll have to encourage his friend Seddon Howard to buy a place down here. Roberta wired from the ship that the Howards are on their way to Miami. It's been years since the Firestones and the Howards visited, but hopefully they can spend some time together this season.

■ ■ ■

"Did you get the money?" Bryce asks anxiously.

Janice is standing in front of her new Buick, parked behind the grandstands of the polo field. It's a shiny blue coupe and she loves it dearly. Just being near Baby Blue, as she calls her car, makes her feel better. Because Bryce certainly doesn't.

"I told you I would."

"Oh, that's great, Janice! I can't tell you how happy I am!"

"I'm glad you're happy, Bryce."

Janice puts her hand on Baby Blue's front quarter panel and lovingly caresses it as she saunters toward the backseat, where the money is. She had a little trouble coming up with so much cash. She had to sit down with the bank manager and he grilled her for a few minutes, but Janice just kept saying the same thing: *It's an emergency, I'm sorry.* It took about an hour, which gave Janice time to think. Sometimes it's good to sit in the lobby of a bank and just think. Everywhere people are scrounging after money. They count it, they count it again, they put it behind big steel doors, and no one ever smiles. Because money doesn't make people happy. It makes them miserable, mostly. The manager seemed like he was going to explode. *Ten thousand in cash!* He sounded as though Janice had set his hair on fire.

She reaches down and lifts up the brown paper bag from Piggly Wiggly. She almost bought Bryce an elegant briefcase but then decided he didn't deserve one.

"Here you go."

He doesn't smile. His face becomes hard the minute he touches the money.

"I really appreciate this. I can't tell you how much it means."

He leans down and kisses her. He smells like a horse. He has to go and clean up. He'll swing by later and bring her to the party his uncle is throwing for his aunt. He gives her one more kiss.

Then Janice hops into Baby Blue and sticks the key in the ignition. "Are you ready, Baby Blue? We have some exciting work ahead of us."

■ ■ ■

Lying down: that has been foremost on Irene's mind for the past hour. Lying down in a darkened room with a pillow over her head. Lying down in complete silence, trying to empty her mind. So when Irene finally reaches her room, she collapses onto the four-poster bed. The mattress is so soft it feels like she's sinking into a pit of quicksand.

Her parents will be arriving soon, which means soon, very soon, Irene will have to tell them why Frank won't be joining them for dinner—or anywhere else. But let them enjoy their first night in Florida. They deserve that.

She grabs a fluffy pillow and presses it against her face. Face: she can't forget Nina Randolph's face. Was she pretty? Of course she was. She was blond, too, a hair color that makes men twist into pretzels. And she was young, bubbly, flirtatious. She batted her long lashes and giggled expertly. She must've fallen hard for Frank, who oozed sex appeal like sap from a maple tree.

Did Frank love her?

Harder on the pillow she pulls, fighting against these tortured thoughts like a swimmer struggling against the tide. Nina Randolph. A name but what's that? She was Frank's secretary. That's something. They worked together. They grew intimate being so proximate. He'd ask her to do things and she'd do them. She made his coffee in the morning and picked up his dry cleaning. Kind of like a wife.

But did he really love her?

She sits up as if hoisted by a winch. The afternoon sun has filled her comfortable room with a luscious syrupy haze. She can barely see anything. There's a chesterfield the color of money. There's a fauteuil with upholstery the color of rutabaga. Next to it is a cheval glass. A closet. A bathroom. A table with a telephone on it.

A telephone.

Irene hops off the large bed and lands on the floor with a thud. She inspects the telephone like she's never seen one before. She runs her finger across the receiver. In a drawer she finds a *Polk City Directory* for Miami. She quickly finds the last names beginning with R. She counts ten Randolphs, none with the first name of Nina.

Randolph is a common name.

She puts the directory back and walks over to her window. She has a glorious view of Biscayne Bay and downtown Miami. She was going to live here with Frank Hearn as man and wife. This was going to be where they played house.

Maybe he didn't love Nina. Maybe there's much, much more to this horrible situation than meets the eye. The Frank Hearn Irene knows and loves (loved?) would not kill anyone. But the police say he did. And how did Nina Randolph end up in his apartment this morning? Why did she crawl through a window rather than answer questions from the police?

That man Irene met this afternoon—Horace Dyer—seemed polite. Intelligent. Sophisticated. Poised. Irene might have said things to him that sounded wrong. He gave Irene his card and told her to call him whenever she wanted. Well, the truth is, she'd really like to speak with him, so she goes and fishes the card out of her purse.

Irene glides over to the phone and dials the number. But no one answers. So Irene is still right where she started, choking on speculation, her worst fears rampaging through her brain like a drunken crew of pirates. The idea of Frank loving someone else.

But did he?

If Frank loves Nina, as seems to be the case, there have to be mementos, evidence, traces of their life together. Lipstick cases, combs, things only a woman would use. Possibly letters. Something. After all, she had to have been a frequent visitor to his apartment.

Irene has to know. She can't stay cooped up in this room another minute. So Irene slips on her Deauville sandals and grabs her beaded purse, heading out to find the answers to her questions. The first place she'll start is Frank's room at the Crozier. She's not sure how she's getting in there, but she'll cross that bridge when she comes to it.

Then she'll go meet the arrival of her parent's ship. Oh joy.

■ ■ ■

It never ceases to amaze him. Whenever Horace Dyer drives the streets of Miami, he can't help but gawk slack-jawed at the startling contrasts. On the one hand there is a burgeoning business district that is home to some of the tallest buildings south of Washington, D.C. Anyone who visits can't help but be impressed by downtown Miami. This is a city that is going places. But not even a few blocks away there resides another city altogether. This city is in shambles and its people poor and mostly colored. Gambling and prostitution are rampant. The city sends its cops in on raids to clean up the crime. And yet, farther out still, lie the broken dreams and sun-faded billboards directing motorists to unfinished subdivisions like Sweetwater. The city looked the other way while those criminals ran roughshod over people's life savings. Criminals like Parker Anderson. And maybe Frank Hearn.

But maybe not Frank Hearn. Frank Hearn claims to have an alibi. He said he couldn't have killed Parker because he was in jail. There's no record of the arrest, which doesn't exactly support Hearn's story. But he also mentioned that Parker and he had bet on jai alai, and that the owner, a man named Delaney, sent his goons after them. He said Delaney might be behind Parker's death.

It was at that point during the interview when Quigg pulled the plug.

Dyer can't forget about that as he parks in front of the Palmetto Jai Alai Fronton, an immense building that looks like a large temple, with white columns and rounded windows. There is only one reason why it exists: gambling. Everyone knows it goes on, but yet no one dares shut it down. Least of all Quigg, who protects most of the illegal gaming operations in the city. Even the worst gangster of all, Al Capone, has taken up residence here. The newspapers are in an uproar about that: *What about the city's image?* The mayor is under pressure to do something about Capone, about gambling, about the Negroes. These are tense times in the city. Someone will have to take the fall for all that's wrong in Miami.

Dyer gets out and decides on a plan of attack. He's not exactly sure what he's looking for. Hearn said something about a car with a rear window shot out. No such cars fit that description in the expansive front parking lot, but often around back there is a smaller lot for employees. Maybe he'll take a gander before he sees if he can get inside the fortress.

He follows a sidewalk around the building. The front is well maintained, with neat rows of crotons planted around palm trees. Not a speck of litter anywhere. Off to the east sits a much smaller building, a long, narrow box that looks like a jail. A sidewalk connects it to the grounds of the main fronton, so the two buildings are related in some way.

As Dyer suspected, there is another parking lot in back. Some flashy cars are parked there, long and sleek and dark. One is even a black Chrysler, but it isn't missing a back window. Maybe it was replaced. The glass looks new. He jots down the license plate just in case it comes in handy.

He turns and looks around. He hears no sounds, not even of traffic. This place is in the middle of nowhere. Should he go in alone looking for Delaney? If Hearn is telling the truth, then this Delaney is a real bad apple. Dangerous and cold-blooded. Maybe he killed Parker Anderson or ordered him killed. If he did, then what's the connection with Nina Randolph? Nothing adds up. This is the kind of puzzle that's missing several big pieces.

He decides to poke around. After all, as a federal officer, he has some protection. The badge might feel light but it carries a lot of weight. He walks over to the jai alai fronton. He tries to open each door, but all are locked. He walks back around to the front and presses his face against a rectangular glass window to peer inside. He sees a row of betting windows, all shuttered. He sees a concessions counter and a door marked HAT CHECK. Dyer checks his watch. Almost five. When will they open up? It should be soon.

He takes one last look and is surprised to see a group of brown-skinned men wearing brilliant white uniforms with large black numbers emblazoned on the back. They are walking across the lobby, laughing at something.

Dyer pounds on the door. They stop, frozen in place.

"Where's Delaney?" he shouts. They don't look like English speakers, but luckily Dyer picked up some Spanish in Tampa. "¿Donde está Delaney?"

A tall, angular-faced man steps forward. "No sé, amigo. No lo he visto hoy."

For some reason Dyer thinks to hold up a picture of Parker Anderson. He presses the mug shot flat against the window. *"Por favor, mira. Esta hombre está muerto."*

A few shuffle forward to get a better look. Through the door Dyer can hear them muttering. Then the door swings open, nearly bashing him in the nose. The tall man eases himself out, keeping the door open with his foot.

"Who are you?" he asks, his voice heavily accented. His black eyes squint distrustfully, like he'd run at the first sign of trouble.

Dyer produces his badge. The tall man swallows hard.

"This man is dead, no?" he whispers.

Dyer leans forward. "He was murdered. Did you know him?"

"Please, we cannot talk here. *Es muy peligroso.*"

"Here, take my card."

"Hey!" comes an angry voice from inside. The tall jai alai player quickly disappears and the door slams shut. Dyer crouches down low and moves away from the door. He doesn't have a gun, but it feels like he could use one.

The door swings open and out steps a short, compact man in a black suit, black felt hat, silver tie, and orange shirt. He moves with the prancing anger of a bear on the prowl. A thick carpet of stubble covers his fat cheeks. Sweat drips down his furrowed brow. When he spots Dyer, his scowl grows menacing. A hand darts into one of his pockets, where there is probably a rod.

"Who are you?" he growls.

Dyer holds his ground. "I'm a federal investigator, the name is Dyer." He flashes his badge. Delaney acts like it came from a box of Cracker Jacks.

"What do you want?"

"Are you Delaney?"

"You got a warrant?"

Delaney seems like he's about ready to pounce and start tearing at Dyer's flesh. A real tough guy, this one. Probably has a high-priced mouthpiece and Chief Quigg in his back pocket.

"No, I just want to ask you some questions."

"About what?"

"About this." Dyer shows Delaney the photo of Parker Anderson. "You know him?"

"No."

"He won big last night. Is your memory improving?"

"So what? I don't run no clip joint. If he won, I paid him, same as any other winner."

"This winner turned up dead this morning. Shot in the face at close range."

Delaney sniffs like a dog picking up on a scent. "Too bad for him."

"Yeah, too bad." Dyer smiles and then shifts gears. It's obvious he's not getting any useful information, but it won't hurt to plant a seed or two of fear. Maybe something will grow. "Who drives that black Chrysler parked in back?"

"My mother."

"Do you know why somebody might have taken a shot at her last night?"

A stubby finger comes rising up and stops within an inch of Dyer's thin nose. "You're wearing out your welcome, understand? I don't like people pushing me around. I didn't kill no one, understand? If you want to ask me any more questions, we'll do it downtown. Until then, get lost, Boy Scout."

Delaney disappears back into the fronton. Seconds later, the neon sign blinks to life, shining bright blue in the gathering dusk. Dyer walks back to his car. Something rotten is happening at this jai alai fronton.

THE UNDERSIDE

L et's go, Hearn."

Frank pulls himself up from the cold concrete floor. He's been trying to sleep for the past couple of hours. But if he doesn't get some food soon, he's going to black out. He's starting to feel very light-headed and weak. But chances are the guard isn't taking him to the chow line.

"Don't bring him back, Jonesy!" T.R. yells. "We don't want him!"

"I'm just doing what they tell me."

"Where are we going?" Frank grumbles.

"Somebody wants to talk to you."

"Is it my lawyer?"

Buddy hoots like an owl. "You're one cool cucumber, Frank!"

"Shut up and come on!" Jonesy yanks on Frank. "I don't got all day!"

The shackles go back on his ankles and wrists. Jonesy leads Frank down the narrow corridor to the elevator. Frank is really starting to feel woozy. Those two jailbirds might be right after all. "Where are we going?" he asks again, trying to sound polite.

"You'll see."

They take the elevator down to the basement. The guard pulls the door open and waiting are two cops Frank's never seen before. Both are bruisers and look meaner than junkyard dogs.

"Thanks, Jonesy," one says. "We'll take it from here."

The guard gets on the elevator and leaves. The boiler hums ferociously. It's the biggest one Frank's ever seen. Has to be, for a building this huge.

"Are you ready to sign a confession, Hearn?" one asks. "Ready to admit you killed Parker Anderson?"

"I didn't kill anyone."

A nightstick strikes him in the back of the head. Frank drops to one knee.

"The confession's right here, Hearn. Just sign it and we're done."

Frank doesn't say a word. He'll never sign a confession to a murder he didn't do. He covers his head with his arms and falls to the ground in a fetal position. He's been beaten up before, plenty of times. The blows rain down on his arms and rib cage, but then stop.

"Ready to sign?"

Frank holds his tongue. He's not sure he can talk anyway.

"Next time will be worse, Hearn. You can think about that. Get up!"

■ ■ ■

Headaches. Nothing but headaches. That's what owning a jai alai fronton gives a man. As soon as one thing gets taken care of, something else comes along and takes its place. Delaney leans back in his chair and shakes his pounding head. His shoulders are pinched from the body brace he sent away for last month. The contraption is supposed to overcome "weakness and organic ailments" but all it's done is pinch him like a mean crab. He ought to chuck the stupid thing in the garbage.

"What's wrong with the world?" he laments to Lonigan as light from the late-afternoon sun streams through the lace curtains blowing in the gentle breeze. Delaney unwraps a piece of Black Jack chewing gum. Last week he entered a contest the company was sponsoring. You came up with a title to a picture of a little boy and girl in a store point-

ing at a box of the gum. The winner got a thousand bones. Delaney's
entry was "Chew on That, Mister!" which was pretty damn clever.

"Who was that guy, boss?"

Delaney shrugs his shoulders and works on the gum. If his head
would just stop torturing him, maybe he could think. "I don't know.
Said his name was Dyer and he's a fed."

"A fed?"

"A stinking fed. This is bad. I thought we were in the clear."

"Me, too. What did he want?"

Another forlorn sigh. "He was asking about a car window that got
shot out. So he's talked to Frank Hearn."

"Hearn?"

"Somebody was able to find the mutt! How hard can it be?"

"We'll find him, boss. It's about time I went to relieve Figgins anyway. I'll find Hearn if it's the last thing I do."

"I can't spare you that long. I got some high-hatters coming tonight.
I need someone to watch the counter while I show them a good time."
Delaney drums his fingers against his desk. He knows what he has to
do, but he doesn't want to do it. It's swimming through a sea of sharks
to reach a distant shore. "Looks like I need Blott."

"Blott? You sure, boss?"

"I got no other choice! It's just one headache after another! Get
moving. Go over to Hearn's apartment and send Figgins back. I'll get
Blott to meet you over there, and then you come back. Understand?"

"Who's going to take Garate's place tonight?" asks Lonigan, standing up. A smart kid. Always on the ball. Pays attention to details.

"We'll let Gomez in."

"Think he's ready?"

"Sure. He can handle it."

Delaney chomps on the gum. It feels better to have a plan. You
don't go around like a chicken with your head cut off. "Okay, we got it
under control now. Let's keep it that way."

Lonigan leaves. Now Delaney is alone in his office. Is it too early
for a drink? He reaches into a drawer and pulls out a flask. It's silver

and his initials are carved in it. Set him back a few plunks but when a man gets to a certain station in life, he should have nice things to show for it. He's worked hard to get where he is, and that's why he's not going to let some pampered rich kid and some greasy spics take what he has.

When the players see Gomez's name on the board instead of Garate's, chances are no one will put the fix on ever again.

He picks up the phone and places a call.

■ ■ ■

Daniel Turner. The stuff you think about. Daniel Turner was the retarded kid who lived across the street. Figgins didn't mind him. If you tried hard enough you could understand some of what he was saying. He liked looking at the flowers growing in the window boxes during the summer. So did Figgins. The geraniums were best. Daniel Turner called them "ninnies." But you could tell what he meant.

Figgins sighs and sinks lower in the front seat. He's been watching a building for the past couple of hours waiting for Frank Hearn to show up, but so far, nothing. Boring, boring, boring.

Lonigan used to take a slingshot and hurl rocks at Daniel Turner. One hit him in the face and he started to bleed. That made Lonigan famous on the street. A deadly shot.

One time Figgins threw a snowball at Danny. They were both thirteen. Papa was dead by then. The snowball missed. It landed three feet from the stoop where Danny was sitting. Then Lonigan creamed him in the face. Danny started to cry.

"Hey," Figgins hears. He opens his eyes. It's Lonigan.

"Were you asleep?"

"No."

"Your eyes were closed. Anything happening?"

"I don't think so."

"You okay?"

"Yeah."

"Good job taking care of Garate today. Dumb spic had it coming."

Figgins can feel the snowball in his hand. He didn't want to throw it but everybody else was. So he did. The shock on Danny's face. His mouth dropped open. That's how dead people look.

"Delaney wants you to go back," says Lonigan.

SOIRÉE

ow do I look?"

Henri de la Falaise outstretches his arms to show his wife the dinner jacket he just slipped on. Tonight they are off to a grand soirée being thrown by Mr. and Mrs. Edward T. Stotesbury, whose fortune has come from one railroad or another. Who can keep track? Doesn't every American own a railroad? Joe Kennedy eats them for lunch and brushes his teeth with banks.

"Divine, darling. Simply divine." Gloria sounds happy tonight. Like a woman in love. You know the look they get: the eyes sparkle and the laughter comes bubbling forth like the springs at Perrier. They flit like butterflies in the spring, soaring effortlessly before alighting on a newly blossomed flower.

"Do you mind terribly if I drive tonight?"

"You drive? We don't have a car."

"I just haven't driven for a few weeks, since we left Los Angeles. I'm rather fond of automobiles, you know."

She rolls her eyes. "Men and their toys. Your species is a strange one."

"There's nothing like sitting behind a powerful engine."

"How much have you had to drink today?"

His eyes drop toward the empty highball in his hands. He doesn't feel drunk. It's probably impossible for him to get drunk anymore, even though he's been drinking for most of the day. Intoxication is a reward for souls at full sail. In the dead calm, you sink to the bottom.

"Not enough," he answers softly.

"I don't mean to act the part of the lecturing harridan, but automobiles and booze a good marriage don't make."

"I promise to be *très bon*."

"I know, darling. I just wouldn't want anything untoward to happen in Florida."

She keeps trying on gowns, unhappy with each one so far. She's standing before him in a chemise of brilliant white silk, acting like he's not even there. She's dressing not for him but for Joe Kennedy. She's trying to find the gown that will unlock the safe deposit box of the tycoon's bloodless heart.

"What did you do while I was fishing?" he hears his voice ask her. Actually, it doesn't sound like his voice. It sounds like his father's when he was an old widower who sat in a rocking chair at the home for pensioners and asked: *When will I see you again?*

"I rested. I was exhausted."

"Did you see Joe? He didn't come fishing with us."

"From the sound of it, he didn't miss much. You told me you caught no fish."

"That's right, nothing was biting."

"Darling, is something the matter?"

She's looking at him gravely, the way one inspects the infirm for signs of worsening. She's holding a gown in her hands. It looks like it was spun from gold.

"No. I'm talking to my wife about her day. Isn't that normal?"

"No, it isn't. Your face is sunburned. Doesn't it hurt?"

"No. I don't feel anything. Care for a drink?"

"Not yet, darling."

She turns back around and keeps on dressing. Henri imagines killing him in front of her. Pulling the trigger as he begs for his life. There will be little joy. This is a duty, not a whim.

She'll ask him why. He will not respond. He will never speak to her again.

■ ■ ■

The phone rings. It is Joe Kennedy. He wants to know if Gloria is—um, they are—ready. She begins to accelerate her preparations now that she knows he is waiting for her—them—in the lobby. She starts to skip around the suite in a hurried fandango, looking for the right pair of shoes to go with her shimmering René Hubert gown of bengaline crepe laced with delicate skeins of alençon. Her voice bounces allegro and he can understand little of what she says. He studiously finishes his gin and tonic, the way a scientist might work in a lab. His movements are careful and repetitive. Glass to lips, place back on coaster, pick up the cigarette, inhale.

"Okay," she sings. "I'm ready."

"You look ravishing."

She blushes at his tone, mumbling thanks like he's a stranger who's just wandered into her room.

He extends his arm to lead her out.

REAR WINDOW

For the third time today, Irene Howard pulls up in front of the Crozier, Frank's apartment building. A group of kids is skipping rope on the sidewalk. Their faces shine with unbridled joy, and why shouldn't they? Their lives are uncomplicated and full of possibility. Until this morning, Irene felt something like that youthful exuberance bursting inside her. But the world can turn on a dime.

"Please wait," she tells the driver. "Keep the meter running."

"No problem."

She steps out of the cab and looks up and down the street. A humdrum, drab street. A barbershop on the corner. Second-rate apartments. The Crozier. The Lawrence Court. Vacant lots overgrown with weeds. Flivvers and pickup trucks parked on the street. The great unwashed, and among them her future husband, whose apartment Irene wants to break into so that she can search for evidence that Frank was sleeping with his secretary.

Playful, laughing children go romping off and into the Lawrence Court Apartments. They make it look so easy, happiness.

Breaking and entering? Isn't that a crime?

Technically, perhaps. Frank is still her fiancé. She's not going to take anything. Answers, that's what she wants. Since she can't talk to Frank, the closest thing is to roam through his junk. You could also say snoop.

Her face cringes. She's snooping on him.

So what?

Frank is sitting in jail, charged with murder, and Irene has no idea what's going on. She's always hated feeling helpless. And anyway, she's probably not going to find anything. This is all one big exercise in futility. The only thing worse is sitting and waiting, waiting, for a telephone call, for her parents to arrive. At least now she's doing something, even if it's stupid.

Irene gazes at the building and quickly realizes she has no earthly idea how she's getting inside. She can't exactly ask the landlord for a key.

The children come tearing back out. "Where's Landon?" she hears one chirp.

"On the fire escape!"

"Oh! He'll get in trouble! He's not supposed to climb up there!"

So back inside they go to retrieve their wayward friend. Meanwhile, Irene starts walking down the block and around the corner so she can double back up the alley to the fire escape. Sometimes it takes a child to show you the way. A lousy burglar she'd make.

The sun still hovers on the horizon, casting a few last rays of glorious warmth. A gentle breeze blows in from the southwest. A thermometer at the hotel read seventy-four degrees. What perfect weather! The fun she could've had with Frank today. Instead she's creeping down a trash-strewn alley, getting ready to sneak into his apartment.

Laundry lines crisscross the alley overhead, and various garments flutter in the breeze. The smell of garlic from smoking kitchens fills the air. A hirsute woman leans out of a window, a cigarette dangling from liver-colored lips. "Get off that fire escape!" she yells at the kids. They comply and go scattering away, like billiard balls at the break.

There is a lull. While the Lawrence Court teems with life and noise, next door the Crozier sits in relative quiet. One light shines from the top floor. The second floor, where Frank's apartment is, looks unoccupied, dark and lonely. The ladder from the fire escape, thanks to the children, has been pulled down, as if awaiting her arrival. Now it's just a matter of climbing up and crawling in an open window into Frank's drab apartment.

She treads lightly up the ladder, trying to act like a cat. The critics in London said she had no acting talent. Her friends told her not to read the reviews. But advice is easy enough to ignore. The bad notices cured her of the acting bug. Maybe this visit to Frank's lair will cure her of him.

So far, so good. She's made it to the second floor.

"Hey!" a voice bellows angrily.

Irene freezes.

"Get me my dinner!"

"I'm too tired! You're not the only one around here who works."

"The hell with you!"

"The hell with you, too!"

Never has open hostility sounded so lovely to Irene's ears. Frank's kind neighbors on the third floor keep screaming at each other as Irene scurries on by one floor below. The first window she gets to looks into Frank's living room. It's open a few inches already. She places her hands beneath the lower sash of the double-hung window and lifts up gently. It doesn't budge. She exerts more upward pressure, but nothing. Perspiration is now streaming down her face. She can't dally too long, so she tiptoes over to the other window. This one too is open about five inches. She lifts up on the sash and it starts to move. Irene feels a flood of relief mixed with a healthy dose of fear. Because now she's got to step inside. What's waiting for her in there?

No use gnawing on the unknown, it's time to get the inside dope. She leans down and stretches a long leg into Frank's bedroom, followed by her torso and the rest of her body. She closes the window back to the way it was and then stands perfectly still. The only noises she can hear come from above, where the shouting continues, although somewhat muffled.

■ ■ ■

"What is that screwy skirt doing?" Lonigan mutters to himself. Did he see what he thought he saw? A black-haired knockout pulled up in a cab in front of the Crozier. To do what? Visit Frank Hearn? Instead of using the front door, the skirt scooted around to the alley. Lonigan decided to tail her and damn if she didn't climb the fire escape and crawl into Hearn's apartment through a window.

Now what?

Did Hearn slip back home while Figgins was watching? Is he up there now? Where the hell is Blott? Delaney said he'd call the station and get word to Blott to come to the Crozier as soon as possible. A cop has the kind of muscle to do this job right. A badge, a billy club, handcuffs. Those would go a long way to solving the problem.

Where is he?

Lonigan can feel the clock in his chest beating, beating, telling him that time is running out. He has to do something. He can't wait any longer. Blott might not show for another hour.

Figgins! How could he have let Hearn get up to the apartment without seeing him? That watery-eyed dope, he can't do anything right.

Can't cry over spilled milk. Lonigan has a rod with a silencer screwed on the end of the barrel. Not the same kind of muscle as a cop, but it can do the job.

■ ■ ■

Irene's eyes go first to the bed. It is unmade, sheets and blanket entwined in a mad embrace. A pillow is on the floor. Evidence of passionate lovemaking? Or just Frank being a slob? Clothes lie littered across the floor, along with towels and newspapers. Every drawer of his dresser is still open from the police search that morning.

She feels sad seeing these artifacts of Frank's life. But she can't wallow. She needs to know much more. She starts by walking over to his dresser. His billfold is lying on top. She picks it up and starts going through it. There's no money in it, just some scraps of paper. One she recognizes. It's an IOU from Babe Ruth he always carries around for good luck. It's worthless now but he didn't care. He said he'd keep it forever.

"Oh, Frank," she hears herself say. But she instantly steels herself against remorse. On another scrap he has written "Klieman's, Olympia Bldg." She's not sure what that is. A clue? Or just one of those random notes that mean nothing? She can't decide so she puts the wallet down and keeps going. Next she starts searching through the drawers of his dresser. Among his socks she finds an envelope, addressed to Miss Irene Howard, 53 Kings Road, London. But there is no postage.

It's a letter he never sent.

"Oh no," she mutters, staring at his mangled cursive. His letters were never long, and this one feels as light as the others, a single page. She can guess what it says. It's his explanation. It's his attempt to come clean about Nina but then he chickened out and never mailed it. So she angrily tears it open and starts to read:

Christmas, 1927

Hey Kiddo,

It's real late, after midnight. So I guess it's not Xmas anymore. I had dinner at the diner down the street. My fork was dirty but the pie was good. Parker invited me over but I don't like the guy as much as I used to. Funny how things can work out.

Last year was nice. Remember? We were in Spain. Barcelona, right? I never should have left you, honey. This was a mistake. That thousand bucks your papa lent me is about gone. No one is buying, everyone's selling, and Parker is just a smooth talker. I don't know. I keep trying my best but everybody's clawing at the same prize. They say things get better in January. You're still coming home, aren't you?

Then he stopped, as though he was ashamed of delving into matters that showed him to be vulnerable and confused. Irene manages to smile. This is Frank's handwriting but the letter doesn't sound like Frank. Usually he wrote short, to-the-point letters that emphasized how busy he was. That didn't really bother her because Frank wasn't the introspective kind. But it's touching to see in plain view evidence of why she fell in love with him. Behind the muscles and the eye patch is a stray dog looking for a home.

But the letter doesn't prove he wasn't having an affair. In fact, its sadness makes it appear likely that he would seek out solace with his fiancée an ocean away. She can imagine him growing frustrated with his business dealings, increasingly lonely in a city where he knew no one, and one night, after working late, falling into the arms of a stunning young woman like Nina Randolph. And worse, the letter describes irritation with Parker Anderson. Given Frank's violent background, Irene can't be sure that he didn't do something he'd regret.

So instead of finding evidence to clear him, Irene has only added to her doubts. She doesn't feel better at all. In fact, this apartment is beginning to give her the creeps. It is at once familiar and alien. She recognizes his clothes, a shirt she sent him from Harrods, shoes she bought for him in Milan, and yet the rest seems to belong to the man on the moon.

She stuffs the letter into a pocket and keeps on going, morbidly curious now about this man she loves—loved. There isn't much left to examine. A stack of *True Detective* magazines. A pile of newspapers. An address book.

An address book? Why didn't the police enter it into evidence?

She knows Nina Randolph's name will be in there. Nervously she leafs to the R section, filled with Frank's nearly illegible chicken scratch. There it is. He took more care writing her name and address than the others. Perhaps it means something. Then again, she might be driving herself insane.

742 Jackson Street. Coconut Grove.

Maybe he sent her a Christmas card. After all, he sent one to Irene's parents and brother at Groton.

She hears footsteps out on the fire escape and her heart nearly leaps into her throat.

■ ■ ■

Where is she?

That's what Bryce Shoat wants to know. It's now officially a few minutes after five o'clock and he's standing right in front of the band-stand in the middle of Royal Palm Park, just like Nina Randolph told him to. Some workers are stringing up a banner: WELCOME, MR. PRES-IDENT! MIAMI WELCOMES YOU! First Gloria Swanson, now Coolidge. But nothing will lift the curse. This city is doomed. He'll be glad when he can finally get away. Hopefully that will be soon.

Under his arm is a brown bag stuffed full of cash, $10,000. He's followed her commands to the tee and all he wants is for this entire episode to come to an end. Once he gets the real estate documents from Nina, he'll be in the clear, once and for all.

So what game is the stupid skirt playing now?

He sinks angrily onto a park bench. The sun is low in the sky, and the air is growing a little chilly. A light jacket would be nice, but Bryce left his back in his car. Didn't think he'd be waiting very long. All around people are enjoying the park. Some are walking dogs on leashes, and others are reading the newspaper, smoking pipes, and looking very relaxed. The checkers tables are mostly full, and some old-timers have started up a rousing game of horseshoes. His eyes drift over to the McAllister Hotel, where Parker Anderson liked to play roulette in the private penthouse casino. Next door is the Southern Cross Observatory. He took Janice there last week so they could see Jupiter. They even banged a reefer beforehand and giggled when they looked through the telescope. Didn't see much of outer space, though.

He checks his watch again. Still no Nina.

Bryce gazes farther south, at the Royal Palm Hotel, an enormous L-shaped structure that takes up four city blocks on a prime piece of real estate, where the Miami River meets up with Biscayne Bay. The old-timers talk about how elegant it was, how Henry Flagler built it and virtually created the city thirty years ago. You can see the pool and the tennis courts, but no one is using either. That's because the hotel looks like a dump now. It's shuttered up, with lots of broken windows. The 1926 hurricane badly damaged it and it hasn't reopened. Bryce can sympathize. He's in the middle of a storm, too, and he doesn't know yet if he'll escape unscathed. Parker Anderson, the poor bastard, bit off more than he could chew and paid for it with his life. Bryce won't let some stupid skirt get the better of him.

He looks down at the brown paper bag. Maybe he should tell Nina Randolph to go fly a kite. No, can't do that. Otherwise Uncle Harvey will send him to Africa.

This stupid city!

"Bryce?"

He spins around. Somehow Nina Randolph snuck up from behind.

"You're late," he says, standing up.

"Sit down."

He sits, and she joins him on the bench. She smells like she just stepped out of the shower. Fresh coat of red lipstick. A slinky dress that shows off her figure. Cloche hat pulled tight against her face.

"Is that the money?"

"Do you have the files?"

"The money first."

"I'm not stupid, Nina. I'm not giving you something for nothing."

"I'm leaving."

"Hold on. For the love of Mike. Why do you have it in for me so bad? What did I ever do to you? I thought we had something pretty special."

He tries to brush her cheek, but she shoos his hand away. The strange part is, he likes her more this way. She's not the callow, pliable secretary anymore, but a real tigress on the prowl. "You're a liar, Bryce. You always will be."

"Was I lying when we made love? It's hard to lie about that."

"You were using me. Now I'm using you. Give me the money."

"We could run off together right now, Nina. We could take this money and go to Europe. Just me and you."

"It's too late, Bryce. You blew it."

"How did I blow it? I told you I needed some time to milk Janice for cash—and here's the cash."

She shakes her head. "I'm not talking to you. Give me the money or I'm calling the cops."

"Okay, okay. Here you go. It's all there." He pushes the brown paper bag across to her. "Now where are the files?"

She hands him something small and silver. A key.

"What's this?"

"It goes to a post office box, number forty-eight at the main branch downtown. That's where you'll find the Sweetwater files and the other stuff."

"Oh, that's dirty pool! I want everything now!"

"You'll get everything, Bryce. I checked before I came. The envelope's been delivered to the main branch downtown."

She's got the money in her hands, and he wants to grab the bag back from her. She's playing him for a rube. But what can he do about it now, with all these people in the park? Not one thing.

"You better not be lying," he says, sounding more wounded than angry.

"I'm not like you, Bryce."

"You got me all wrong, Nina. I was starting to fall for you. You can call it balloon juice if you want, but it's true."

"Don't follow me. Someone is watching you. If you get up before five-thirty, they're calling the police."

Bryce looks around. He doesn't see anything out of the ordinary.

"You got it all planned, huh? So what's next?"

"Good-bye, Bryce."

She stands up and walks away. He watches her go, admiring the smooth contours of her long legs. What a tomato.

■ ■ ■

Janice Pendergast ducks down in the front seat of Baby Blue, parked on Third Avenue in front of the First Presbyterian Church. Coming right at her, with a brown paper bag stuffed with her cash, is the woman Bryce met in the park. It just happens to be the same blonde he chatted with last night at the party for Gloria Swanson—the same one! Janice smelled the rat a mile away and she was right. She's glad she followed him. Happy, even. Delighted. Because now she knows the truth. Bryce was lying. About what? Good question. Janice has no idea why he just gave the blonde ten thousand bones. Blackmail? Hush money?

She hears a car door slam and slowly she inches up, peering just above the dashboard. The blonde is sitting in a car parked at the corner of Flagler Street. How about that? Janice watches as the Model T lurches forward and turns left, heading toward Biscayne Boulevard.

"Let's go, Baby Blue," Janice mutters as she turns the key in the ignition.

From across the park Janice sees the Model T hang another left, heading north on Biscayne. She presses down on the accelerator and the engine roars. One day she can laugh about this pathetic episode. Not now. It's not funny yet. But it's starting to feel like an adventure. When she followed Bryce from the Nautilus Hotel to the park, she figured she would go bursting in and confront him if she caught him lying. But she didn't. She's become intrigued. Now she can't help herself. She wants to see where the blonde will go next. Maybe she has another lover. The possibilities are endless.

On Fifth Street the blonde cuts over to the Dixie Highway and then heads north. A mile or so later, the terrain changes drastically. Wispy pine trees stretch in all directions, hovering above dwarf palmettos. The only signs of civilization are the runty little motels and greasy filling stations that pop up out of nowhere, sitting in stark isolation. The road grows narrow, and southbound cars whiz past just a few feet away. Where is the blonde going? Fort Lauderdale? Night is starting to fall and Janice doesn't see very well in the dark without her glasses. She doesn't like wearing them, though. They make her look like a stodgy librarian.

Finally, to Janice's relief, the blonde pulls her car over. The Sandman Motel. A series of small shacks painted white nestled among a sweep of treeless desolation. Across the street is a filling station. Janice needs some gas. Baby Blue is thirsty. She pulls up to the pump and a grungy-looking attendant with black smears on his face emerges from the garage. She tells him to fill her up and then she gets out so she can look across the highway at the Sandman Motel. The blonde has parked in front of one of the shacks. It looks like the one Bryce rented a month ago near Palm Beach. He threw a potlatch party. Everyone dressed up like an Indian. Janice drank so much gin that she had to vomit in the woods. What did Bryce do? Nothing. Didn't lift his pinkie to help her. The bum.

What game is this little bird playing? Janice half expects Bryce to appear any second. But then why did they meet in the park if they were planning on a rendezvous in the middle of nowhere? No, somebody else is coming. The blonde's partner in crime. A man. Handsome and rugged, she imagines.

"She's ready, miss."

Janice pays for her gas. "Is there a telephone?"

"Inside, miss."

"Thanks."

Janice hurries into the office of the filling station. A red-faced man with no teeth is sitting behind a desk reading a book. The title on the spine surprises her: *Main Street*. She's heard of that one before. She dated a boy once, he loved it. Couldn't stop blabbing on about it. He was a killjoy.

"Can I use your telephone? It's urgent."

"It's on the blink."

Janice frowns. The attendant might've mentioned that. "Is there another close by?"

"The Sandman across the street. But he's pretty fussy about letting people make calls. Your best bet is to head a mile south and stop at Tim's. There's a pay phone outside."

"Tim's?"

The attendant comes back and gives the red-faced man the money with which Janice paid for the gas. "You make your call, miss?"

"The phone doesn't work! Thanks for nothing."

"It don't?" He looks at the red-faced man. "Ain't we paid the bill?"

"She doesn't care about our paltry lives, Norm. Excuse Norm. He's barely civilized."

Janice is eager to get going. No more small talk with these buffoons. She mutters thanks and then dashes back to her car. She checks across the street. The blonde's flivver is still parked in front of one of the shacks. She hops into the car and revs the engine. Baby Blue sounds very happy. Then she drops into gear and pulls away. A hundred yards later, Janice feels something cold poking her in the head from behind.

"Don't move." A woman's voice. "Just keep driving."

Janice can't see who it is behind her, but she can take a guess. The blonde she was following must've gotten wise. What started out as a lark has suddenly become very scary. There's a gun at her head. She's going to die! Tears start flowing down her reddened cheeks, like lava from a volcano.

"Don't kill me! Don't kill me! You can keep the money! I won't tell anyone! Don't kill me! Please don't kill me!"

"Why did you follow me? Why didn't you just stay out of it?"

"That was my money! Bryce lied to me!" The sobs grow louder. Janice's hatred for Bryce explodes inside her like a Roman candle. It isn't fair! He's the one who should die!

"He lied to me, too. He lies to everyone, or haven't you noticed?"

"Please don't kill me! I swear, I'll do anything you want. I can get you more money."

"Turn around."

"What?"

"I said turn around. Drive back to the motel."

Janice does as she is told.

■ ■ ■

A jazz trio starts playing the tune to "Sometimes I'm Happy" as the gangplank of the SS *Algonquin* comes distending out. Stewards in neatly pressed white uniforms string tropical flowers along the rope handrails. Then the passengers begin disembarking. Most seem very pleased to be in paradise. It is a beautiful January evening.

A handsome couple emerges and begins a careful stroll down the gangplank. Seddon Howard is wearing a gleaming white suit and a Panama hat, while his wife, Lauren, has on a sheer chiffon frock the color of watermelon and enough pearls to hang a man with. He is fifteen years her senior, but both of them appear tanned, impeccable, and stately. Upon closer inspection, however, one detects unease. The way Lauren Howard's eyes rove along the pier, past the jazz trio, and into the gathered crowd.

"I don't see her," she tells her husband.

"Who can see anyone amid this throng?" Seddon responds, giving his wife a squeeze on her shoulder. "And we're a little early, are we not?"

"He wears an eye patch. I don't see anyone in an eye patch."

"And we're the better for it," he sings merrily. "Perhaps Irene has come to her senses after all. Ah, the tropics! It stirs the soul."

They shuffle along down the gangplank and head directly toward a sign bearing the letter *H*. Luggage will be distributed according to last name. A grid with twenty-six letters has been painted onto a large section of the pier. All around is evidence of happy reunions: couples hugging, children greeting parents, but no sign of Irene.

"I'm worried about her," Lauren sighs, wringing her hands. "I just want to see her face and know she's well."

"Maybe she was delayed in Havana," offers Seddon clinically. "Those Cubans move at a slow pace, I can vouch for that firsthand. Remember when I bought into that sugar plantation? I rued that investment for the next five years."

"Delayed in Cuba? Isn't Havana the most sinful city in the world?"

"It is indeed. Scandalous, to tell the truth." Seddon Howard surveys the pier with his usual fierce gaze. "Where the devil is our luggage?"

"I don't want her to be stuck in Havana."

A voice calls out. A short, rotund woman with curly gray hair, a flabby neck, and bright red lips that look garish on a face with skin the color of a ghost is waving and hooting like an owl, with a crew of porters hauling her luggage on four hand trucks behind her.

Seddon Howard forces a smile and returns a lame wave. Mrs. Roberta Firestone, sister-in-law of the tire magnate.

"You must come tonight!" the spry dame effuses. "Harvey will insist on it."

"That is certainly kind of you," stammers Lauren Howard, glancing up at her husband.

"Eight o'clock then. And be sure to bring your daughter. I haven't seen her since she was in grade school. Isn't she meeting you?"

"Something must've detained her," says Lauren with perfect poise. "We'll check in at our hotel and see if there isn't a message from her."

"I hope there is nothing wrong! Please come if it's convenient. It was a pleasure traveling with you both."

Roberta Firestone waddles away just as another porter arrives with the Howards' luggage. Now it's time to hail a cab and head to the hotel. The Flamingo, on Miami Beach.

"Well, where is Frank Hearn?" Seddon demands, voice dripping with scorn. "He should be here, shouldn't he, if she was delayed in Havana? If it were me, I'd greet the parents of my fiancée."

"Oh, Seddon. Let's hurry to the hotel. I can hardly breathe!"

■ ■ ■

"Where's Hearn?" the man growls at her.

Irene can't take her eyes off the gun. It's got something funny attached to the end of it, making it resemble a toy. If only this were a game. This ruffian means business. He's backed her against a wall. He's vowed to kill her if she moves a muscle.

"I don't know."

"You don't know? That's a lie. I can see right through you. You're pretty but you're dumb. I'm going to ask you one more time. Where is Hearn?"

He's young and despite the swagger in his voice, he sounds scared, too. His mouth is quivering and his nostrils flare like a bull about to charge. She has no doubt that he'll shoot her once he gets the information he wants. But the fact remains: Frank is in jail! He could find that out simple enough, it would seem. A telephone call to police headquarters.

"If I knew that, why would I have come here looking for him?"

"I don't like riddles, got it! Tell me where Hearn is!"

Before Irene can answer, noises come breaking in from outside. The sounds of several feet pounding against the fire escape, followed by shouting.

"Hey, kids!" Irene shouts. "Come on in!"

"Shut up!" her assailant barks, to no avail. Seconds later the faces of several urchins are pressed against the glass of the window. Irene waves to them.

"Want some candy?"

"Yeah, lady! Give us some candy!"

"Hold on!" Irene traipses past the young assassin and heads to the children. "What kind of candy do you want?"

"Taffy!"

"Taffy, huh? Let me see. Let me make a call. The police have candy." She glares at the man with the gun. He's got it stuffed in a pocket and very quickly and quietly he goes running toward the front door.

"The police have candy?" the largest boy asks, truly befuddled.

■ ■ ■

Now what. Now what. Now what.

Lonigan slams on the brakes to let a streetcar ramble up Miami Avenue.

What'm I supposed to tell Delaney?

That skirt saw him. She could pick him out of police lineup. Not good. Not good at all. He presses down on the accelerator. The Buick roars like a lion.

I've got to find her.

How? He doesn't know onions about her. She probably called the cops. That's why he scrammed. Sticking around was too dangerous.

She broke in there, too. Went in through the fire escape.

Maybe she didn't call the cops. Lonigan looks behind him, as though somewhere in the wake lies the answer he's seeking.

I've got to get that skirt.

■ ■ ■

"They got you pretty good, huh?"

Frank opens his good eye and sees Buddy hovering over him like a demonic nurse. He kneels down and puts a tin cup to Frank's lips. The water is warm but it still tastes good.

"Thanks."

"Take a biscuit. You gotta get your strength back."

He helps Frank sit up. High above in the top bunk T.R. scowls down like a vulture ready to swoop. With his harelip curled up in disgust, revealing a set of yellow teeth, he watches Frank chew.

"This ain't right, Buddy," he calls down.

"Just shut up now, T.R. What the hell can we do about it?"

"We can kill him."

Frank stops chewing. His head and ribs may ache, but he's not so bad off that he can't defend himself from being jumped by some wispy stick of a man.

"I wouldn't try it," Frank says evenly.

"Don't listen to him. T.R. got a bad temper."

"Because it ain't right! He can't climb down no hundred feet! Look at him! He's all busted up!"

Frank looks to Buddy for an explanation. "Who's climbing where?"

"We're getting out of here," claims Buddy, matter-of-factly, the way you might describe the color of a shirt. No doubt, no hesitancy. And for a second Frank believes him. Then he remembers: they're twenty floors up. The only window has steel bars across it.

"Really? How's that gonna happen? Is there an airplane I don't see?"

"Let's just kill him, Buddy! Stop horsing around!"

Frank stands up. "You say that one more time and you're gonna eat a knuckle sandwich."

T.R. pulls out a long shiv and brandishes it. "Yeah, slugger?"

"Shut up, both of you! Listen, T.R., you ever consider that you might be the one who eats that shiv? So clam up! He's coming with us."

"Wait a second!" Frank waves his arms. "Who said I want to escape? I'm not guilty of anything. If I run, the cops'll think I have a reason to."

"Because you got a reason."

"You lost me."

"Hearn, you don't get it, do you? They're gonna keep beating you until you confess. And if you don't confess, they'll take you out and—you don't believe me, do you? Listen, I don't care what you do. But we're getting out of here tonight. If you're still here and your brain still works, you ought to come with us. I know how these cops work around here."

Frank weighs his options. Getting beat up again isn't appealing, and there's no doubt the cops in this town are crooked enough to kill him. If he can get out of here, he can call Irene. She can get him a lawyer. That's what he needs, a mouthpiece. Then he'll turn himself back in. And he'll get to see Irene. He has to see her. But escaping is dangerous. They're twenty stories up. The guards will shoot to kill. Escaping just doesn't seem possible.

Frank swallows hard. "Okay, tell me one thing. How are you getting out of here?"

Buddy points. "Through that window."

"That window?"

"It comes out."

"It comes out?"

Buddy walks over and lifts the window out and holds it up for Frank to see. "We took a chisel and carved it right out."

"That's awfully enterprising of you. How'd you get the chisel?"

"Ain't none of your business how," snaps T.R.

"It's an inside job. Same with the sheets." Buddy nods toward the bed. Frank looks over.

"What sheets?"

"In the mattress. We made a rope out of sheets. We'll scale down to the landing on the seventeenth floor. The next landing is on the fourth."

Frank does a quick calculation. "That's what, a hundred and thirty feet? You got enough sheets for that?"

"We'll see. It'll be dang close."

Frank whistles and shakes his head. "I don't know."

T.R. hops down and holds the shiv in front of Frank's face. "What don't you know? You're coming now. Ain't nobody gonna mess it up. We done worked too long and hard. You're coming or you're dying right here. We told you too much already."

"Put that thing away!" Frank growls. He'd cut that idiot's throat except it would complicate his legal case.

"T.R., don't be stupid. It's almost time for the shift change. We better get ready." Buddy goes to his mattress and starts unfurling the rope of sheets. Frank inspects the knots. They look like they can hold. But a hundred and thirty feet? That's a long, long way down. But Frank can hear the voice of the cop who clubbed him: *Next time will be worse.*

And T.R. is still holding the shiv.

■ ■ ■

Officer Jackson Blott parks his motorcycle in front of the Crozier. He eases off the seat and takes a look around. He scratches his bushy sorrel mustache with his thick fingers. Where is that boob Lonigan anyway? He hitches up his belt and starts to walk. From the open windows of the Lawrence Court Apartments he can hear radios blaring. Seems like everyone in the world owns one now.

No sign of Lonigan. Blott has told Delaney a hundred times that those guppies from Philly couldn't screw in a lightbulb. Like this job. Frank Hearn is in jail and those two boobs've been staking out his apartment all day! One phone call downtown would've cleared everything up. Frank Hearn ain't going nowhere except Raiford to die, with that double homicide charge wrapped around his neck.

People are stupid. That's really all Blott could say about the human race. Look at the damn Miami Police Department. Who got passed over for promotion last year? Who didn't make sergeant? *We're eliminating positions, Jack. The city commission voted to cut our budget.* Then came the cuts in pay, on top of increased workloads. The criminals sure didn't cut back their budgets! Hell no, but the city of Miami did, and now men like Blott had to pick up the slack.

And he was picking up the slack, damn right he was. Blott gets back onto his motorcycle and decides to head up to Colored Town. It'd be nice to find a card game to bust up. That thousand bucks he got last night on a traffic stop was gone after a bad stretch of luck at the Seminole Club playing roulette. So he's short on cash again. But it's easy to fix that problem in a city like Miami where greenbacks seem to grow on trees.

■ ■ ■

Lauren Howard opens the door of her hotel room and greets her daughter with a look of polished incredulity. Irene had called from the lobby and said she would be right up, so her entry is no surprise. But her demeanor is.

"Hi!" Irene squeals and throws her arms around Lauren's neck. "Sorry I didn't meet you at the boat! I was doing something for Frank."

A mother can tell when one of her children isn't happy, and Irene in particular was never good at hiding her emotions. Even as a little girl, Irene always tipped her hand when trying to fib. Her voice choked up and her eyes darted around the room—much like now. She looks as nervous as a turkey on Thanksgiving.

"Where is the young man?" Seddon jumps in. "Hard at work, I presume?"

"He's busy as a beaver," answers Irene with false gaiety. She scoots by them both and walks across the hotel room, over to a bay window.

She throws open the curtains and drinks in the cool breeze. "Some place, huh? Great view. How was the trip?"

Lauren gives her husband a worried glance. Irene seems out of sorts, short of breath, frenetic. She's acting like some kind of zoo animal, complete with the herky-jerky mannerisms.

"Fine, dear. And yours?"

"Oh, interesting. You meet the grandest people on ocean liners. I met a man who fought in the Crimean War. He knew Florence Nightingale." She waltzes from the window and sinks into a chair. Then she bursts into tears.

Lauren and Seddon go to comfort her at once. She keeps her face buried in her hands, however, and won't divulge the genesis of this tumult. Lauren suspects the worst—or the best, depending on how one looks at the situation. It's no secret how Seddon feels about Frank. But it's obvious something has come between them.

"Did you and Frank have a fight, dear?"

"No," she sobs. "Not really."

"Oh, sugar! Look at you!"

"Mummy, this has been the worst day ever!"

"What happened, Peanut?" Seddon tenderly strokes his daughter's ink-black hair.

"I can't tell you! It's too terrible!"

"Is it another woman?" asks Lauren knowingly, a hard edge to her soft Southern twang. But this question elicits more sobs and a reproving glare from Seddon. Lauren's heart sinks. Just once she wishes she could find the right words to comfort Irene. Seddon has the knack to soothe his daughter's troubled waters.

"Whatever is the matter, we'll fix it," Seddon coos. "But I can't help you unless I know how to, Peanut."

"I'll be okay," she sniffles. "You two just got here. I don't want to be a bother."

"You have us worried sick, honey!"

Irene wipes the tears from her eyes and then stands up. "No, everything is fine. I just thought things would be different. I thought tonight would be so special."

"Where's Frank, honey?"

"In jail!"

The tears come flowing again and Irene sinks back into the chair, as if pushed down by a burdensome weight.

▪ ▪ ▪

Horace Dyer's office is about the same size as a broom closet. There is room for a desk and a file cabinet, but not much else. The federal attorney for this region of Florida claimed it was the best he could do until the new courthouse officially opens sometime in the coming fall. As it is, Dyer is stuck on the tenth floor of a building that isn't open for business yet. All day long work crews come and go outside his office, making a racket and killing his concentration. He has no secretary to speak of. He can go to the old courthouse downstairs (the new one is literally being constructed on top of it) and get typing help, but mostly he doesn't bother. Instead, he chooses to work at night when it is quiet. It's not like he has anyone at home waiting for him.

Tonight his goal is to complete a rather lengthy memorandum detailing developments in his far-ranging investigation of real estate fraud in Dade County. His superiors in Tampa have been clamoring for information, and after Dyer was able to get good dope from Parker Anderson, he started a memo to tout this seemingly positive turn of events. But now he will have to begin again from scratch.

Dyer begins to reexamine the notes he took during the interrogation of Frank Hearn. Sometimes Dyer writes so quickly and sloppily that he has trouble reading his own chicken scratch. Such shoddy investigative work won't cut it if he ever hopes to work for the Federal Bureau of Investigation, which has been Dyer's dream since high school. Two years ago he interviewed with the director, J. Edgar Hoover, and Dyer thought he was making a good impression. But then Hoover asked if he had a wife or fiancée, and when Dyer said he was getting married, Hoover's tone quickly changed. Suddenly Hoover was unsure of the "rigor" of Dyer's legal background, which was fairly slight. But what young attorney doesn't have thin experience? It was almost as if Hoover disapproved of the impending nuptials. But how could that be? Married men make good employees. They don't stay out late chasing skirts. Why would Hoover frown on marriage?

No, it had to be something else in Dyer's application that raised doubts in Hoover's eyes. The sting of being rejected led Dyer first to Tampa and now to Miami, all to prove to J. Edgar Hoover that he had what it takes to be a G-man. The sad part is, when Dyer moved to Florida, his fiancée called the wedding off. She didn't want to live in Florida. So now Dyer is a bachelor again. Who knows, maybe it will help him win over Hoover, odd as that sounds.

There is a knock at the door. Dyer springs up to answer it. A visitor! He doesn't get many on the tenth floor.

"Working late again, Horace?"

It is Vernon Hawthorne, a county prosecutor and a man of the highest caliber. Dyer had called him earlier in the day. Rumor has it that Hawthorne is going to impanel a grand jury to look into corruption at the MPD and that he's taking his case all the way to the top, meaning he'll target Chief of Police Leslie Quigg. Hawthorne is just the man to answer some questions about Delaney and the jai alai fronton, and whether there were any known associations with rogue elements within the MPD.

"It's when I think best. Thanks for coming up. I hear you're pretty busy these days."

Hawthorne whistles and shakes his head. "You don't know the half of it. Another suspect died while in police custody. They found his body in Colored Town an hour ago, filled with bullets. I'm headed over there now."

"Let me guess. Quigg is saying the officers fired in self-defense, right?"

"Five times at point-blank range. So what did you want to chew my ear off about?"

"What do you know about a man named Delaney who owns the Palmetto Jai Alai Fronton?"

"Delaney?" Hawthorne rubs his chin thoughtfully. "His name's been popping up a lot. He's got a couple of traffic cops who work for him. One's named Blott and Blott is a terror. He likes to cruise Colored Town and bust up card games, except no one gets arrested. He just cracks skulls and takes the money."

"So Delaney is trouble then? He'd kill someone who crossed him?"

"Oh, I wouldn't doubt it. From what I can tell, he has connections to the underworld in Philadelphia. How does this work into real estate fraud, old man?"

Dyer squints as if staring into the sun. "I'm not sure yet. But it might have something to do with the murder of Parker Anderson."

Hawthorne does a double take. "I thought they already had a suspect in custody."

"They do, but I'm not so sure it's the right guy." Dyer leans closer and speaks in a hushed voice. "See, I think someone in the department is covering for Delaney. The guy they arrested, he's just a patsy. That's why I needed a word with you. I suspected Delaney might own a cop or two."

"From the looks of it, he does. But Horace, you'd better tread lightly. These aren't con men selling swampland. These guys are very dangerous. If you knew what I did about how this police department operates—torturing suspects, killing others—it is truly staggering in a democracy such as ours." His voice trails off into soft dejection. Then he points to the fraternity paddle on the wall, Dyer's sole decoration. "You were a Sigma Chi, were you?"

"At Ohio State."

"I pledged Kappa Alpha but dropped out because I couldn't afford the dues. Those were some fun times. Beats this. I tell you, it's a tragedy what's going on in this city."

"I'm starting to see that from a whole new angle." Then the phone rings. "I better get that." The two men shake hands good-bye and Hawthorne rushes out to go see about another outrage. Poor bastard looks like he's been through the wringer.

Dyer answers the phone and at once recognizes the voice as belonging to Irene Howard.

"Mr. Dyer? You sure do work late."

"Got nowhere else to be. What can I do for you, Miss Howard?"

She pauses and he can hear her breathing on the other end. What's she so unnerved by? "I have something to tell you. It's about Frank."

"I'm listening."

"Somebody broke into his apartment about an hour ago, and I think they were looking to kill him."

Dyer bolts up in his chair. Nothing today has happened the way he expected it to. It's like everyone has started speaking in tongues. "How do you know this?"

"Because he had a gun."

"Did you see him? I'm confused, Miss Howard."

She pauses and then blurts: "I was in the apartment! Don't get mad at me!"

"What were you doing in there? How did you even get in there? Don't answer that. Just—Miss Howard, you could've been killed!"

"I know, but I thought you'd be interested. Somebody was looking for Frank."

"You're quite the detective, Miss Howard. But I don't remember deputizing you."

"Do you think Frank is guilty?"

"I don't know, but what difference does it make if you die snooping around? You are lucky to be alive, from the sound of it. How do you know you weren't followed?"

"I took three different cabs back to the hotel. I wasn't followed."

Dyer taps his pencil against a legal pad. "Let's hope not."

"I'm going to hire Frank a lawyer. And a private dick. I want to get to the bottom of this. I don't think he's guilty."

"If you bring a private dick into it, he might just gum up the works. I'm working on a few leads right now. You have to trust me. If Frank is innocent, I'll find out."

"Have you found the secretary?" She pronounces the word with hostility.

"No. That's another problem. Nina Randolph could make my life much easier. But she melted into thin air."

"Are the police looking for her?"

"I have no idea. You'll have to ask them."

"If nothing has changed by the morning, I'm going to pay a dick to find her. She's the key to all of this."

"Maybe. Maybe not."

"What do you mean?"

"I don't know what I mean, Miss Howard. Rest assured, I'll be working late tonight to get to the bottom of this."

"I'm impressed, Mr. Dyer, by your dedication."

He laughs sardonically. "Don't be. I just don't have anyone at home waiting for me. It's fairly pathetic, actually."

"I wish I had a sister I could marry you off to."

Dyer winces. What he wouldn't do to have the likes of Irene Howard for a wife. It's been going on two years now since the wedding was called off. Dyer feels like saying: *Hey, even if Frank Hearn isn't a killer, he's still a thug! You should drop him like a bad habit!*

But he doesn't. That's unprofessional. "Thanks," he mutters instead. "I'll take all the help I can get. And Miss Howard, please stop breaking into apartments. It's against the law."

■ ■ ■

Something catches Lonigan's eye. He's been poking around Frank Hearn's apartment trying to get a lead on the skirt with the black hair. As he suspected, no cops were called to the Crozier. The skirt didn't bother calling because she wanted to avoid them as much as he did. So that was his second mistake, leaving too soon. He should've called her bluff but he panicked, and that was his first mistake. He let those kids spook him. He should've plugged that skirt when he had the chance. What were those kids going to do? Arrest him?

He picks up a piece of scrap paper he found beneath some letters and other junk on a table.

Flamingo Hotel, 2 rooms
Irene/parents, Jan. 13

Today is January 13.

"Irene, is that your name?" he mutters under his breath. He keeps looking a little longer and hits the mother lode, a shoe box of photos of the same black-haired skirt. On the back are little captions. *Irene at Duomo. Irene in Pisa.*

"You're Frank's girl, huh? That why you came looking for him?"

Maybe she came to get something for Hearn. Maybe he's hiding at the Flamingo.

Lonigan stuffs a few photos in a pocket on his way out.

▪ ▪ ▪

Nina Randolph has just finished gagging poor little Janice Pendergast with a pair of nylon stockings. Now with another pair she is going to bind the pampered princess to a chair in the tourist cabin Nina rented for the day. Although everything is still on schedule, you couldn't say it's gone swimmingly. It seemed like every time Nina turned her head, another mishap was brewing. But she's got the money now. There's only one thing left to do.

"You'll be okay, Little Miss Muffett," Nina tells Janice, whose eyes are still wide with fright. "The maid cleans the rooms in the morning. But I guess you know all about maids."

Nina takes Janice's hands and pulls them behind the wooden chair. Then she lashes the nylons around her wrists and loops them through the bars in the chair's straight back. She pulls hard on the knot, just to make sure the heiress will stay put for at least the next hour. That's all the time Nina needs. Then it's smooth sailing.

"How does that feel, pumpkin? Does it hurty-wurty wo' wittle hands? Maybe next time you won't be such a buttinski."

What about the feet?

Nina is out of nylons. Pretty soon she'll never be out of anything for as long as she lives, but she'd better come up with something. A bra? No, that won't hold her down. A shirtwaist? That should do the trick. It's an old thing, with a frayed lace collar from about 1907. Nina bends down and notices Janice's shoes. They're all scuffed up and ratty. That's when you know you're rich—when you don't care what you look like when you go out.

Nina ties Janice's feet to the legs of the chair. Then she stands up. Janice bats her eyes a few times, and tears dribble out. Nina lifts the gun and places the barrel right at Janice's temple. Strange sounds come from her mouth. It sounds like she's choking.

Nina fingers the trigger. Then the gun falls, as if her arm can no longer sustain the weight of it. "You're so lucky," she mutters. "You're living on borrowed time now. Make the most of it, sweetheart."

Janice closes her eyes. Her mascara has washed down her face, leaving a thin layer of what looks like moist charcoal. Nina stuffs the paper bag in her suitcase and heads out the door.

THE LAST RESORT

Before they left for the gala being thrown in her honor, Gloria Swanson pinned red carnations on the lapels of the dinner jackets of the two men escorting her. Joe Kennedy is still wearing his. Every so often he looks over at her and smiles, and it feels like a blast of sunshine. It's a good thing she's been dousing herself with champagne, otherwise her blushing would be a dead giveaway that she was in love.

Henri's carnation has come off. So has his tie. He's standing beneath a crystal-and-gold chandelier in the dining room, drink unsteadily in hand. In fact, he's spilled a few drops of gin onto the gorgeous Aubusson rug that must've cost an arm and a leg. This mansion, estate, palace—all three rolled into one—rivals anything Gloria has ever seen in Beverly Hills. El Mirasol, it's called, and everything about it screams old money. The owners and hosts, Ned and Eva Stotesbury, spend some of the year in Philadelphia, summers in Bar Harbor, Maine, and January and February in Palm Beach. They are a lovely couple. He made his fortune with J.P. Morgan and after his first wife passed away, married a woman thirty years his junior. Eva, however, is no gold digger. She is pushing fifty and carries herself with that gracious, regal air of someone for whom good taste is like a second skin. Portraits of deceased relatives hang in gilded frames on the walls. Also on the walls are tapestries so beautiful and intricate that they seem unlikely to have been crafted by human hands. Someone told her that there is a gardener for every acre of the grounds, and since El Mirasol sits on forty-two acres, even an actress can do the math. The Stotesburys employ a total of seventy-five servants, and tonight each of them is carrying a tray of something exquisite.

This is luxury on a scale that even Hollywood moguls are awed by. When they first arrived, entering through an arched Moorish gateway, Joe Kennedy said: *I'll have to buy one of these.*

Henri's reply: *Buy two. We can be neighbors.*

And so now there is the problem of Henri. Gloria knows her husband well enough that she can tell when something is bothering him. He is not a man given to excessive drunkenness. Like most European men, he can hold his liquor. He has never incapacitated himself with drink. He always stood erect, chin held high, back straight, hair combed, and clothes pressed. His manners were unfailingly impeccable, the kind you can only get at Swiss boarding schools. But look at him now. His face is puffy, like an Irish cop. His voice booms and his laugh is a tiresome cackle. He keeps spilling his drink. There is a red stain on his shirt, near his heart. It looks like blood but tomato paste is a safer bet.

His heart. He knows. That's it right there. He knows about Joe.

Eva Stotesbury waltzes up with a man and woman in tow. He is pushing seventy, stooped, wrinkled, and tanned, with a bald head speckled with age spots. She is about sixteen and weighed down with gold and diamonds like a pack animal from the Andes.

"Gloria, dear, please meet my lovely friends, Mr. and Mrs. Rodney Farkleberry," says the hostess as she introduces the couple. "They just moved here from Ohio. He is the Soap King."

"Dish soap," he corrects her. Eva covers her mouth as if she just cursed.

"Of course, dear. The Dish Soap King."

"I love you!" giggles Mrs. Farkleberry, blushing at Gloria. "I mean, I love your pictures!"

Gloria smiles. This is roughly the tenth couple she's met tonight where you could've sworn they were father and daughter, not husband and wife. Although she's come three thousand miles, in many ways it feels like she never left Hollywood.

"And I love your gown! Who designed it?"

"René Hubert."

"Oh, Rod, I want one just like it." She tugs on her husband's sleeve like a little girl in a toy store. The old man beams down at her as if she just awarded him the Nobel Prize. The Dish Soap King and his fetching lass. Gloria slurps more bubbly so that her mouth remains occupied and silent. Eva Stotesbury goes flitting away, promising to be right back. Gloria's glass is almost empty. What's she supposed to do now? What more could she possibly say to the Farkleberrys? They're standing there gawking at her like she's in a zoo.

Luckily Joe sidles up and tells a wonderful white lie: "The star is urgently needed by the photographer." Rescued by a prince in shining armor! He takes her by the elbow and leads her down a long corridor, past the scurrying help outfitted in sharp uniforms, through the bustling kitchen, and back into a lush, tropical courtyard. A cage of parakeets starts to serenade them. A fountain is spraying a cool mist of water into the air. They sit on a bench beneath a chinaberry tree.

"What's gotten into your husband?" he asks her calmly.

"A lot of booze. He's been drinking all day."

"Eddie Moore told me that he was making insinuations about us while they were fishing. That could spell big trouble."

She lights a cigarette and blows a plume of smoke skyward. "I was never a very good speller."

"We might need to get him out of here before he ruins one of those carpets."

Gloria looks down at her small feet, size two and a half. The new shoes she bought this morning on Worth Avenue are starting to wear blisters on her pinkie toes. What she most wants to do is curl up in bed next to Joe, just the two of them beneath a ceiling fan. "You're right," she finally says.

"He won't go willingly, I suppose."

"No, not in the mood he's in. I've never seen him like this before. I just want him to take that job you offered him, the one in Europe. Things will be much easier that way."

"I hope he takes the job, too. Then I can rent a house in Los Angeles."

He squeezes her hand. She closes her eyes. Life is moving very fast. The years have blurred past. When will things slow down? Does she even want them to? She was never cut out for an ordinary existence.

"I would like that," she says, pulling her hand away.

"There you are!" comes Henri's booming voice. He staggers toward them, smiling broadly and waving his glass. He's disheveled, like a starving artist in Montmartre. Gloria half expects him to start panhandling. "I was looking all over for you two lovebirds!"

"Henri, you're drunk," snaps Gloria, standing up and stamping out her cigarette.

"I am not drunk. I am inebriated. There is a difference. One word is Latinate, and the other—oh, bugger, German, I think." He cackles merrily, sitting down on the ledge of the fountain. He teeters as if he might fall in.

"You can't stay here in this condition."

"I am very well behaved. And well mannered. And just swell. *Je suis poli!*"

"I need a drink," says Joe. "I'll meet you back inside. Let me know when you're ready to go."

Then he leaves. Henri reaches into the fountain and cups water into his hands. Then he splashes it on his face. Now he is soaking wet from head to toe. Gloria shakes her head angrily. He does it again, bellowing an aria from Puccini. Gloria starts laughing. She can't help it. The sight of this French aristocrat bathing in a fountain is amusing.

"Feeling better?" she asks.

"No. I feel the same."

"We need to get you home."

"Why? Because Joe Kennedy says so? He's not my boss. He'll never be my boss! *C'est un fils de pute!* Do you know what that means?" His voice cracks with sadness.

She goes to sit next to him. Maybe she can talk sense into him.

"No. I can't speak French. That's why they hired you as my translator."

"Then I'll translate." He takes a deep breath, water dripping off his nose. "It means: 'He is a son of a whore.' Huh? Do you see now?"

"No. Can't we go now?"

She stands up and pulls on his arm. He feels lifeless, clammy and cold from the water he splashed himself with.

"I just want you to be happy, *mon petit papillon.*"

"Then let's go back to the hotel."

"I need a drink first."

He bolts up and breezes past her, brushing her arm with his side. She feels something poke her, like he's got a club or hammer in his dinner jacket. *Oh no!* she gasps to herself, watching Henri staggering away. *He's stolen one of the valuables!*

BUSMAN'S HOLIDAY

rank Hearn sticks his head through the barless window of the jail cell and looks down thirty feet to the landing on the seventeenth floor. He can see the two others standing beneath him. They made it down no problem. Now it's Frank's turn. Buddy is holding on to the rope of sheets, the extra length spooled at his feet like a snake. The other end is by Frank's ear, lashed to the bunk bed that has been pulled flush against the back wall. Frank has checked that knot and rechecked it, and it sure looks tight enough to hold him. But there is another knot, the one inside his stomach. Although he's about to hoist himself through the window, Frank is wavering. He knows he's got to hurry but for some reason his body won't move.

Are you sure? He hears the voice of caution that has gotten him out of plenty of jams. He's learned to trust this voice. It wasn't always easy. He had to take a few lumps on the noggin first, but in time he started to wise up. But this might be the most important decision of his life.

Buddy starts waving frantically. T.R. is already cutting the rope with the shiv so they can tie down the remaining length for the next descent. It's now or never. It all boils down to this: Frank Hearn will not go down without putting up a fight. He's not going to let those bastard cops beat him into a bum confession. If he's going to die, he's going to die on his feet and not on his knees.

Frank wraps both of his meaty hands around the rope and, using the bunk as a ladder, angles his long body up and through the window. Now he's out, hovering thirty feet above the landing, both feet against the white stucco of the courthouse. He begins to walk his way down, arms straining against the force of gravity pulling at him. He doesn't dare steal a glance below because his entire focus is on the next step. One slipup and he goes splat like a bug on a windshield.

Concentrate, he tells himself. He's getting close because he can hear Buddy's voice: "Almost there, just a few more feet."

Finally Frank looks down. He's about ten feet from them. Seconds later he lands with a thud. Now he is standing on a roof that wraps around the entire middle elevation of the building. The lights of Miami sparkle beneath him like a glittering field of diamonds. Farther in the distance the soft flicker of light gives way to a blackness so thick it seems to be alive.

"Let's go!" shouts Buddy excitedly. "The next one is the doozy."

There is a railing that runs along the edge of the roof. It's wrought iron and bolted into the concrete. It sure looks sturdy enough to support their weight. Looks can be deceiving, though. Especially in Florida. Anything built here, there's a good chance the contractor cut every corner in the book.

Buddy shows them the best spot for the next descent. It's a long way down. A long, long way. You can talk about thirteen floors but seeing the drop is another thing entirely. It's like they're standing on the moon and are trying to get back to earth with a piece of kite string.

Buddy kneels and starts tying down an end. He uses a double bowman, and pulls it tight. That knot won't slip. The railing might break off and a sheet might shred, but the knot won't slip. At least there's some comfort in that.

"Let's see how far she makes it," says Buddy, picking up the spool of sheets and tossing it over the railing. The three men lean over and watch the sheet rope unfurl like the tongue of a huge frog. Then, nothing. The other end isn't visible. They might be fifteen feet short or forty. There's no way of knowing.

"Who's going first?" asks Frank.

No one speaks up. Danger is licking at their faces like a roaring fire. Who knows what awaits them at the bottom?

"Hell, we don't got time to wait no longer," gripes Buddy. "I'll go."

"I'll listen for a thud," cracks T.R.

"That ain't funny."

Down goes Buddy, his angular frame fighting against the wall like a stubborn horse being led to a stall. He's kicking and bucking and groaning, and he's not even halfway down. This is crazy. There's no way this will work. Frank stares at the knot again, looking for any evidence that it's slipping. It seems fine. The railing is holding up, too. For now.

"You gettin' yella?" asks T.R.

"Just being careful."

T.R. then sucks in a gulp of air and gives Frank a hard look. "You go last since you came in last."

"Just mind your own onions."

Out of the corner of his good eye Frank sees T.R. wave the shiv, its sharp blade tied to a broken section of a mop handle.

"I don't much cotton to your bossiness," T.R. says in a frog voice.

"Put that blade away."

"What if I don't?" T.R. is brandishing the shiv like he's a fearless samurai. Frank has a notion of shoving it down the rat's throat, but Buddy should be at the bottom by now. The bottom, though, is hard to make out, especially for a man with one eye. Frank can't tell if Buddy made it safely or not.

"Stop wasting time. You see him down there?"

Finally T.R. regains his senses enough to take a look.

"I see him," he says after a quick inspection. "Don't hear no hollering. Looks like he made it. Well, I'm next. Remember, don't fiddle with the rope."

"I won't, cowboy."

"Damn straight."

You'll get yours, thinks Frank, standing alone on the seventeenth floor of a building that until today he always admired. Only a growing, robust city could build a courthouse of nearly thirty stories. It towered over the landscape, radiating confidence in the future. The big gala opening is just a few months away. The city plans on throwing a lavish party. Too bad Frank will have to miss that shindig.

The sheet tied to the railing is starting to look frayed because it's been rubbing against the building. If you pull a piece of string as taut as you can, just a flick with a dull knife will cut it in two. And Frank will be going last. He's also the heaviest, so he'll be putting the most strain on the sheets. He's got to be sure not to swing back and forth. He's got to go down as straight as he can. Any more rubbing against the building could be a disaster.

■ ■ ■

Inside the players' dormitory, Figgins hears someone screaming.

"Help! Help!"

It's coming from room 8. Uranga's room. He's the one who can speak English. What time is it anyway? Almost eight? Uranga's match isn't until later.

Figgins fumbles for a key and unlocks the padlock, then throws the door open so hard it nearly bounces back and hits him in the face.

"What's wrong?" he asks. The light is off, so he can't see very much. He can make out the faint outline of the bed. It looks empty, though. "Uranga, for the love of Mike, what's going on?"

He takes a step inside the room. Someone jumps on Figgins and pulls a pillowcase over his head. Then he gets pushed to the ground. His keys! They took his keys! He struggles to stand up but it's too late. The door slams shut and the padlock goes back on. It's only then that Figgins can get the pillowcase off his head.

■ ■ ■

Frank Hearn has literally reached the end of his rope. Now he's got a drop of fifteen feet. Not as bad as it could've been. That slapdash rope managed to stretch down eleven stories.

"Hurry it up!" Frank hears.

He lets go of the last section of sheet and feels his body falling. *Hit and roll*, he tells himself, knowing he has to break the fall. He's jumped out of plenty of windows to get away from cops, so he's no stranger to taking a plunge. Growing up, he was the best at climbing trees, jumping from roofs, scaling fences. It feels like he's a kid again as he falls through the night air, a kid doing something dangerous on a dare.

He hits the ground and instantly does a somersault. He then springs to his feet. His ribs really ache now. He doubles over in agony, not sure about taking another step.

"This way!" Buddy says, pointing toward the part of the fourth-story roof that overlooks the bus station. Buddy and T.R. sprint across the gravel roof and stop at the edge. Frank forces himself to stand straight and staggers toward them, willing himself past the pain. As a kid he'd sometimes go days without eating. He never went to a doctor, no matter how bad he was beat up or cut. Pain was a friend he knew on a first-name basis. And he knows how to ignore it, too.

"Hurry it up!"

"Told you we shoulda killed him!"

"Just go, T.R. We'll catch up."

Frank makes it to the edge and joins Buddy. Down below and across an alley is the elongated tin roof of the bus terminal. It looks about twenty feet high and as comfortable as a bed of nails.

"We'll jump on that."

"Okay."

"It ain't hard. See, T.R. already made it."

Then Buddy jumps. He looks like a giant eagle, arms spread wide as he cuts through the air. He lands with a thud on the tin roof and starts rolling. He comes to a stop and gives Frank a thumbs-up. Then

Buddy shimmies down a drainpipe to the ground, making it look much easier than it is.

Frank sighs and leaps. But he didn't get his all behind his takeoff. His legs lacked energy and his arms felt like spaghetti. In midair, a horror seizes him. It looks like he's going to miss the roof. He starts flapping his arms like a wounded duck.

He lands on the front edge of the roof with about an inch to spare, otherwise he might have sliced himself in two. Then he starts rolling across the tin and sort of swims toward the drainpipe. He makes it to the brick pavement, feetfirst. An acrobat couldn't have done better. A puzzled black woman looks at him with fearful eyes.

"Good job," says Buddy, grinning. "We have to run for it. Come on, follow me."

Frank isn't sure where they're headed or what they'll do once they get there. But the fact is, Buddy waited for him. Why? Why is it so important to Buddy that Frank comes along? Does he want something? Frank has no clue. He has to get out of this jam alive first. Then he can worry about the future.

■ ■ ■

It's moving!

The cruise ship is moving, finally, after an agonizing wait during which Nina Randolph was sure that any minute the police would come busting into this fetid second-class cabin and slap a pair of handcuffs on her. With her rotten luck, she was expecting the worst.

The truth is, you make your own luck in this world. She's proven that today, getting away from the cops and soaking money from Bryce Shoat because she followed a plan. She outsmarted people who dismissed her because she was just a secretary. A dumb little bird. What did she know besides some shorthand and how to brew coffee? But now she's sailing aboard the SS *Munsorleans* bound for Havana, Cuba, with ten grand in cash.

She checks on the money again like an anxious parent fussing over a newborn baby. The bills are in a suitcase and the suitcase is in a narrow closet. She'd never seen so much dough at one time. At first she thought it was play money, but then she smelled it. She ran her fingers across the sturdy parchment and examined the faces of Benjamin Franklin and Alexander Hamilton. Franklin she knew something about, but Hamilton? Which president was he?

Now it's time to speak to the purser about moving to a first-class cabin. She waited this long because she didn't want to draw attention to herself. But her ship has finally sailed and it's time to enjoy the fruits of her triumph. From now on, it's first-class all the way.

■ ■ ■

The three men follow the gravel bed of the tracks of the East Coast Railway to Fourth Street, where they veer off and start running west. This section of downtown is industrial, smoky, and since it is night, pretty quiet. But it's still too risky being out in the open like this. They haven't changed clothes yet. These jail uniforms are dead giveaways. With one phone call from a concerned citizen, patrol cars will be swarming like hornets.

"Where are we headed?" asks Frank, ribs aching, sweat stinging his eyes, and confusion rattling his brain. He's got to break off on his own and soon. He's got nothing to do with whatever scheme these two hoodlums have hatched. But he's got to play along and pick the perfect spot, otherwise they will turn on him.

Escaping from an escape: not something Frank's done too much of.

"There's a taxi garage up here," Buddy explains, huffing and puffing. "There'll be a truck waiting. And clothes. At least, there'd better be."

That sounds promising, so Frank keeps following. After all, he's got to get off the street and out of the zebra suit.

"There it is, Buddy!" T.R. points at the taxi garage. A faded wooden sign reads Guardian Taxi Company. No lights are on inside the brick building. There are two service wells but it's impossible to say whether there is a truck waiting.

Buddy hustles over to a side door and opens it. Everyone ducks inside and Frank starts to breathe a little easier. They've made it this far, and it feels good to be off the street. Now they're huddled in a musty office that smells like burned coffee. A Penzoil calendar from 1922 hangs on a wall. Carbon copies litter a wobbly wooden desk like confetti from a ticker-tape parade.

"About time," says a voice from the shadows.

"Barely enough sheets, Jonesy."

Frank recognizes the guard from the jail. He's in street clothes now, gray flannel and two-tone shoes. His hair is slicked back and it looks like he cut himself shaving.

"What's he doing here?" Jonesy nearly spits at Frank.

T.R. and Buddy start removing their prison uniforms. Jonesy has a change of clothes for them, the wrinkled garments stuffed into a brown paper bag.

"You don't need no clothes," T.R. says to Frank, voice dripping with scorn. "You ain't going nowhere else tonight."

Frank doesn't bat an eye. "That's fine with me. I got to call a lawyer. You guys have fun."

"Why is he here?" barks Jonesy, louder now, voice full of fear and anger. "That was stupid, Buddy. Real stupid."

"I told him, Jonesy," T.R. quips.

Jonesy lifts a gun and points it right at Frank's face, point-blank range.

"Don't be stupid, Jonesy," counsels Buddy. "We don't got to kill him. That's a murder charge we don't need. We got to think, boys. Use our noggins. Put the piece down."

"He ain't coming with us, is he? I ain't giving up my share, that's for damn sure!"

"Me neither," T.R. seconds.

"Put the piece down, Jonesy."

"He knows too much, Buddy."

"He don't know squat and he ain't coming with us. Let's don't make it harder than it already is. Put that dang piece away." Buddy sounds sterner now. "I mean it, Jonesy. This is my show."

"Your show? Who got you out?"

"We all did. And now we're gonna do what we need to. But it ain't gonna happen if we act all stupid and such. Put it away! Do you want your share of the money or not?"

Frank's heard that right before you die, your life flashes before your eyes. All your memories come flooding at you. That's when you know you've reached the end. But that hasn't happened so far. No memories, no nothing except the sound of his breathing. Maybe it's not his turn.

Jonesy finally relents. The gun drops down to his side. Frank lets out a big sigh of relief. The faster he can get away from these boobs, the better. He tells himself to keep quiet as he inches closer to the door they came in. Just a few more feet.

"You got the truck?" T.R. asks.

"It's out back. That Seminole gal of yours, she's all right." Jonesy flashes a devilish grin.

"What the hell you mean by that?"

"I mean she's all right."

"All right how?"

"She's real nice."

"Did you—you son of a bitch!"

T.R. looks like steam is coming out of his ears. His face turns crimson but before he says another word, Buddy drives a paper spike into Jonesy's left eye. He must've grabbed it off the desk. Jonesy screams in agony, bringing his hands to his face. Buddy takes the gun from him and quick as a cat turns and shoots T.R. in the forehead. He crumples to the ground at Frank's feet. Frank cringes and turns away, ears ringing from the loud report. The 1922 Penzoil calendar is now spattered with blood.

Jonesy is still moaning in agony, until Buddy shoots him, too. Frank stares at the door two feet away. So close.

"Hurry up and change," barks Buddy at Frank. "Get those overalls on."

"What?"

"Do it! We ain't got much time!"

Frank does as he's told, hands shaking like a boozer who needs a drink first thing in the morning. He steps into a pair of overalls that fit him very snugly and show most of his ankles.

"You just saved me sixty thousand bones, Hearn."

"I did?"

"You sure did. I don't got to pay T.R. or Jonesy a cut of nothing."

"A cut of what?"

"I'll tell you on the way. Come on."

But Frank doesn't budge. He's not going anywhere with Buddy. That wasn't part of the deal. "I got to call a lawyer," he announces evenly, like he's reading from a script.

"After you do something for me." Buddy pauses as he buttons up his pair of overalls that once belonged to a car mechanic named Slick. The name's stitched on the breast pocket. Buddy is having some trouble with the buttons because he's still holding the gun. "If you don't want to help me, I guess I can kill you right now."

From the frying pan into the fire. "Take it easy. Just understand one thing. I ain't rubbing nobody out. If that's the ticket, count me out. You might as well shoot me right here." Frank almost can't believe these words came out of his mouth. It wasn't long ago he made his living beating people up to collect debts.

"Who said you had to?"

Frank shakes his head slowly, still confused by all of this. "Then what the hell do you want from me? I want to see my girl. We're getting married. I don't want no trouble with anyone. I'm just a regular Joe trying to live my life on the up-and-up." He can feel tears in his eyes and they burn like cigarette butts.

"This'll be like stealing candy from a baby—and as soon as you're done, you can go see your girl or fly a kite, I don't give a rat's ass. But I need you to do something and as long as you do what I say, you'll live. Now let's move."

▪ ▪ ▪

Until a few seconds ago, Delaney was in the clear and it felt real good. Frank Hearn was in jail, charged with killing Parker Anderson. That was like a gift from God. The players knew Delaney meant business when they saw Gomez filling in for Garate in tonight's lineup. The high rollers were having a good time, spending money like it was going out of style. Maybe that's why his body brace wasn't chafing so much. His spine was actually getting pulled into alignment, and his chronically aching head wasn't aching so bad. He was showered, cleanly shaven, and wearing new cuff links. Who knows, he was thinking he'd cruise Flagler Street tonight and pick up a couple of skirts.

But now this.

"Tell me again what happened."

Figgins shifts uncomfortably in his chair. He's got a pillowcase on his lap like a little pet.

"I heard some yelling coming from Uranga's room so I went in there." The words stagger out of his mouth like a platoon of raw recruits at first reveille. They bump into each other and then stop suddenly.

"And he got away. That's the bottom line."

"Yeah."

"Using a pillowcase."

"He threw it over my head, Uncle Gene!"

"Thank God he didn't have a teddy bear! Hell's bells, kid, you're the one packing heat!"

Figgins stares down at the pillowcase. "I don't like hurting people."

Delaney throws open his arms like greeting a long lost friend. "No one does, kid. No one does. But if you don't hurt the mutts who want to hurt you, guess who gets hurt? You do. It's simple self-defense."

"Want me to go find him?"

Delaney winces and shakes his head. "Somebody's got to make sure these matches go off! Get back out there and do your job. Where the hell is Lonigan anyway? Hearn's in jail, so who's he looking for?"

"I don't know."

"My soul, I should send you two back to Philly. You dumbbells aren't worth a damn!"

There's a knock at the office door. "Come in!" Delaney yells, head pounding again. He could use a BC powder.

In walks a large, menacing cop, with bleary red eyes and a missing front tooth.

"Blott!" spouts Delaney like a nervous host. But Blott has that effect on people. It's like seeing a shark when you're swimming. You know they're dangerous even when they're far away.

"Scram, punk," Blott tells Figgins, who nearly trips over his feet scrambling out the door.

"Did you find Lonigan and tell him about Hearn?"

"No. He wasn't there like you said he'd be. It was a waste of my valuable time."

Delaney holds up his hand like a conductor leading an orchestra. "I apologize. But I can make it up to you. I got a job, a big job."

"How big?"

"One of the spics got away. Name's Uranga. Here's a picture." Delaney slides a glossy head shot across his desk. Blott doesn't reach for it.

"How big?"

"A thousand."

"Let's call it two."

"Fifteen hundred."

"Two."

"Fine. I need you to hunt him down. There was a fed sniffing around here today, named Horace Dyer. You know him?"

"Nope."

"Well, I think Uranga went to find him. I checked and didn't see no Dyer listed in the city directory."

"He's a fed, you say?"

"Yeah. A stinking fed."

"That's going to cost you three. Half now, half when it's done."

"I thought we had a deal!"

"Three. It's a dang fed you're wanting, Delaney. Not some spic."

"Do it tonight. It can't wait." Delaney reaches into his desk and counts out fifteen one-hundred-dollar bills.

■ ■ ■

Frank parks the pickup truck in an empty gravel lot next to a life-size wooden cutout of an Indian chief pointing northward. Up ahead flows the smooth black water of the Miami River and the entrance to the Seminole village on Musa Isle, where tourists pay two bits to see Indian weddings and alligator wrestling. People say it's a hoot. A man jumps into a pit with a dangerous animal. Kind of like being with Buddy.

"Let's go," Buddy says politely but firmly, still leveling the gun at Frank. Wordlessly Frank gets out and heads toward the chief, feet crunching against the gravel.

"What about the alligators? They feed at night, don't they?"

"They keep them in pens."

"They'd better."

The two men jump a waist-high concrete fence. They skirt along it as they jog back toward the north side of the village. About a hundred yards away Frank can see the little huts the Indians live in. Can smell the food they're cooking, too. Whatever it is, he'd devour. It's been a long time since he had a good meal. And it doesn't look like Buddy has any plans to stop for a bite to eat.

■ ■ ■

A short woman with reddish-brown skin stands in the middle of a large treeless square dotted with thatched huts. Hundreds of beads encircle her thick neck. Her round face glows from the flames of a nearby fire. Her black eyes dance and dart like mosquitoes. Sally Tiger rubs her hands nervously against her colorful patchwork skirt. T.R. said it would happen tonight during the guard's shift change. That's when Jonesy would make sure no one would bother them. And then they would meet up at the garage and come here for the boat.

She looks at the night sky. Should be anytime now.

Smoke billows thinly out of the cooking chickee. Minnie Willie is stewing sofkee again. She makes that soupy mush taste pretty good. She's showed Sally Tiger how she does it, first pounding the corn, then adding some sugar, but Sally doesn't speak the Seminole tongue as well as she once did so it's hard to understand what the old woman is saying.

One expression she knows by heart. *Este étu fullat.* That's what they call Sally Tiger at Musa Isle. The words literally mean "two strangers walking past," translated best into English as "outsider." Sally Tiger came to Musa Isle because she had nowhere else to go. T.R. was back in jail.

And tonight he's busting out. Sally Tiger gazes into the murky distance, on the lookout for any sign of him and Buddy Upthegrove. They'll get on a boat Sally got from Musa Isle's caretaker, a drunk named Moose. It wasn't easy. She had to sleep with him, and his breath tasted like rotten meat. Worse was the guard, Jonesy. He enjoyed hurting her. But T.R. told her to do whatever she had to.

A baby begins to cry. The mother is one of Sally Tiger's cousins. Yesterday a stupid white tourist pointed at her and said: *Look at the squaw suckling that babe!* Then they all crowded around the chickee and snorted and snickered, acting like the Indians weren't real. Sally Tiger wanted to get a gun and fill them with lead. No one stays at the village long. It's too degrading. If Sally never spends another day here, that'll suit her fine. But once T.R. gets his share of the money, she won't have to.

The baby keeps crying. Sally Tiger decides to go see if she can help her cousin, who is very young and homesick for Big Cypress, the swamp that was her home. She and her husband will return there as soon as he sells his alligator hides.

Sally Tiger crawls up the short ladder to the chickee she shares with her cousin. The floor sits three feet off the ground and is made of roughly hewn half logs of cabbage palm. The fronds of the tree form the thatched roof overhead. There are no walls or windows, just six posts. Between two of the posts hangs a small hammock. Sally Tiger's cousin is rocking the baby in it, and both mother and child look very sad.

The baby's eyes finally fall closed. Sally Tiger sits down and lets her legs hang over the side. She looks out across the back of the property on the north side of the island. The tourists aren't allowed to wander into that section, because there the midwives have erected a birthing chickee. They keep it separate so that in case the mother dies during labor, the entire village won't have to be burned, as is Seminole custom.

Then she hears a strange noise and it stirs her heart. It sounds like a boat engine. T.R. made it! Sally Tiger scrambles back down the ladder and skirts along the edge of the square until she comes to the path leading to the birthing chickee. Her heart beats wildly in her chest as she runs as fast as her stubby legs will carry her. T.R. made it! The plan worked! Sally Tiger can barely contain her glee. Her life will never be the same. She and T.R. will move to Cuba and never work again.

When she gets close enough to the boat she sees two men, and neither of them is T.R. One is tall and is wearing an eye patch. The other one must be Buddy Upthegrove. But where is T.R.? Where is Jonesy?

"Let's go," she hears a man say above the din of the engine. She made sure there was gas and food enough on board for the trip to Canal Point. That's where they're going. It's a small town on Lake Okeechobee where Buddy Upthegrove's sister lives. That's where they'll find the money.

But something isn't right. Something happened to T.R. The wind in the trees seems to be whispering a message from him. They killed him. They used T.R. to spring them from jail and then they killed him.

Sally Tiger crouches low beneath a saw palmetto. She doesn't dare show herself. If they killed T.R., they'll kill her, too. So she remains silent and watches as the boat pulls away.

Then she sprints back toward the village. They left the pickup truck parked in the lot across the river. Sally was supposed to drive it back to Moose's house. But she needs it for something else now.

BEND YOUR EAR

L onigan is sitting in the crowded lobby of the Flamingo Hotel, with an edition of *The Miami Herald* shielding his face. From this vantage he can see a bank of elevators twenty yards away. For the past hour he's been waiting for Irene to show her pretty face. But is she even staying at this hotel? If only he knew her last name, he could bribe a bellhop with a sawbuck and get her room number.

He knows Delaney must be pulling his hair out. Lonigan has been gone a long time. The jai alai matches have started and there's work to do. Lonigan thinks about finding a pay phone and calling in. But the fact is, he's afraid to. Delaney learned the ropes from Boo Boo Hoff. You cross him once and you're finished. When he gives you a job, he wants it done right. So there's no way Lonigan can show his face back at the fronton without a trophy in hand. But he can't sit here all night, either. At some point he's got to throw in the towel.

"Come on," he grouses, snapping the newspaper angrily. Just like his old man used to do at breakfast when the kids got too loud. Funny the things you remember.

How much longer?

Lonigan snaps the paper again. Just then he sees a face he recognizes. It's her. It's the skirt Irene with an older couple. Her parents, just like the note said. Lonigan keeps the paper in front of his face and peers around it. He watches them walk past. That Irene is a real tomato. What a pair of legs.

He waits until they walk past and then he springs up. The three of them are headed for the stairs that lead down to the circular drive. They're going somewhere nice, the way they're dressed to the nines. Lonigan's car is parked in the visitor's lot behind the tennis courts. He can't lose them now. He's worked so hard to find Irene!

But there she is getting into a cab with her parents. It pulls away right as Lonigan reaches the bottom step. He waves down a cab. He'll leave his car where it is for now.

"Follow that cab," he tells the driver. "I'll make it worth your while."

For a few minutes Lonigan feels something like satisfaction. He's always prided himself on his ability to think on his feet. But there's one last hurdle: icing the skirt. That won't be easy. She's with her parents, headed to Collins Avenue by the looks of it.

But the cab speeds past all the usual spots. Roney Plaza, Bouche Villa, Roman Pools.

Huh?

Half a mile later the cab slows down and pulls into a huge beach-front estate surrounded by a fence and protected by a guard at a gate.

"Keep going," barks Lonigan, befuddled by this turn of events. "What is that place?"

"That belongs to Harvey Firestone."

Lonigan falls silent. What is he going to do now? He's not breaking into the Firestone mansion.

"Where to?" the driver asks.

"Hell's bells! Ah, take me back to the Flamingo. What a load of applesauce!"

▪ ▪ ▪

Where's Janice? That's what Bryce Shoat would like to know. He went to pick her up so he could bring her to the party being thrown for Aunt

Roberta, but when he got to her house, Mrs. Pendergast said she wasn't home and she didn't know where she was. *I thought she was with you!* The hag was fretting and Bryce started to worry. It wasn't like Janice to stand him up. The last time he saw her was at the polo match, where she gave him the money so he could pay off Nina Randolph.

As Bryce stands in the drawing room, next to a potted rubber tree, gurgling on ginger ale, he starts to think that maybe Janice *is* standing him up after all. Maybe she got good and steamed about the money. Maybe she's trying to prove a point. It's hard to say. But Bryce would feel a lot better about everything if Janice were here.

"Did you hear I'm hosting a little party for the president?" Bryce hears Uncle Harvey boast to Aunt Roberta, who cackles in delight.

"Is that so?"

"He won't be staying long. He's catching a boat for Havana. You know how he is. He can be a fusspot." Then Uncle Harvey pats Bryce on the back. "You excited about meeting the president?"

"Sure thing! Ought to be swell."

"Are you going to invite the gal you've been courting?"

"Who is that, pray tell?" gushes Aunt Roberta, who loves sticking her nose in his affairs. Like everyone else in the family, she thinks he's damaged goods because of his father, a man Bryce barely remembers. They say he was a drinker and a gambler, unfit to marry into such a prominent family. He died on a business trip to Colombia when Bryce was three. Mother still hasn't recovered.

"No one, really."

"Did you hear your cousin is getting married? She's from California! Her family owns several banks."

Uncle Harvey jumps in. "Bryce's gal is no slouch, either! He's seeing a Pendergast! A real fine family here in Miami."

"Do I hear marriage bells in your future, Bryce?"

Bryce snickers nervously. If he just knew where Janice was—see, that's the thing, the not knowing. What is that skirt up to anyway? God knows who she's been blabbing to. Probably telling the whole world about the money she gave him. Fine, let her. It doesn't matter any-more. No one can prove anything. How does she know he didn't pay off a gambling debt? It's not like there's anyone to ask.

"Marriage is what makes a man," intones Uncle Harvey, repeating one of his favorite maxims. "If you'll excuse me. My dear friend Sed-don Howard and his wife, Lauren, have just arrived."

Bryce looks over at the newcomers as Aunt Roberta starts singing like a drunk canary: "The Howards are here! Oh, let me say hello!"

She goes scurrying over to the older couple. Then someone catches Bryce's attention. A tall, gorgeous young woman with black hair and a look of irritation that makes her smolder. She's standing by the Howards. Their daughter? That would be a nice surprise. That dish sure would help take his mind off Janice Pendergast. He drifts over toward Aunt Roberta. Who needs Janice Pendergast anyway? She can just stew in it if she's sore at him about the money. While the cat's away, the mice will play. And Bryce feels like playing.

Formal introductions are made. Bryce shakes hands with all of the Howards. Irene's skin feels smooth as silk, and she is a shapely drink of water, with long legs that would look very good wrapped around his neck. Stylish clothes. High cheekbones. Straight nose. White teeth. Full, red lips. Delicate neck.

"First time in Miami?" he asks casually, sidling up next to her.

"I came when I was little."

"How do you like it so far?"

"Not very much at the moment."

"Why's that?"

"It's a long story."

This one is cool as a cucumber. Not much for small talk. But there's a remedy for that. He's got a flask of bourbon upstairs that he was saving for Janice, but she's not here . . . and there's a beautiful woman who's bored. Time for the heavy artillery.

"How about a drink?" he whispers. "A real one. I mean, if you're interested."

"That's a nice offer, but I can't indulge right now."

Although her voice is throaty and quite sexy, Irene sounds all balled up about something. She's watching Seddon Howard and Uncle Harvey huddle together for a private talk. Uncle Harvey's great impassive face is twitching, and that spells trouble. God knows Bryce has seen that twitch plenty of times.

"Let's go up to my study," Bryce hears his uncle say to Seddon Howard. Seconds later, everyone goes marching off with Uncle Harvey, leaving Bryce with Aunt Roberta.

"So," Roberta starts, "tell me about this girl you've been seeing."

But he's not going to endure that kind of torture. Aunt Roberta likes to carve him up like a surgeon. "I need to visit the restroom. I'll fill you in when I get back."

Bryce starts off for his bedroom. He'd better have that flask of bourbon handy in case Irene Howard changes her tune. He also wouldn't mind listening in to what the Howards are discussing with Uncle Harvey. Sure enough, at the top of the stairs he hears voices coming from the study. He creeps down a majestic hallway lined with satinwood love seats and Italian lace curtains. A series of Savonnerie rugs masks the sound of his footsteps. He stands outside Uncle Harvey's office. The door rests open, slightly ajar. He can see no one inside the room.

"Irene, Frank Hearn is no good for you! What additional evidence do you need?"

Frank Hearn? The name itself sends a shiver down Bryce's spine. That was the last person he expected to hear about. Nina said the cops think Frank Hearn killed Parker. Pretty clever of her, framing him like that.

"Mother, Frank might be innocent. Even the police say so."

"Heavens, Seddon, will you please talk to your daughter?"

"Honey, they wouldn't have arrested him without just cause. You can't know all the facts."

"There is this one investigator, Horace Dyer. He thinks this case is more complicated than it seems. He thinks other people might be involved."

"Sweetie, let the authorities handle the matter. That's why we all pay taxes, so we don't have to do the jobs of public officials."

"He needs a good lawyer. And a private investigator."

"We'll hire him a lawyer," Lauren promises.

"We will?" her husband replies angrily. She flashes Seddon a withering glare.

"The best one in Miami."

"And an investigator to work with Dyer. What if Frank is innocent, Daddy? Someone might be making it look like he's guilty. He didn't kill Parker Anderson!"

"You sound like a dime novel!"

"I don't care."

"My nephew, whom you just met, was friends with Parker," says Uncle Harvey in a sad, plaintive voice. "I'll have to tell him about this. I don't think he knows. As far as a lawyer, I know several we can call."

Bryce's mind starts to tumble like a pair of dice. His legs take him away from the study and up a flight of stairs to his bedroom on the third floor. Once in his room, he dashes over to a closet and finds the flask of bourbon buried in a box of old riding boots. He takes a deep chug and the burn in his throat soothes him a little. Now it's time for the performance: pretending to be shocked by Parker's murder.

Back downstairs he goes. At the foot of the stairs Irene points and declares: "There he is." Then to Bryce she says in a softer voice, full of tenderness: "Your uncle is looking for you."

■　■　■

"Parker's been killed?" Bryce chokes like he just bit into a lemon. "How? What happened?"

They have reconvened in Uncle Harvey's study to break the bad news to Bryce. Irene Howard is hovering above him as he sinks into a Chippendale chair. She smells like a ripe peach that he'd love to take a bite out of.

"He was murdered," announces Uncle Harvey gravely.

"By who?"

"They think someone named Frank Hearn did it."

"What? No, that's impossible! I don't see how that could ever be possible."

Irene points to Bryce like he's a statue in an art gallery, evidence of something shadowy and powerful. "See, I'm not the only one who thinks that." She kneels down in front of him and bats those big brown eyes. Bryce is trying hard to evince anguish, not so easy with a pretty broad nestled between your legs. "How do you know Frank?"

"I met him once or twice. He worked with Parker, didn't he? How do you know him?"

"He's my fiancé. You haven't spoken to the police, have you?" she asks hopefully.

"No," he mutters. *Fiancé? Frank Hearn? Is that a joke?*

"Would you mind terribly helping me out? You said yourself you don't think Frank was capable of murder. You knew Parker—perhaps you knew his secretary, too? She might be involved but no one seems to know where she is."

"Oh, I didn't know the secretary," he replies uneasily, sobering up quickly and becoming a little scared now by the direction this is headed. The last thing he wants to do is answer questions about Nina Randolph. Or Parker Anderson, for that matter. "Parker and I were old friends, but as far as who would do something like this, I couldn't venture to guess. Frank seemed like a nice guy."

"Did Parker associate with bad people?"

"Irene, let the poor boy alone!" Thankfully Seddon Howard intervenes, allowing Bryce a moment to gather his wits. "He's told you he doesn't know anything, and he's just found out his friend is dead."

"I know, Daddy. We don't have the luxury of time. Frank is sitting in jail, and the real killer could be getting away. Leaving the country, even!"

"I want to help. I really do." Bryce finds himself again gazing longingly at Irene. She in turn smiles back at him.

"I would greatly appreciate it. I'm going to do everything in my power to prove Frank is innocent." She gives her mother a hard look. Mrs. Howard lets out a small, disappointed sigh.

"I don't know much, really," Bryce offers, as meekly as a church mouse.

"Didn't you and Parker have some kind of business relationship?" asks Uncle Harvey.

"We talked about some real estate junk a few times," replies Bryce vaguely.

"Could you spare a few minutes to speak with someone tonight?" Irene presses.

"Now Irene, aren't you making too many demands on this poor fellow?" her mother objects.

"The investigator working the case told me he'd be at his office late tonight. I could call and see if he's in."

Bryce checks his watch. His hand is shaking like a leaf on a tree. "Sure, you go ahead and call. I told you already, though, I don't know anything."

"But even the smallest detail might be useful!" Irene reaches out and touches his arm. Bryce grins sheepishly. He just has to remember that no one can prove anything. But still, he doesn't need this right now. And where the hell is Janice anyway? Why is everything going so wrong all of a sudden?

■ ■ ■

Dyer can't help it. He's excited about the prospect of seeing Irene Howard again. She called and asked if she could bring in someone who knew Parker Anderson and Frank Hearn. Of course he agreed to such a request. But after he hung up the phone, his mind started to drift. It's been a long, long time since a woman has made his pulse quicken. It's a good feeling. Maybe a little too good. Because now he can't concentrate.

Get a hold of yourself, pal.

It can't hurt to dream a little. Anything to break the tedium of writing the memorandum to his boss in Tampa. So far it's been slow going. Every time Dyer thought he understood the case, a loose thread would lead to a huge hole in his story. Since he isn't the world's fastest typist, starting over meant another laborious hunt-and-peck expedition on the keyboard. What bothers Dyer the most is the way Hearn was arrested at the Flamingo Hotel, attired in just a bath towel. That makes no sense. If he killed Parker Anderson, why would he show up at the Flamingo half naked? Unless he was telling the truth: he was looking for Irene. And if he's telling the truth, then Hearn might also be telling the truth about not being mixed up in Sweetwater. Which means Parker Anderson was a con man. Throw in Delaney and a crooked cop named Blott, and Dyer is writing a memo that drifts all over the place. Nothing adds up.

Then the phone rings again. It startles him, like the cry of a baby in the middle of the night. Irene Howard calling back to cancel?

He answers haltingly. The voice on the other end surprises him.

"Me-star Die-are?"

Heavy Spanish accent. "This is Dyer. Who are you?"

"I meet you today. At the jai alai."

The lanky jai alai player. Bingo! This could be something.

"I remember."

"I am near Silver Slipper."

"The nightclub?"

"Yes. I must tell you of bad things."

"Don't move. I'll be there in a few minutes."

Dyer hangs up and then remembers Irene Howard is on the way to see him. But he can't leave that jai alai player out on the streets where Delaney might finish him off. And this just might be the break in the case that springs her fiancé, Frank Hearn. So he's got to go.

He decides to leave a note and Scotch tape it to the door. Scotch tape is a miracle of progress. It's like a ghost can stick anything anywhere.

Irene:
Something came up. Will return soon.
Horace Dyer

■ ■ ■

Bryce Shoat reminds Irene of an old boyfriend she used to have, Jimmy Woodman, a handsome, dashing young man blessed with family money and an ability to make bland conversation. Jimmy always wore the right clothes, shaved carefully, and drove expensive cars, like the Nash roadster now humming in front of her, a finely tuned machine that exuded speed and power.

"Should I put the top down?" Bryce asks politely.

"It's a bit chilly tonight."

"Up it stays."

He opens her door for her and in Irene slides. The interior is neat and trig, not a speck of dirt anywhere.

"I don't mind helping you out," he says before putting the car in gear. "But I don't think I'll be much help. I didn't know much about Parker's business affairs."

"Anything you can do will be copacetic." Those were the words out of Irene's mouth. But what she thought was: *Why did he mention Parker's business affairs? Isn't that odd? Why is he assuming business affairs had any connection to Parker's murder?*

"I only knew him socially. Real estate wasn't my kind of racket."

The car goes tearing off down the long driveway which winds through the Firestone estate. Right off he proves he is rather reckless and proud of it, stealing glances at her when he makes a sharp turn. Yes, she's known plenty of boys like Bryce Shoat. And she knows just how to play him.

"You're a good driver," she gushes girlishly. It's like she's back in prep school again.

"It's all in the timing. Timing is everything."

"Driving scares me."

"I've never wrecked. Well, once. But it wasn't my fault."

In a sweet voice. "So you didn't know Nina Randolph?"

"No. Not really. I mean, we said hello to each other."

Even sweeter, like lemonade. "You stopped by the office sometimes?"

"Sometimes. Not much, though."

Hmmm. Doesn't know much about Parker's business but stopped by the office.

"And that's how you got to know Frank?"

"I didn't really know Frank very well."

Irene falls silent with a smile on her face, as if she is marveling at his automotive acumen, when in fact she is wondering about this Bryce Shoat. He talks in circles and contradictions. He is cocky and full of himself. But she can't pry too much or he'll grow suspicious of her. He already seems to be getting defensive. Like he's got something to hide.

He turns right and heads over a bridge across the bay. Atop the tall hotels clustered along Biscayne Boulevard, neon signs glow in garish, screaming colors. Bryce brags about the high-stakes casinos that operate in most of them. But Irene is hardly impressed. She's found Miami to be a cluttered, haphazard city that seems to be going through an awkward adolescence. Boastful and insecure, beautiful in places and wretched in others. To think Frank wanted to live here as man and wife—Irene shudders at the prospect.

"Do you sell tires, too?" she asks, expertly changing the subject.

"No, no. Maybe one day. I mean, I'd like to. It's the family business." He seems very uncomfortable talking about that subject as well. He turns the tables on her. "Enough about me. What about you?"

"Me? Until today I thought I'd be happily married to Frank Hearn."

"Oh yeah? Engaged, you two lovebirds were?"

"Something like that."

"Lucky him."

"He might not feel so lucky where he is right now."

"I didn't mean it like that. I just meant the man who ends up marrying you will be a lucky man indeed."

"Thank you."

"You're welcome."

He's flirting with me. What a cad! My fiancé is in jail and he is feeding me lines older than my grandmother.

As they near the Miami end of the causeway, he asks: "Where we headed? The police station?"

"I want you to talk to this man named Dyer. He isn't a cop. He works out of the courthouse, wherever that is."

"Who's this Dyer? What are you talking about?"

He sounds skittish now, like a kid who doesn't want to eat his vegetables. She tries to keep her voice as sweet as before. "There's a federal investigator named Dyer who is looking into Frank's case. He's the one to speak with."

"He always works this late?"

"Apparently so. He's expecting us."

"I wonder what's wrong with him." Then brightening. "When this is over, maybe we'll go get a drink somewhere. How does that sound?"

"I don't think I'd make very good company tonight."

"We'll have to do something about that, won't we?"

Nothing seems to faze this would-be Valentino. Irene is getting the impression that his sole motivation to help Frank was to be next to her, alone in his fancy car.

"Here's the new courthouse!" he sings proudly. "Tallest building south of Baltimore. Wow, this place is crawling with cops!"

A true statement. Men in uniform are scurrying everywhere. "It looks like a St. Patrick's Day parade," she quips.

Bryce drives past the building. But the traffic is heavy on Flagler Street and they crawl along, looking for a place to park.

"We're right near the Mammoth Cave." He winks at her. "It's a speakeasy. We can improve your mood in a hurry."

"My mood is fine. I want to go in the courthouse and do what we said we were going to do."

"Okay, okay. But I'm telling you, the Mammoth Cave is hotter than a griddle!"

He doesn't sound serious at all. His flip attitude is most annoying. It's time for Irene to call his bluff. "You don't have to help me if you have other things to do."

"Oh, now, see? You're mad at me! What'd I do? Can't a fellow have a little fun?"

"Let's just go see Dyer."

Grumbling under his breath, finally he finds a place to park in front of the Miami Recreation Academy. He starts telling her an inane story about fencing lessons. Irene thinks: *Under no circumstances am I getting back in this car.* She doesn't trust Bryce, and getting away from him will be not only a pleasure but a necessity. Hopefully Dyer will be able to poke so many holes in him that Bryce will look like Swiss cheese.

■ ■ ■

The Silver Slipper sits on the corner of northwest Twenty-second Avenue and Fourteenth Street, a plain-looking building in the middle of a mostly residential neighborhood a few blocks from the river. But the Silver Slipper just might be Miami's most notorious speakeasy. Flashy cars are parked in the vacant lots around it, because tonight the featured performer is Smiling Sam Macy and His Hawaiian Paradise of the Pacific Revue.

Horace Dyer picks a table in back, so he can see the front door. He's already loped through the crowd, looking for the person he's supposed to meet, presumably a lanky Spanish man whose brown skin will identify him in this all-white club.

He orders a club soda and then settles back, the loud island music of the four-piece band acting as a welcome tonic. The pretty dancers are also nice to look at, although the show borders on being indecent. They flash too much skin for any cultured person. This show proves that the times are changing fast. If his mother could see him now, she'd keel over and die. Dyer has heard of clubs in Miami where the girls take off their tops and parade around shamelessly. The police won't close any down because, big surprise, the owners pay them off. What a sham this city is.

Why is he even bothering? It doesn't seem like anyone in Miami wants him to clean up the real estate racket. Assume for a moment that he could untangle the mess. A few men would go to jail. Parker Anderson's killer would be brought to justice. And tomorrow someone else would open a false office and lure easily fooled northerners into signing contracts for submerged land. And the gambling, the bootlegging, the prostitution, all would proceed full steam ahead.

His drink arrives and he downs it with eyes blazing. No, he won't quit just because it's a useless struggle. Life is a useless struggle. No matter how hard you try, you end up dead. The key is making a difference. Protecting the innocent. He is just one man, but one man who can help. Look at Vernon Hawthorne and what he's doing. If Dyer needs some inspiration, that's it. Vernon Hawthorne is going after the biggest fish in the sea, the chief of police. Vernon Hawthorne is fighting to protect the rights Americans have fought and died for—and so can he.

Horace Dyer looks around. There is no sign of a jai alai player anywhere. Very strange and eerie: it feels like someone is watching him. Is this a setup? Will Delaney suddenly appear with a couple of goons and make subtle threats? There are a couple of hundred witnesses, so that scenario is unlikely.

Finally Dyer sees the jai alai player. The Spaniard has a noble countenance, slender lips, and weary eyes that dart around the club. He looks frightened but manages a quick smile when he spies Dyer.

But Dyer doesn't smile back. In fact, he starts to wonder if this isn't part of the setup. Delaney obviously called Quigg after Dyer's visit, and Quigg told him to back off. Now this. A little too neat a package, wrapped, with a bow on it.

"Thank you much to coming," the Spaniard says, wearing not his white uniform but street clothes that seem to be a few sizes too small for his lanky frame. He sits down, exuding nervous agitation. "I need help of you."

Dyer keeps his cool. "What's your name?"

"My name is Uranga. Listen, sir, my friend I think he has dead."

"Who do you think is dead?"

"His name is Garate. Sir, I think they kill him."

Dyer studies the man's noble face, twisted in panic and dread that no actor could fake. This Uranga is in trouble. But Dyer isn't ready to take the bait yet. His first impressions have been wrong of late. This is a city where you have to be careful every second. "Why do you think Garate has been killed?"

"They take him away."

"Delaney did?" Dyer leans forward, voice lowered as he looks around the club. "Did you see him do it?"

"No. I am locked in room. I hear him scream."

"You were locked in a building?" Dyer doesn't quite understand what Uranga is getting at.

"*Sí*, locked. *El jefe* keeps locked the doors. Like dogs we are."

"Delaney locks you in?"

Uranga nods his head vigorously. "He is a very bad man. He kill Garate. You show me a picture of that man, Parker Anderson. We working with Parker Anderson. I know Parker Anderson. And he is dead, too."

"Wait, wait, wait. You're going too fast for me."

But Uranga can't put the brakes on. "I can call no police. Everyone scared of Delaney. He has police. How do you say? They are his police."

Dyer's instinct is to get in his car and drive over to confront Delaney, but a frontal assault would be suicide. No, what Dyer needs to do is protect this witness and figure out a way to present his testimony to the grand jury that is looking into the other abuses of the police department. Dyer needs to get Uranga to give a statement to Vernon Hawthorne, and that means going back to the office, where Dyer was supposed to meet Irene Howard anyway. He can call Hawthorne from there.

Dyer tosses a one-dollar bill on the table. "You'll have to come with me," he tells Uranga. "We need to go to my office. I want you to talk to someone. He's a lawyer."

"No, no. I go now."

"Wait! You have to testify against Delaney!"

"No. I go home now."

"Home?"

"To Spain. On a ship."

"What about Delaney? What about the others you're leaving behind? Don't you want Delaney to pay?" Dyer's voice trills with emotion. Uranga looks like a decent, standup sort of fellow. He risked his life getting away from Delaney. He possesses strength and character, two traits jurors love.

"You have to help us," Dyer whispers as Uranga folds his hands beneath his chin. "We can make sure you get home to Spain. In a first-class cabin. Huh? Will you help us?"

Uranga closes his eyes like he's trying to see into the future. His future. When he opens them, he is smiling and shaking his head. Dyer winces. What's he trying to say?

"I can guarantee your safety. Delaney can't get you anymore. You'll be safe."

Uranga smiles a little more.

"*Sí.*"

■ ■ ■

Blott parks the motorcycle in front of the Central Grammar School on First Avenue. Across the street is the Realty Board Building, but it might as well be the jail, the way those real estate crooks operate. Busting up card games in Colored Town will get you a few smackers, but that's balloon juice compared to what those white-collar cons are raking in. No one ever said life was fair. The only way to get ahead is to play the game by your own rules.

As Blott doubles back toward the Fink Apartments on Fourth Street, he gazes at the grammar school. He can almost feel the boredom emanating from it. He hated school with a passion and stopped going as soon as he was big enough to pick cotton. Ma tried to get him to go but he didn't mind her. Pa beat the snot out of him, so Blott left home when he was ten. Learned a trick or two along the way courtesy of Uncle Sam's army and then he landed in Miami after the war.

Now they make recruits go to a police academy before Quigg'll hire them. Mr. Fancy Pants, the Big Reformer. But when he needs something done, he don't call no police academy grads, that's for sure. He calls men who know how to use a nightstick and crack skulls. Quigg used to call Blott sometimes, but they got into it a few years back and Quigg moved Blott out of Vice and into Traffic. Traffic! Don't take no brains to direct traffic.

That's when Blott started working for Delaney. It sure helped make up for the lost income. Yeah, ole Delaney, he's forked over some real cool kale. This ought to be an easy three grand. Three grand! One good night at the craps table could set him right for the rest of his natural-born life.

The Fink looks like a well-kept place. Four stories, yellow stucco, old men sitting out front playing cards. No good. Blott doesn't want anyone to see him. He cuts around to the alley to see about a back entrance. He's looking for number 12. An old friend who works for the phone company came up with Horace Dyer's address. Blott said: *We got to find this guy. He's in serious trouble. Somebody's trying to kill him.* In this business it pays to have a sense of humor.

Now it's just a question of how. Usually folks will open their door when it's an officer of the law who's knocking. His pistol has a silencer. Not his MPD-issued Colt revolver. But a Smith and Wesson he copped off a jig a few weeks back. Blott figured it'd come in handy. As usual, he was right.

In the alley Blott picks up his pace. He hasn't checked in at the station for a few hours. The louie on duty tonight is Grizzard, a vet who likes to tell stories about his grandkids and complain about how no one can do anything right. Hell, Grizzard is the kind who'll hop on a motorcycle and drive around looking for you if he gets his dander up.

Blott bounds up a few rickety wooden stairs. The back door to the

Fink is propped open with a brick. He steps into a musty hallway. There's a narrow staircase to his right and he starts up, thinking 12 must be on the third floor. As usual, he's right.

Sir, there's been an emergency. Might I come in?

That works almost every time. He strides right up to number 12 and knocks. He puts his ear against the door. Nothing. No one is home, seems like.

"Are you looking for Mr. Dyer, officer?"

It's a woman's voice. Blott spins to look. Standing at number 11 is a battered old hen with stick legs and a bathrobe that fits her like a fur coat. Her hair is orange and her lips are red, but her skin is ghostly white and sags down in drooping layers, like bunting.

"Yes, ma'am," he answers, tight-lipped. "It's an emergency."

"He works late most every night. You might try his office. It's at the new courthouse."

"Thanks, ma'am." Blott tries to avoid eye contact and he doesn't smile as he hurries away. The missing teeth give him away. Not that it matters. Even after someone finds Dyer's body tomorrow morning, that old woman, after the shock wears off, will think the police were trying to save her neighbor, not kill him.

▪ ▪ ▪

Figgins is perched on a stool in the locker room as the players in the fifth match pull on their cestas. That's what those long gloves are called. Usually there is playful banter, some of it directed at Figgins, who can't speak Spanish but can tell what they mean. Just like when the retarded kid Danny Turner talked. None of the words made sense but Figgins could still get through. That's how it is with the players.

But not tonight. The players are mum like they're getting ready to attend a wake. No one even looks in his direction. They know about Garate. They know about Uranga getting away. They don't like being locked down like animals in a zoo.

If only one of them would laugh. But they don't. You can even hear the showers dripping.

Why did he leave Philly? Because Mr. Hoff told him to.

Why does he always do what he's told? He looks down at the gun he's holding. He's never liked guns. He's pretended to like them so he could be friends with Lonigan because everyone liked Lonigan, especially the girls. Maybe they could meet some tonight. Lonigan always knows what to say.

"Hey!"

Figgins turns. It's Lonigan, all dressed up and ready to be alert. Hair slicked back. Gold cuff links.

"Where were you?"

"Looking for someone. You all right?"

"Yeah."

"I heard you had some trouble."

Figgins scratches his nose. It's a big nose, the nose of an animal, not a person. "I guess so."

"I'm sure it'll turn out okay." Lonigan pats him on the shoulder. "I better get back to the windows. I'll see you later."

"Sure." Figgins looks at the six players sitting on two benches, cestas attached to their right hands like giant claws. It's almost time. This was when Garate would start hooting like an owl. He'd get them all so excited. They really love playing the sport of jai alai. It does look fun. Uranga said he'd teach him one day.

Fat chance.

B.C.

his place is spiffy, *n'est-ce pas?*" Henri observes acidly. They are standing beneath a green awning in front of a porte cochere corner entrance to a sprawling white building. You have to look closely to see a sign frosted onto the window of the front door: B.C., it reads. It stands for beach club. Bradley's Beach Club, to be precise. The world's most exclusive casino, according to Joe Kennedy. "Isn't that the word? Spiffy?"

"You wanted to come here," Gloria reminds her husband. Joe is seeing to the valet who parked the car.

"Indeed I did, *ma chérie.* I feel lucky tonight. Very lucky."

Gloria rolls her eyes. So now they will gamble. With that carrot they lured Henri away from the party, where he was making a first-class ass of himself. Coming here was Joe's idea. He is a member and convinced Henri that spending some time at the beach club would be memorable. *Last year I saw a man whose name you'll recognize lose half a million dollars in one night!* That testimonial won Henri over. He loved going to Monte Carlo, although Gloria doesn't recall having seen him win. But the stakes here dwarf those at Monte Carlo (so Joe claimed). Henri had to see for himself. Thank goodness they were finally able to shove him into the backseat and get away from El Mirasol before Henri crashed into an ancient Greek urn.

"Ready?" Joe Kennedy comes bounding up the steps, exuding restless energy with each stride. He greets the doorman with a hearty slap on the back and a generous tip. Then the three of them step inside. The reception room is small though elegant. Joe makes his way over to a flat-topped mahogany desk and chats up an impeccably attired man with a neatly trimmed mustache and knowing, watchful eyes.

Henri stands behind Gloria, his booze-fouled breath licking at her neck. If he'd just stop drinking, he might pull himself together.

"We're all set," Joe says, waving them over. The man behind the desk stands up and offers his hand to Gloria.

"It is our pleasure, Marquise de la Falaise." He nods to Henri. *"Bonne chance, marquis."*

"J'essayerai de bien me tenir," Henri quips, his words starting to slur.

"What's that, Hank?" asks Joe nervously.

Henri translates. "I said I'm going to behave myself."

Gloria groans. Her husband needs to go home and go to bed. He can barely stand up straight. But apparently he needs to prove a point or some such nonsense.

"You're such a cutup, Hank! Come on, let me show you around."

They walk through a door marked ENTRANCE FOR CLUB MEMBERS ONLY. Greeting them is a hall with thick green carpet and pure white walls. To one side is a restaurant, where handsome couples dine in wondrous splendor, the candlelight dancing off their beaming eyes. It looks like a romantic spot, the kind of place Gloria would love to enjoy with Joe.

"Who wants a drink?" asks Henri.

"You can't have drinks in the game room," Joe replies.

"We must drink first."

"Let's go to the game room," says Gloria, pulling on the sleeve of Henri's evening coat. "I think I see the roulette table."

Henri says nothing and instead staggers off toward the restaurant. Gloria starts after him but Joe catches her arm.

"Let him go," he says gently. "They'll serve him something and maybe he'll be ready to call it quits. If not, Colonel Bradley will have him escorted out of here. Acting drunk at the beach club is a no-no. They won't stand for it."

His touch thrills her. Was it just today they made love for the first time? It seems like a thousand years ago. So much has changed in her life. Her feelings for Joe are overwhelming, the culmination of months of flirting and lusting, with him rearranging her life, her finances, her career, and ultimately her marriage. Joe will never divorce his wife, but that steadfastness only makes him more attractive. They can never become entangled in the trivial disputes that mar most marriages. They can love and laugh, come and go, without the added weight of forever lashed to their backs. The one obstacle, the only obstacle, is Henri.

"I've never seen him like this," she whispers.

"He's no fool."

"No, he's not. But he's drunk and he never gets drunk."

"He should take the job in Europe. It's what he wants. He just can't admit it to himself yet. But he will."

"I don't know. I wouldn't be so sure."

"No, he'll come around."

"He's pretty mad. You should've heard the names he was calling you."

"He'll get over it. He's just blowing off some steam."

Joe has a way of making her feel safe and secure. She listens carefully to what he says, because he is usually two steps ahead of everyone else. His is a brilliant, calculating mind. She loves matching wits with him. No man has ever appealed to her more.

But about Henri, he might just be wrong.

■ ■ ■

Henri sits at a table and waits for his drink to come. *Cocu! Cocu!* It's that infernal bird again, chirping in his head. The cuckold bird. What dreadful clatter! Why won't it just shut up? Maybe the better question is: Why won't he just shoot the bastard between the eyes? Right here, right now, in front of all of his nouveau riche pals, these *très gauche* buffoons with waxed-on smiles and garish toupees which look like they came from carpet remnants. These *fils de putes* with money to burn and confidence oozing from their scaly skin—shoot the bastard, right here, right now.

"Your drink, sir."

The waiter sets down the highball of gin Henri ordered. He stares at it with profound sorrow. As drinks go, it is perfect. Perfection everywhere, as is optimism and can-do spirit and new cars for every man, woman, and child. The land of milk and honey and electric toasters.

Descendre le bâtard.

Henri lifts the highball and drains it in one long gulp.

Shoot the bastard.

Which bastard? The bastard screwing his wife or the bastard who can't make his wife happy? Huh? Which deserves to live and which deserves to die?

He stands up. The couple at the next table examines him carefully. Henri offers a lame smile. They seem so pleasant, so comfortable. A nice meal just devoured. An empty bottle of wine. It will be unfortunate, what happens next.

Onward he walks and nearly plows into a waiter carrying a tray of china and cut glass. He sees Gloria and Joe, still standing in the hall, talking rapturously. Then they notice him. They stop talking. Another lame smile.

"Finish that drink, old sport?" says Joe Kennedy manfully.

"Might I have a word with you in private?"

"Sure, sure." He sounds flummoxed. For the first time, Henri hears in Joe Kennedy's voice the aching strains of doubt. *Mon Dieu!* One might mistake him for European!

"Henri, don't make a scene." Gloria sounds angry, the way she gets at the help back home when they forget to iron the sheets.

"I will not make a scene, love."

She glares at him crossly. Was it just four years ago that they roamed the streets of Paris, arm in arm, lolling along the Seine, she giggling at his whimsical jokes and falling in love with him? They were in costume then. She loved her part, that of the ravishing marquise. But he wasn't a leading man.

"Please don't, for my sake."

"I will not make a scene." He brushes her face. So lovely, so unique. Her pout can melt a heart of stone. Her eyes smolder like coals.

■ ■ ■

He's felt this way before. The first night before he faced combat. His nerves were jangling like rocks in a tin can. But he did what he had to do.

"What's on your mind, Hank?"

Joe Kennedy's voice sounds like that of a greengrocer addressing a housewife who can't decide on kiwi or carambola. Pleasant, businesslike, with a hint of exasperation. They're standing on the sidewalk in front of the club. Sleek limousines deposit their masters, mostly demimonde blondes escorted by stooped benefactors, with numbing regularity.

Take the gun out. Let him fear you.

"I have something to tell you."

"Shoot. I'm all ears."

Henri can't help but laugh. These quaint Americanisms! They say "shoot" when they mean "talk"! It's all quite droll.

Henri reaches inside his dinner jacket and pulls out a case of cigarettes. He offers one to Joe Kennedy. Soon smoke enshrouds their faces, and Henri clears his throat. He has something important to say and he wants to say it clearly, so there is no misunderstanding.

"I'd like to take that job in Europe you spoke of. The one with Pathé Studios."

Suddenly Joe Kennedy seems delighted. A wide grin creases his round, handsome face. He waves his cigarette like a baton. "Great news, Hank! We'd love to have you!"

"I think that Europe is where I belong. No need fooling myself any longer."

"You're making a wise move, Hank. I've got big plans for Pathé in Europe, and you're just the man I need to head up the operation. Wait till Gloria hears. She'll be thrilled."

Henri winces at this true and painful statement that cuts like a knife across his soul. But he has never been one to lick his wounds. He takes a long drag off his cigarette. The barrel of the pistol is poking him in the ribs like an insistent child who wants something very badly.

"Come on, let's go tell her! Let's celebrate!"

Celebrate the end of a marriage? "Thanks, no. I am feeling rather tired."

"Let's shake hands, huh? Glad to have you on board, Hank!"

He extends a meaty paw and the two men share a manly hand-shake. But Henri feels sick to his stomach. He starts sweating and the world goes wobbly. He feels a small, delicate hand on his back.

"Are you not well, honey?"

It's Gloria, gazing at him with motherly concern. Henri reaches into his dinner jacket to get a silk handkerchief. "I'm better now, thanks."

"You should go home and sleep."

"I think I will leave."

"The hotel is just a block away. I'll walk you home."

"No, please don't. I don't want to spoil your evening."

"Nonsense."

"I won't get in your way, love. I am man enough to concede defeat."

"What on earth are you talking about?"

He smiles and pats her delicate shoulder. Then he turns away from her and hops into a waiting taxi. Gloria trails behind, nearly stumbling over her gown.

"Henri! Wait!"

"Go," he tells the driver.

"Where to?"

"Anywhere. Hurry!"

The driver speeds off just as Gloria Swanson reaches the sidewalk, waving frantically at the taillights of the departing taxi. A few seconds later Joe Kennedy sidles up beside her.

"What did he tell you?" she asks her lover, sounding both afraid and annoyed. But she never takes her eyes off the taxi. She can see it cruising over the bridge that leads across the lake to West Palm Beach.

"He's taking the job in Europe I offered him."

"He is?"

"That's what he said."

A GATHERING OF SCORPIONS

ally Tiger is driving a small black Ford truck with a broken muffler as she pulls into the dirt-swept parking lot of a service station at the intersection of the Conners Highway and State Road 25 in the village of Canal Point. She cruises past the lone gas pump standing vigil over the quiet night. Lights shine from within the clapboard store with a slanting tin roof dappled with rust. She keeps on driving until she reaches the pump house of the West Palm Beach Canal. She circles around it, putting two tires on the steep bank of the levee that holds in the waters of Lake Okeechobee.

Sally Tiger parks, pulling hard on the brake to keep the truck from rolling. From here she can see the store, but she's still hidden by the pump house. This is the place. She asked the toll collector when she got on the Conners Highway if he knew where Laura Upthegrove stayed. She was John Ashley's wife. John Ashley used to be the biggest gangster in Florida. He and his gang made thousands robbing banks and smuggling booze from the Bahamas. But John Ashley was gunned down a few years back, and most of the rest of the gang is either dead or behind bars. Buddy Upthegrove belonged to the Ashley gang. He told T.R. that John Ashley hid a hundred grand somewhere in the

Everglades and if they could bust out, they'd go find it, with Laura Up-thegrove's help.

Sally Tiger reaches into the glove compartment and pulls out a small pistol. It belongs to her cousin. There are three bullets in the chamber. She'll need at least two because there are two of them, Buddy Upthegrove and the other one with the eye patch.

Sally Tiger found T.R.'s body at the garage, lying next to Jonesy. Both of them were shot in the face. Only one of them deserved it.

She grips the gun with tenderness. She's shot guns her whole life. She's seen men aplenty die in all kinds of horrible ways. But she loved T.R. Wilson. He only hit her when he was drunk. He was brave and he never backed down. And they killed him. Maybe they think they're going to get away with it. Maybe they think they'll find the money John Ashley hid in the swamp and not give T.R. his share. But they're wrong.

Sally Tiger settles back and waits. She is a patient woman. She knows they're coming. She'll have the element of surprise on her side. She'll spring on them like a panther chasing down a deer. If T.R. isn't getting his share after all he did to help Buddy Upthegrove bust out, no one is getting that money. It is the Seminole way: all starve before one does.

▪ ▪ ▪

The small boat churns through the still waters of the Miami Canal, passing beneath a train trestle that spans the narrow ribbon of water like the arm of a giant black spider. For miles, on both sides of the canal, stretch fields of beans, acre after acre, row after row. Holding a flashlight, his hands lashed together, Frank Hearn sits at the bow, shining a beam of light into the red eyes of alligators that swarm on the banks. He's seen dozens so far, and to be honest, they're giving him a bad case of the leaps. Some have been huge, as long as the boat or longer, twelve or thirteen feet. What's stopping them from attacking the boat and eating them alive? That pistol of Buddy's won't stop them. This is nature, raw and unadorned, something Frank hasn't much experienced in his life. But here he is, wearing dirty overalls, sitting in a boat, going God knows where to do God knows what. The cops have to be swarming all over south Florida looking for them.

"The canal locks is just up ahead," Buddy announces. "We're almost there."

"Then what?"

"I'll tell you when I see if them locks is open or not."

"What do you mean?"

"The canal drains from Lake Okeechobee. In rainy season they let the water rush out, all the way down to Miami. But it ain't the rainy season. They liable to close them locks at night. If they is closed, we ain't getting through."

"Then what?"

"We'll have to get us a car."

Frank lets these words sink in. As far as he can tell, they're in the middle of nowhere. They haven't seen anything but gators the whole way up from Miami, red eyes glowing in the shine of a flashlight. Like they're waiting, biding their time, before they attack. He always wanted to see a man wrestle an alligator, and tonight he might get his wish.

And now Buddy wants to steal a car. Fat chance of that happening. But with his hands literally tied, what can Frank do about it? That's a question he's been asking himself a lot. He hasn't come up with any good answers. But it's like playing poker. You have to wait until you get the cards. So far it's been nothing but slop. But a good poker player can win with slop by bluffing.

"Hey, Buddy, let's kick this around a minute." Frank keeps shining the flashlight forward as he cranes his neck to talk. "What exactly do you need me for? You know I don't want the money you're after. I don't want nothing to do with getting in more trouble, either. I'll only get in the way."

"No, you won't. I just need you to do one thing."

"But what? How'm I supposed to do something if I don't know what it is?"

"I need to find out what a person knows."

"Why don't you ask him?"

"He won't say unless we make him say."

"I told you I don't want to get involved in the rough stuff."

"You won't! All you need to do is go into a service station and say your truck broke down. That's it. Someone named Cecil'll go get his truck to tow you back to the station. I'll jump him when he comes out. That's what T.R. was gonna do. But he wanted to split the money with me."

Frank turns away from Buddy. The night sky is littered with a million stars. It reminds him of the first night he spent with Irene in Asbury Park. They were holding hands on the boardwalk and then he coaxed her for a walk on the beach. Those are the same stars that were shining back then, lighting the path to his future. He has to get back to her. He can't die out here in this desolate place.

"If I do that, I can go?"

"You can go."

"No strings attached?"

"No strings attached. Them's the locks, right up there. Damn if they ain't opened up wider than a hooker's snatch."

Frank turns to look. Two steel doors sit open and water is flowing out of the lake. Surrounding the lake is an earthen levee about six feet tall. Off to the right is a small building and outside it a lone lightbulb glows. Insects are swarming around the yellow globe. Buddy eases back on the throttle and the engine begins to idle as he guides the boat slowly through the locks. There isn't much room to spare. The skiff squeezes through and once on the lake, Buddy guns the engine and they take off again.

Now it's too loud to talk. So Frank drinks in the surroundings. The isolation of the lake hits Frank between the eyes like a brick. He shouldn't have been surprised. But the reality is hard to digest. He can't help but wonder about a few things. Even if you assume that, as unlikely as it seems, everything works just like Buddy said it would, is Buddy going to let him walk away? Probably not. He's killed two men tonight. What difference would a third make? Buddy is already staring at a death sentence. The man has nothing to lose.

But say Buddy lets him leave when the job is done. The next question is where is Frank supposed to go? He's out here in the middle of the boondocks, he doesn't know a soul, and he is still a fugitive from the law, wanted for murder. Go where? He doesn't even know where he is right now. Lake Okeechobee? What the hell is that? Plus, there's the exhaustion. Frank's tried sleeping a little but it's hard to stretch out. His stomach is growling, his head is killing him, and his heart is shattered right now. This is it. This is the bottom.

COMEBACK

Standing in front of a locked door on the tenth floor of the almost-finished Dade County courthouse, Irene Howard reads aloud a note left by Horace Dyer. As she does, Bryce Shoat starts acting like his feet are on fire.

"Too bad, nobody's home," Bryce chirps. Then he turns like he's ready to go.

Irene doesn't intend to give up that quickly. She very much wants Bryce to answer some questions, because he is as slippery as a snake and can't keep his trap shut. Once he started blabbing, he wouldn't stop, and an investigator as bright and professional as Horace Dyer would pick up on the fact that Bryce is hiding something. So she knocks again, in case Dyer came back and forgot to take down the note.

"You're going to break your arm! Give it a rest! We can come back in the morning."

"This is important. A man's life is at stake."

"I know, I know, believe me. Hey, my friend got killed today, don't forget. I'm not thrilled about that."

But he doesn't sound upset. He sounds bored. Irene glares at him, not sure of anything except this: she'd love to see him squirm. He knows something about this case but he won't say what.

"Come on," he grins, offering his arm gallantly, "let's go get a drink. For the love of Mike, we deserve one."

"Let's wait for Dyer to come back."

"Ah, don't be a sourpuss! Just one drink."

Irene strains to keep from yelling in his face. "Maybe another time."

"Boy, you're a tough nut to crack! You'll change your mind about me once you get to know me better. I'm not the ogre you think I am."

"You'll have to excuse me. It's been a long day."

"Oh, play the chill all you want! I won't take no for an answer!"

What will it take for this playboy to settle down? A drink? Will he behave himself then? Irene doesn't want to let him go alone because then he might never come back. "Oh, fine. One drink and one drink only. Then we come back to see Dyer. Fifteen minutes is all. Got it?"

"Got it!"

He starts off down the hallway toward the elevator, whistling a tune. It's not exactly a funeral dirge. He seems to be enjoying himself, while inside she feels revulsion. She's going to get to the bottom of this. She'll change his tune, all right. He'll be the one in the hot seat. Dyer will make short work of this chucklehead.

She pushes a black button and waits for the elevator.

"I'll say this," she hears him say. He's standing behind her and she'd rather not turn to face him. "Frank Hearn is one lucky man, because you are one beautiful doll."

"Thank you," she mumbles, hoping the elevator will come soon.

■ ■ ■

Blott pushes the stop button on the service elevator. The doors freeze in place and he steps out and looks both ways, peering down long hallways floored with new linoleum. The glue is so fresh that it still stinks. The plaster on the walls is unpainted and so are the baseboards. The new courthouse is empty, just as he thought it would be. After all, it doesn't open for a few more months. The county keeps some of its prisoners way up on the top floors, and the old courthouse still occupies the bottom four floors, so Blott figures Dyer's office is somewhere between the fifth and the tenth floors, future home of Dade County's administrators, lawyers, inspectors, and tax collectors.

Blott starts walking and checking each room of the fifth floor. As he walks, the soles of his brogans squeak against the new linoleum. Every step sounds like a mouse squealing. He tries walking on his tiptoes and that helps a little. It's hard, though, being so big. He passes by one empty office after another. He looks beneath a tarp covering buckets of paint.

But his shoes keep squeaking, so he stops and takes them off. Now he can move silently, like a tiger through the jungle. He places them by the elevator on the fifth floor and heads up to the sixth.

■ ■ ■

A long mirror runs behind the bar of the Mammoth Cave, and in it Irene can see the jovial patrons elbowing their way to get a bartender's attention. Some shout, some whistle, and all wave bills of various denominations. On a cramped stage a chanteuse and her pianist do their best to entertain, but the poor bird seems very nervous. Her voice cracks on the high notes. Next to Irene a thin young woman with too much mascara opines, after lighting a cigarette and blowing smoke toward the ceiling: "She is dreadful."

Irene doesn't respond. She might've said something like *It takes guts to get onstage.* But she doesn't feel like talking at all. She's barely touched her drink, something called a madras that Bryce ordered for her. He's sitting on a stool to Irene's left, waving at other well-bred tyros and their vapid dates. If ever a man seemed in his element, this is it.

And this is ridiculous.

"I'm going back there," she tells him firmly. "The fifteen minutes is up. I'm sure Dyer is back by now."

"We just got here!"

She ignores his porcine plea. Why did she let him talk her into this? She should've insisted that they wait for Dyer's return. Is everyone in

Florida just plain lazy? Only out for a good time? Everyone, it seems, but Horace Dyer, who's burning the midnight oil while Irene delights herself at a speakeasy.

"You haven't finished your drink," he tries again.

"We're going back."

"Don't be a killjoy."

"Come on, you promised. What, aren't you a man of your word?"

"Can't a man finish his drink?" he whines like a spoiled child. Pity the poor woman who marries this cad. Irene feels like dragging him down the street by the ear.

■ ■ ■

Janice Pendergast has been kicking her feet for hours, trapped in a dark cottage that reeks of stale smoke. Her legs burn with pain. She can't feel her arms anymore. Any second now her bladder will explode. But she keeps on trying to break that knot around her ankles. For the first hour she couldn't budge her feet at all. It's like they were frozen in blocks of ice. But she kept at it, fighting through the pain and the tears that gave way in time to a grim determination. She's never had to fight for anything this hard before. So much has been given to her. Clothes, cars, trips to Europe. She's always gotten exactly what she wanted. Until now.

Kick! Kick! Kick!

With all her might she struggles against the shirtwaist tied to her feet. Sweat streams down her anguished face, grimacing in agony and exertion. She's not giving up. She's going to kick Bryce Shoat right in the groin the first chance she gets. She's going to flush the blonde's head down the toilet.

Kick! Kick! Kick!

She hears fabric ripping! It worked! It really worked! Janice carefully stands up, bringing the chair with her like some kind of delirious hunchback. She sees that the knot didn't break, but the fabric split from all her kicking. Her feet are still lashed together. She can take baby steps, though. One false move and she'll go tumbling down, with no guarantee that she can stand back up. She moves carefully toward the front door of the cottage, one tiny step at a time, inching along like a centipede.

Finally she makes it. Now what? She's got to get this blasted chair off her back. Her shoulders feel like they might pop out any second. Pain stabs her in the neck. She leans her head against the wall, which takes some of the pressure off. Then she starts swinging the chair into the door, swiveling her hips like she's inventing a crazy new dance.

Thud! Thud! Thud!

She keeps pounding the chair into the door, hoping someone will hear the racket and come see what's causing it. But no one comes. She keeps at it, even as she begins to feel light-headed. She might pass out. She knows the feeling. But then something happens she wasn't expecting. The chair starts to crack! First one leg and then another. Emboldened, thrilled beyond words, Janice savagely attacks the door with what remains of the chair until it splinters so badly that she can slip her hands free of it. Like her feet, though, they are still bound together behind her. She can't reach up and take the gag out of her mouth. The smell of nylon is making her sick! Breathing fresh air will be like eating caviar.

Time to get out of here. She spins around slowly so that her back faces the door. Just barely she can reach the knob with one hand. She has to stand on her tiptoes, rising up as high as she can go. Her fingers can barely brush the knob. Just a little more and she can grab it—done!

The door swings open. Janice is outside, a place she wasn't sure she'd ever see again. And right in front of her is Baby Blue, waiting for her like a faithful pet. She just has to get these stupid knots undone and she'll be off. Bryce Shoat had better say his prayers tonight.

▪ ▪ ▪

What was that? Irene thought she heard a noise, some footsteps and then a jarring clang, the sounds echoing through the empty hallways of the tenth floor of the courthouse. She turns to look and doesn't see anything. Yet she heard something. She keeps listening, but there's only silence. Her mind must be playing tricks on her. It's dark and the only light comes from a bare bulb hanging in the hallway, which casts menacing shadows that seem to be moving.

Is someone else up here?

She's not waiting to find out. This is just too creepy. She turns away from the office door where Dyer has taped the note and starts walking fast down the hall, back toward the elevators. But before she arrives, two men step out of an elevator. One of them is Horace Dyer. The other is a Mexican-looking fellow.

"Thank God it's you!" Irene calls out.

"Women routinely have that kind of reaction when they see me." Dyer smiles coyly and Irene finds herself feeling very glad to see him. All of a sudden the world seems to be in a recognizable order.

"Is that so?" she pouts playfully.

"Sorry I had to run. This is the reason why." Dyer pats the brown-skinned man on the back. "I'll explain it all in my office."

Irene feels confident that Horace Dyer will take care of everything. He exudes calm and intelligence, mostly through his demeanor. He never gets flustered. He's always ready with a quip. These qualities are rare in people.

And Horace Dyer is handsome, something she's been trying not to notice.

■ ■ ■

Blott has reached the tenth floor, and still no sign of Dyer.

In stocking feet Blott steps out of the service elevator. Immediately he hears an office door open and shut, the thud echoing down the hall-way. That's a good sign, Blott decides. A very good sign. Like shooting fish in a barrel. Hopefully he can wrap this up quick and still make it to the casino before too long.

THE GRAND TOUR

loria Swanson leans back and blows a smoke ring to the ceiling. Her bright blue, almond-shaped eyes regard the trailing smoke with curious indecision. On the silver screen she comes across as sexy, glamorous, and alluring, but tonight she seems puzzled, even frightened. Is her life going up in flames again? Will yet another one of her husbands wither and die beneath the white-hot glare of her fame? Does she fall in love too easily? Why hasn't she met her match?

Or has she?

Over in a corner, Joe Kennedy is whispering to Eddie Moore. They are talking about David Sarnoff and the RCA deal Joe has been cooking up, while waiting for the arrival of the hotel detective. Joe Kennedy takes charge. Joe Kennedy exudes vitality.

Joe Kennedy is married.

Another sad smoke ring drifts away. He's a married man and she's a married woman. Do such scripts ever have happy endings?

Henri still has not returned from his misbegotten sojourn into the unknown. A private investigator might have to go looking for him. Joe especially is concerned about Henri's state of mind. One false move by Gloria Swanson's husband, and every newspaper in the world will have a field day trashing her.

And one false, tragic move Henri could make. On the outside he comes across as incredibly debonair, poised, and polished, the epitome of Old World refinement. Those are the qualities she loves about him. Yet there is a side to every husband that only a wife gets to see. Gloria knows something about Henri which she hasn't told Joe. Something that has been bothering her ever since Henri drove off in that cab.

Back during the war, Henri fell in love with a Romanian singer named Alice Cocéa. Henri was just twenty and had seen horrible combat for two years. He met Alice in Paris and they spent a glorious two weeks together. Then Henri had to return to the war, but he promised to come back to Paris on his next leave. Ever dutiful, Henri did just that, only to find Alice in the arms of an older, wealthier gentleman.

Henri was crushed. He tried to kill himself.

Gloria winces. Henri is a proud man, and proud men don't allow themselves to be humiliated. What if he tries something like that again? She can't stand to think of it.

"He's fine," she says in a husky voice her film audiences have never heard. Barely over five feet, Gloria doesn't seem capable of having such a voice. But she is a child of the Midwest, of Polish and Swedish stock, and the twang of Chicago is unmistakable. "He's just thinking, that's all."

"Sure he is," Joe agrees warmly, leaving Eddie Moore to go to her. "But he's also boiled and upset. It's best if we find him before he does something stupid. You can't afford that kind of publicity right now, not with *Sadie Thompson* on the horizon."

"I don't care about the stupid censors!"

"I know you're feeling bad, you."

"Oh, you."

That was their particular way of addressing each other. It was playful and eased the tension. Gloria sighs and walks over to the window. Everything was going so well. Her finances were getting straightened out. Joe has agreed to hire the brilliant director Erich von Stroheim for her next picture. Last month they all met for lunch in New York and von Stroheim laid out the story he envisioned for Gloria to star in. It was going to be lavish and thrilling and romantic, an epic that would endure through the ages. All they needed was a new title. Von Stroheim entitled his script *The Swamp*. That would never do, of course. Swamps are things to be drained.

▪ ▪ ▪

The cab begins to slow, and the cessation of speed, of cold wind blowing in his face, causes Henri to frown. For miles he's seen no trace of mankind, only a vast, sweeping, flat plain of uninhabited swamp. He had no idea such a place as this ever existed. The Everglades, the driver called it.

He's holding the gun in his lap like a pet.

"Are we stopping?" Henri asks, his usually neatly combed hair windblown from sticking his head out the open window of the backseat. The enormity of the night has become crystal clear. His life will change again. The ground has shifted beneath his feet.

"There's a tollgate up here."

"A toll?"

"For the Conners Highway. Do you want me to keep going?"

He's given the driver two twenties, with the instruction to keep driving. "Please."

"I'm gonna need to stop for some gas."

They've reached the tollgate, consisting of a covered arch over both halves of the road and a small booth in between. Henri can't wait to get going again, to set sail through this forbidding sea of grass. Stopping only reminds him of what he's running from. Failure. Another abject failure.

"There a filling station around here, boss?" the driver asks the toll collector, a dour, squat-faced peasant with fiery eyes and a jutting chin.

"Up in Canal Point is the closest one."

"How far, boss?"

"Ten miles."

"Thanks, boss."

"You all be careful now. The sheriff's been on the lookout for some hoodlums that busted out of the jug in Miami."

"I ain't stoppin' for no hitchhikers, boss."

But Henri isn't listening. He has entered that phase of drunkenness in which the past rises up like a monster from the deep. What does he know about Gloria Swanson anyway? Walked out after eight weeks of marriage to the lecherous Wallace Beery. Had a daughter with Herbert Somborn but left him after a year. Took up with the womanizing director Mickey Neilan. There were countless others floating in and out. Gloria handled men like she handled money—she most enjoyed spending what she got, not saving what she earned. *Une drague par excellence.* The world's biggest flirt.

So why is he surprised? Now she has fixed her sights on Joe Kennedy. It was predictable. Inevitable. Months in the making.

During the war, there were times when either the Germans or the French would ask for a cease-fire and then the enemies would go swimming in the same river. They would play football on a pitch soaked with blood. The next day they would return to trying to kill each other.

C'est la vie.

The cab is speeding off again. Henri settles back in the seat. What a long night. A long terrible night. *La nuit noire de l'esprit.* The dark night of the soul. If one could just rest. A little rest. *Faire dodo. Un petit dodo.*

He looks down at the gun. How easy it would be, here in the middle of nowhere.

A WOMAN SCORNED

The boat's engine sputters to idle as Buddy eases the skiff toward a small dock. Its stubby pilings poke up into the air like the ruins of a lost civilization. Almost nothing of the dock remains. Just some rotten boards and collapsed planks. Frank jumps out as soon as the boat drifts to a stop. Now he's standing on a berm covered with salt bush and wax myrtle. It feels good to be on land again. He still can't see over the berm. He has no idea of what awaits him on the other side.

"Well," says Buddy, tying up the skiff and landing in knee-deep water. "We made it. Now let's take care of business."

This is crazy. That's what Frank wants to say. But he didn't come all the way up here to get shot in the back. If Buddy wants him to go into some hick store and ask for Cecil, that's what Frank will do. If there's a way for Frank to escape, he'll take it.

"Remember what you're doing?"

"Yeah. I'm going in a store and saying my truck broke down."

"That's right. Then when Cecil leads you outside, I'll take over from there."

"What if he asks me where my truck is?"

"You tell him State Road 25. Near Clewiston."

"State Road 25."

"You got it?" Then Buddy unties Frank's hands. "Don't do nothing stupid, Frank. I won't think twice about filling you with lead."

"I'll keep that in mind."

The two men scramble up the berm, Frank in front and Buddy a step behind. The soil is hard and breaks up with each footstep. At the top finally Frank sees the store. Inside some lights are shining, so the joint must be open. There's one gas pump standing in lonely vigil beneath the star-filled sky. Not far away the West Palm Beach Canal feeds into the lake surrounded by an earthen levee. Down the road a bit is a general store, with barrels of animal feed on the front porch. The remnants of a hotel that burned last year stand in blackened testimony to the capricious nature of life on the frontier. The town of Canal Point hardly seems thriving. It's the last place Frank would pick to look for loot. It doesn't look like you could find two dimes to rub together around here. But back in Miami, Buddy had mentioned something about saving him sixty grand, so there must be more about this dump than meets the eye.

"It's open," Buddy crows. "I knew it would be. They sell corn liquor here, right out of the store."

"I could use a belt."

"You got a good sense of humor, Frank."

"Thanks."

"Now go on. I see the tow truck. It's over on the side by the garage."

Neither man takes note of the pickup truck parked at the bottom of the berm, near the pump house of the West Palm Beach Canal. It doesn't look like anyone is sitting in it. Just another abandoned, broken-down flivver.

■ ■ ■

Well well well. Look what the cat dragged in. Just when you thought a Friday night couldn't get much worse, in walks a tall, handsome stranger with chiseled features and an eye patch that makes Laura Upthegrove's heart go pitter-patter. He's dressed like a mechanic and could use a shower, from the looks of it. He probably cleans up real nice, though.

"Help you?" she asks, batting her dark eyes. A woman of nearly forty, acting like a clumsy schoolgirl.

"My truck broke down."

"That's too bad, sugar."

"I was wondering if I could get a tow. Noticed you had a truck outside."

"Who's out there?" Cecil Tracey shouts from the back office. Laura's half brother is good and boiled tonight. A load of corn liquor just arrived from Pahokee and he's been helping himself like a field hand. He's no happy drunk, either. Every five seconds he's been asking her about the money. *Where's the money? Where's the money John Ashley hid?* Like she would tell him if she did know. God, how she despises this place!

"Somebody needs a tow!"

Then Laura turns her attention back to the mystery man. "You ain't from around here. I ain't never seen you and you got a Yankee accent. You just passing through?"

"You could say that."

Cecil comes charging out, stinking of corn liquor. He's liable to drink the whole load himself. "You need a tow?"

"My truck broke down."

"That so?"

Cecil starts nodding his head like a puppet on a string. Then he reaches behind the counter and lifts up the shotgun. He levels it right at the mystery man's chest, not four feet away.

"Who sent you? Buddy Upthegrove?"

"Nobody sent me. My truck broke down."

"You're a liar, mister! Where is he, outside?"

"You got it wrong, friend. I don't know a Buddy Upthegrove and nobody sent me."

"I killed men bigger than you, mister. I ain't no fool. I know Buddy Upthegrove busted out of jail tonight. News travels fast on the lake."

"Buddy busted out?" Laura asks, incredulous. "Funny you never mentioned it to me, considering he's my brother and all."

"He ain't getting the money over me, Laura!"

"Shut up about that money, would ya? Don't worry, I hate Buddy almost as much as I hate you."

Outside a horn starts blaring. It makes Cecil jump. "Is that the signal, huh? Is it?"

"Don't kill him in the store!" Laura growls at her half brother. "You'll have the sheriff here in no time. I'll see who it is first. Could be nothing."

She walks past the mystery man, giving him a good inspection. It's like having the sun shining on your face after a long winter. There's not a man within a hundred miles of here who could hold a candle to this one. No way Cecil is killing him, he's too damn pretty.

She peers out a window. "There's a cab at the gas pump."

"A cab? Ain't no cabs in Canal Point!"

"It's from Palm Beach."

"Hell's bells, go see what they want."

"They want gas, Cecil. That ain't my job, it's yours."

Cecil's face wrinkles up like he just bit into a sour pickle. "I ain't going out there." He waves the gun at the mystery man. "You go. You're dressed like a mechanic. Go fill the tank up and bring in the money. I'll be watching every move you make."

■ ■ ■

Sally Tiger can see Buddy Upthegrove hunched down behind a tow truck. He's got a gun and a look on his face like he intends to use it. What's the other one doing in the store?

She could shoot Buddy Upthegrove right now. It's a clear shot, like a rabbit nibbling on some grass in a meadow. But if she kills him, then what? If they're after the money, it's better to wait and let them lead her to the cash.

Just then a cab pulls up and stops in front of the gas pump. The driver sounds the horn.

Is this part of it?

Sally Tiger checks Buddy Upthegrove. He's still hunched down like a tiger. The cabbie gets out. The one with the eye patch comes out of the store. He's alone. He looks confused.

■ ■ ■

"Fill'er up."

Frank stands impassively at the door, looking over at the cabbie. Somewhere nearby a bullfrog belches out a mating call. A gentle breeze blows in from the southeast. Smoke from a chimney fills the air with a scent of burned wood.

Two people are itching to kill him. One is hiding behind the tow truck around the corner. The other is inside the store. Damned if you do and damned if you don't.

The greasy overalls. Frank looks like a mechanic. "Sure thing."

"Check the oil while you're at it. Where's the john?"

Frank has no idea. "Around back." He points vaguely behind the store.

The cabbie starts off at a lope and Frank saunters over to the cab like he's on the clock. He can feel two sets of eyes on him, the way a deer must feel during hunting season. He peers inside the cab to check the gauges. Not much gas is in the tank. But the keys are still in the ignition.

There's someone sleeping in the backseat.

Frank looks up. He can see the outline of a figure behind the screen door. He can see the shotgun in silhouette. He takes a step toward the rear of the car, closer to the gas pump. He shoots a glance over at where Buddy is waiting. With only one eye, it's hard to see that far.

It's either now or never. He can't stay here or he's a dead man. Soon the cabbie will come back. A little more gas wouldn't hurt, though. Frank cranks the pump a few times. It's one of those old-fashioned kinds. The bell starts clanging as the gas dribbles out. Sweat starts to roll down his nose. Filling up will take forever.

Now, a voice tells him.

He drops the hose and hops into the cab just as the cabbie rounds the corner, still zipping his pants. The engine fires right up and Frank presses down hard on the accelerator, spraying sand and dust as he speeds away.

"Hey!" he hears someone shouting. He can see the one with the shotgun, aiming the thing right at him. Frank swerves hard on the wheel and spins the cab in a wild arcing sphere that takes him onto a paved road.

Slowly it occurs to him, as he hurtles through the moist night in a stolen cab, that somehow he's still alive. No one even took a shot at him.

▪ ▪ ▪

"Drop the gun, Cecil."

Cecil does as he's told. The shotgun now lies at his feet like a faithful dog. Buddy Upthegrove takes another step forward, brandishing the gun at both Cecil and the cabbie, who's choking back tears and muttering what sounds like a prayer.

"You gonna kill me, Buddy? You do and you'll never get your hands on that money."

"Where is it?"

"I don't know yet."

"Where's Laura?"

"Inside the store."

"Get her out here."

Cecil turns his head and yells a name that sounds like Laura, but Sally Tiger can't tell from where she's squatting behind the pump house. A few seconds later, a tall woman emerges from the store. She looks vaguely familiar. Sally Tiger might've seen her a few years ago in Big Cypress swamp.

"Hey, Buddy," she says. "You bust out?"

"We're going after the money. You're gonna take me there."

The sister smiles and shakes her head. She's the one who knows.

That's why Buddy Upthegrove came here in the first place. Sally Tiger brings her gun up and expertly aims it at Buddy Upthegrove's head. An easy shot. Like shooting a tin can off a fence.

The bullet hits him in the ear and he drops like a rag doll. Cecil reaches for the shotgun but he's too late. Sally Tiger shoots him in the top of his head and he pitches forward like a daredevil trying to do a somersault down the steps.

"Nobody move!" Sally Tiger yells. The cabbie is wailing now, like a lost child. The sister, Laura, remains stoic. She's at least part Indian, Sally Tiger can see that now. The straight black hair and broad nose. "We're all getting in this truck and we're going after that money. Hurry up!"

"Don't kill me!" the cabbie bawls.

"I won't," Sally Tiger replies calmly. "You're driving."

BLOW THE GAFF

arvey Firestone returns to the party with a worried look. His mouth has creased into a frown and his brown eyes register a swirl of disquiet. Before he was summoned for an important phone call, he was telling humorous stories about President Coolidge, all in the effort to enliven what has become a very somber party. The news of Parker Anderson's murder and Frank Hearn's arrest has cast a pall over the affair. Many guests have left. The Howards remain, awaiting news from Irene.

"Is something wrong?" Idabelle Firestone asks. She's a lovely woman, unfailingly polite and a gracious hostess. But tonight has been very difficult.

"That was Georgia Pendergast," answers Harvey, softly, as if the words cause pain upon their utterance. "She still hasn't seen or heard from Janice since this afternoon."

"She hasn't turned up yet?"

"Apparently not. Georgia is quite concerned. Janice usually calls if she misses dinner."

"Oh, dear!"

"There's more. Georgia said that earlier today Janice withdrew ten thousand dollars from the bank."

Idabelle's eyes grow wide with fear. "You don't think Bryce is some-how involved?" Her trembling voice answers her own question. If Lauren Howard was worried before, now she is petrified. What ex-actly are they saying about Bryce, the man who has whisked Irene away?

Roberta Firestone picks up on the scent. "Do you think Bryce is in trouble?"

Harvey tries to remain calm. "Let's don't jump to conclusions."

Lauren Howard can't contain herself another minute. "Can some-one please tell me what is going on?"

"Bryce would never do anything to hurt anyone. I'm sure there's an explanation for everything."

Roberta snorts at this declaration. Lauren shoots a glance at her husband, who inhales sharply and stands up. "Harvey's right. Let's not go overboard. But just the same, old man, my daughter is with him and you need to tell me if we should be concerned. I don't know what the devil is going on."

Roberta doesn't let her brother answer. "Bryce has been in trouble his entire life. He's never held a steady job and he flunked out of four colleges."

Harvey cuts her off. "I'll handle Bryce. He knows he's run out of chances and that's why I can't believe he'd do anything as stupid as— well, he wouldn't do anything so stupid."

Roberta rolls her eyes. "I wish it were true, little brother."

"Let's call the police," Lauren Howard suggests anxiously. "That's where they were going. I want to know if she made it."

"Fine, we'll call the police."

"I'll go with you," offers Seddon Howard, and the two barons of in-dustry head off together, leaving the three women behind. A pot of cof-fee steams on a silver tray. No one has touched the slices of fresh strawberry. Lauren Howard's stomach feels queasy. Not once on the ocean liner from New York did she get seasick. This was supposed to be a happy time. Her daughter home from Europe. A party for the president. Polo matches and shopping.

"He's up to no good," says Roberta sadly. "That boy is trouble and has been since the day he was born."

"Now, Roberta, Bryce has suffered a great deal. He didn't ask for his father to die." Idabelle Firestone is compassionate and caring, perhaps to a fault.

"Bryce only has himself to blame for his problems," sniffs Roberta.

"His mother gave him up! Imagine what that does to a child!"

At that moment a servant enters and whispers something in Idabelle's ear. The poor dear jumps up in delight and claps her hands. "Show her in, by all means! Janice Pendergast is here! Oh, this is wonderful news!"

■ ▨ ▨

"Here's what I think happened," says Dyer, perched on a corner of his desk with one leg kicking free. He's wearing argyle socks that look frayed. His office is small but neat and organized. The only decoration is a fraternity paddle that hangs on the wall at a jaunty angle. Sigma Chi. Ohio State University. How droll.

"Delaney found out that Parker Anderson was trying to fix jai alai matches. We know Frank and Parker went to bet on jai alai last night, and Frank said he joined in on the action. Then he and Parker went to La Vida Club to celebrate and when Frank left, somebody tried to kill him. Probably one of Delaney's goons."

Dyer pats the jai alai player on the back.

"Now Uranga here backs up Frank's story. Uranga knew Parker Anderson was trying to get players to fix matches. Uranga also says Delaney mistreated the players and possibly even had one of them killed, although I haven't confirmed that."

"Okay," Irene answers uneasily, "so why did you suspect Frank at first?"

"Because Parker said Frank was involved in selling bogus real estate. I thought Frank killed Parker to shut him up. But Parker was most likely lying to throw me off."

"What about Nina Randolph, the secretary? Why did she jump out of a window rather than answer your questions? How do you know she didn't kill Parker?"

Dyer purses his lips and furrows his brow. "Maybe she did. It was more likely Delaney, though, because of what happened to Frank. Don't get me wrong, Nina Randolph has something to hide, I just don't know what. I'd like to find her and ask her some questions. She's the part that doesn't fit."

"Do you think she was having an affair with Frank?" Irene tries not to quack like a wounded duck.

"I have found no evidence of it. Nina's mother claimed she was seeing someone who drove a Nash roadster. Parker Anderson drove the same kind of car. Perhaps the two were romantically linked."

Irene sits up straight in the chair. The hinges squeak from the force of her body springing forward. "A Nash roadster! That's why I called you! I met someone who knew Parker and the secretary! His name is Bryce Shoat and I brought him down to answer some questions, but he left when you weren't here. I think he knows something about this. I got a feeling from him. It's hard to describe. And he drives a Nash, too!"

Dyer grins knowingly. "That is very interesting."

"There's more. He's the nephew of Harvey Firestone."

Dyer whistles. "Sounds like someone Parker would know. I'd like to talk to him. But first I need to call Vernon Hawthorne, the county attorney looking into police corruption within the Miami Police Department. I think he'd be very interested in hearing from Mr. Uranga. We need to get him some protection. I'm sure by now Delaney has figured out he's missing."

Dyer reaches across to grab the receiver. Irene can't help but marvel at his confident manner. He is a man who is two steps ahead of everyone else.

"That's funny," he grumbles. "It's dead."

He pushes down on the disconnect button.

"It's always worked before." He hangs up the phone with a shrug.

Then the door flies open.

"Nobody move!" a man shouts. Irene can't see who it is because Dyer is blocking her view of the door. "Now get on the floor! All of you! On the floor!"

Dyer lies down first. Then Irene can see who it is. A cop. A very large cop with a thick mustache. His black eyes seem lifeless, like a shark's. He's missing a few teeth and probably lots of other human qualities. And he's going to kill them. Irene can barely breathe as she scrambles to the ground. There's no one to save them. This is it, the end, thanks to Frank Hearn.

■ ■ ■

"Bryce isn't here, dear," says Idabelle Firestone, standing up to greet Janice Pendergast, who obviously is distraught. Tears have filled her eyes and now stream down her flushed cheeks. "But I know he's been wondering where you were!"

"I bet he has!" she snorts. "I bet he has!"

"Now, Janice, what is the matter? You need to call your mother. She's worried sick about you."

"I'll call her. But first give Bryce a message for me."

"What's that, dear?"

"Tell him I know everything. Everything." The poor girl's eyes blaze like two red-hot coals.

"And he'll know what that means?"

"He'll know. Believe me, he'll know."

Then Seddon and Harvey return, and Harvey is grumbling aloud as Seddon looks panic-stricken. Very seldom has Lauren seen her husband as discomfited as now, and it unnerves her. "No one at the police station knew what the devil I was talking about! It's hard to tell the hoodlums from the cops in this blasted city!"

"Harvey, Janice Pendergast is here," announces Idabelle gently.

"She is!" His eyebrows lift in surprise. "Where have you been? Your mother called looking for you!"

"I've been tied up."

"You need to call her and let her know you're alive and well."

"Is Bryce in trouble?" blurts Roberta, causing Harvey to wince.

"Not yet," replies Janice, rather smugly.

"Are you suggesting he might be?"

"Where is Irene?" asks Lauren, in her most authoritative voice. Everyone stops talking at once.

"We don't know," Seddon admits. "They never showed up at the police station. The officer we spoke to is calling all the substations to see if they went there."

"Oh, dear God!" Lauren covers her face with her hands. Seddon comes over to comfort her.

"You need to tell us if Bryce is in trouble, young lady," barks Roberta. "No more insinuations. We need to find him right away."

"I don't know where he is!" Janice yells back. "The last time I saw him, he was at the band shell in Royal Palm Park giving some blonde ten thousand dollars!"

"What on earth are you talking about?" asks Harvey, in a stunned voice. "Who did he give the money to?"

"I don't know her name. But he lied to me and said he needed the money to pay off a gambling debt! I guess that makes me a sucker, huh?"

"That is the last straw!" Harvey thunders. "Bryce has run out of chances with me! He'll rue this day for the rest of his life!"

"We need to find him first, dear," Idabelle reminds him.

"I'll find him! Then I'll wring his neck! He's getting on the first steamer for Liberia! He wants to learn the rubber business! He'll learn! By God, he'll learn!"

"I'm going to call the police station myself," Seddon whispers to his wife. "I'm going to get to the bottom of this."

■ ■ ■

Irene lies facedown on the smooth, cool floor of Horace Dyer's office. She can't see very much from behind the desk, just a pair of argyle socks and Dyer's two-toned patent-leather shoes. There's no way out. The cop is blocking the door. The office is cramped already. Irene's head is pushing against a file cabinet and her legs are jammed beneath the desk.

"It's not you we want!" Dyer insists. Even now he sounds resolute and forceful, no hint of fear.

"Shut up!"

"It's Delaney who's behind it. You can cooperate with the county attorney's office! That's the way out of this!"

"I said shut up!"

"Killing us doesn't solve anything. It'll just make everything worse."

"We'll see about that."

"Take me! Let the others go! I'll be your insurance policy!"

Irene then hears something she's never heard before. The firing of a gun with a silencer. A loud pop mixed with a sickened thud. The cop shot someone. Was it Dyer? Involuntarily a scream escapes from her lips, a wail of fear and sadness from deep within her.

"Shut up!"

But Irene doesn't shut up. She keeps screaming as loud as she can.

▪ ▪ ▪

Bryce steps out of the elevator on the tenth floor of the courthouse and begins loping down the hallway toward the office they went to before. Hopefully this won't last very long. The sooner this episode ends, the better. *I don't know. I'm not sure.* Those are the answers he needs to give. Friendly answers. Lots of smiling. *I'd love to help you but I just don't know anything. I only saw Nina Randolph once or twice. We never talked.*

After Bryce turns a corner, he can see the door to the office is ajar and light shines from within. Looks like what's his name came back. Dyer. Time to get this over with. Maybe once it's over, Bryce can convince Irene Howard he isn't such a clunk. Of course, it would be nice to know where Janice Pendergast is. What a loon.

Then he hears a scream. A woman's scream. Bryce doesn't hesitate. He starts to run at full tilt.

Then, stepping out of the office, a cop appears. He's got a gun. It's pointed right at Bryce.

THE LEADING MAN

loria Swanson thinks the hotel detective looks like a stunted version of Count Dracula. The same fanglike incisors, hooded eyes, sharp nose, and slicked-back hair, only in miniature. The man is barely taller than she is. It is not a good omen. The netherworld seems to have sent a tiny emissary. If only the detective looked like Douglas Fairbanks! Or even W.C. Fields. The last thing Gloria needs to be reminded of right now is a vampire. Her thoughts are dark enough already.

"I'm sorry to tell you that I haven't found out anything about your husband, Mrs. Swanson," he says gravely. "I've called all around and no one has seen him—or arrested him, I should say."

"That's good news," Gloria quips in a deadpan.

"He's not in a hospital, either."

"Even better."

"Hopefully he'll come back soon, after he sobers up a little."

Joe Kennedy and Eddie Moore whisper to each other. Then Joe breaks away and takes the detective gently by the arm, like a teacher leading a lost child to the office.

"Thank you, Detective. I appreciate your effort. Good night."

"If we hear anything, I'll certainly inform you right away."

Gloria smiles as Joe Kennedy follows the detective out to the hall. It's getting late and Gloria would like nothing more than to crawl into bed and go to sleep. But with the personal secretary, Eddie Moore, standing over her like an Irish gargoyle, that outcome seems rather unlikely. They're hunkered down until Henri shows up. It's like waiting for a bomb to explode. Only you can't see the fuse.

That gallant, foolish Frenchman! Tonight of all nights he gets drunker than a skunk. Ah, who could blame him? Gloria never intended to jump into bed with Joe Kennedy. But she couldn't resist him. Joe Kennedy is a man who gets what he wants. He commands every room he steps into and never slips up.

But maybe this time Joe Kennedy overplayed his hand.

"Hank will be fine," Eddie Moore assures her unconvincingly yet again. Usually he exudes such competence. He's been at Joe's side as they conquered first the world of high finance and now moving pictures. But even Eddie Moore is unsure of himself. "He's just blowing off some steam."

"I'll smack him in the kisser the minute I see him." But Gloria knows she won't. She could never be mean to Henri. Her other husbands made it easy to despise them. They were some combination of haughty, vain, jealous, and unfaithful, but so far Henri has displayed no such traits. Sure, he has his faults. The man lacks all ambition. He has no head for business. He has no money. Little Gloria and Brother love him to death. He has a wicked sense of humor. He shares her love of costume parties. He fell for her without ever having seen one of her pictures. Why won't he come home to her?

Oh, this insipid roller coaster! She was supposed to be sorting out her life, her career, her finances. And Joe Kennedy's wife is ready to give birth any day now! A fine mess she's made of things. Life was so much simpler when she was earning $13 a week making screwball comedies at the Essaney Studios. Now she is the most famous woman in the world, and her heart has a hole the size of Idaho.

Joe Kennedy returns and closes the door behind him. He looks tired because he looks worried. His blue eyes still sparkle, although there are circles beneath them. She's urged him to consider changing his diet. He eats too much meat. He's poisoning his body with bad food.

"Hey, you," he says sadly.

Gloria manages a smile. "Hey, you. Some night this has been. I need my beauty sleep."

"Do you want me to go?" He sounds vulnerable, a stark contrast to the restless conqueror whose eyes never veer from the bottom line. He told her he's never failed at anything. Not once has he tripped and fallen.

"No. Stay and tell me a funny story."

▪ ▪ ▪

"*Arrêtez la voiture!*"

Frank spins his head around to glance toward the backseat. The passenger who had been asleep is now awake and screaming in what sounds like French. That's Frank's guess anyway. It was the language he had the most trouble with when he was traveling in Europe with Irene.

"Stop! Stop!"

The frog speaks English, too. Frank isn't sure what to do. He doesn't want to pull over in the middle of nowhere. Ever since he left the gas station he's seen headlights in the rearview mirror, although a good distance away. The road he's been driving on is straight as an arrow. The last sign read thirty-five miles to Palm Beach. Not much farther to go. But the gas needle is pushing on E.

The passenger in the back starts retching. He's going to get sick. "Hold on! I'm stopping, I'm stopping!"

Frank eases the car onto the narrow shoulder that drops off into a canal that looks a lot like the one Buddy took him up. The frog is really heaving now, leaning out the window and spewing his guts. That kind of sick only comes from drinking. The frog smelled like a distillery so it figures. On and on the frog goes, until the poor guy starts groaning in agony.

"À l'hôtel."

"What's that?"

"Hotel."

"What hotel?"

But the frog doesn't answer. He falls back and curls up into a ball, eyes closed and body shivering. Boy, has Frenchie tied one on tonight. He's gassed.

Frank checks the rearview mirror again. Headlights are approaching fast. He decides to let whoever it is pass on by. Just so it's not a flattie. Frank might have trouble explaining why he's driving a stolen taxi.

Frank keeps checking the mirror. Now it looks like the headlights are pulling up behind him. It's not the cops, either, but a pickup truck. Maybe they want to know if the cab broke down. Or maybe it's something else. No need to find out. Frank throws the cab into gear and presses down hard on the accelerator. The tires kick up rocks and sand before squealing against the pavement.

Frank keeps his pedal pushed to the floor. The engine revs and roars, and the wind howls through the open windows. The inside of the car grows cold but Frank doesn't feel it. The headlights are still in the rearview mirror. Who the hell is giving chase?

■ ■ ■

"I don't know where the money is!" With that, Laura Upthegrove lets out a screeching laugh as the truck the frightened cabbie is driving careens down the Conners Highway. Next to Laura and holding a gun is the woman from the Tiger clan who just shot Buddy and Cecil dead as doornails. Talk about doing the world a favor. They were both mean as snakes and greedier than Wall Street bankers. But the little squaw is off her nut.

"Why did Buddy come up here then?"

"Because he's stupid! Think about it, if I knew where the money was, why would I be living over that smelly filling station and working for my idiot half brother? Do you think I like the smell of gasoline? I got news for you. I don't. I hate it."

"You were John Ashley's wife! Don't lie to me!"

Laura Upthegrove sets her jaw firm. "I ain't lying. He died near five years ago, sweet pea. If the money is out there, I sure don't know where to look. No matter what Buddy said."

The Tiger squaw bites her tongue, because surrounding them is the vastness of the Everglades, stretching for miles in all its desolate glory. Nobody knew the big swamp better than John Ashley. If he hid the money somewhere, he never told Laura about it. But the Tiger squaw isn't buying that story. She's killed two people because of a lie that Buddy and Cecil couldn't stop gnawing on the same way some dogs snap at fleas. Eventually they chew their own skin off.

"That's my cab," says the driver, out of the blue.

Sure enough, up ahead is a red-and-white taxi, the same one that handsome man in the eye patch stole.

"I'm pulling over," he says manfully.

The Tiger squaw is still silent. It's like she can't talk anymore, now that she knows the truth. Won't admit the truth, but at least she knows it's there. The law will be looking for her soon enough. She's liable to grow as dangerous as a rabid coon, frothing at the mouth and not caring who she bites.

"Keep driving," the Tiger squaw finally mutters, voice barely above a whisper.

"To where?" Laura snaps. "There's nowhere to go unless you want me to start lying to you. I can do that. I'm a good liar."

Now the gun swings around and the Tiger squaw points it right at Laura.

"I'll kill you if you don't start talking!"

A twisted, joyous smile never leaves Laura's face. "You think I'm scared of dying? I tried to kill myself two months ago when I was in jail! I cut my hand and got some iodine and I drank it! But it didn't work, and they turned me loose so I wouldn't try it again on their watch. Go ahead and shoot me. Shoot me right here." She points to a spot between her crazed eyes. "You'll never find the money then."

"So there is money!"

The driver slams on the brakes and the two women pitch forward into the dashboard. The gun falls from the Tiger squaw's mitt-size hand. The three of them start wrestling in the cramped space of the truck's cab, like three cats tossed into a burlap sack. The strongest of the three, Laura, comes up with the gun. Blood drips down the side of her face from the collision against the dashboard.

"Listen carefully. There . . . ain't . . . no . . . money."

The Tiger squaw starts crying in great, heaving sobs. She buries her face in her hands and curls up into a sad little ball. "They killed him!"

That's what she keeps saying.

"Who did?" asks Laura a couple of times.

It takes a few minutes but eventually the Tiger squaw starts telling a story about a man named T.R. and a jailbreak that left him dead, thanks to Buddy Upthegrove and the handsome man in the eye patch. Things are finally beginning to make sense, as much as anything does in this stupid world.

■ ■ ■

The engine starts to sputter and then it dies. Frank eases the cab over onto a narrow shoulder. Out of gas, now it's official. Stuck in the middle of nowhere, with a passed-out Frenchman in the backseat of a stolen cab.

Frank checks the rearview mirror and sees headlights again. Who the hell is that? Buddy? Cecil, the one with a shotgun? A deputy sheriff? Or maybe it's nobody at all, but Frank can't take that chance. He has to hide before they get much closer.

But hide where?

The only place is the swamp. Frank jumps out of the cab and starts running into the saw grass muck. The saw grass stands about chest high, perfect for providing some cover. He crouches down and watches, breathing heavily, feet sinking into the mud. He's been tired before but never like this. His entire body aches from weariness and exhaustion. This is one long nightmare that won't seem to end.

A minute later a pickup truck pulls over and parks behind the cab.

He sees three people get out. He recognizes two of them. One is the driver of the taxi and the other is the tall woman he saw in the filling station. She's got a gun now. The third person is a short, round woman who is dressed like an Indian.

He can hear their voices. "Looks like he ditched the cab and took off."

"He couldn't have gone far."

So they're looking for him. But why? He hasn't done anything.

He watches as the tall woman lifts Frenchie from the back of the cab and carries him over to the payload of the pickup. They check his pockets.

"A hotel key. The Royal Poinciana. Pretty fancy digs. What's this? Another gun! Now I got two."

Frenchie starts groaning.

"You're okay, sweet pea. Ol' Laura's gonna take care of you."

Maybe they don't mean any harm. Frank thinks about flagging them down before they take off. Then he sees something that nearly makes his heart stop. Not ten feet away is a gator, eyes shining red from the headlights of the car. He always wanted to take in some alligator wrestling, and it looks like he's going to get his chance. The gator appears to be sizing him up. Frank's been in enough fights to recognize the signs. First you stare down your opponent. Then you strike.

"Hey!" yells the tall woman with the guns. "I know you can hear me! You won't get away with it! We know what you did and you'll pay!"

What in the world are you talking about?

The gator slides forward and Frank nearly jumps out of his skin. He rushes forward through the saw grass, nearly tripping over his own feet. He runs as fast as he can, shoes slurping up the mud. And then he's in the clear again, by the road and staring down the barrels of two guns.

"Hi there, stranger," the tall woman says, smiling brightly. Frank raises his arms over his head.

"Don't shoot! You got it all wrong!"

The Indian woman points at him. "You killed T.R.!"

Now he gets it. "That was Buddy! He made me come up here! I don't know beans about any of this!"

"Liar!"

"No! They threw me in jail this morning! It was Buddy! He's the one you want."

"Give me my gun!" the Indian woman shouts. "I'll kill him right here!"

"You got it wrong. Buddy was gonna kill me if I didn't do what he said. Please. I'm an innocent man. I can prove it, too. Just give me the chance."

The tall woman never stops smiling. And she doesn't let go of either gun. "No one's gonna kill you, honey. You're too pretty. And you're all mine."

"He's a liar."

Frenchie starts groaning. He sounds like he's on death's doorstep.

"Come on, big boy," the tall woman barks at Frank. "Get behind the wheel. Let's take this dandy back to his fancy hotel. Maybe there'll be a reward." Then she turns to the others. "Sorry, but this is a date. You're staying here. I want to be alone with my new friend."

"Wait a second!" the cabbie objects. "You're leaving us here?"

"I'm sure somebody'll be passing by soon enough. Bye-bye!"

FRAT BOY

ryce Shoat throws up his hands and stops on a dime. A cop with a gun? "Don't shoot me!" he yells as he drops to the floor, arms wrapped around his head. He actually hears a bullet go whizzing by, a sound like no other. It grazes his forearm but he won't realize until later that he was hit at all. Because when Bryce opens his eyes he sees someone wrestling with the cop who just took a shot at him. He's a little guy compared to the cop, but he's got a good hold on the arm that's holding the gun. Must be Dyer, the investigator Irene wanted him to talk to.

Bryce jumps to his feet and watches as Irene Howard takes a running leap, landing on the cop and digging her fingernails into the cop's face. He growls like a wounded bear and with incredible strength shakes Dyer off his arm like he's a puppy playing tug-of-war. But Dyer is a scrapper and he brings a knee up into the cop's groin as Irene keeps gouging at him. Dyer is wrestling with the cop and Bryce is frozen in place, not sure what the hell to do.

Then the gun goes skidding across the floor. It stops at Bryce's feet. He bends down and grabs it before Irene does.

"He's going to kill us!" she screams at him. "He tried to kill you!"

Bryce finally notices that his arm is bleeding. But he keeps the gun pointed at the cop. "Somebody better fill me in!"

"There isn't time! Give Dyer the gun!"

Bryce isn't about to give the gun to anybody. The cop is still hunched over on all fours and panting like a rabid dog from the knee to the nuts he took. Dyer is checking on a spic who looks very dead, lying facedown in a pool of blood.

"Is he dead?" asks Irene anyway, as if there were any doubt.

Dyer stands up. "Son of a bitch! Give me that gun!"

"Just stay put, pal! I don't know what the hell is going on yet." Bryce then notices that the cop starts to stir. "You stay put, too, flattie, you hear me? Everybody just stay put!" Bryce backpedals to get a better look at the three of them—Irene, Dyer, and the cop.

"I came here to make an arrest," the cop says painfully, now resting on one knee, his face scratched and bleeding.

"That's a lie!" counters Dyer. The cop ignores him.

"That's when I found the body over there."

"You killed him and I saw it all with my own eyes! You shot him in the head!"

The cop extends an arm toward Bryce like he wants to shake hands. "Son, don't get yourself in trouble. Give me my gun back. I didn't mean to take a shot at you. You scared me good. That's what we're trained to do. Shoot first and ask questions later."

"You got that right," Dyer snarls. A feisty little runt that one is.

"Don't listen to him, Bryce!" pleads Irene. Irene Howard. Daughter of Seddon Howard. No way she'd be involved in killing anyone. But a Miami cop? That's a different story.

"Call for some help, Irene," Bryce says coolly.

"The phone line's been cut."

"The police station is right across the street," Dyer barks at Irene. "Go there and get some help."

Irene takes one step before the cop wheels around and grabs her in a bear hug. He wraps an arm around her neck and lifts her off the floor. Irene struggles against him but her kicking and clawing are futile.

"I'll kill her right here," the cop snarls. "I'll snap her neck like it's a twig. Drop the gun! Drop it now!"

"Do you know who my uncle is?" Bryce hears himself saying. The gun is still in his hand.

"Drop the gun or she dies!"

By now Irene is making some gurgling sounds, like she's choking to death. Bryce lets go of the gun.

"It's Harvey Firestone," he mutters as the gun clatters against the linoleum.

■ ■ ■

"Mr. Firestone, what can I do for you, sir?"

Chief of Police Leslie Quigg had to take that call from Harvey Firestone, and in doing so he interrupted a meeting with City Manager Welton Snow, Traffic Director H.H. Arnold, and, most conspicuously, Colonel E.W. Starling, personal attaché of President Coolidge, all of whom have assembled to go over the plans for the president's arrival by train tomorrow. But foremost on Quigg's mind is capturing the killers who busted out of the new county jail. The scofflaws scaled down twenty floors using bedsheets, presumably obtained from a corrupt guard named Thomas A. Jones, whose arrest is also sought and whose whereabouts are currently unknown.

"They were coming here to the station, sir?" Quigg strains to hear over the noise at the front desk. A couple of rowdy drunks are singing ribald songs. "Will you pardon me?" Quigg covers the receiver with a meaty mitt and points at the drunks. "Shut them up!" Then he turns his attention to the desk sergeant on duty. "Do you know anything about a nephew of Harvey Firestone's coming to speak to anyone here at the station?"

The desk sergeant shrugs his shoulders. Some officers lead the drunks to a jail cell. Quigg gets back on the phone.

"Mr. Firestone, do you know what it was in reference to? Parker Anderson? I think the chief of detectives is leading that investigation, but he's been on detail for the last several hours." Then a thought hits him between the eyes. "Wait a second, sir. It might be possible that your nephew and Miss Howard went to see someone else." Quigg is trying to sound polite but inside he's seething. Dyer has been busy meddling out of his jurisdiction. "His name is Horace Dyer and his office is right across the street in the new courthouse, if memory serves me. I'll get a number you can call."

Quigg instructs the desk sergeant to get the number. It would appear that Horace Dyer is sticking his nose where it doesn't belong. But Quigg has enough to worry about at the moment. He can't concern himself with the intrusions of a low-ranking federal investigator.

"Thanks for calling, Mr. Firestone. Let me know if there's anything else I can do for you."

Quigg hangs up and returns to his meeting. He is just getting an update from Arnold on the roadblocks instituted around Miami when the desk sergeant comes bursting in again. Harvey Firestone has called back. Quigg excuses himself one more time.

"Something's wrong with the phone number?" Quigg sighs in exasperation. He ought to wring Dyer's neck. "I'll send a man over to Dyer's office and he'll get back with you. His name is Sergeant Flagstead."

■ ■ ■

The cop is still holding Irene as the gun slides along the floor. She's gasping for breath as she kicks at him, fighting like a warrior against a much stronger foe. By the looks of it, that ape could break Irene's neck with little effort. Dyer knows that there is no way the cop is letting anyone out of this building alive. He'll kill them all as soon as he gets that gun. He's got to do something fast.

The Sigma Chi paddle.

It's hanging on the wall just a few feet away from Dyer. Everyone said it was a tacky decoration but Dyer always liked it. Reminded him of innocent days in Columbus, when the world seemed knowable and fresh.

Still holding Irene with a death grip around her neck, the cop's hand descends to the ground like a vulture alighting on a corpse. Thick fingers extend to wrap around the pistol, and at that moment Dyer makes his move. With the grace of a gymnast and the explosiveness of a linebacker, Dyer grabs the paddle off the wall and jumps toward the cop, who is just standing up with the gun in hand. Dyer jabs the paddle at the cop's face and catches him square in the nose. The paddle is about three feet long and hefty, and the blow staggers the cop, who manages to get off a shot that punctures the wall a foot away from Dyer's head. Chunks of plaster fall down like dusty snow.

Irene manages to grab onto the cop's gun hand and pulls on it with all her might. Dyer swings the paddle like a baseball bat and hits the barrel of the gun as another shot explodes a window. But in the process the paddle flies out of Dyer's hands. The handle is small and always pretty slippery because he'd sanded it down so smoothly.

With little difficulty the cop hurls Irene off of him. She hits the floor hard with a thud at his feet. Then he points the gun straight down at her, but wisely Irene starts rolling away from him with wild abandon. Dyer screams at the top of his lungs and takes one step toward the cop, who changes his mind and lifts the gun up and aims right at Dyer. Then, coming out of nowhere like a bat out of hell, Bryce slams into the cop with tremendous force, knocking him back and sending the gun flying toward the Sigma Chi paddle. It comes to rest about an inch away from Dyer's treasured keepsake.

"Everybody freeze!" someone yells.

Dyer glances over his shoulder. Another cop has arrived on the scene. More trouble? Or has help finally arrived? It's not easy to tell in this city.

"They attacked me, Flagstead," the big cop croaks as he struggles to his feet. He's wearing socks. No shoes. Where are his shoes?

"I'll talk to you later, Blott," Flagstead says warily. "I got other business first. Which one of you is Firestone?"

"Me," answers Bryce. "Sort of."

"I'm supposed to bring you back to headquarters. Is that a body?" Flagstead sees poor Uranga, lying dead in Dyer's office. "Jesus H. Christ."

"Your associate there killed him," Dyer says calmly, finally gathering his thoughts. He turns his attention to the big cop, Blott, a name Dyer recognizes. "So you're Blott, huh? One of Delaney's triggermen. I've heard plenty about you."

But Blott doesn't answer. Instead he makes a sudden dash for the gun. Irene screams and Dyer instinctively reaches out and grabs her, shielding her from Blott.

"Stop it right there, Blott!" the cop named Flagstead shouts. "I got to sort this out!"

But Blott doesn't stop. Now he's got the gun again.

"I'll shoot, Blott! Freeze, goddamn it!"

A shot rings out.

FEMME FATALE

ehind the wheel of a truck, Frank Hearn is staring at the biggest hotel he's ever seen, and that includes ones in Atlantic City and Europe. But this thing stretches for miles, with a million palm trees planted on a big chunk of prime real estate right on Lake Worth. So this is Palm Beach. This is how the other half lives. Irene would fit right in here.

He turns onto the hotel's long driveway. Who's he kidding? He's never gonna see Irene again, the way things are going now.

"Okay, honey," Laura sings in a throaty drawl. "Let's drag our prize up to his room and see what we can find."

"I just want to make one phone call. Will you let me do that, please?" Frank smiles at his new friend, who seems to have taken a liking to him. Whatever it takes to survive. She's still got two guns and seems nuts enough to use them. "It's not the cops. I swear it's not the cops."

"Where'd you get those muscles anyway?" She reaches over and squeezes a bicep. She's been taking liberties with his body and Frank has let her. It's keeping her mind off killing him.

"Born that way, I guess."

"You're one big side of beef."

"When we get up to his room, I'm making a phone call."

"No, big boy. You got something you have to do first."

He bites his tongue. He can't push her too far, because she seems right on the edge already. So he's keeping his mouth shut—for now. But he won't take too much more of this.

He drives past the front of the hotel, where a long limo is idling, its whitewalls gleaming and chrome shining. People dressed to the nines give the flivver some curious looks as it goes by. Talk about a fish out of water.

"I'll park it up there," says Frank, nodding toward a parking lot beneath a grove of palm trees.

"Muscles and brains. I like that."

After parking, Frank jumps out to go check on Frenchie. The little guy starts to stir but he's still in bad shape. He's soiled his dinner jacket with vomit and his pants are covered with dirt.

"Can you walk?" asks Frank, pushing him a little.

"*Dodo,*" is the reply.

"What does that mean?" asks Laura.

"Means he can't walk, I guess." Frank hoists the frog over his shoulder like a sack of potatoes. He isn't a big guy and doesn't weigh much, so it's no trouble for Frank to carry him, except his ribs still ache. When will this all be over? "What's the room number?"

"Suite 601. We'll go in the side door there."

■ ■ ■

The chief of police leans forward across his desk and gazes wide-eyed at Bryce like he just jumped out of a birthday cake. He isn't the only one reeling from confusion. Irene wasn't sure she heard Bryce right, either. Daddy's ears have turned red and Mr. Firestone looks like he's passing kidney stones. The only person in the chief's office who never changes expression is Dyer. That man possesses a deep reserve of calm.

"Frank Hearn wasn't involved in any real estate scam?" the chief repeats slowly, body rigid and beefy arms hanging limply at his sides.

He's one intimidating person, although at the moment a bit perplexed. And no wonder. He did everything he could to wrap a noose around Frank's neck. "Is that what you're saying?"

"No, sir, he wasn't. But when Parker got caught selling swampland, he blamed it on Frank. That was the plan anyway. Blame everything on Frank Hearn. My mistake was telling Nina Randolph about it."

"That's your only mistake?" asks Mr. Firestone, eyes blazing.

"Well, no. I shouldn't have been involved at all."

Irene tries not to roll her eyes. Even when he's coming clean, Bryce sounds like he's piling lie atop lie. The oily rube did save her and Dyer's lives. Quite by accident. And now he's finally admitting the truth. His version of it anyway.

She shoots a glance over to Dyer. He's not even scribbling notes. He's taking it in like a wizened sage who sees all and knows all. Except his face still has peach fuzz. Or maybe it's he can't hold a pen without his hand trembling. Irene hasn't stopped shaking from the deadly encounter. Two men killed right in front of her. She can still hear the guns, the sickening thud.

"What about Nina Randolph?" the chief asks. "What's she got to do with this?"

"She was the secretary," Dyer interjects. The chief nods his head but he looks rattled, like he doesn't understand. But really, neither does Irene.

"I didn't want my name getting dragged into this investigation," Bryce continues, rather smugly pointing at Dyer. "I didn't trust Parker anymore. For all I knew, he was keeping the paperwork so he could set me up and save his own hide. He dropped hints that he would. My back was against the wall. I wanted the files he kept in his office, the ones with my name on them. I thought I could convince Nina to steal them for me."

"Convince her how?"

Bryce shrugs his shoulders, grinning like a cad. "You know, some flowers, a walk on the beach."

"We get the idea!" Mr. Firestone grumbles.

"But Nina Randolph stabbed me in the back!" Bryce sounds like the idea came from outer space. "She blackmailed me for ten grand."

"So you think Nina Randolph killed Parker Anderson?" Dyer asks, voice flat and dry. It's nearly impossible to tell what's really on his mind.

"I do."

"Why?"

"To put the pressure on me. That's what she told me anyway, in so many words. I got scared and just gave her the money. I got it from my girlfriend."

Mr. Firestone's jaw muscles start twitching as he sits erect in a straight-back chair. But behind the stern exterior is a sadness that flows out of his soft eyes like gentle rain. He's just listened to his nephew admit to some rather despicable things. "Is there anything else, Bryce?" he asks helplessly, as though waving a white flag.

"I'm really sorry about it all. I never meant to hurt anyone."

Dyer looks like he's trying hard to restrain himself. He's tapping a pencil in obvious annoyance. Bryce keeps his eyes focused squarely on his lap, chastened like a puppy that just got his nose whacked with a rolled-up newspaper.

"It's a little late for that," Mr. Firestone sighs.

The chief of police clears his throat. He's trying hard to act like he's in control of a situation that he has no grip on. "We need to find Nina Randolph."

"You won't," Dyer snaps.

"Why not?" The chief seems stunned.

"Because she's long gone by now. I went by the house where she lives with her mother. All her clothes were packed up. She had this planned out."

The chief's face turns crimson and Dyer to his credit holds his tongue, showing the same poise that Irene has come to admire. "We'll put out an APB on Nina Randolph. Mr. Dyer, can you provide a physical description?"

Irene can, no problem. A tall, shapely blonde with long legs. No matter how hard she tries, in the back of her mind she can't forget seeing that woman in Frank's apartment. By the sound of it, Frank didn't kill Parker Anderson. Dyer said he hadn't found any evidence that Frank was having an affair. But what was Nina Randolph doing in the apartment in the first place? He claims to have been arrested but there is no record of it. Again, given the shoddy and corrupt nature of the Miami police, Frank might very well be telling the truth. Nonetheless, the image of the gorgeous Nina Randolph bringing Frank his breakfast is hard to suppress.

"Are you going to drop the charges against Frank Hearn?" Seddon Howard asks, as if he can read his daughter's mind. "It's apparent now that he isn't guilty of anything except perhaps rank stupidity."

Irene glares at her father. But she knows he's right.

"I don't see that being a problem," the chief replies.

Her father nods at her but Irene isn't as happy as she thought she'd be. People have died. There's still so much she doesn't understand. If Nina Randolph killed Parker, why did that copper Blott kill the poor jai alai player? If it hadn't been for Bryce, Blott would've killed her and Dyer as well. Did he work for the owner of the jai alai fronton, Delaney? Frank told the police Delaney tried to kill him.

Those are the questions Irene wants answered. And the biggest of all: Why did any of this have to happen? It just strikes her as so pointless and sordid. Real estate scams, gambling fixes, blackmailing secretaries, crooked cops. This isn't the life Irene imagined she'd have.

Can a leopard really change its spots?

▪ ▪ ▪

"I hear voices," says Frank, after cupping his ear against the door to suite 601. "People are in there." He's still got Frenchie perched up on his shoulder like he bagged the guy hunting.

"So what?" Laura scoffs. "They're fat cats with buckets of kale and they'll pay us for bringing this frog back."

"Put those guns away, how about it? We don't need any more trouble."

"I like trouble, big boy." Her eyes are glinting like two black stones. She's more nuts than Buddy, if that's possible. At least that bastard had a plan. This broad is doing everything on the fly.

"Put the guns away."

"Keep your shorts on, lover." At last she sticks the pistols into the side pockets of the long dress she's wearing. The thing looks like it was made in 1879. Smells like it, too. "Ready?"

She's got the key out. Frank rolls his eyes. He should just put Frenchie down and run. This is about the craziest thing he's ever done. They don't know who's in that hotel room. Could be a roomful of flatties. Or a bunch of triggermen from Detroit.

No, he's had enough. He carefully takes the Frenchmen off his shoulder and puts him on the carpet of the hallway, so that he's resting in the fetal position. He starts to groan a little.

"What are you doing?" she gasps.

"I'm finished with this."

The guns come back out. Both of them. "Pick him up and carry him inside. I'm not finished with you yet."

There's an angry emptiness in her voice that Frank recognizes as raw desperation. He has no doubt that she'll kill him, right here, because she doesn't care. But Frank does care, so he picks the drunk back up and snarls: "Go ahead and open the door. Let's get this over with."

"That's a good boy." Then she sticks the key in the door, a neat trick because she's also holding on to the small .22. The .38 is in the other hand. She kicks the door open with a foot and motions for Frank to go first.

■ ■ ■

The door swings open and in walks a hulking specimen of a man, curiously dressed in a befouled uniform of a common auto mechanic. He's wearing an eye patch and has what looks like a dead body draped over his broad shoulders. Behind him stands a very tall and very homely woman with long black hair and a plain-spun dress.

"Who the hell are you?" shouts Joe Kennedy, who nearly spills his drink all over himself.

The one-eyed mechanic stops and then slowly and gently, like a mover handling a delicate piece of glass, drops the person he was carrying down to the ground.

"My God, that's Henri! Is he dead?" Gloria jumps up and rushes over to her husband. Right away she can see he isn't dead. Just passed-out drunk and stinking like a bum from the Bowery. She tenderly strokes his dirty face. "You foolish, foolish man," she coos, a trace of bitterness in her throaty voice. "At least you're home."

Closure at last. But no. Right in front of Gloria's disbelieving eyes, she notices that the tall woman is brandishing a gun. No, two guns. Real guns. Not props, although you couldn't tell one from the other. Obviously this woman has had some experience in this line of work.

Cut! That's what Gloria expects to hear. *Get me rewrite!* This script isn't making any sense. Is this some kind of practical joke? Henri does love to pull people's legs. Any minute he'll pop up and shout *Surprise!*

Except he doesn't.

Then Joe looks at Gloria, and Gloria looks at the one-eyed mechanic. "Is this a stickup?" she asks politely.

The tall woman snorts out a laugh. "We found him by the side of the road and brought him home. Is there a reward?"

"I just want everybody to know," adds the mechanic, sounding like a scared child, "I got nothing to do with this." He nods emphatically toward the tall woman. Then his mouth opens in a rictus of shock as he stares at Gloria. "Hey, is that—get a load of that! It's Gloria Swanson!"

The tall woman does a double take. Shorn of all her bravado, the ostrich seems like she's going to have a heart attack. The guns start shaking like leaves on a tree and her mouth gapes open, wide enough for a train to rumble through.

"Oh my God!" she exclaims. "Gloria Swanson!"

Then Joe takes over, bless his heart. "Now listen very carefully. You two can't be here. I've got five hundred dollars in cash." He shows them his bankroll. "Take it and go. No one's calling the cops because we don't need the publicity. So just take the money and run. Right this instant."

Henri starts groaning. He lifts his head and his eyes blink open.

"I don't want the money," the mechanic says again. "I got nothing to do with this. I was just making sure he got home alive. She picked us up after my car ran out of gas."

"*J'ai mal à la tête,*" mutters Henri.

"You know I don't speak French," Gloria whispers.

Joe gives the money to the tall woman. She still has the guns pointed at them, one in each hand, cowboy-style. "Please go," Joe tells them. The master of the moment. In command and in control.

Thankfully they leave.

■ ■ ■

"We can go have ourselves a good time now. Five hundred bones!"

They're walking down a sumptuous hallway, back toward the elevator. Each step only makes Frank more steamed. Time to take off the kid gloves. This has gone on long enough. Barging into Gloria Swanson's hotel room! Every cop in Palm Beach is probably on the way. Or maybe not. The publicity wouldn't be good for her. So they could be in the clear but Frank isn't exactly doing cartwheels. This broad still has two guns and she's liable to do anything. If he started running, she'd shoot him in the back.

"I told you I got to make a phone call," Frank snaps.

"Don't be sore, big boy." She pats him on the rear and gives a good squeeze. Frank spins and grabs both of her arms at once, pushing her back against a wall.

"I don't like it when you do that."

"Give it to me rough, lover."

He keeps squeezing her arms until he's able to get both guns from her. An elegant couple walks past, looks of horror on their tanned faces. They go scurrying away and duck into their room, the door slamming with a thud. If no one has called the cops yet, that's about to change.

"I'm leaving, okay? The cops'll be here any minute."

"Take me with you! We can go to Bimini."

Frank doesn't answer. He turns and runs down the hall. But he can hear her calling to him from behind. She sounds like a bird dog, the way she's howling. This is a disaster. Everybody in the hotel can hear that nutty skirt.

"Wait! Take me with you!"

Stairs, stairs. Where are the stairs? Ribs still very sore and weary from the long day, Frank somehow manages to summon the strength to run as fast as he can. But to where? After he rounds the next corner, he quickly realizes he's about out of hallway. A dead end! He must've gotten himself all turned around.

"Wait! Wait!"

Now what? Surrounding him are walls and closed doors. And a laundry chute. He dives through the swinging metal door and then plunges headlong down a curling, twisting slide, down, down he goes through perfect blackness, feeling a strange sense of joy, because he used to do this at the Berkeley Carteret in Asbury Park. He and his buddies would sneak in and slide down seven, eight floors and land in a big tub of towels and sheets. It was the greatest fun in the world.

But they always made sure there would be a soft landing. What's at the other end of this ride?

A few seconds later Frank crawls out of a large vat of linens with a pillowcase on his head. It looks like a nightcap but quickly falls off after he starts running through the cavernous laundry room of this gigantic hotel. The black laundresses stop their scrubbing to regard this curious interloper with an eye patch and two pistols.

One of the workers screams. But Frank doesn't have time to explain. "How do I get out of here?" he asks, trying to keep his voice calm even as his heart pounds away.

A large lady points to a door, finger trembling.

"Thanks!"

Off he scampers, out into the cool Florida night. But then he hears a chilling sound.

"Wait!"

He turns and sees that tall broad running out of the same door he just left. He's still got about fifty yards on her. Now it'll be a race to the truck. Where is it? He parked in a lot near the front. But it's hard to get oriented, this hotel is so huge. He lowers his head and pumps his legs as forcefully as he can, heading toward a grove of palm trees beneath which are arrayed elegant tables where some guests are taking in the pleasant evening.

"Don't leave me here!"

She's getting closer and even worse, he can hear sirens off in the distance. When will anything ever work out?

The truck! There it is! The flivver appears before him like a vision of hope. He starts to giggle like a maniac, unable to stop because it seems like he's going to get away. Just a few more steps.

YES, WE HAVE NO BANANAS

The night air licks at her face like a hungry cat. Nina Randolph closes her eyes and leans her thin body out over the railing of the promenade. Nothing beats a midnight cruise through the Florida Straits. The stars above twinkle like a brilliant rhinestone gown. The smell of salt water fills your head with notions of romance. She is taking precisely the sort of glamorous, exciting trip that wealthy young women embark upon. Already she's met a stockbroker and an accountant, and both have asked her to dine with them in Havana. She won't be staying there long, however. She has her heart set on Paris. Paris in winter, then Paris in spring.

Soon she'll have to pinch herself to make sure she isn't dreaming. She actually pulled it off. The girl no one noticed, the girl whom men treated like a door prize, the stupid little secretary, yes, that girl, the one standing on an ocean liner surrounded by high rollers of every stripe, that girl is going to Paris with a suitcase full of money.

What Nina would like at the moment is more to drink. The champagne she ordered at dinner was simply divine. The accountant promised her it was the best in the world. Roger. Roger Robertson. Balding. Double chin. Expensive watch. Tailored suit. The stockbroker was more handsome but also more untrustworthy. He asked too many questions, most involving her finances. Obviously he was trying to drum up business. Nina had him figured out from the starting line. Takes one to know one.

A yawn suddenly overpowers her. Maybe she should forego a drink and try to get some sleep. It's been a long day. A long and wonderful day. Nina bids good night to the ocean and starts off for her second-class cabin. The purser had rather rudely informed her that no first-class cabins were available.

Sleepily Nina descends the stairs to the bowels of the ship. Already the air smells poorer. Somewhere a baby is crying. These miserable wretches! They'll never know the silken pleasures of true luxury.

Outside her door she fumbles for the key to her monkish berth. A Murphy bed. A bathroom. A dresser. All crammed together like sardines. Her last night of privation. To think Mother is still back in that miserable hovel, with the leaky everything and the rotten fruit on the ground. Mother will be worried tomorrow when she sobers up. But poor Noodles, the kitty! Oh, she can't think about her cat now. One day, once everything blows over, Nina will come back for Noodles.

No! Don't start to cry! Not tonight of all nights!

One thing will always cheer her up. The money. Might as well say good night to her new best friends, all ten thousand of them.

She gets the suitcase out from the small, narrow closet. Right away she knows something is wrong. It feels too light. Empty. Panic grips her around the throat. The air grows poisonous and breathing pains her.

She unsnaps the buckles and throws open the top part.

Gone.

The purser. The goddamn purser. She asked him about a first-class berth and that tipped him off. He's not getting away with it. No way in hell.

■ ■ ■

"So, I guess I'm not sure what to say." Irene is standing with Horace Dyer on First Street outside of the City Hall Annex. Steam from the municipal high-pressure station floats through the air in a fine mist. Train tracks go trailing off southward into the warehouse district, where acres of lumber wait to become houses. The madness of Florida real estate. Its siren call seduced Frank and nearly destroyed him.

Harvey Firestone and Daddy have already jumped into a waiting limo, but Irene first has to say good-bye. A few simple words she's stumbling over, like roller-skating on gravel. "Thank you just seems so inadequate after all you've done."

Dyer grimaces at the compliment. "I didn't do anything except get a man killed."

"No." She reaches out and touches his arm. "Don't say that. You didn't do anything wrong."

"We may never know what really happened."

"You mean with Nina Randolph?"

"With everything. That cop Blott was just the tip of the iceberg. He worked for Delaney. Why else would he have shown up at my office? Look at who he killed first. The jai alai player who could testify against Delaney. That's who they need to bring in for questioning. But will these clowns lift a finger? We'll see." Dyer whistles sullenly. "This city, I don't know. Sometimes it feels like you're living in another country."

"What will do you?" Irene feels silly asking about his future. It's none of her business. But she still wants to know.

"Well, I'll keep on plugging, I guess. The county attorney will be very interested in what happened tonight. What he can do about it is another question."

Irene knows the others are waiting for her, yet for some reason she can't pull herself away from Horace Dyer. She's grown fond of him very quickly. He exudes strength of character and grace under fire. But is that all she's feeling for him?

"Do you think you'll stay in Miami after it's all over?"

"I don't know. I'll file a report with my boss in Tampa and I imagine he'll pull me out of here." He chuckles and kicks at the sidewalk. "I don't want to die, either, you know."

"Do you think they'll come after you again? Tonight even?"

"I don't think so. But I'm not taking any chances. I think I'll stay in a hotel."

"How about the Flamingo?" Irene blurts and immediately she starts to blush. What in the world is wrong with her? She's engaged to be married!

"That's out of my price range."

Daddy calls for her from the limo. Everyone is ready to go back to the Firestone estate. Mummy must be pulling her hair out.

"It would be my treat. It's the least I can do."

Finally he looks her in the eyes. It's dark out, so he can only see the flicker of an overhead streetlight in them. "It wouldn't be right. Someone might say you're bribing a federal employee."

"Fiddlesticks."

"I guess you'd better go."

"Again, thanks for everything. Drop me a line in case you change your mind. Even federal employees deserve a break every now and then."

"I hope Frank turns up safe and sound."

Frank. Now Irene is flooded with guilt. "I've been trying not to worry about him."

"I'm sure everything will be fine."

"Let's hope so anyway."

They shake hands. His palms feel sweaty. Was he as nervous as she was?

■ ■ ■

Harvey Firestone bids good-bye to the Howards, making sure they will attend tomorrow's reception for President Coolidge. But there is one person who will not be, and he's standing right behind him.

"Uncle Harvey, don't be sore at me!" Bryce pleads, using the same voice as he did when he begged forgiveness for being expelled from college, for wrecking a slew of automobiles, and for getting the servants drunk, among his various and sundry transgressions. It is a thin and reedy voice, not unlike a French horn.

"I am not sore," Harvey Firestone announces sourly. "I am disappointed."

"But I saved everyone's life! You heard Irene! If I hadn't come back to that office, she and that Dyer fellow would be dead and gone!" Bryce is hopping around like a prairie dog trying to stay in front of him, but Harvey Firestone is in no mood to hash this out. Idabelle has retreated to her bedroom. He would like to kiss his wife good night and crawl into bed himself.

"No one is questioning your bravery, Bryce. Your judgment is another story."

"Don't send me to Liberia! Please, Uncle Harvey, I know I futzed up, but give me another chance."

"There is nothing wrong with learning the business of tires from one end to the other. The fact is, we could use some brave and stout men to help quell the natives. We need those primitives to harvest rubber much faster than they currently are. I think you would learn a great deal in Africa. You could prove to me that you can handle stressful situations, for one thing."

"Couldn't you just send me to Ohio instead?"

"In time, boy, in time."

The fact is, he should've shunted Bryce off to Liberia long ago. He has the physique of a man and the heart of a boy. Except on a polo field. There Bryce was confident and strong. He could anticipate the play before anyone else. He was fearless and deadly accurate. But away from the polo field, Bryce let others push and pull him. The hot African sun will be his teacher for six months. It's the best gift he could give the boy.

"The first thing in the morning you will give Janice Pendergast a check from me for ten thousand dollars, along with a note of apology to her and her mother. Do you understand?"

"Yes, sir."

"Very well. I'll see you at breakfast."

▪ ▪ ▪

Horace Dyer is staring at the big map of the world Chief Quigg has hanging on a wall in his spacious office. His eyes rove over the continents from Africa to Asia to Australia before settling on small atolls in the middle of the Pacific Ocean. He leans close to inspect the names of these islands. Yap is one. Palau another. Bora-Bora. Tahiti. Islands where simple savages live simple lives. He closes his eyes and shakes his tired head. Tonight he was supposed to die. But instead he still breathes. It was a sheer accident. But being lucky is no excuse.

The door swings open. "Mr. Dyer, you're still here?" Quigg sounds a bit peevish.

"I want you to bring a man named Gene Delaney in for questioning."

"Mr. Dyer, you aren't an officer in my police department. We'll handle this investigation."

Dyer fixes a gaze on the larger man, imposing in his uniform. "I have an investigation, too, Chief."

"I suggest you lower your voice, Mr. Dyer."

"I'm not lowering anything! Delaney sent Blott to kill me."

"We don't know that."

"He sent him to kill me and he would have if that kid hadn't stumbled in."

"The matter is being investigated and we'll get to the bottom of it, Mr. Dyer. I think you could use some sleep. We all could."

"I don't need sleep. I need answers. Bring Delaney in now."

Quigg's voice lifts like a preacher delivering a sermon. "If the evidence points toward Delaney, Delaney will be arrested. But until then, he is a free man. That's how our system works, Mr. Dyer. Innocent until proven guilty."

Dyer's jaw juts out and he feels the hairs on the back of his neck stand up. The last thing he needs at this hour is a lecture on jurisprudence from a chief of police who will soon be under grand jury investigation. "Everyone will have their day in court, Chief. Everyone. Even you."

"What the hell does that mean, Mr. Dyer?"

Dyer walks out without another word passing between them.

■ ■ ■

"Who was that, boss?" asks Lonigan, peeking his head in the door of Delaney's office. A couple of plainclothes flatties stopped in to see Delaney. They stayed for about twenty minutes and then left. The whole time Lonigan was pacing back and forth as the janitor swept up the trash left over from a night of gaming. Figgins is sitting in the players' dorm. Lonigan is supposed to join him but first he has to know what's going on.

"Some old friends." Delaney looks anxious, with dark circles beneath his eyes. No one has gotten much sleep lately, not the way things have been going. "They had something to tell me. One of my players turned up dead."

Lonigan cracks a smile. "Way to go, Blott. That didn't take him long. Did he get Dyer, too?"

"No, he didn't."

There's something strange in Delaney's voice, a catch that Lonigan doesn't quite get. Uranga deep-sixed is good news. But Delaney isn't acting like it. "What is it, boss? What happened?"

"There was a problem. Blott killed Uranga all right, and then he killed himself."

"He killed himself? Why?"

"I don't know, something went wrong. Blott followed Dyer to his office and I don't know what the hell happened after that. All I know is Uranga and Blott are both dead and I'd better be ready to answer some questions." Delaney reaches into his desk and pulls out a flask. He pours a drink but doesn't offer Lonigan one. "It's that fed, Dyer. He's raising a stink. But they got nothing on me, the bastards. Right?"

Lonigan tries to keep a straight face. He still hasn't told Delaney everything. But there's time to fix it. "Right. They got nothing."

But Delaney isn't buying it. His face darkens and his mouth starts to quiver. "What are you holding out, huh?" he rasps, voice froggy and broken. Lonigan shakes his head, trying to rein in his emotions. He can't show weakness to Delaney. Or fear.

"Nothing, boss."

"Where were you today? Why didn't you come back like you were supposed to?"

"I told you already, I was looking for Hearn."

"What else?"

"Nothing."

Delaney puzzles over this denial, smiling like a man at the end of his wits. Delaney is starting to go nuts. The pressure is getting to him.

"Go over and help Figgins take the locks off the doors in the dorm. The cops'll be back poking around here. We got to keep this joint clean."

"Sure, boss."

"They got nothing on us. Blott can't talk and neither can Uranga. They think Frank Hearn killed Parker Anderson. We just need to lay low and this will blow over."

"Go get some rest, boss. We'll lock up."

Lonigan turns and leaves. That skirt Irene is the only loose thread. What if she picked out his mug shot? He ain't going to prison. He's got a murder charge to face back in Philly, so this is the last problem he needs. Maybe he should head over to the Flamingo Hotel and see what's cooking. This might be the perfect time to take care of unfinished business.

He'll take the locks off the doors first. He jogs over to the dorm and throws open the door. He takes a step inside and pokes his head into the room he shares with Figgins.

"Hey, no sleeping!" he calls out playfully. But there is no answer. Figgins isn't there.

ON BENDED KNEE

rank parks the pickup truck across the street from the Flamingo Hotel. For all he knows the cops are sitting on this place, so he needs to check out the landscape before he tries to get in touch with Irene. He's already been arrested at this hotel once today. No need to double his money.

He looks up and down Alton Road. Nothing seems out of the ordinary. Traffic is heavy since it's a Friday night. Frank starts off down the circular drive that leads to the hotel's entrance. The cover of night gives him some comfort. He stays in the shadows of the Australian pine trees as he cuts over toward the tennis courts. He doesn't spot any suspicious vehicles parked as if staking out the hotel. Still, you can't ever be sure, so he needs to be careful.

He loops around the tennis courts and makes his way to a side entrance. Now he just needs to find a house phone and call Irene. His heart starts pounding because he can almost taste her now. It's been so long, and soon he'll have her in his arms again. An hour ago he was sure he was going to die. Now his dreams are about to come true. He will be with Irene.

A phone! It's sitting on a table in an alcove, along with two chairs and a potted palm. He rushes over and picks it up. Hands shaking, he dials zero. An operator comes on.

"Irene Howard's room," he croaks, throat parched from the ride down the Dixie Highway in a pickup truck.

"I'll connect you."

■ ■ ■

The ringing of the phone awakens Irene from a fitful sleep. She reaches for the receiver and knocks over an alarm clock. It clangs to the floor, its glass face shattering.

"Hello?" Irene mumbles, dreading the news she's going to get. They found Frank. He's dead.

"Hey, doll."

The deep masculine voice hits her like a splash of cold water. She jerks up and feels fluttering in her stomach. "Frank? Is that you?"

"Alive and kicking."

"Where are you?"

"Downstairs."

"You're downstairs?" Emotions crash through her like waves against a rocky shore. She's happy, confused, and scared all at once. She wasn't expecting this. But life with Frank is never dull. "Oh my God, Frank, you're in the hotel? Are you okay?"

"I miss you, doll. Let me come up and see you. We got some junk to talk about, huh?" He sounds tired but the same old Frank.

"My parents are in the room next door. I'll come down. I need to get dressed first, though."

"Irene, I never touched her."

Irene pauses and lets his words sink in. The playful tone is gone from his voice. He wants her to believe him. But that's not the same thing as telling the truth.

"You were in the shower and she was bringing you breakfast."

"I stank. I'd been in jail all night after taking a swim in a canal."

"The police never found any record of you being in jail."

He sighs deeply. "Just come down here so we can talk. I'll meet you in the lobby."

■ ■ ■

The Flamingo Hotel looms in the distance, its dome lit up in splashes of red and green. Lonigan parks the Buick beneath a grove of Australian pines. He gets out and starts hoofing it toward the hotel. He doesn't know what room Irene is in, and by the looks of it, there are a couple of hundred rooms. He can't exactly go knock on each door. But it can't hurt to snoop around a little first and see what there is to see. It's late and the hotel should be quiet. He might be able to steal a list of registered guests from somewhere. It's not hard to pump people for information. You just smile and act polite, then flash some green. Works every time.

■ ■ ■

For the past two hours, Figgins has been sitting on a bench a block away from the police station. He's watched the cops come and go. His favorites are the ones who ride the motorcycles. The engines on those things really hum! But then he remembers they're just stupid cops. Flatties. They're no good, more crooked than an old man's cane.

Aren't they?

There was a cop who used to walk the beat in Society Hill. His name was Carneal. A big Scot with a friendly smile. He'd walk down Pine Street giving away candy and telling the boys to stay out of trouble. He made a lasting impression on Figgins, that's for sure. Carneal was manly, kind, and considerate. One of his front teeth was turning black but Carneal never stopped smiling. Figgins really enjoyed seeing Carneal. He started to wonder if being a police officer wouldn't be exciting. When he was seven he mentioned it once to Papa and he nearly exploded. *No son of mine'll ever be a cop! You got that!*

The belt came off and Papa spanked him hard. After that he never mentioned it again.

In time you learn about life. When Figgins got older and started working for Mr. Hoff, he came to know that plenty of cops in the ward where he grew up were crooked. Then when Papa was killed by one, Figgins hated the police with utter and unredeemable vehemence. And until today never did he question this hatred. It burned inside him like an unquenchable flame.

But now he's not so sure. He never had to hurt anybody working for Mr. Hoff. Figgins answered the phone in the warehouse where the booze came in. Hundreds of others were doing the same. It was a big operation. But then Lonigan got into trouble, and now this.

Figgins struggles to his feet. His legs are numb. He starts shaking them awake and then it hits him. He can't hurt anybody anymore. He's *not* going to hurt anyone anymore. But he can't snitch, either.

His legs start to feel better. He takes a step and then another. He's got some money in his pocket and a full tank of gas. Maybe he'll just start driving and see where he ends up.

■ ■ ■

"I don't know, Frank Hearn, trouble seems to follow you around."

They're sitting in wicker chairs with a table in between them, like two strangers passing the time. A gentle breeze is blowing tonight and it's starting to get cool. No one else is sitting on the wide porch overlooking Biscayne Bay. Gondolas are docked at a wharf and rock gently to and fro. It's as quiet as a church on the porch, and just as chaste. When Irene greeted him, after months apart, she barely kissed him. She gave him a little peck on the lips and then said he tasted like a gutter. She wasn't ribbing, either. She had that tone she gets when she's not pleased. It's like she's talking with a clothespin on her nose.

So Frank has a lot of ground to make up. He's got to convince her that he's a changed man and not the slugger from Asbury Park always on the lookout for easy dough. Words alone won't do it. He's got to show her. But will she stick around long enough to give him a second look? Or is it already strike three, you're out?

"Me and trouble, we're getting a divorce." The words barely escape his lips. Just seeing her a few feet away is enough to send him into a trance. It doesn't seem real. The setting. The stupid clothes he's wearing. How beautiful she looks.

She frowns and rolls her eyes. "Yeah, right."

"I'm serious. From now on, no more stupid stunts like going in on fixed jai alai matches." That lame excuse is met with stony silence. He scoots up closer to her, the feet of his chair scraping against the Spanish tile floor. Time to lay all the cards on the table. He's losing her, so no need to hold anything back. "You know why I did it? To pay back your old man. Some good that did. He must really hate my guts now, huh?"

"He hasn't even met you."

"I know what your mom thinks. I wouldn't blame them if they did hate me. I haven't done much with my life except nearly get you killed."

"I'm alive," she whispers angrily. "That's more than you can say about that poor jai alai player I saw get killed tonight because of you."

So that's it. Irene blames him in some roundabout way for everything that happened. He stares up at the sky. A thin layer of clouds now covers the stars. Everything appears murky and indistinct. When he looks back at her, she's got her arms folded across her chest. If she had a rolling pin, she'd probably whack him with it. "I know I screwed up, kid. It was stupid what I did. I should've learned my lesson but I wanted to show you I could be somebody."

"You are somebody, Frank."

"Yeah, I'm somebody who borrows money and can't pay it back. What kind of man is that?"

"You'd pay it back when you could. Daddy doesn't need a thousand dollars, Frank."

Her tone slices him like a razor blade. But he's not going to let her carve him up with it. If the train is leaving the station, he's not stupid enough to stand on the tracks. "Do you want me, Irene? Answer me that question. Yes or no."

She wipes tears that have welled in her eyes. "Oh Frank, of course I want you."

"Why?" He laughs bitterly. "Why the hell do you want me of all people?"

"Because I love you."

"But I'm no good for you! A blind man can see that! I got a sixth-grade education and no money!"

"Are you calling it off?" More tears. They dribble down her cheeks like raindrops on a freshly waxed car.

"No. Are you?"

"No." Now she's sobbing. He can't do anything right anymore. The more he talks, the more she cries. "You sound like you don't want me."

"I want to marry you, doll. But I don't want to ruin your life, either. What if I'm just one of those bums who can't stay clear of cops and thieves, who chase stupid pipe dreams because they don't know any better. Huh? Is that what you want? To marry a bum?"

"You're not a bum."

"Without you, I'd be in jail right now. I'd be called a killer."

"You're not a killer."

"Irene, I want to change. I really do. I want to make an honest buck. But scrambling is all I know."

She buries her face in her hands. They shouldn't be doing this here, in public. They need to be alone, so he can show her what he's feeling. Words have always betrayed him. In bed, though, they've never had any trouble connecting. And that's where he needs to take her.

He reaches out and brushes her leg. "Let's go back to my place," he says softly.

■ ■ ■

Nina Randolph stands outside the door to room 3, which is a stateroom currently occupied by Roger Robertson, certified public accountant. She moistens her lips and smooths out her taffeta dress. Then she knocks.

Nothing happens.

She knocks a little louder and presses her ear against the door. She can hear footsteps padding on the floor. This is her only hope. A bald, chubby accountant with asparagus-thin fingers and a gold wristwatch. She never did confront the purser. She can't report the missing money because she can't draw any attention to herself.

So she must survive by her wits. It's all she's known.

"Who is it?" comes his anxious voice.

"It's Janice." That's her name from now on. Janice Owens.

"Oh. I'm in my nightclothes."

"Something terrible has happened!"

Roger opens the door a crack and peers at her with some suspicion. She pushes her way in and, sobbing, throws herself against his soft chest. His body feels like a pillow. A pillow stuffed with money.

"What's wrong?"

"I've been robbed!"

"Dear heavens! Did you report it?"

"It didn't do any good. All my money, my passport, everything! I'm so scared!"

More tears that stain his bathrobe with his initials embroidered on a lapel. He strokes her blond hair with his paper-thin hand. She'll do whatever it takes. That's the quality of character that separates the winners from the losers.

"There, there," he coos.

"I'm so scared."

"No need for that. You're safe now."

Although still crying, she breaks into a wry smile that he can't see.

▪ ▪ ▪

It's the skirt! And Hearn!

Lonigan ducks behind a potted palm as the couple strolls arm in arm through the lobby of the Flamingo Hotel. He watches them prance down the big set of steps that leads to the circular drive below. From the potted palm he dashes over to a wooden railing overlooking the entrance. He sees the happy couple jump into a waiting cab.

Hearn's place.

Where else would they be going at this time of night? And besides, what the hell is Frank Hearn doing walking the streets? He's a fugitive from the law who busted out of jail just tonight, a wanted murderer, and now he's free? Don't the cops know he's here? Wouldn't they suspect that he'd come find his broad?

Lonigan hustles down the front steps and back toward his car parked far away up the front drive. As he runs he can see the cab's red taillights disappear into the night. But he's not worried. He knows where the Crozier is.

This couldn't be better. Hearn and the skirt, two birds with one stone. Then there won't be nothing to worry about.

COOLIDGE IS COMING

eneath the shade of a Barbados nut tree, Janice Pendergast sits in a wicker chair with the morning paper spread open in front of her. She is reading through the society page. There is a picture of a stern-looking woman sitting at a bake sale in front of Burdines. The photograph of Mother makes her look like a snarling guard dog. She'll hate this picture. She'll see it and want to faint. Just as Janice wanted to faint after she read the front page. PARKER ANDERSON MURDERED. SECRETARY SUSPECTED. COOLIDGE IS COMING.

But not a word about Bryce Shoat.

No, Bryce avoided having his name dragged through the mud. One call from Uncle Harvey to *The Miami Herald* most likely did the trick. After all, who's hosting a party for the president? Harvey Firestone, that's who! Whose nephew is a lying creep that stole ten thousand dollars from her?

Janice sighs and puts the newspaper down. She picks up a cup of steaming breakfast tea and squeezes a wedge of lemon into it. She picked it off a tree just this morning, in an effort to try to feel more chipper. But that's pretty much impossible, given what a fool she was. Mother won't talk to her. Janice tried once this morning but Mother's face turned beet red and she decided on the spot to go shopping. Just as well. What on earth could Janice possibly say?

Janice brings the cup of tea to her lips when Miss Fannie comes out. "Mr. Tire is here to see y'all," she announces matter-of-factly.

That's what Miss Fannie calls Bryce. *Mr. Tire.*

"Tell him to go to—" Janice almost says *hell* but stops herself. Miss Fannie goes to church three times a week. "Jump in a lake."

"Why y'all want Mr. Tire to jump in a lake? Ain't you sweet on him?"

"Tell him to go away and never come back."

"You two been fussin', ain't no doubt."

Miss Fannie goes back inside. Janice stands up and nearly knocks over her hot tea. Above her a parakeet is singing. Dozens flit about the backyard, having returned to the wild after escaping their cages. You can't catch them, either. Not even peanut butter works. They've won a second chance at freedom and nothing will trick them again.

Miss Fannie comes back. She is wringing her hands in her white apron. "Mr. Tire say he ain't goin' nowhere."

"Fine. I'll throw him out myself."

Janice marches around the table and inside the house. *Punch him in the kisser or kick him between the legs?* That's a tough decision for a gal to make.

Bryce is waiting for her in the foyer, near the bust of Father. He's holding a bouquet of white roses. It appears that he shaved this morning. His hair is slicked back with tonic. His suit is pressed and his shoes shine.

"I know you hate my guts," he says grimly. "I don't blame you."

"You know where you can stick those flowers."

"They didn't fit."

"Want me to try?"

"Sure, go ahead." He tosses her the roses and then spins around and bends over at the waist. Janice can't help it. She smiles. A laugh even escapes her lips. More like a giggle. But still, why does she act like that around this creep?

With his head dangling between his legs he says: "I got something for you."

She folds her arms across her chest. She wants to stay mad at him. He's a no-good liar. He should be in jail, is what.

"Want to know what it is?"

"No."

"Too bad. I'll just drink it all by myself."

"You have booze?"

He stands up and winks at her. "Just came back from Colored Town. Guess what we can do?"

"What?"

"Get gassed and go meet the president!" A crazed look gleams in his gorgeous eyes. "Wouldn't that be screwy?"

"I hate you."

"You're lying."

"No, I really, really hate you."

He shrugs his muscular shoulders. "Uncle Harvey is sending me to Africa tomorrow. I can't even go to Parker's funeral. So you only have one more day to hate me."

"I don't like funerals."

"Me either. Here's a check for ten grand from Uncle Harv. And a letter from me to your mother saying I'm a screwup." He drops an envelope on the table right beneath Father. "Come on, let's go get boiled. Coolidge will be here soon."

▪ ▪ ▪

"Have you heard from Irene yet?" Lauren Howard asks her husband, who as usual has his face buried in a newspaper. They need to get going to make it to the brunch the Firestones are having for the president. After the long turmoil Irene had yesterday, Lauren figured that her daughter needed to sleep as long as possible. But now she should be readying herself.

"She must still be sleeping."

"I'll go wake her. I'd hate to be late."

"Silent Cal could care less. Never have I met a more phlegmatic man."

"Still, I would hate to embarrass Idabelle Firestone. She is a dear, sweet thing."

Seddon sniffs and snaps the paper. He is in a foul mood. The stock market must've done poorly yesterday. Oh, truth be told, Lauren feels dispirited as well. Irene's life has again become a source of great anxiety. The idea that she was nearly killed—by a police officer, no less—caused Lauren to toss and turn for most of the night. Seddon had trouble getting settled as well.

But today is a new day. Lauren darts next door and raps on her daughter's door. In a flash Lauren remembers waking Irene for grammar school and how she would protest and beg for more sleep. It seems just like yesterday. Where have the years gone?

"Honey, time to wake up!"

But no one is answering. Lauren tries the door but it's locked. She then hurries back to her own room. "She's not answering," Lauren says evenly, although her insides roil. "I'll call her on the phone."

Seddon puts the paper down and silently waits. Lauren listens to the phone ringing. No one there. Irene is gone.

"Maybe she stepped out," suggests Seddon without much conviction. "Maybe she's downstairs shopping."

"I'll call the front desk." But Lauren knows her daughter well. She wouldn't go shopping alone, not when they hadn't gone shopping together in months. No, something is wrong. A mother knows these things.

"She didn't leave a message for us. That isn't like her."

"What are you saying?"

Lauren covers her face with her hands. When will this stop? Last night she put her daughter to bed, safe and sound. Now she is gone.

There are noises coming from next door. Lauren bolts out the door.

"Irene!"

"Hi, Mummy."

Joy overcomes Lauren Howard. Her daughter is alive and well after all. But then she notices that Irene is wearing the same clothes she had on last night. Her hair is a mess and she isn't wearing any makeup. She went out in public looking like a washerwoman.

"Where have you been?"

Irene's face lights up like a Christmas tree. "I got some great news! Frank is fine! He's talked to the police and squared everything away. He's going to meet us at the Firestones'. Isn't that wonderful?"

At first Lauren is too shocked to speak. Then it all becomes scandalously clear. The hair. The clothes. She draws her mouth tight and stands as straight as a ruler. "We're running late, Irene. We need to leave soon."

■ ■ ■

"Hey, no sleeping, you bum!"

A flattie taps Lonigan on the shoulder with a nightstick. Lonigan sits up, having slumped beneath the steering wheel of the Buick. He's parked in front of a barbershop across the street from Hearn's apartment. Luckily his gun stays hidden beneath his thigh and the flattie can't see it.

"Sorry, Officer," offers Lonigan solicitously. "It was a late night. I'll drive on home now."

"Yeah? You from around here? What's your name?" The flattie pulls out a notebook and he's ready to write.

"Daniel Turner." That was the name of a retarded kid who lived across the street from Lonigan back in Philly. He sat on the steps in front of his house and squawked like a parrot. They used him as target practice. Rocks, snowballs, bottle caps.

The flattie's eyebrows lift in disbelief. "Turner, is it? We'll see about that. Hand over a driver's license, how about it?"

Lonigan keeps a smile plastered on his face. "I left it at home, Officer. Sorry."

"Is that so? Where's home?"

"The Bachellor."

"What's your line of work, Turner?"

"I work at the Roney Plaza."

"You know Sergio then."

"Maybe. Which one is he?"

"The manager."

"I should introduce myself."

The flattie pulls out a piece before Lonigan can react. He's got the barrel about four inches from his temple.

"Hands on your head, punk!"

"What? It's against the law to sleep in this city?"

"Hands on your head! Now!"

■ ■ ■

Frank steps into the new suit Irene bought for him first thing this morning. Dark brown with pinstripes and wide lapels. He's got on a new shirt, a new tie, new skivvies, and new socks. Soon he'll slip into a new pair of Italian shoes, all purchased downstairs in the lobby of the McAllister Hotel. Irene paid extra for a tailor to do the fitting. Now he's ready to go meet the president—not to mention Irene's father.

Irene refused to step foot into his apartment last night and further insisted that he never go back there. *You don't know if they're still looking for you. Don't risk it, Frank. Promise me you won't.* And what could he say? It was all part of the long process of making up. At first it was hard because she was so angry with him and he smelled so bad. But then he said: *I'm taking a shower.* He needed to cool down and clean himself up. He was still wearing that stupid mechanic's uniform. No wonder she looked at him like he was diseased.

Next a funny thing happened. She joined him in the shower. After that, everything went like it always did. They started acting like themselves again and fell asleep in each other's arms, until Irene had to get up and go rushing back before her parents started to worry.

The suit fits perfectly. He looks at himself in the mirror. The eye patch. Seddon Howard will never get past it, because it'll always remind him of the way Frank used to be. Rough. Dangerous. Ill-bred. Bad for Irene. What in the world is Frank going to say to that man? Frank doesn't have the money he owes him. Yesterday he was charged with murder and escaped from jail. Not the kind of topics to discuss with the man whose daughter you hope to marry. Ask for Irene's hand? Seddon Howard might punch him in the bazoo instead.

That's it! Frank starts smiling as he readjusts his tie. He met Gloria Swanson! That's how he'll break the ice with Irene's old man. That's a story that'll bring a smile to anyone's lips. Ought to, anyway. It's all he's got, other than slobbering *I'm sorry* a million times.

■ ■ ■

Delaney tugs on the last strap of his body brace when he hears the sirens outside the window to his office. "What the hell do they want?" he mutters bitterly as he puts on a pair of cream-colored knickers and an ocean-blue shirt with white piping along the collar.

The door bursts open. An army of cops comes rushing in, led by Chief Detective Guy Reeve.

"Gene Delaney, you're under arrest."

Delaney raises his hands. "It'll never stick, Reeve."

"The charge is operating an illegal gambling establishment in violation of the Florida statutes. Here's the warrant."

Reeve throws him onto the desk and slaps a pair of cuffs on him, digging hard into Delaney's wrists. Delaney growls like a bear and out of the corner of his eye he sees someone familiar. That Boy Scout fed, Dyer. The one who came around yesterday asking a lot of questions.

"I'll go find where the players are locked up," Dyer says, taking a couple of cops with him.

"Say your prayers, Dyer!" yells Delaney. "I'll be on the street by nightfall!"

Dyer cups a hand to an ear. "Did somebody say something?"

Reeve starts cackling like it's the funniest thing since Will Rogers. These cops are all such rubes.

▪ ▪ ▪

"Mr. President, I'd like you to meet my daughter, Irene."

Frank shifts his weight from one foot to the other. The new shoes are killing him, rubbing him raw just like Seddon Howard. The man is acting like Frank doesn't exist. Has barely said two words to him, and now, after waiting for twenty minutes in a greeting line at the train station, they are finally getting to shake hands with Coolidge himself. But what does Seddon Howard do? Gives Frank the cold shoulder, is what. Now Frank is standing in front of the president of the United States, the leader of the free world, like a complete buffoon.

"Daddy," Frank hears Irene whisper after shaking Coolidge's hand. "And this is Frank Hearn."

All of a sudden it feels like a million spotlights are shining on him. Coolidge looks him up and down for a second, and then he extends a hand and Frank grips it. The president's skin feels hot and sweaty from all the flesh he's been pressing. Frank can feel his mouth twist into a stupid smile, but he can't help it. Just yesterday he busted out of jail, and today he's rubbing elbows with big shots as far as the eye can see. The president. The first lady. The secretary of state. Harvey Firestone. Thomas Edison.

Not bad for a kid who used to toss dice at the Asbury Park boardwalk. Not bad at all.

BLACK EYE

ebruary 20, 1928, finds the city of Boston gripped by bone-chilling cold. Rose Fitzgerald Kennedy is giving birth to her eighth child. The labor isn't progressing, although she started dilating yesterday afternoon. It is now approaching the hour of 7:00 AM.

"Push," Rose Kennedy hears. She does so, and waves of horrible pain grip her plump, strong body. She clings to the sweat-stained mattress and groans. This is God's way. She knows better than to question His wisdom. Just as she knows better than to confront her husband with the rumor that he is having an affair with Gloria Swanson. Rose's own mother told her of the rumor.

What will you do, Rosie?

In a word, nothing. Rose doesn't need to confront Joe because it doesn't matter if he is or isn't having an affair. A marriage is made by God and only He can unmake one, not some cheap floozy actress.

"Push! You're getting closer!"

A person must learn restraint. A person must learn the value of hard work. A good marriage depends on both. Without restraint and the effort required to apply it, a spouse might recklessly shatter a family over trivial matters. Women especially must learn to suffer in silence. Men are what they are and cannot be changed. There will be eight wonderful children in this family, and Rose will not harm them to satisfy a lust for revenge. And anyway, she knows Joe loves her.

"Push as hard you can!"

Rose cries out in pain, the blessed pain of motherhood, consecrated by the blood of Jesus and the tears of the Holy Mother. This pain is proof that pleasure isn't a legitimate reason for intercourse. A righteous euphoria riots in her pounding heart. She will never have sex again.

"Here's the head! Push, Rose, once more."

The child is born. A girl who will be named Jean. Three days later Joe Kennedy will stop in to see mother and child. For Rose he will bring three diamond bracelets. Each is stunning, and Rose will put on all three at once to compare them and then select the one she likes best. Spending his money, that is revenge enough.

Joe Kennedy will be asked: *What will you give Rose if she has a ninth child?*

His reply: *A black eye.*

A joke, of course. Four years later a ninth child will come, named Edward.

■ ■ ■

It is March 23, 1928. Within the last month, a grand jury has indicted five Miami police officers, all charged with murder. Three were implicated in the killing of Harry Kier in July 1925, and the other two for the execution of John Mabry in January 1928. Both victims had been in police custody at the time of their deaths. Each had been shot multiple times from point-blank range. In the past month Chief of Police Leslie Quigg has issued a series of statements all but exonerating his men. Each bore a "splendid record," according to Quigg. They were merely acting in self-defense, bringing safety to a city where outlaws in the Negro neighborhoods ran wild.

At 10:00 AM Quigg hears a knock on his door. He stands to answer it. The man he sees neither surprises nor angers him. It is W.E. Van Loon, chief of the criminal department of the sheriff's office.

"Leslie Quigg, you are under arrest."

"What's the charge?"

"Murder in the first degree."

"Who is the victim?"

"H. Kier, a Negro." Quigg already knew from leaked grand jury testimony that Officer William Beechey testified that Quigg ordered that Kier "be taken care of." Later, after Kier was killed, he told his men to keep their stories straight.

"I've never seen the man in my life."

"You must come with me."

Quigg flashes a sheepish grin. "Van Loon, it's my daughter's sixth birthday. I have a present for her. It's a new bicycle. Can we stop by my house so I can give it to her?"

Van Loon quickly agrees. In the newspapers the next day, this demonstration of paternal affection is given prominent coverage. On April 30, after a ten-day trial, Quigg and three other officers are found not guilty by a jury after three hours of deliberation.

SOMETHING BLUE

You nervous?"

Enrico brushes some lint off the lapels of Frank's tuxedo. They're standing in a Sunday school classroom of Christ Church in Greenwich, Connecticut. Enrico is Frank's best man and oldest friend, chums since their earliest days in Asbury Park, New Jersey. Irene sent out at least two hundred invitations, while Frank asked just Enrico and his family. Thankfully there won't be a groom's side or a bride's side. Everybody will sit wherever they want.

"A little," Frank replies, still trying to get used to the monkey suit. It doesn't really fit. It was hard pinning on the white carnation. But that's not all that's bothering him. "Irene was acting strange last night."

"She seemed fine to me."

"No, she was strange. She's calling it off. She'll never go through with it."

"Come on, Frankie! Listen to yourself! You sound like me!"

"You wait. This wedding is a no go."

"Bushwa! Tonight you two lovebirds will be on a ship for Greece! Now that's a honeymoon. I took Paula to Atlantic City for one night."

"I like A.C. Wish we were going there."

"Frankie, you need a drink."

"You got any?"

"No. I'm just saying, you need a drink."

"Tell me something I don't know. Does my eye look okay?"

Enrico throws his hands up in exasperation. Frank still isn't sure about his new glass eye. Irene claims to like it better than the eye patch, but the thing is, you can see how badly scarred his face is around the socket. But Irene says she wants to see all of him, scars or no scars. It was what she wanted, so he did it for her.

"It's fine. Don't ask me again!"

There's a knock on the door. Both men call out "Come in!" at the same time. A man pokes his head in. It is Seddon Howard, looking every inch like the baron of industry that he is. Impeccably groomed, exquisitely tailored, and in command. He scares the bejeezus out of Frank. Every time Seddon Howard opens his mouth, Frank starts to quake in his shoes. Frank hasn't said one intelligent thing to the man yet.

"Frank, might I have a word with you?"

"Sure thing."

Enrico silently slips out, and Frank starts to feel a little dizzy. Seddon Howard isn't smiling. He looks as serious as a heart attack, jaw set firmly, shoulders thrown back, head held high. If he were Frank's boss, Frank would be getting fired. Like a rag doll, Frank's mouth twists into an awkward smile as his limbs go limp.

"Frank, we need to talk."

"Sure thing. I'm all ears."

"It's about Irene."

Frank holds up his hands. "I know what you're gonna say, Mr. Howard. I've been expecting it. She's calling it off and I don't blame her."

"No, Frank. She's not calling it off."

Frank blinks a few times. "She's not?"

"No. She loves you. And I presume you love her."

"I do, Mr. Howard."

"Good, Frank. This is what I wanted to tell you about Irene. She's my only daughter and I care for her more than I can express. I want you to know that if you fail to take care of her, I'll personally break your neck with my own hands."

Frank swallows hard. "I'll take care of her, Mr. Howard."

Then the silver-haired man breaks into a wide grin. "Just kidding, Frank. I had you going, didn't I? Here, shake my hand. Welcome to the family. You're going to make a fine son-in-law."

It takes a few seconds before Frank starts breathing easily. "Boy, Mr. Howard, you're some kidder."

"In my youth, Frank, I was known as something of a comedian." He puts his arm around Frank's shoulders. "You'll have to tell me that story about how you kissed Gloria Swanson."

"Hold on! I didn't kiss Gloria Swanson. I just met her."

"You didn't kiss her? I'm disappointed. I was told you kissed her." They start walking toward the door. Enrico is waiting outside. Seddon Howard sweeps past him and heads back toward the church.

"What did he want?" asks Enrico in a hushed tone.

"He wanted to know if I kissed Gloria Swanson."

"Did you?"

Frank punches his friend in the shoulder, hard enough for Enrico to wince in pain. "No," Frank grumbles playfully. "Where do these stories get started anyway?"